SATURDAY AM

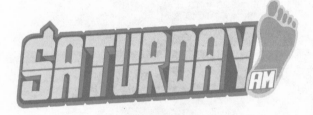

PRESENTS...

YELLOW STRINGER

VOLUME 1

Fake News Provocateurs

BY GOEFFREY JEAN-LOUIS
with FREDERICK L. JONES

ROCKPORT

Contents

Article 1   New in Town   5

Article 2   Late-Night Fun   35

Article 3   Zombie Apocalypse   65

Article 4   Dawn of the Dead   93

Article 5   Sleepy Desert Hollow   125

Article 6   Meet-Cute   145

Article 7   Birthday Boy   169

Article 8   Date-Night Jitters   194

Special Article   Sketch Gallery   218

Article 1: New in Town

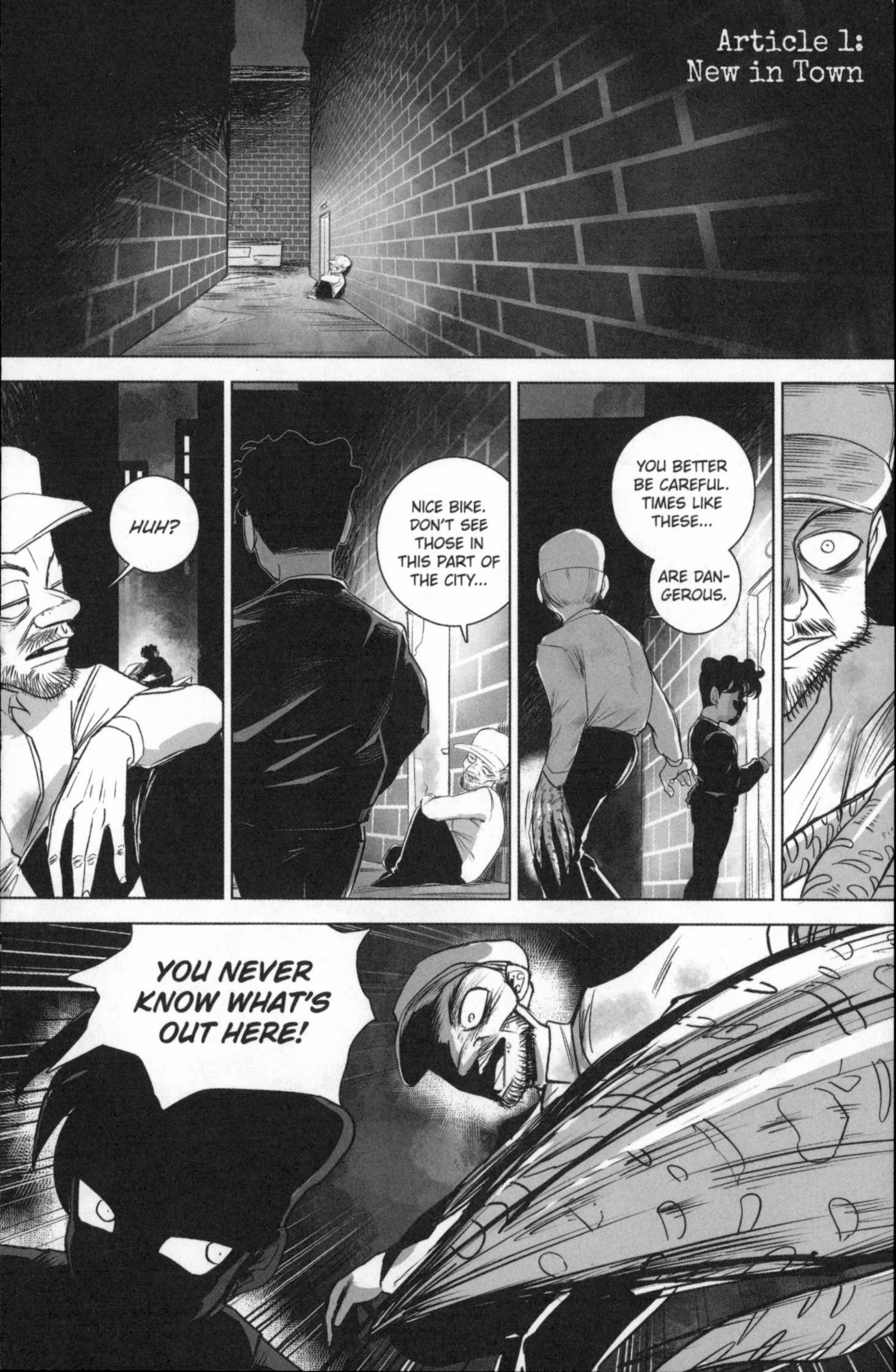
HUH?
NICE BIKE. DON'T SEE THOSE IN THIS PART OF THE CITY...
YOU BETTER BE CAREFUL. TIMES LIKE THESE...
ARE DAN-GEROUS.
YOU NEVER KNOW WHAT'S OUT HERE!

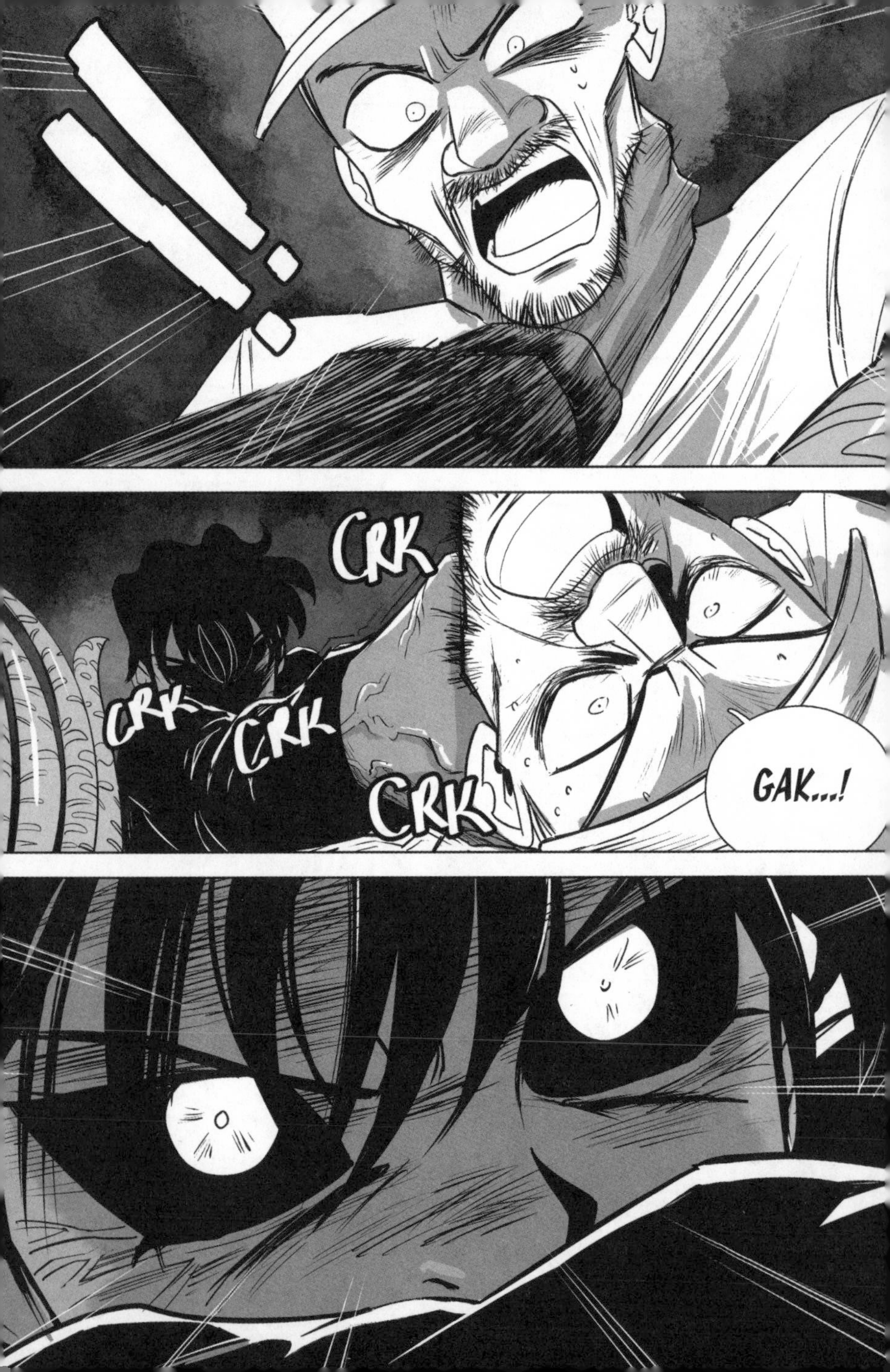
!!
CRK
CRK
CRK
CRK
GAK...!

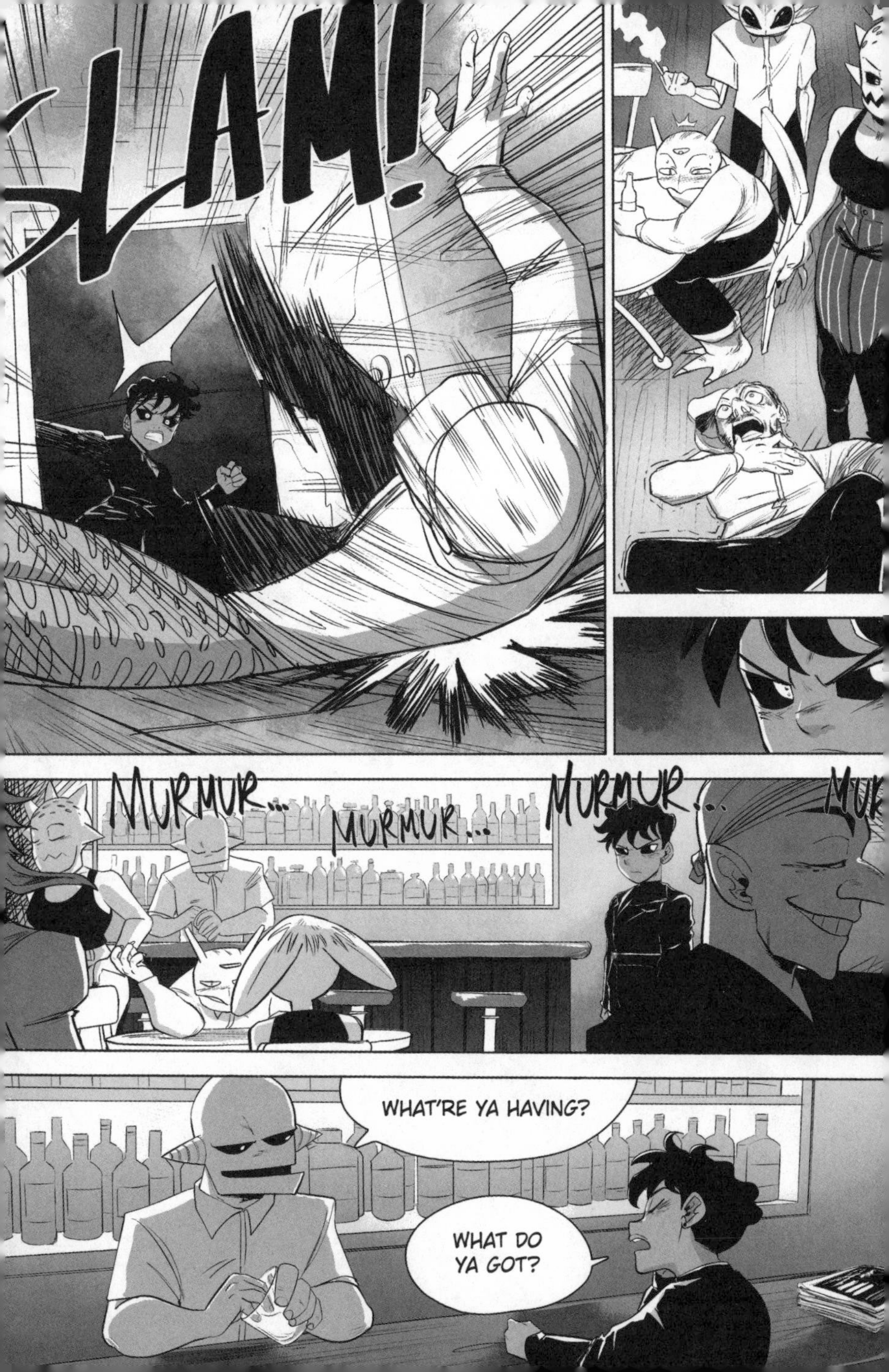
SLAM!
MURMUR...
MURMUR...
MURMUR...
MUR
WHAT'RE YA HAVING?
WHAT DO YA GOT?

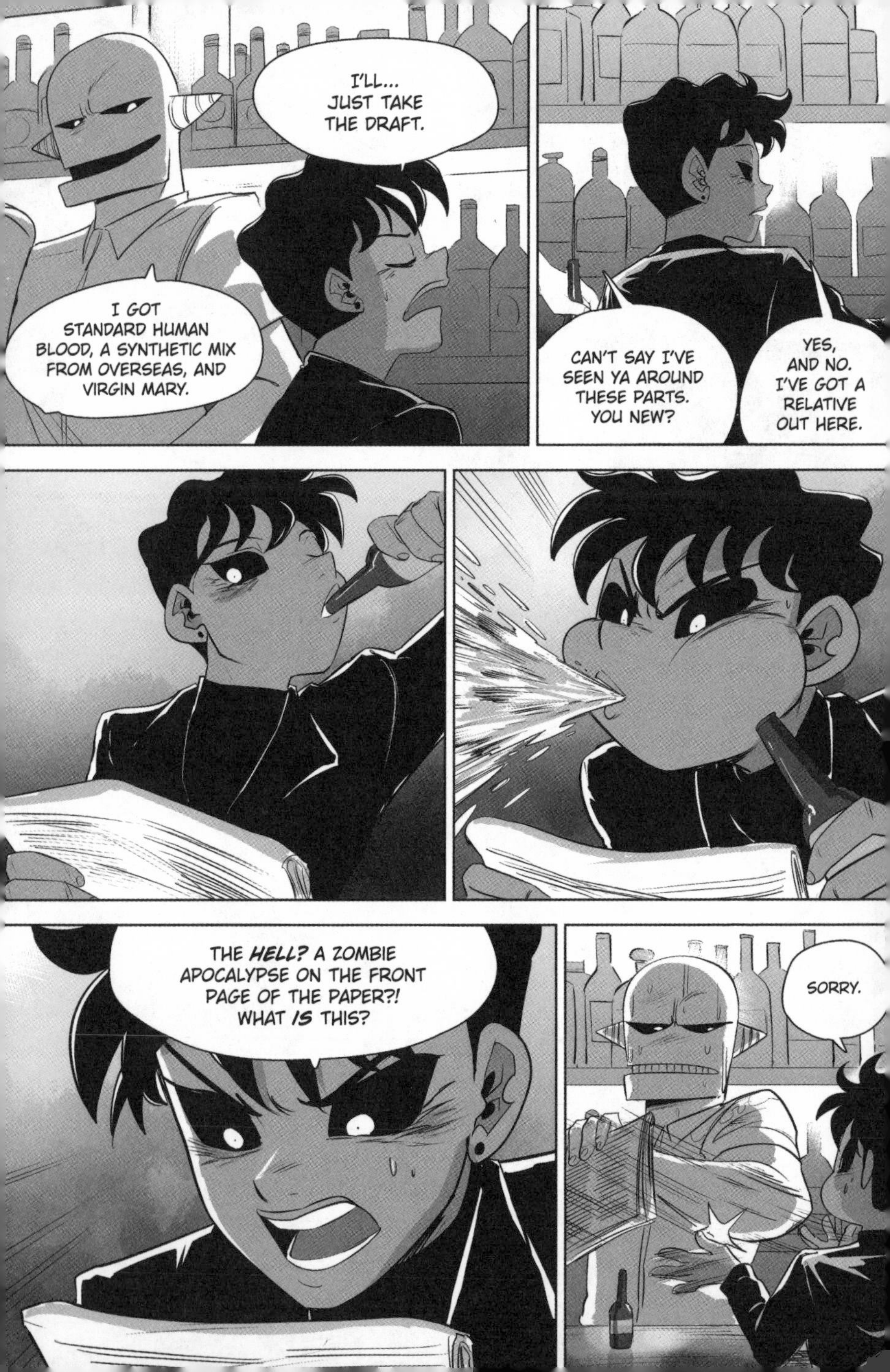
I'LL... JUST TAKE THE DRAFT.
I GOT STANDARD HUMAN BLOOD, A SYNTHETIC MIX FROM OVERSEAS, AND VIRGIN MARY.
CAN'T SAY I'VE SEEN YA AROUND THESE PARTS. YOU NEW?
YES, AND NO. I'VE GOT A RELATIVE OUT HERE.
THE *HELL?* A ZOMBIE APOCALYPSE ON THE FRONT PAGE OF THE PAPER?! WHAT *IS* THIS?
SORRY.

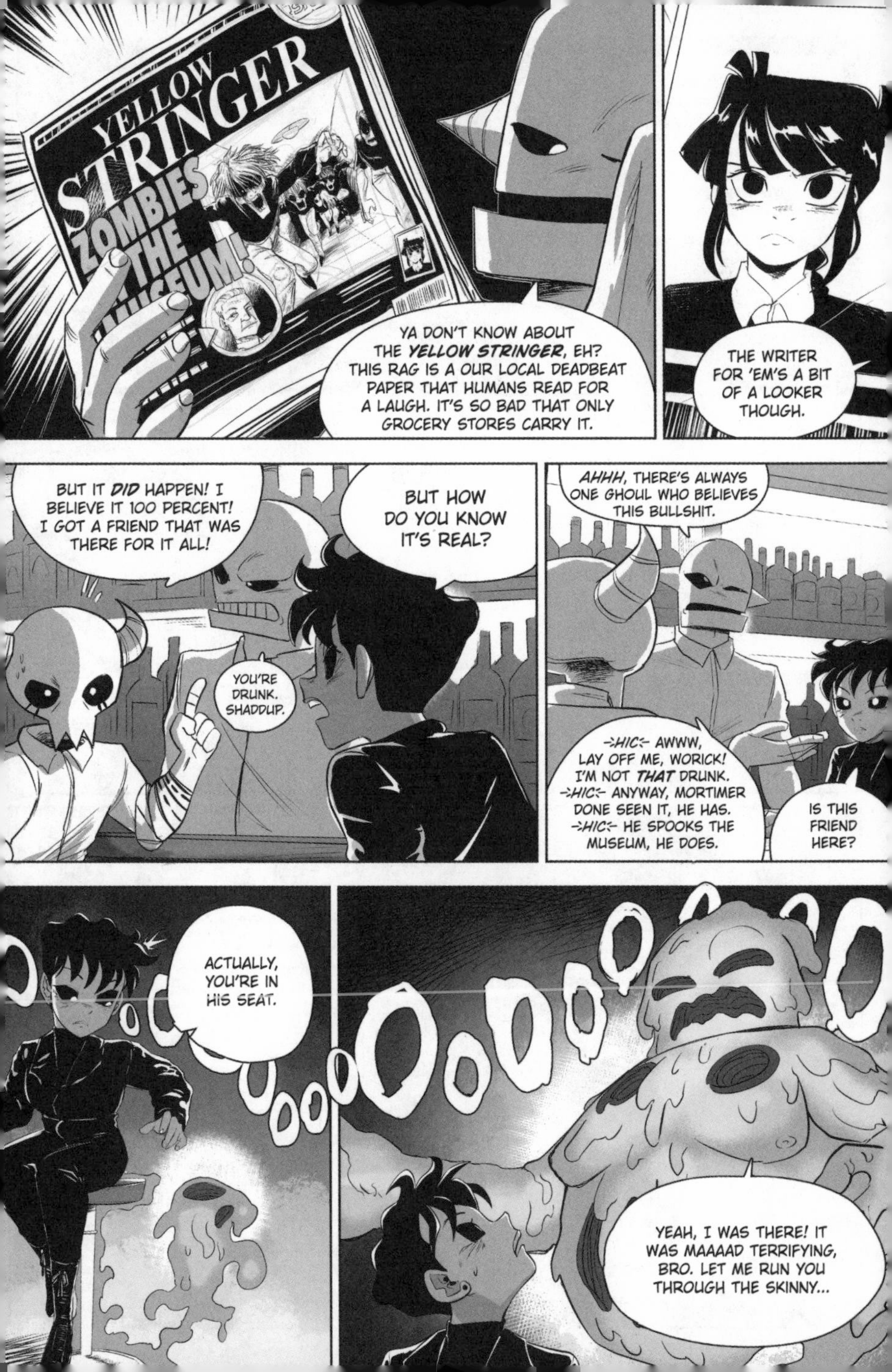
YELLOW STRINGER
ZOMBIES
THE
YA DON'T KNOW ABOUT THE *YELLOW STRINGER*, EH? THIS RAG IS A OUR LOCAL DEADBEAT PAPER THAT HUMANS READ FOR A LAUGH. IT'S SO BAD THAT ONLY GROCERY STORES CARRY IT.
THE WRITER FOR 'EM'S A BIT OF A LOOKER THOUGH.
BUT IT *DID* HAPPEN! I BELIEVE IT 100 PERCENT! I GOT A FRIEND THAT WAS THERE FOR IT ALL!
BUT HOW DO YOU KNOW IT'S REAL?
YOU'RE DRUNK. SHADDUP.
AHHH, THERE'S ALWAYS ONE GHOUL WHO BELIEVES THIS BULLSHIT.
-HIC- AWWW, LAY OFF ME, WORICK! I'M NOT *THAT* DRUNK. -HIC- ANYWAY, MORTIMER DONE SEEN IT, HE HAS. -HIC- HE SPOOKS THE MUSEUM, HE DOES.
IS THIS FRIEND HERE?
ACTUALLY, YOU'RE IN HIS SEAT.
YEAH, I WAS THERE! IT WAS MAAAAD TERRIFYING, BRO. LET ME RUN YOU THROUGH THE SKINNY...

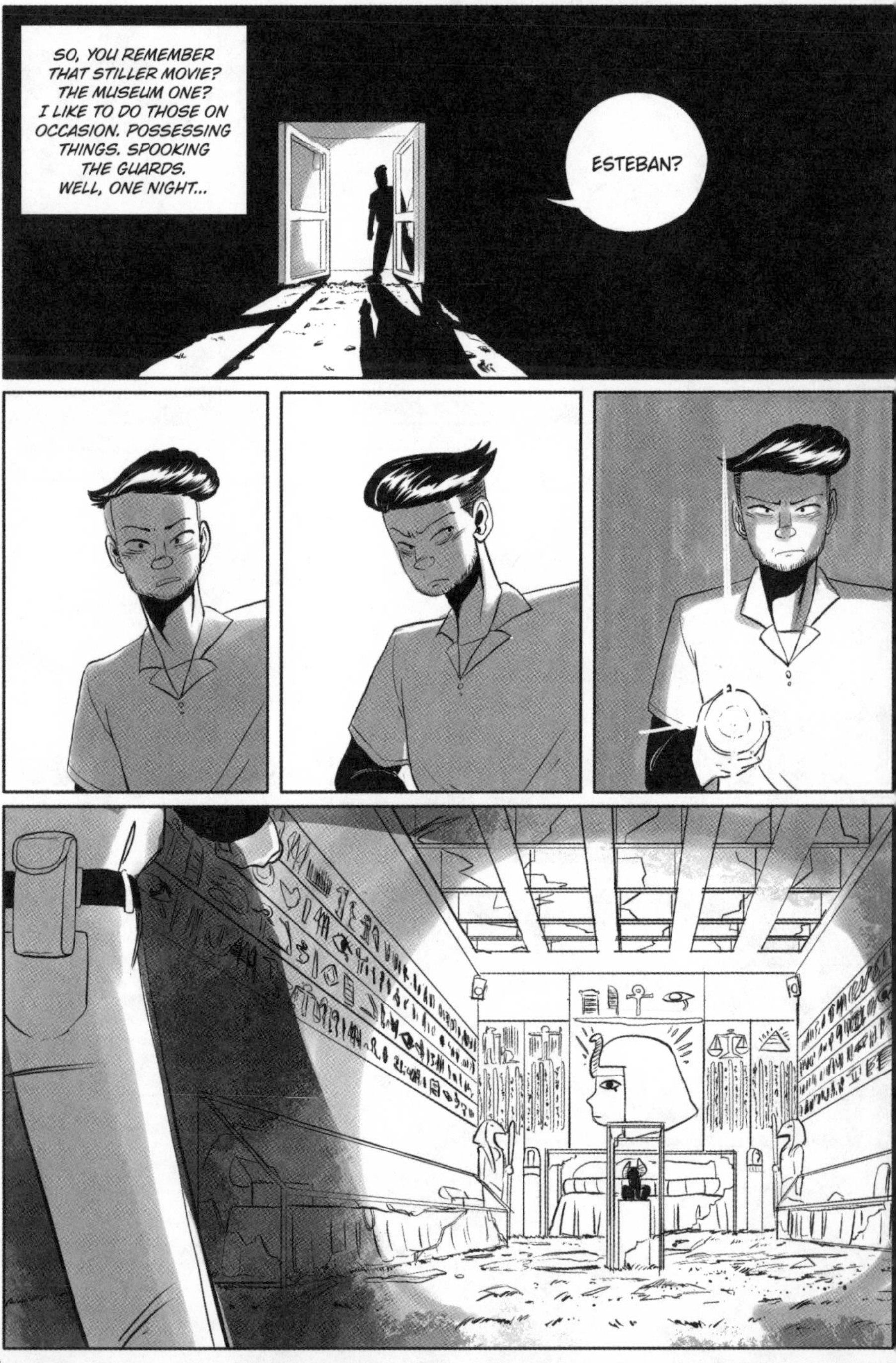
SO, YOU REMEMBER THAT STILLER MOVIE? THE MUSEUM ONE? I LIKE TO DO THOSE ON OCCASION. POSSESSING THINGS. SPOOKING THE GUARDS. WELL, ONE NIGHT...
ESTEBAN?

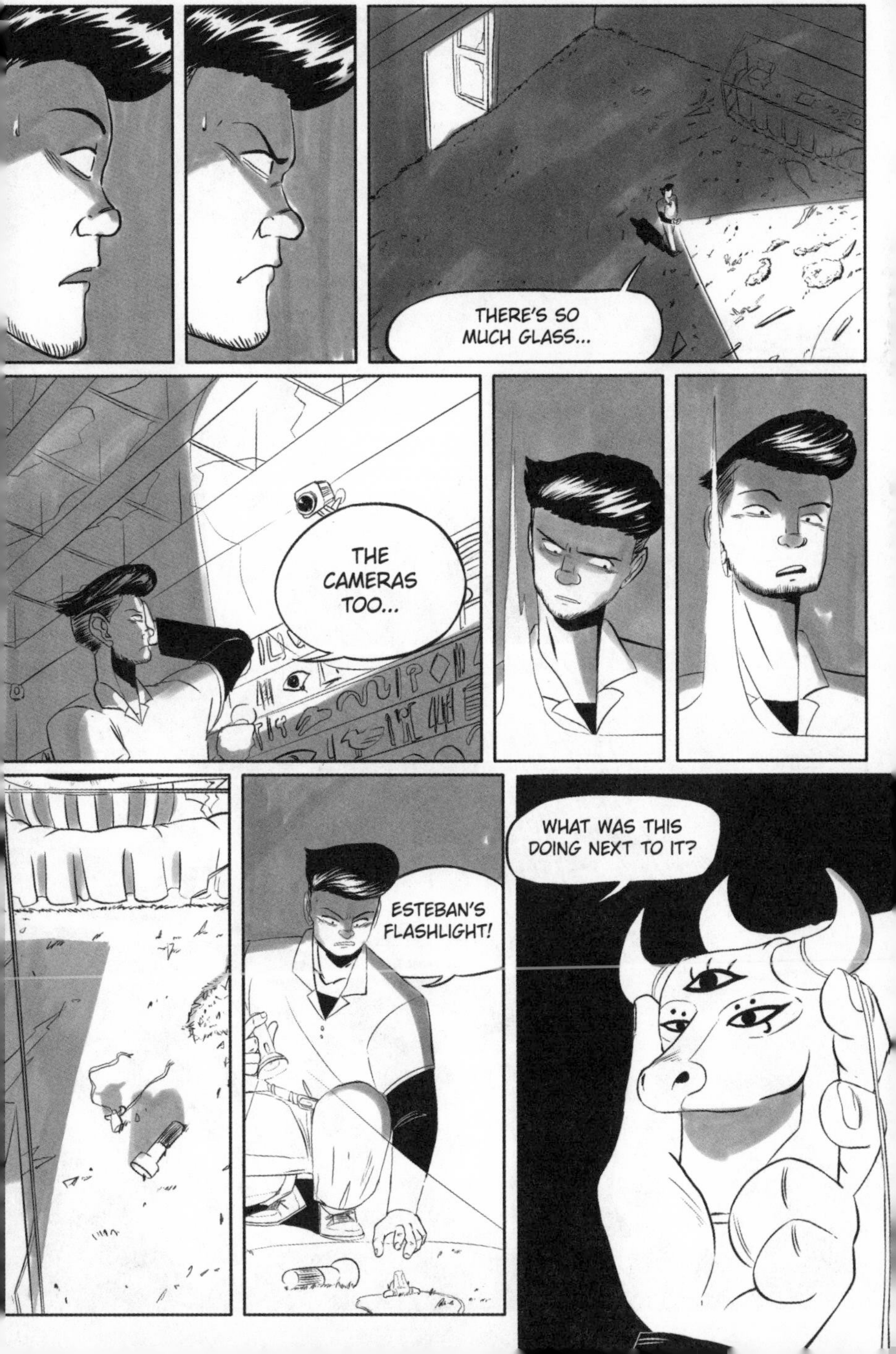
THERE'S SO MUCH GLASS...
THE CAMERAS TOO...
ESTEBAN'S FLASHLIGHT!
WHAT WAS THIS DOING NEXT TO IT?

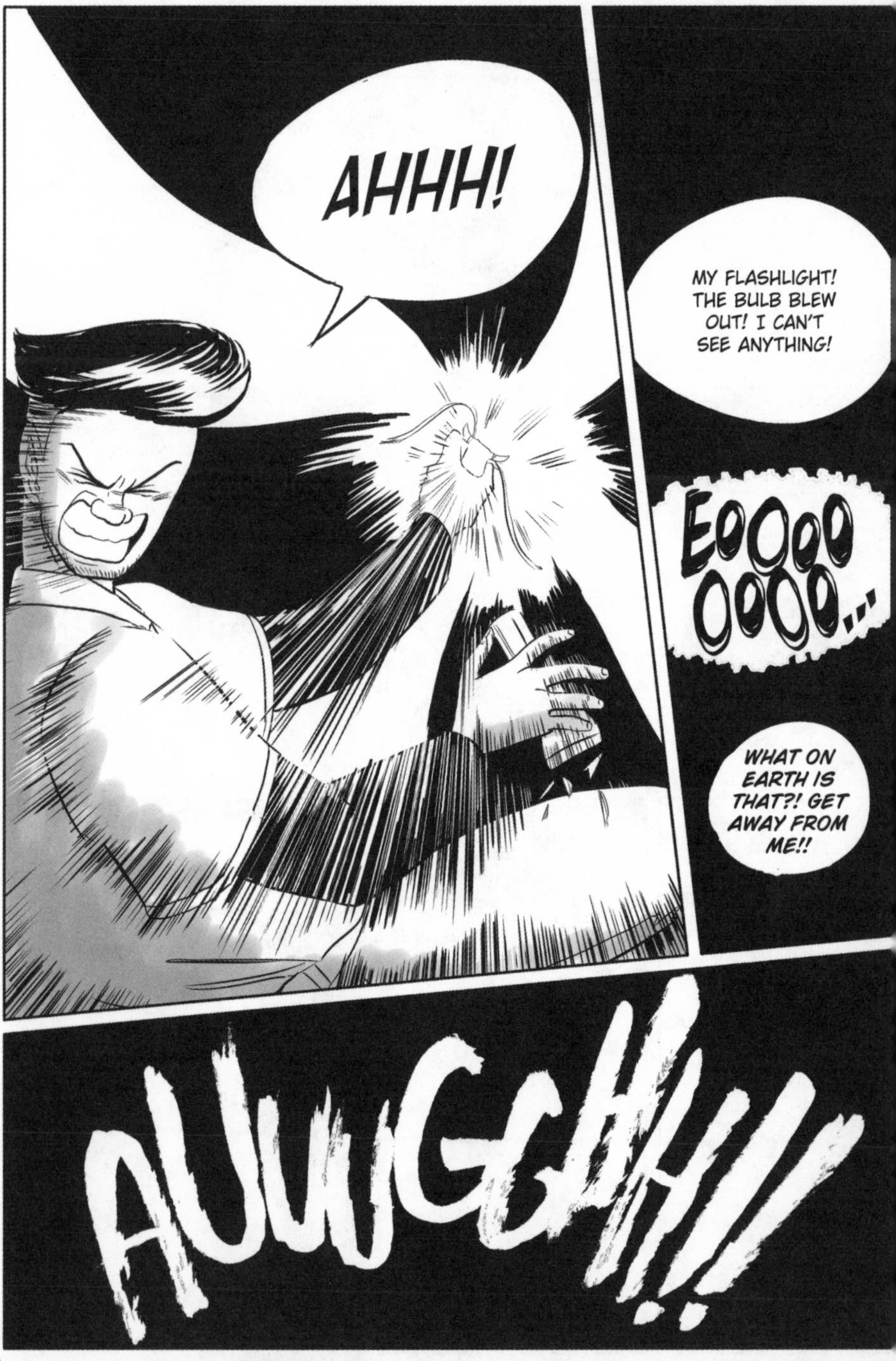
AHHH!
MY FLASHLIGHT! THE BULB BLEW OUT! I CAN'T SEE ANYTHING!
EOOOO OOOO...
WHAT ON EARTH IS THAT?! GET AWAY FROM ME!!
AUUGHH!!

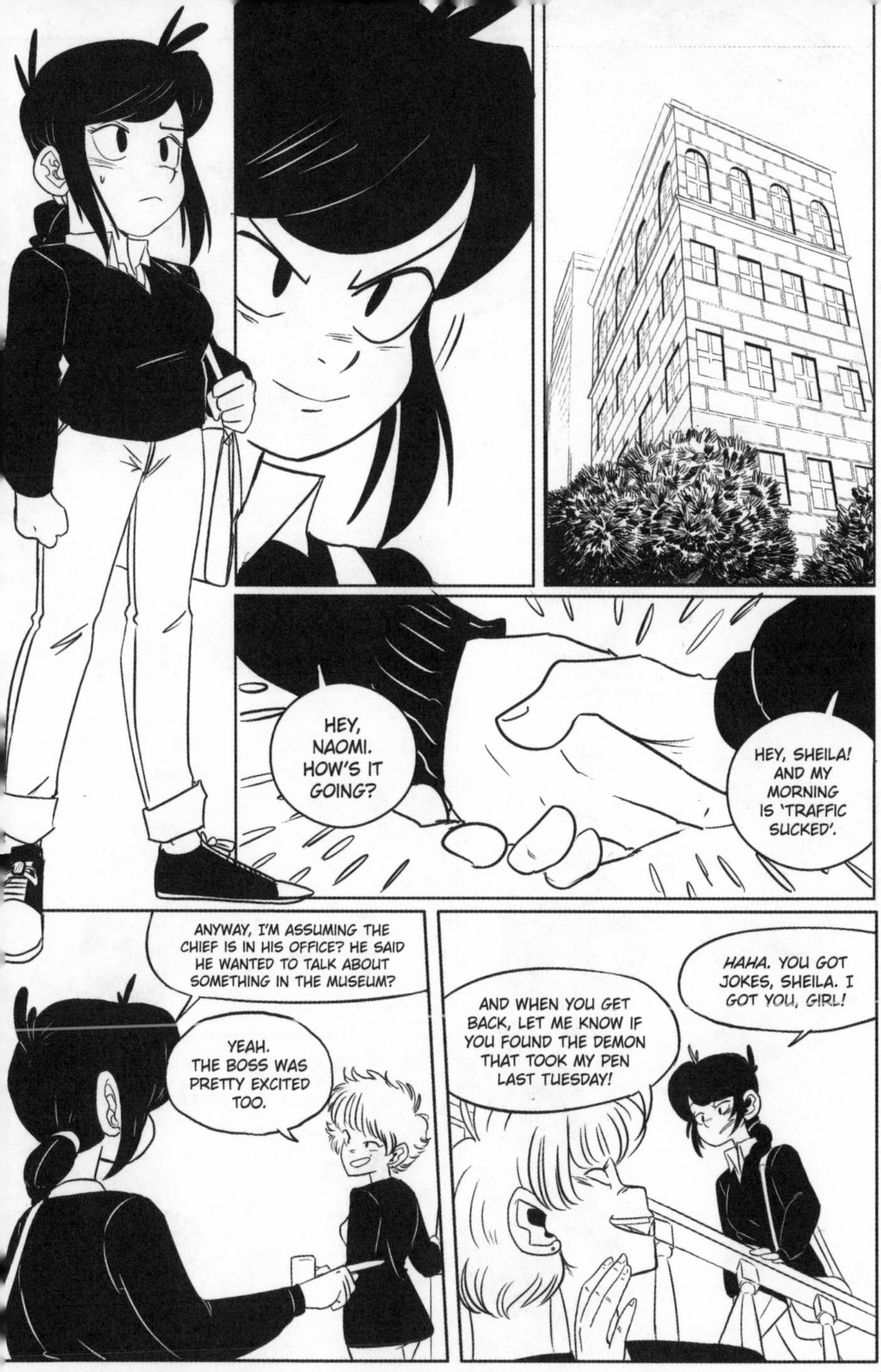
HEY, NAOMI. HOW'S IT GOING?
HEY, SHEILA! AND MY MORNING IS 'TRAFFIC SUCKED'.
ANYWAY, I'M ASSUMING THE CHIEF IS IN HIS OFFICE? HE SAID HE WANTED TO TALK ABOUT SOMETHING IN THE MUSEUM?
YEAH. THE BOSS WAS PRETTY EXCITED TOO.
AND WHEN YOU GET BACK, LET ME KNOW IF YOU FOUND THE DEMON THAT TOOK MY PEN LAST TUESDAY!
HAHA. YOU GOT JOKES, SHEILA. I GOT YOU, GIRL!

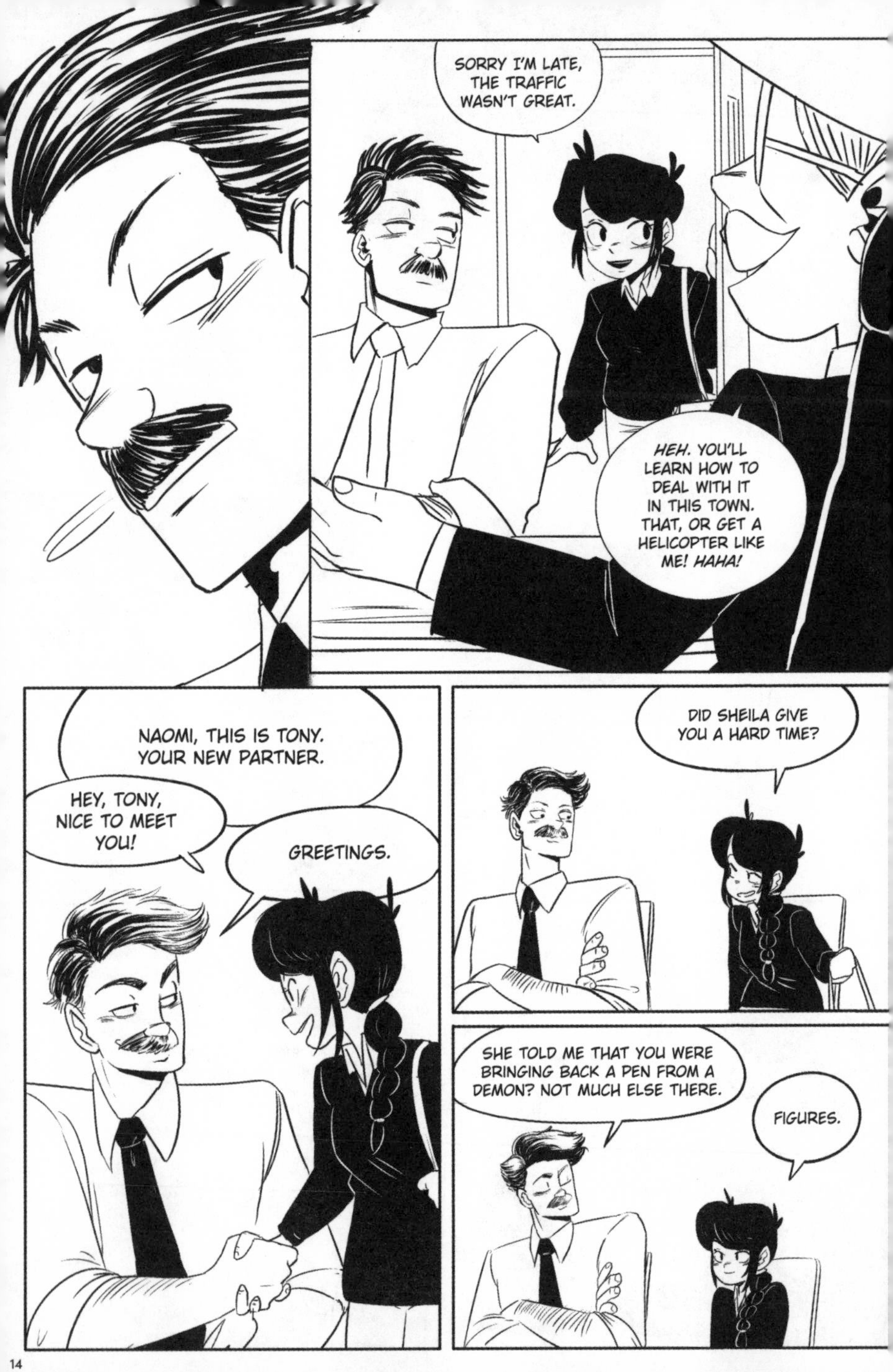
SORRY I'M LATE, THE TRAFFIC WASN'T GREAT.
HEH. YOU'LL LEARN HOW TO DEAL WITH IT IN THIS TOWN. THAT, OR GET A HELICOPTER LIKE ME! *HAHA!*
NAOMI, THIS IS TONY. YOUR NEW PARTNER.
HEY, TONY, NICE TO MEET YOU!
GREETINGS.
DID SHEILA GIVE YOU A HARD TIME?
SHE TOLD ME THAT YOU WERE BRINGING BACK A PEN FROM A DEMON? NOT MUCH ELSE THERE.
FIGURES.

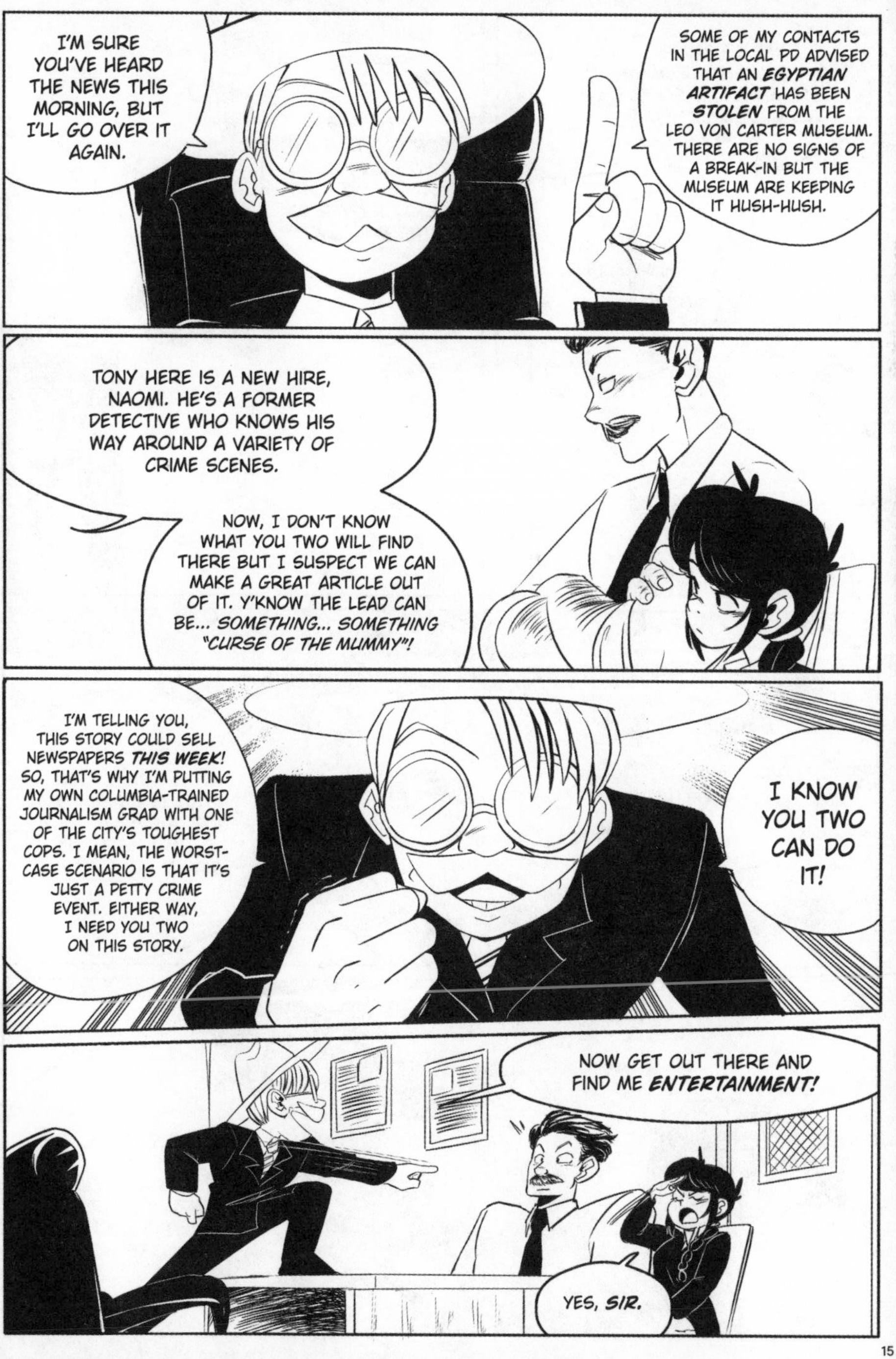
I'M SURE YOU'VE HEARD THE NEWS THIS MORNING, BUT I'LL GO OVER IT AGAIN.
SOME OF MY CONTACTS IN THE LOCAL PD ADVISED THAT AN *EGYPTIAN ARTIFACT* HAS BEEN *STOLEN* FROM THE LEO VON CARTER MUSEUM. THERE ARE NO SIGNS OF A BREAK-IN BUT THE MUSEUM ARE KEEPING IT HUSH-HUSH.
TONY HERE IS A NEW HIRE, NAOMI. HE'S A FORMER DETECTIVE WHO KNOWS HIS WAY AROUND A VARIETY OF CRIME SCENES.
NOW, I DON'T KNOW WHAT YOU TWO WILL FIND THERE BUT I SUSPECT WE CAN MAKE A GREAT ARTICLE OUT OF IT. Y'KNOW THE LEAD CAN BE... *SOMETHING... SOMETHING "CURSE OF THE MUMMY"*!
I'M TELLING YOU, THIS STORY COULD SELL NEWSPAPERS *THIS WEEK*! SO, THAT'S WHY I'M PUTTING MY OWN COLUMBIA-TRAINED JOURNALISM GRAD WITH ONE OF THE CITY'S TOUGHEST COPS. I MEAN, THE WORST-CASE SCENARIO IS THAT IT'S JUST A PETTY CRIME EVENT. EITHER WAY, I NEED YOU TWO ON THIS STORY.
I KNOW YOU TWO CAN DO IT!
NOW GET OUT THERE AND FIND ME *ENTERTAINMENT!*
YES, *SIR.*

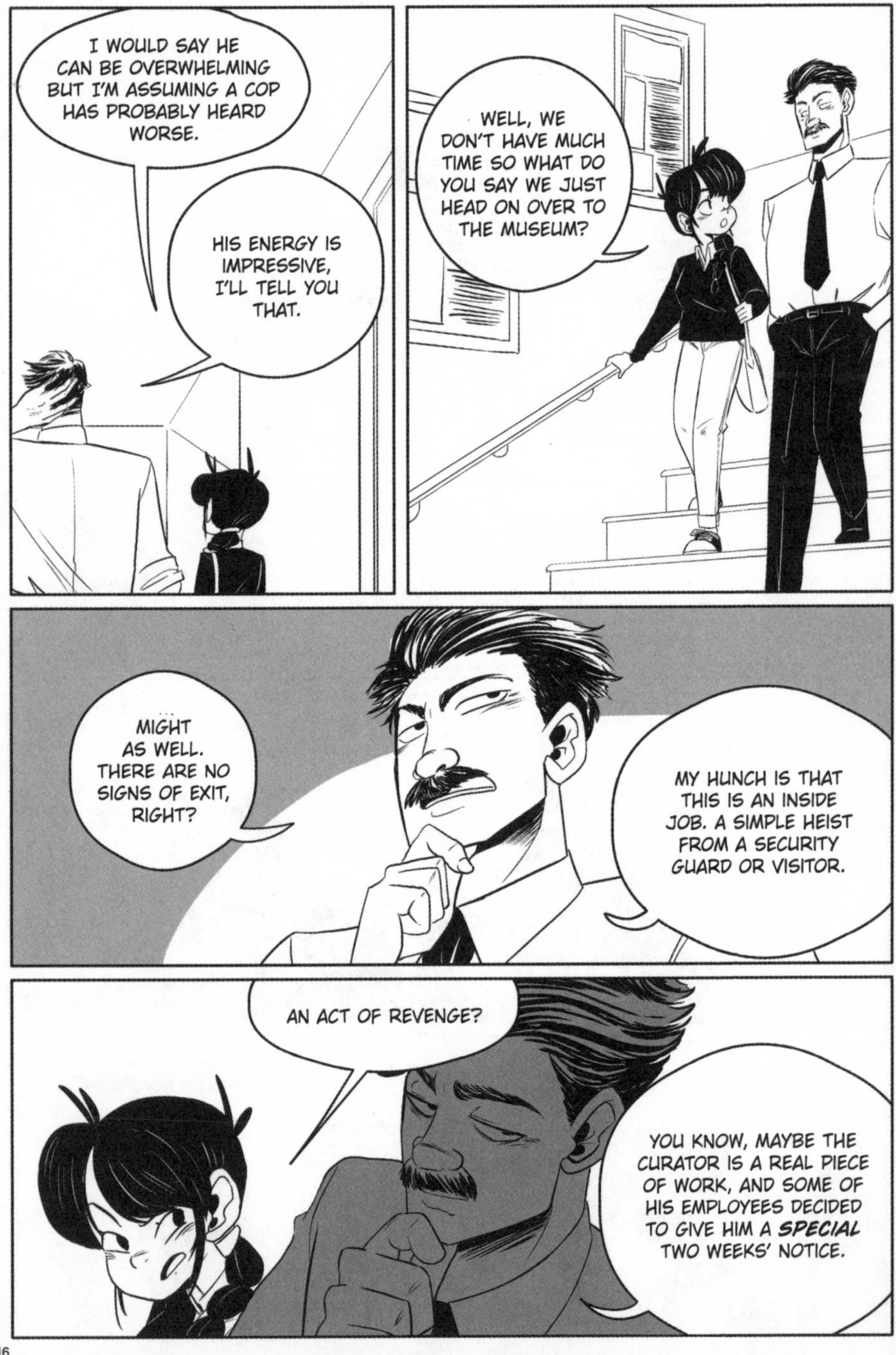
I WOULD SAY HE CAN BE OVERWHELMING BUT I'M ASSUMING A COP HAS PROBABLY HEARD WORSE.
HIS ENERGY IS IMPRESSIVE, I'LL TELL YOU THAT.
WELL, WE DON'T HAVE MUCH TIME SO WHAT DO YOU SAY WE JUST HEAD ON OVER TO THE MUSEUM?
... MIGHT AS WELL. THERE ARE NO SIGNS OF EXIT, RIGHT?
MY HUNCH IS THAT THIS IS AN INSIDE JOB. A SIMPLE HEIST FROM A SECURITY GUARD OR VISITOR.
AN ACT OF REVENGE?
YOU KNOW, MAYBE THE CURATOR IS A REAL PIECE OF WORK, AND SOME OF HIS EMPLOYEES DECIDED TO GIVE HIM A ***SPECIAL*** TWO WEEKS' NOTICE.

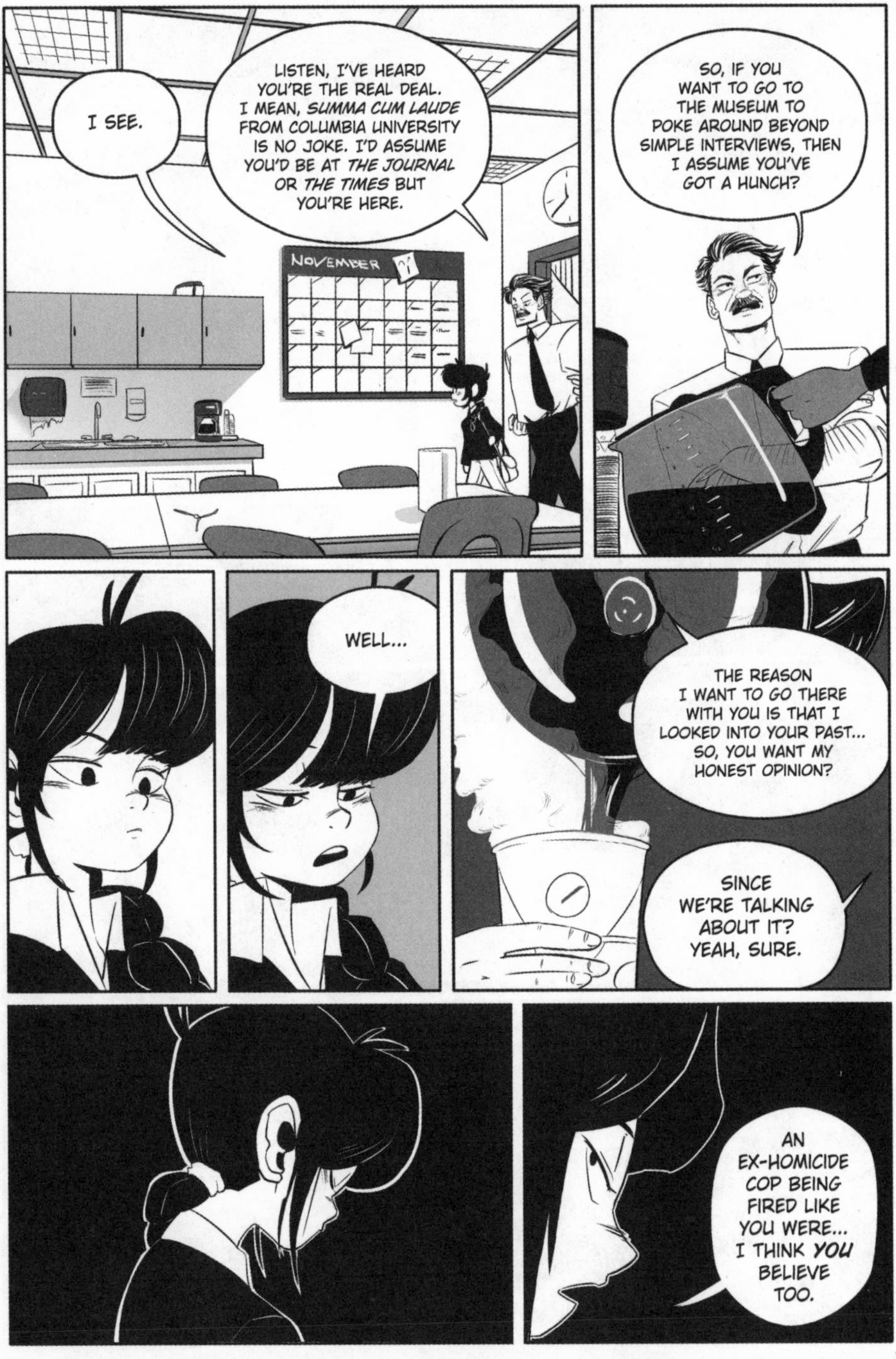
I SEE.
LISTEN, I'VE HEARD YOU'RE THE REAL DEAL. I MEAN, *SUMMA CUM LAUDE* FROM COLUMBIA UNIVERSITY IS NO JOKE. I'D ASSUME YOU'D BE AT *THE JOURNAL* OR *THE TIMES* BUT YOU'RE HERE.
NOVEMBER
SO, IF YOU WANT TO GO TO THE MUSEUM TO POKE AROUND BEYOND SIMPLE INTERVIEWS, THEN I ASSUME YOU'VE GOT A HUNCH?
WELL...
THE REASON I WANT TO GO THERE WITH YOU IS THAT I LOOKED INTO YOUR PAST... SO, YOU WANT MY HONEST OPINION?
SINCE WE'RE TALKING ABOUT IT? YEAH, SURE.
AN EX-HOMICIDE COP BEING FIRED LIKE YOU WERE... I THINK *YOU* BELIEVE TOO.

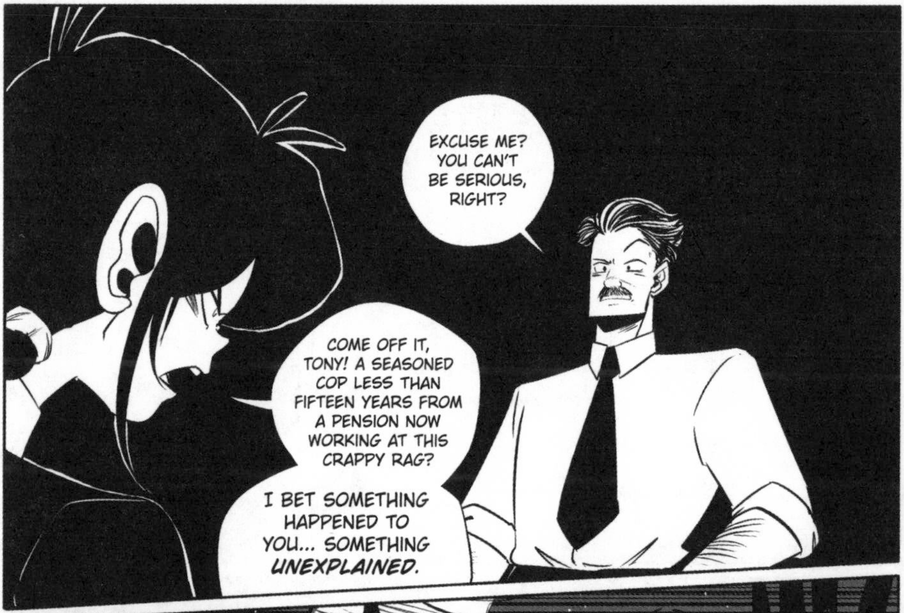

EXCUSE ME? YOU CAN'T BE SERIOUS, RIGHT?
COME OFF IT, TONY! A SEASONED COP LESS THAN FIFTEEN YEARS FROM A PENSION NOW WORKING AT THIS CRAPPY RAG?
I BET SOMETHING HAPPENED TO YOU... SOMETHING *UNEXPLAINED*.

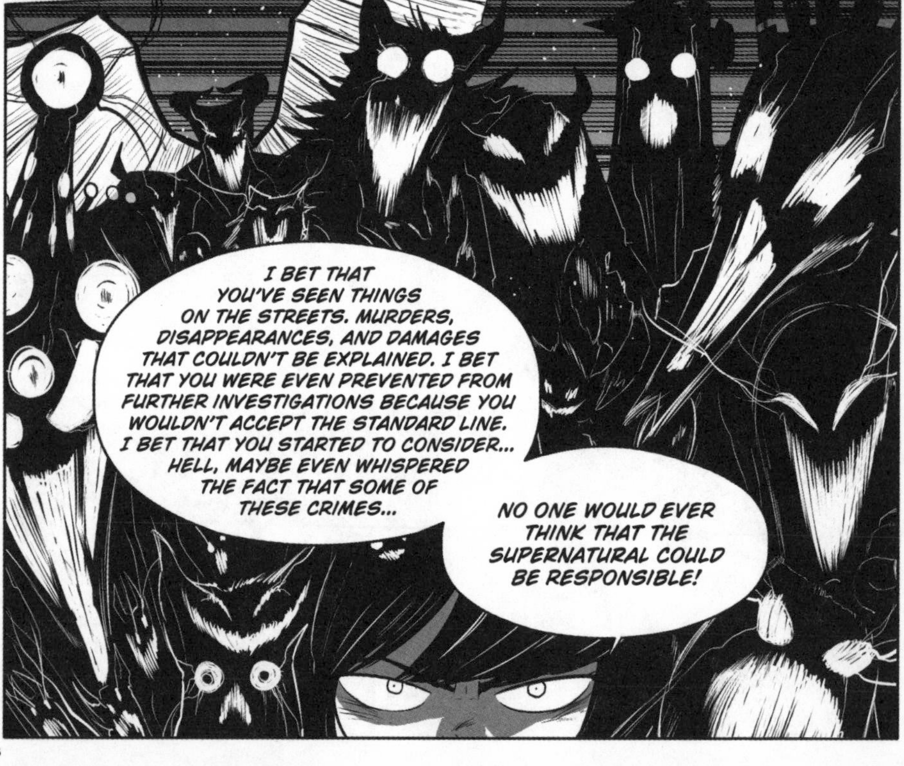

I BET THAT YOU'VE SEEN THINGS ON THE STREETS. MURDERS, DISAPPEARANCES, AND DAMAGES THAT COULDN'T BE EXPLAINED. I BET THAT YOU WERE EVEN PREVENTED FROM FURTHER INVESTIGATIONS BECAUSE YOU WOULDN'T ACCEPT THE STANDARD LINE. I BET THAT YOU STARTED TO CONSIDER... HELL, MAYBE EVEN WHISPERED THE FACT THAT SOME OF THESE CRIMES...
NO ONE WOULD EVER THINK THAT THE SUPERNATURAL COULD BE RESPONSIBLE!

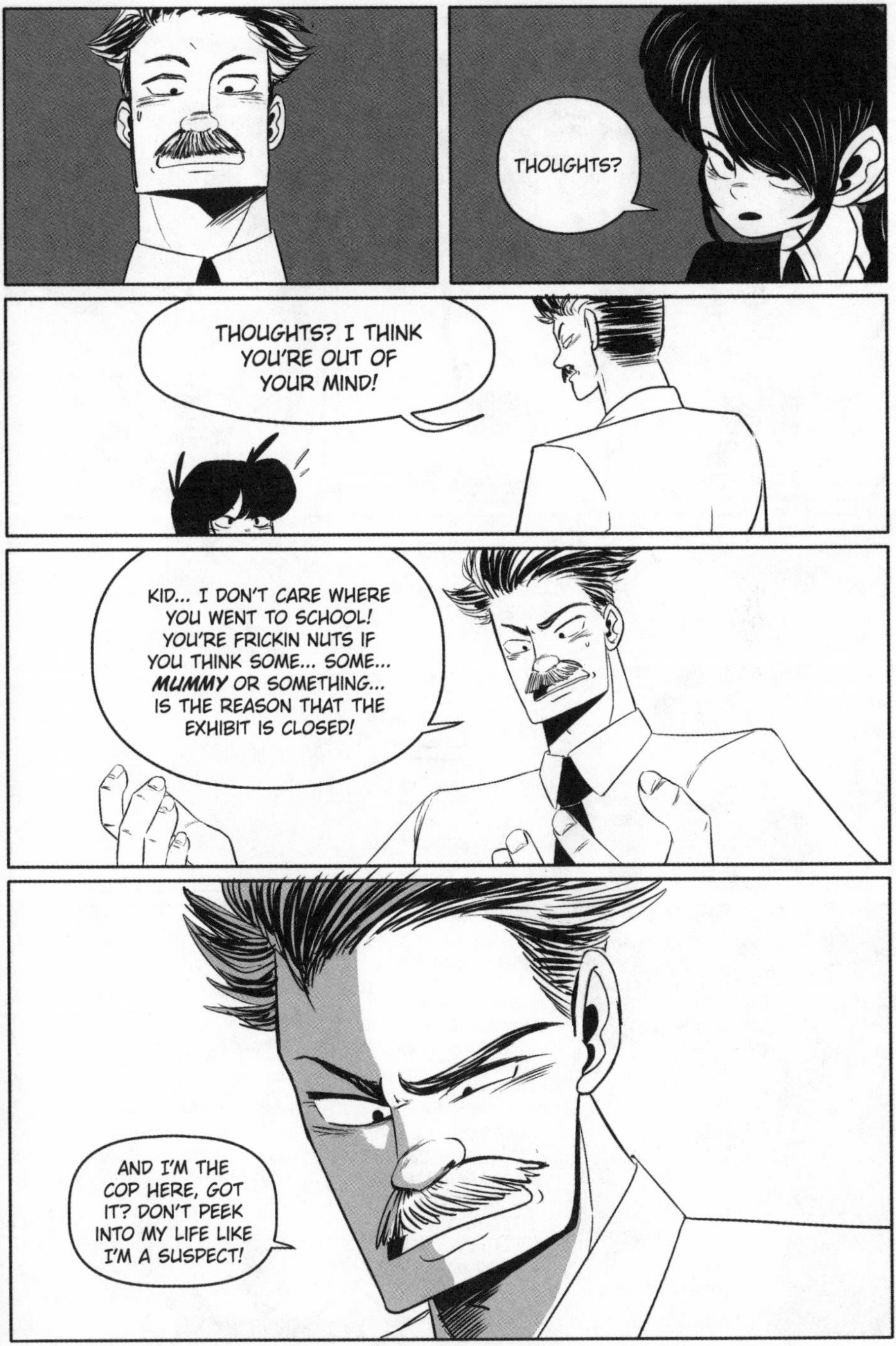
THOUGHTS?
THOUGHTS? I THINK YOU'RE OUT OF YOUR MIND!
KID... I DON'T CARE WHERE YOU WENT TO SCHOOL! YOU'RE FRICKIN NUTS IF YOU THINK SOME... SOME... *MUMMY* OR SOMETHING... IS THE REASON THAT THE EXHIBIT IS CLOSED!
AND I'M THE COP HERE, GOT IT? DON'T PEEK INTO MY LIFE LIKE I'M A SUSPECT!

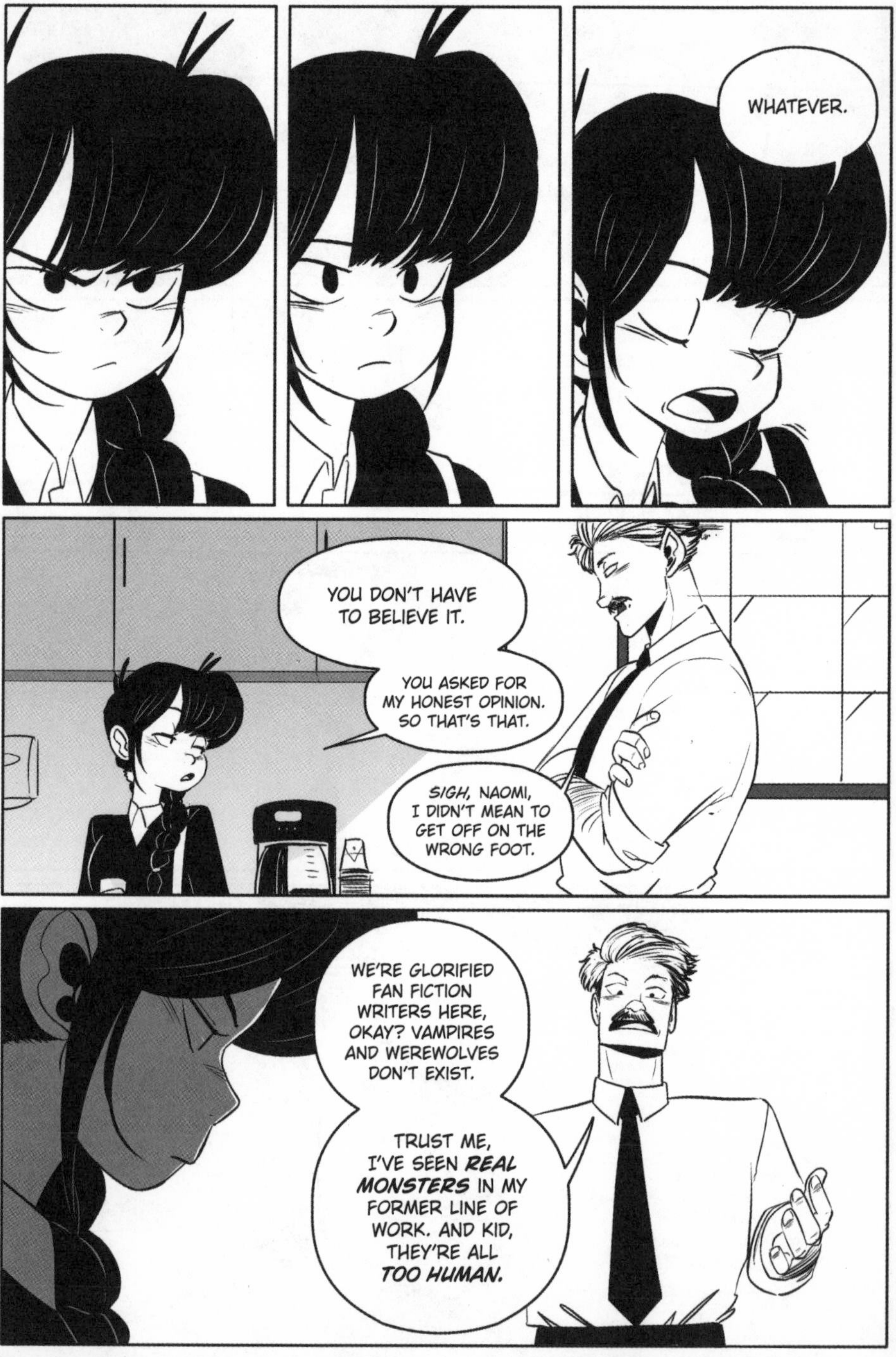
WHATEVER.
YOU DON'T HAVE TO BELIEVE IT.
YOU ASKED FOR MY HONEST OPINION. SO THAT'S THAT.
SIGH, NAOMI, I DIDN'T MEAN TO GET OFF ON THE WRONG FOOT.
WE'RE GLORIFIED FAN FICTION WRITERS HERE, OKAY? VAMPIRES AND WEREWOLVES DON'T EXIST.
TRUST ME, I'VE SEEN ***REAL MONSTERS*** IN MY FORMER LINE OF WORK. AND KID, THEY'RE ALL ***TOO HUMAN.***

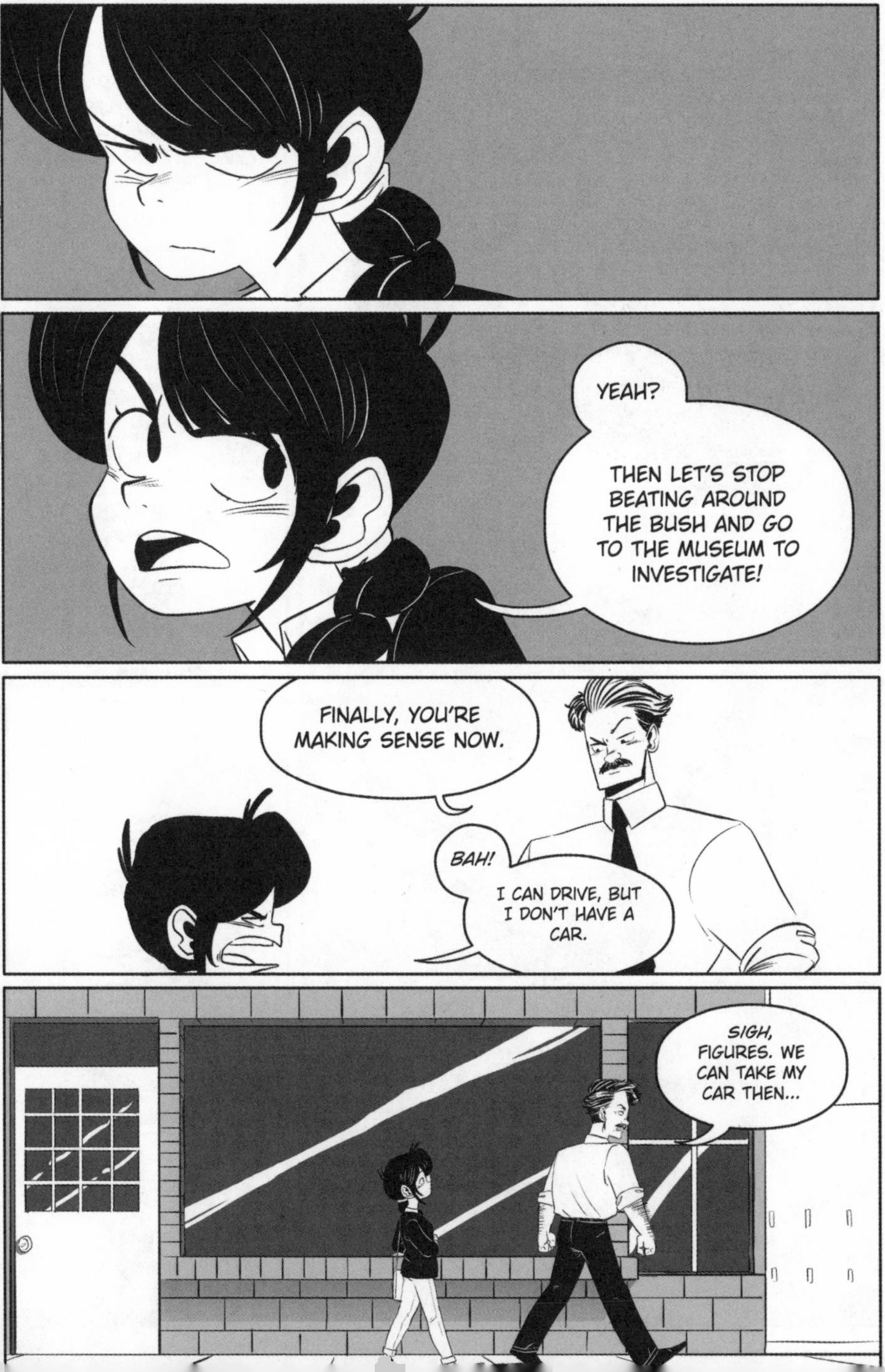
YEAH?
THEN LET'S STOP BEATING AROUND THE BUSH AND GO TO THE MUSEUM TO INVESTIGATE!
FINALLY, YOU'RE MAKING SENSE NOW.
BAH!
I CAN DRIVE, BUT I DON'T HAVE A CAR.
SIGH, FIGURES. WE CAN TAKE MY CAR THEN...

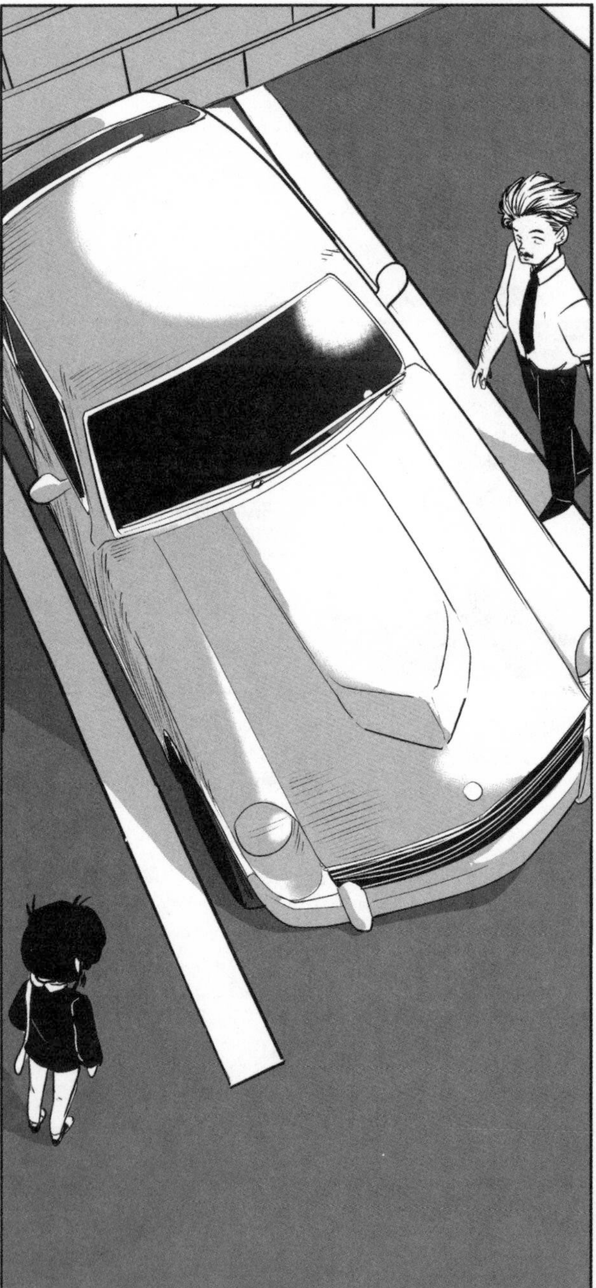

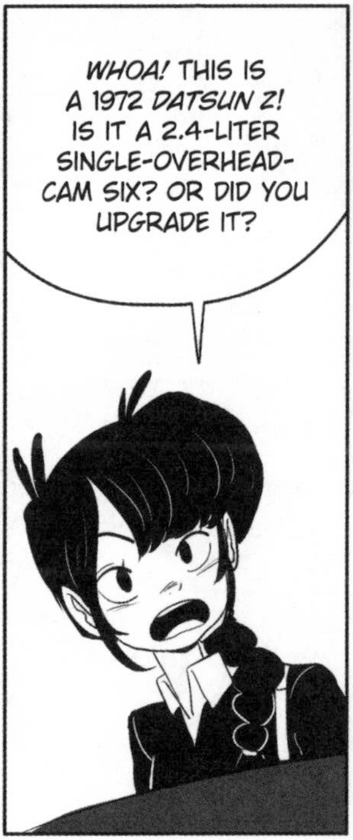
WHOA! THIS IS A 1972 DATSUN Z! IS IT A 2.4-LITER SINGLE-OVERHEAD-CAM SIX? OR DID YOU UPGRADE IT?

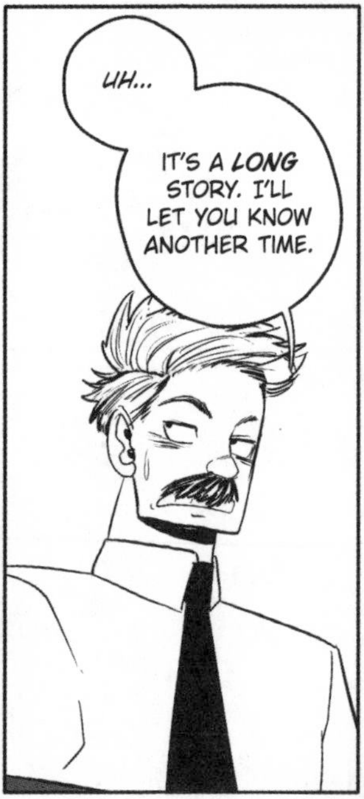
UH...
IT'S A LONG STORY. I'LL LET YOU KNOW ANOTHER TIME.

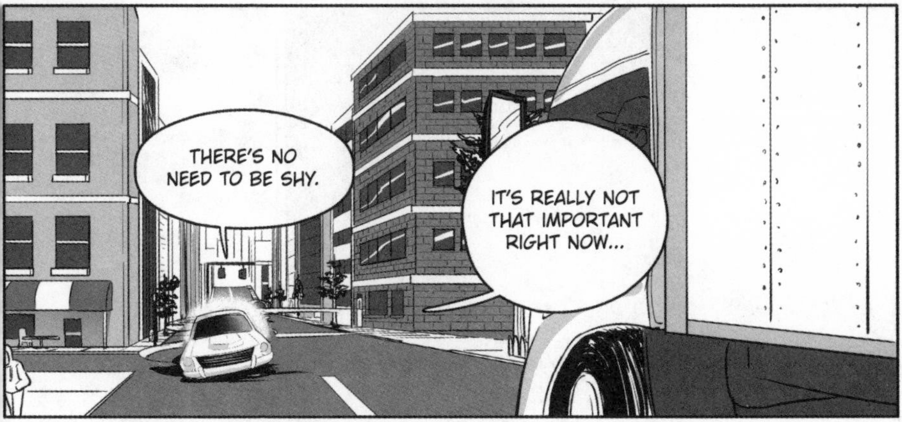
THERE'S NO NEED TO BE SHY.
IT'S REALLY NOT THAT IMPORTANT RIGHT NOW...

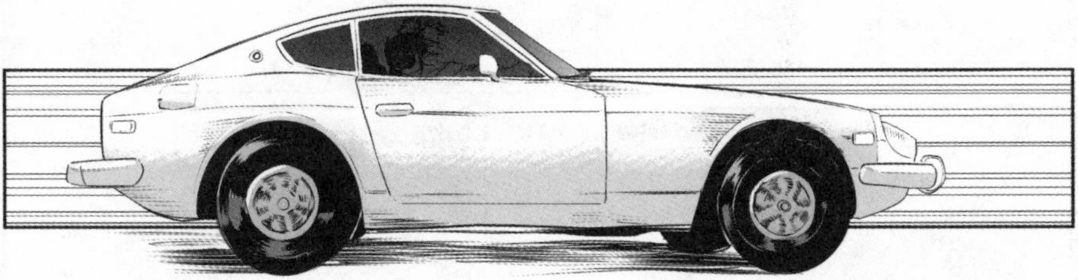

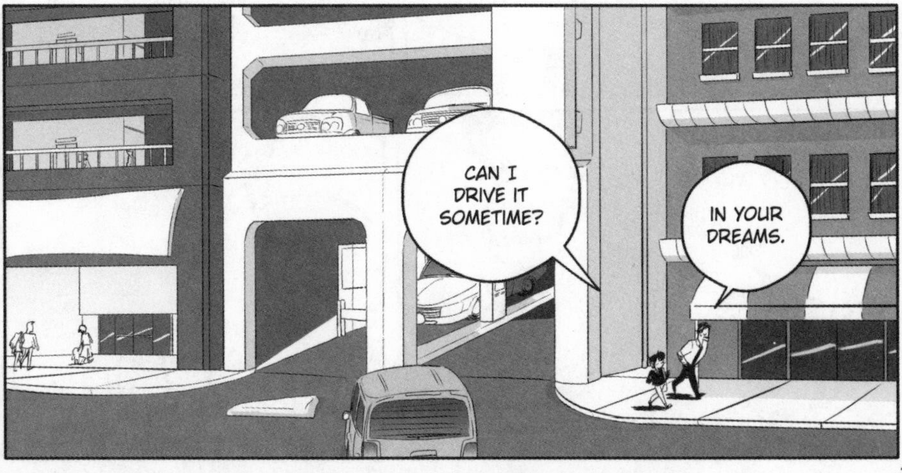
CAN I DRIVE IT SOMETIME?
IN YOUR DREAMS.

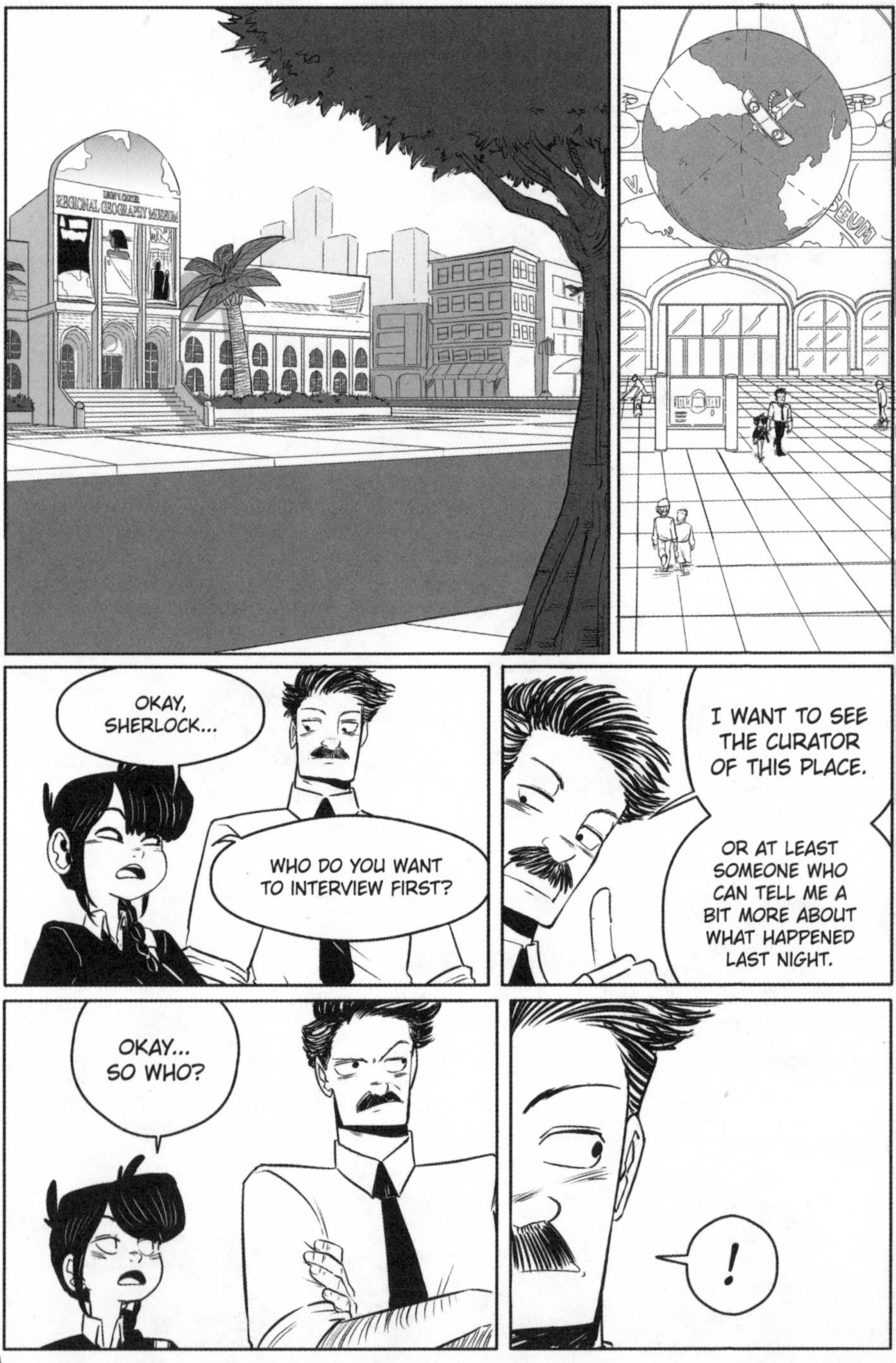
REGIONAL GEOGRAPHY MUSEUM
OKAY, SHERLOCK...
WHO DO YOU WANT TO INTERVIEW FIRST?
I WANT TO SEE THE CURATOR OF THIS PLACE.
OR AT LEAST SOMEONE WHO CAN TELL ME A BIT MORE ABOUT WHAT HAPPENED LAST NIGHT.
OKAY... SO WHO?
!

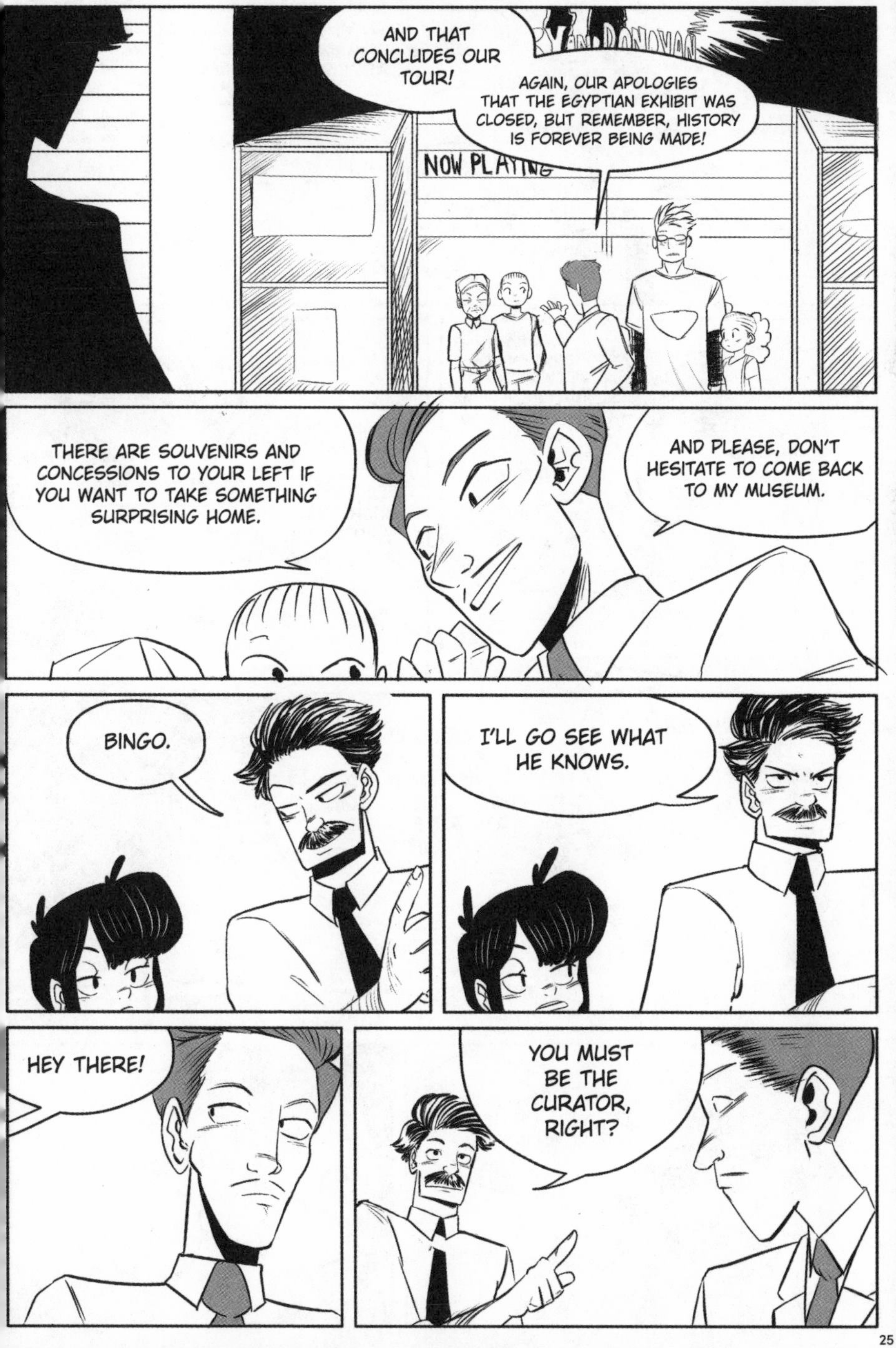
AND THAT CONCLUDES OUR TOUR!
AGAIN, OUR APOLOGIES THAT THE EGYPTIAN EXHIBIT WAS CLOSED, BUT REMEMBER, HISTORY IS FOREVER BEING MADE!
THERE ARE SOUVENIRS AND CONCESSIONS TO YOUR LEFT IF YOU WANT TO TAKE SOMETHING SURPRISING HOME.
AND PLEASE, DON'T HESITATE TO COME BACK TO MY MUSEUM.
BINGO.
I'LL GO SEE WHAT HE KNOWS.
HEY THERE!
YOU MUST BE THE CURATOR, RIGHT?

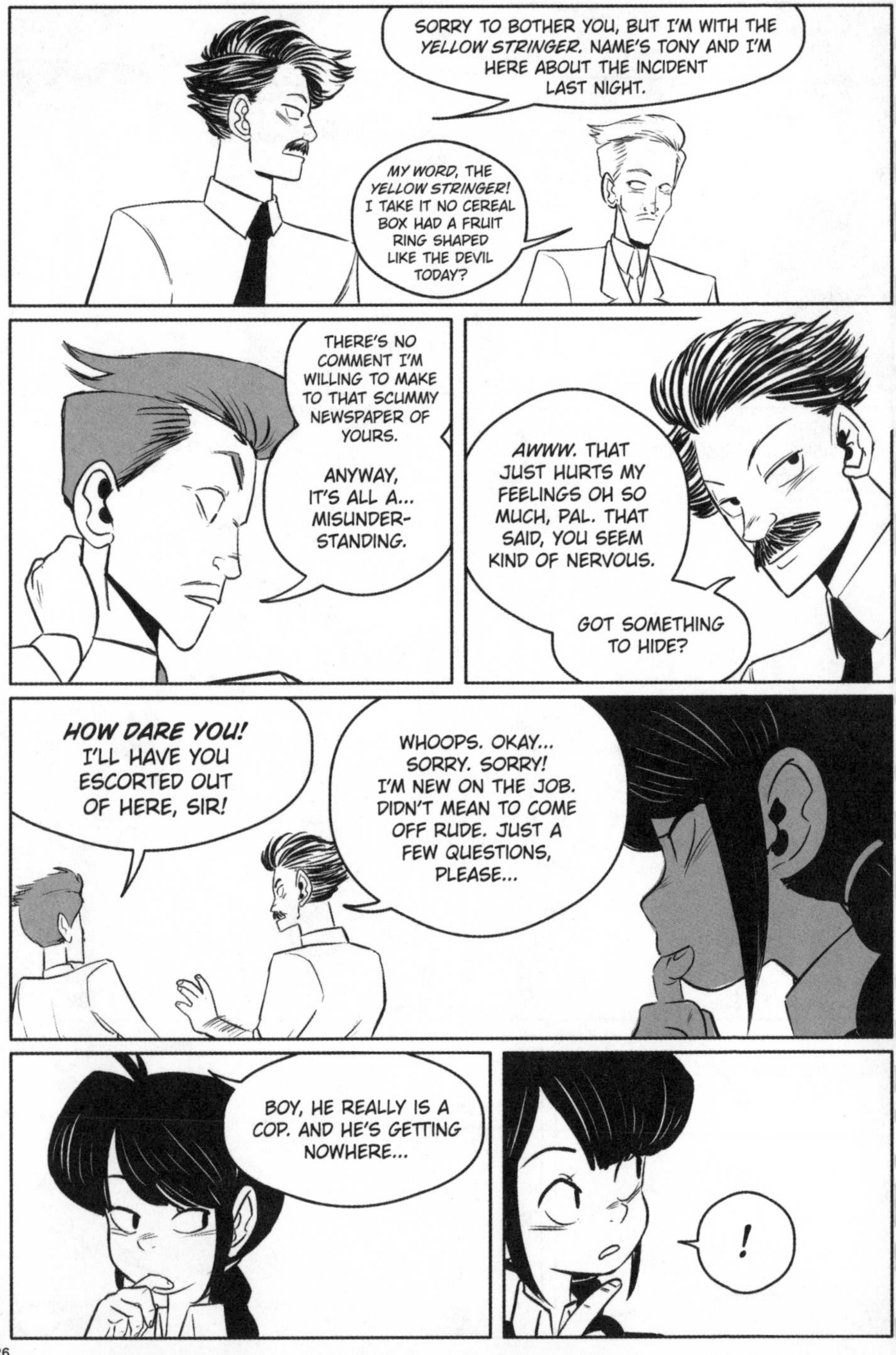
SORRY TO BOTHER YOU, BUT I'M WITH THE *YELLOW STRINGER*. NAME'S TONY AND I'M HERE ABOUT THE INCIDENT LAST NIGHT.
MY WORD, THE *YELLOW STRINGER!* I TAKE IT NO CEREAL BOX HAD A FRUIT RING SHAPED LIKE THE DEVIL TODAY?
THERE'S NO COMMENT I'M WILLING TO MAKE TO THAT SCUMMY NEWSPAPER OF YOURS.
ANYWAY, IT'S ALL A... MISUNDER-STANDING.
AWWW. THAT JUST HURTS MY FEELINGS OH SO MUCH, PAL. THAT SAID, YOU SEEM KIND OF NERVOUS.
GOT SOMETHING TO HIDE?
HOW DARE YOU! I'LL HAVE YOU ESCORTED OUT OF HERE, SIR!
WHOOPS. OKAY... SORRY. SORRY! I'M NEW ON THE JOB. DIDN'T MEAN TO COME OFF RUDE. JUST A FEW QUESTIONS, PLEASE...
BOY, HE REALLY IS A COP. AND HE'S GETTING NOWHERE...
!

THAT'S WHERE THE EXHIBIT IS...

Y'KNOW... I'M A BIT OF A HISTORY BUFF, MYSELF. I'VE GOT A MICHAEL JORDAN JERSEY FROM HIS ROOKIE YEAR.

I'M SURE I WANT TO RETURN TO MY JOB...

WOOSH!!

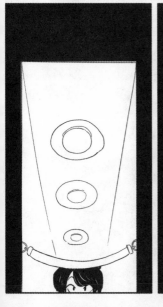

WOW...

THEY SHUT DOWN THE WHOLE ROOM.

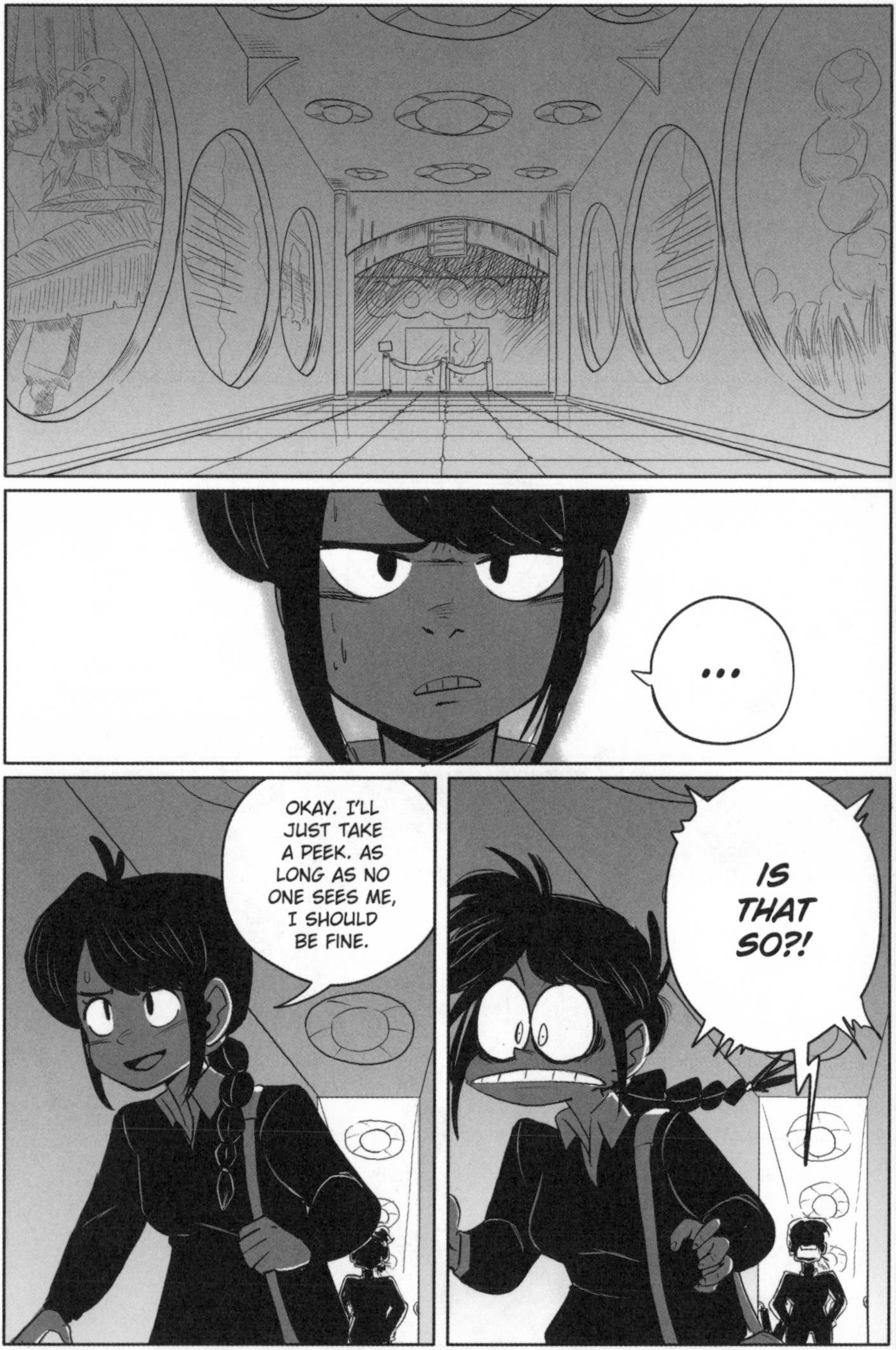
...
OKAY. I'LL JUST TAKE A PEEK. AS LONG AS NO ONE SEES ME, I SHOULD BE FINE.
IS THAT SO?!

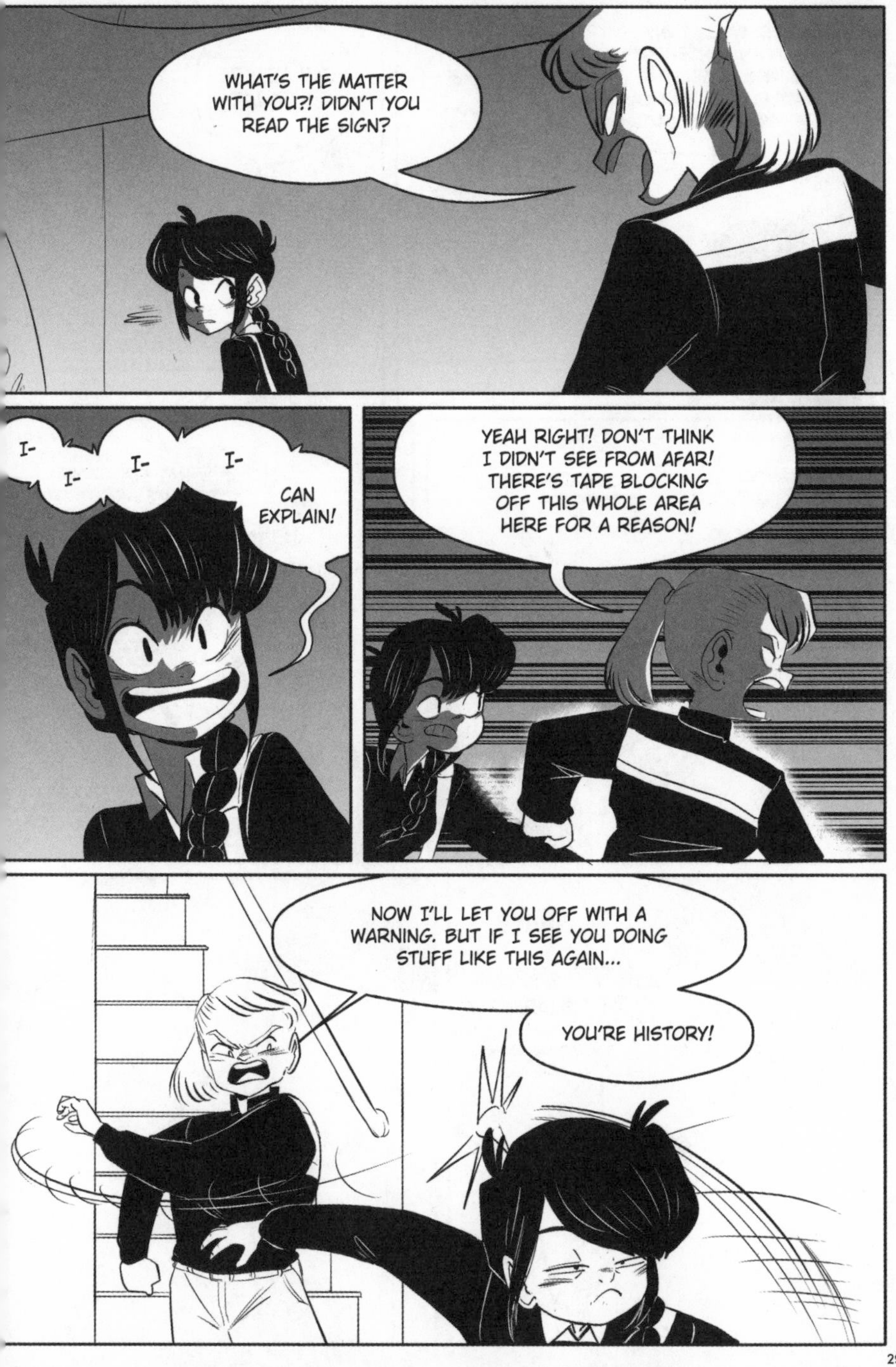
WHAT'S THE MATTER WITH YOU?! DIDN'T YOU READ THE SIGN?
I- I- I- I- CAN EXPLAIN!
YEAH RIGHT! DON'T THINK I DIDN'T SEE FROM AFAR! THERE'S TAPE BLOCKING OFF THIS WHOLE AREA HERE FOR A REASON!
NOW I'LL LET YOU OFF WITH A WARNING. BUT IF I SEE YOU DOING STUFF LIKE THIS AGAIN...
YOU'RE HISTORY!

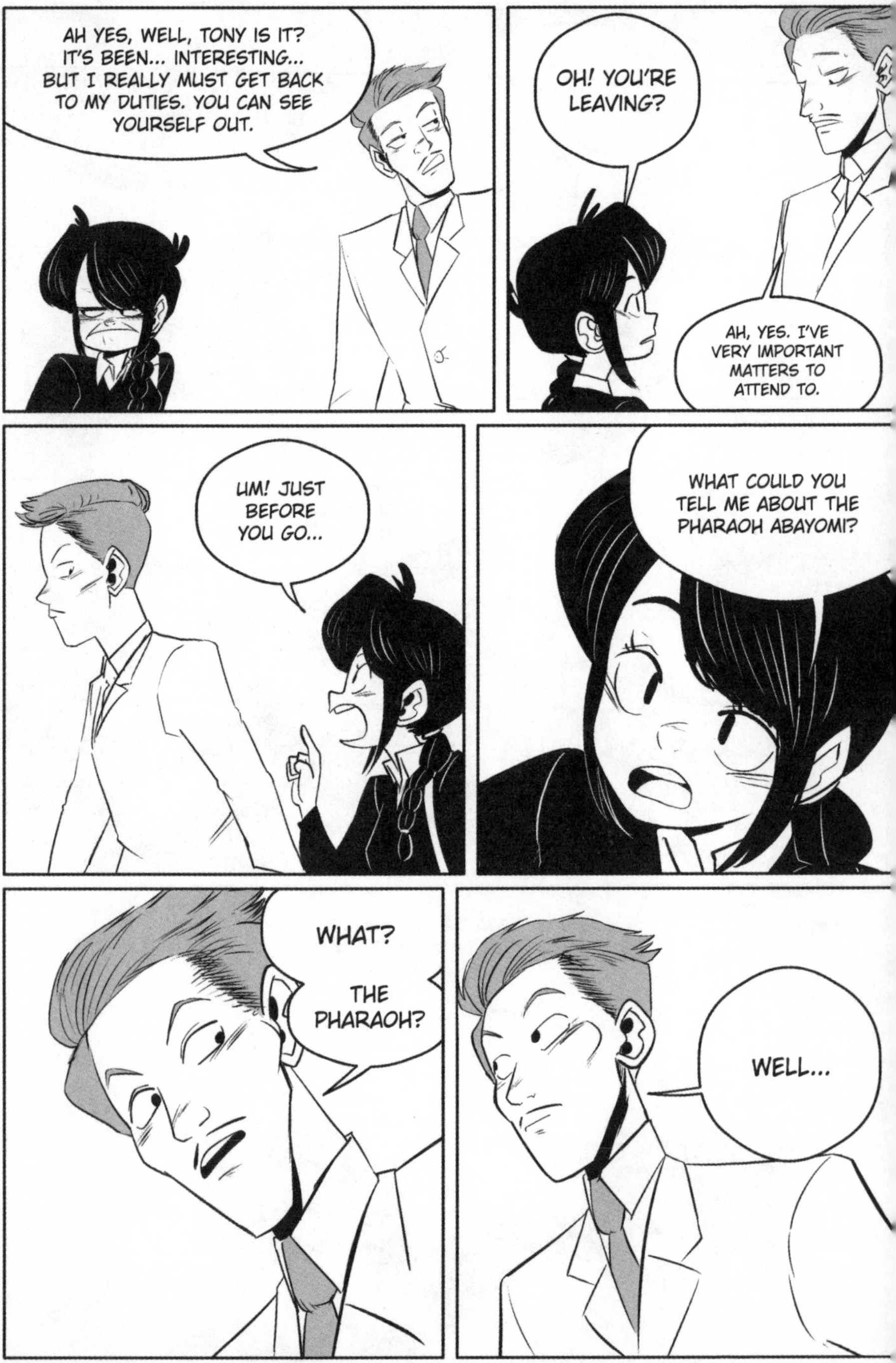
AH YES, WELL, TONY IS IT? IT'S BEEN... INTERESTING... BUT I REALLY MUST GET BACK TO MY DUTIES. YOU CAN SEE YOURSELF OUT.
OH! YOU'RE LEAVING?
AH, YES. I'VE VERY IMPORTANT MATTERS TO ATTEND TO.
UM! JUST BEFORE YOU GO...
WHAT COULD YOU TELL ME ABOUT THE PHARAOH ABAYOMI?
WHAT?
THE PHARAOH?
WELL...

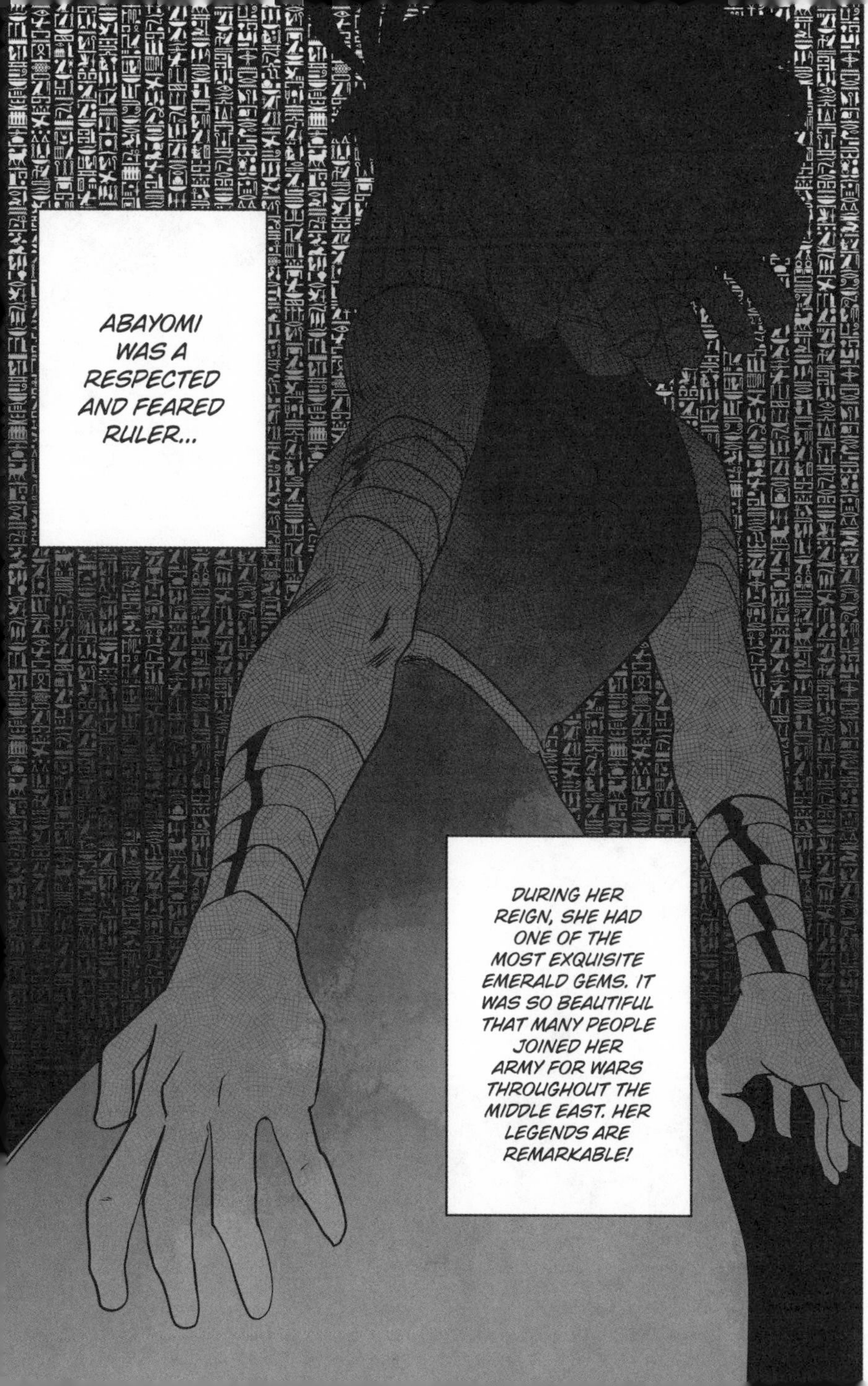
ABAYOMI WAS A RESPECTED AND FEARED RULER...
DURING HER REIGN, SHE HAD ONE OF THE MOST EXQUISITE EMERALD GEMS. IT WAS SO BEAUTIFUL THAT MANY PEOPLE JOINED HER ARMY FOR WARS THROUGHOUT THE MIDDLE EAST. HER LEGENDS ARE REMARKABLE!

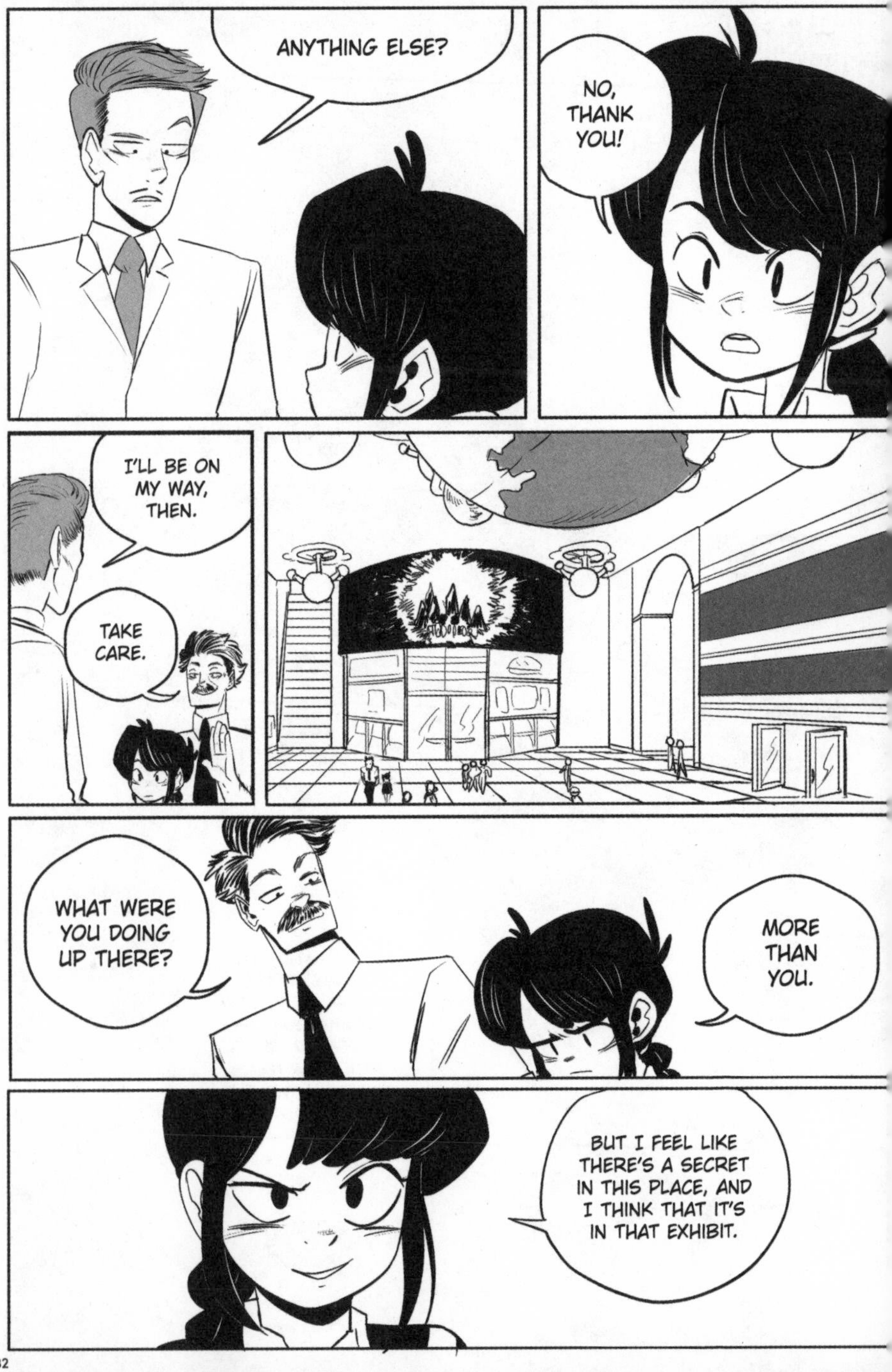
ANYTHING ELSE?
NO, THANK YOU!
I'LL BE ON MY WAY, THEN.
TAKE CARE.
WHAT WERE YOU DOING UP THERE?
MORE THAN YOU.
BUT I FEEL LIKE THERE'S A SECRET IN THIS PLACE, AND I THINK THAT IT'S IN THAT EXHIBIT.

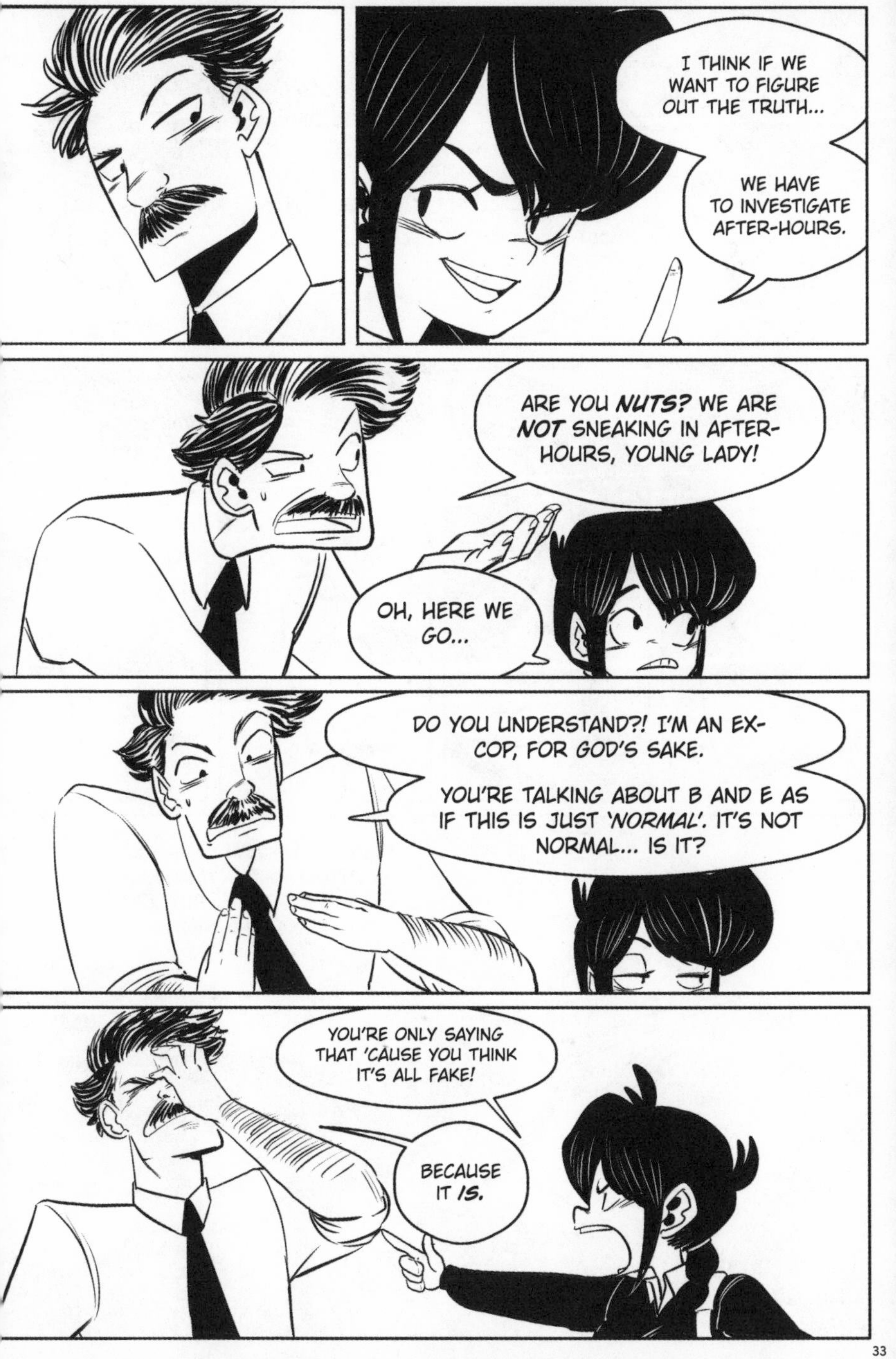
I THINK IF WE WANT TO FIGURE OUT THE TRUTH...
WE HAVE TO INVESTIGATE AFTER-HOURS.
ARE YOU *NUTS?* WE ARE *NOT* SNEAKING IN AFTER-HOURS, YOUNG LADY!
OH, HERE WE GO...
DO YOU UNDERSTAND?! I'M AN EX-COP, FOR GOD'S SAKE.
YOU'RE TALKING ABOUT B AND E AS IF THIS IS JUST '*NORMAL*'. IT'S NOT NORMAL... IS IT?
YOU'RE ONLY SAYING THAT 'CAUSE YOU THINK IT'S ALL FAKE!
BECAUSE IT *IS.*

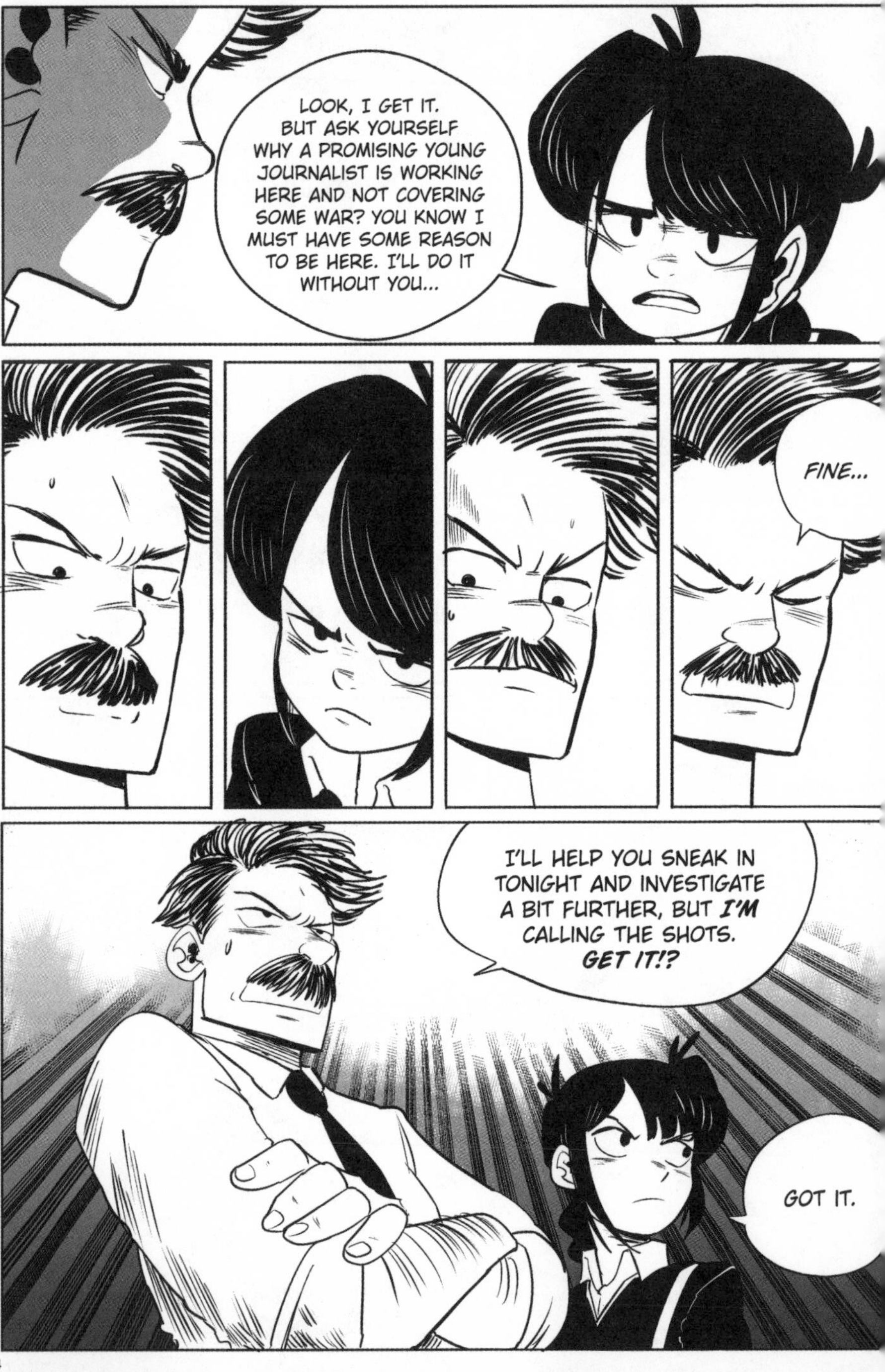
LOOK, I GET IT. BUT ASK YOURSELF WHY A PROMISING YOUNG JOURNALIST IS WORKING HERE AND NOT COVERING SOME WAR? YOU KNOW I MUST HAVE SOME REASON TO BE HERE. I'LL DO IT WITHOUT YOU...
FINE...
I'LL HELP YOU SNEAK IN TONIGHT AND INVESTIGATE A BIT FURTHER, BUT ***I'M*** CALLING THE SHOTS. ***GET IT!?***
GOT IT.

Article 2: Late-Night Fun

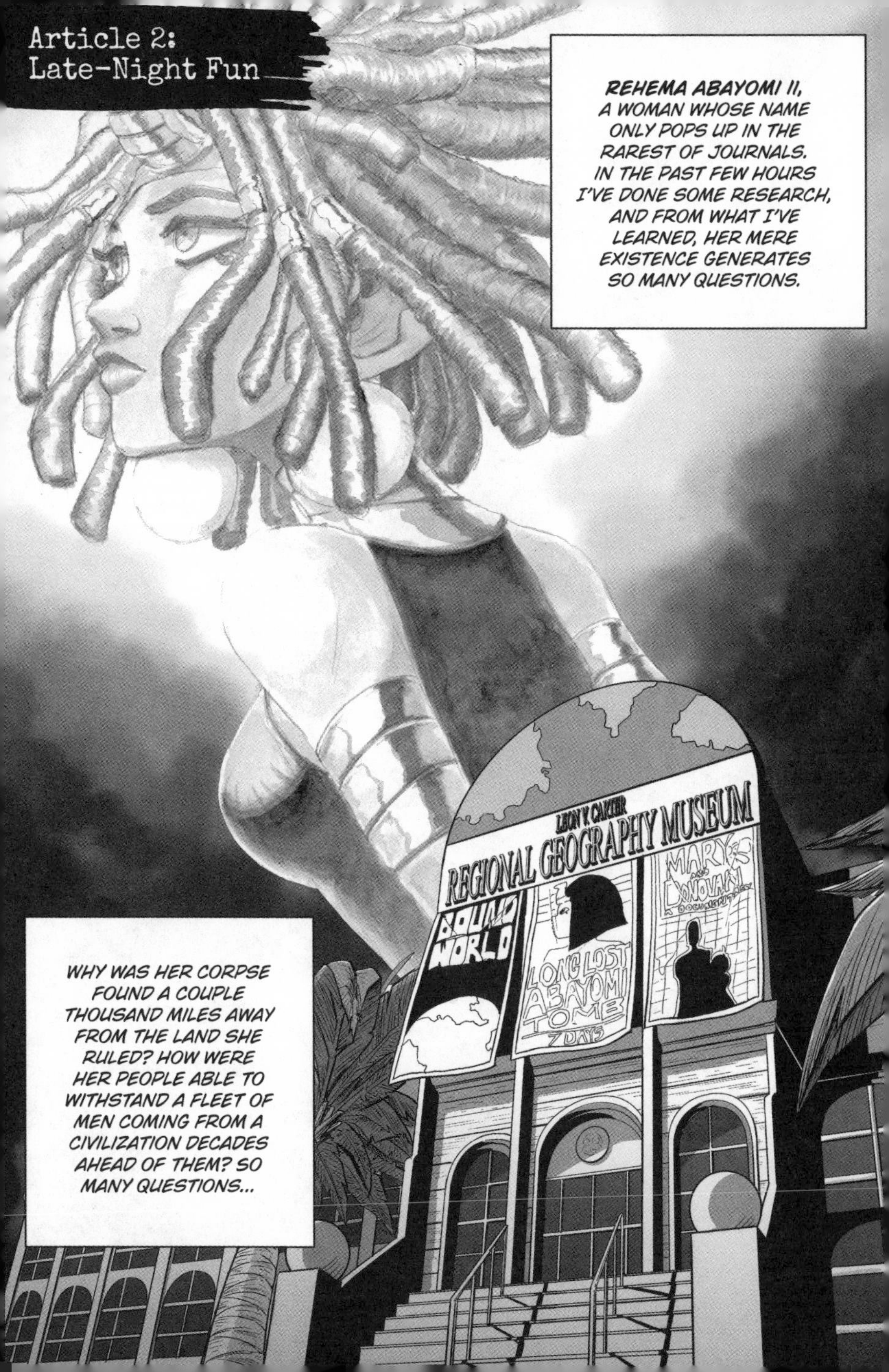
REHEMA ABAYOMI II, A WOMAN WHOSE NAME ONLY POPS UP IN THE RAREST OF JOURNALS. IN THE PAST FEW HOURS I'VE DONE SOME RESEARCH, AND FROM WHAT I'VE LEARNED, HER MERE EXISTENCE GENERATES SO MANY QUESTIONS.
LEON V. CARTER
REGIONAL GEOGRAPHY MUSEUM
LONG LOST ABAYOMI TOMB
7 DAYS
MARY AND DONOVAN
WHY WAS HER CORPSE FOUND A COUPLE THOUSAND MILES AWAY FROM THE LAND SHE RULED? HOW WERE HER PEOPLE ABLE TO WITHSTAND A FLEET OF MEN COMING FROM A CIVILIZATION DECADES AHEAD OF THEM? SO MANY QUESTIONS...

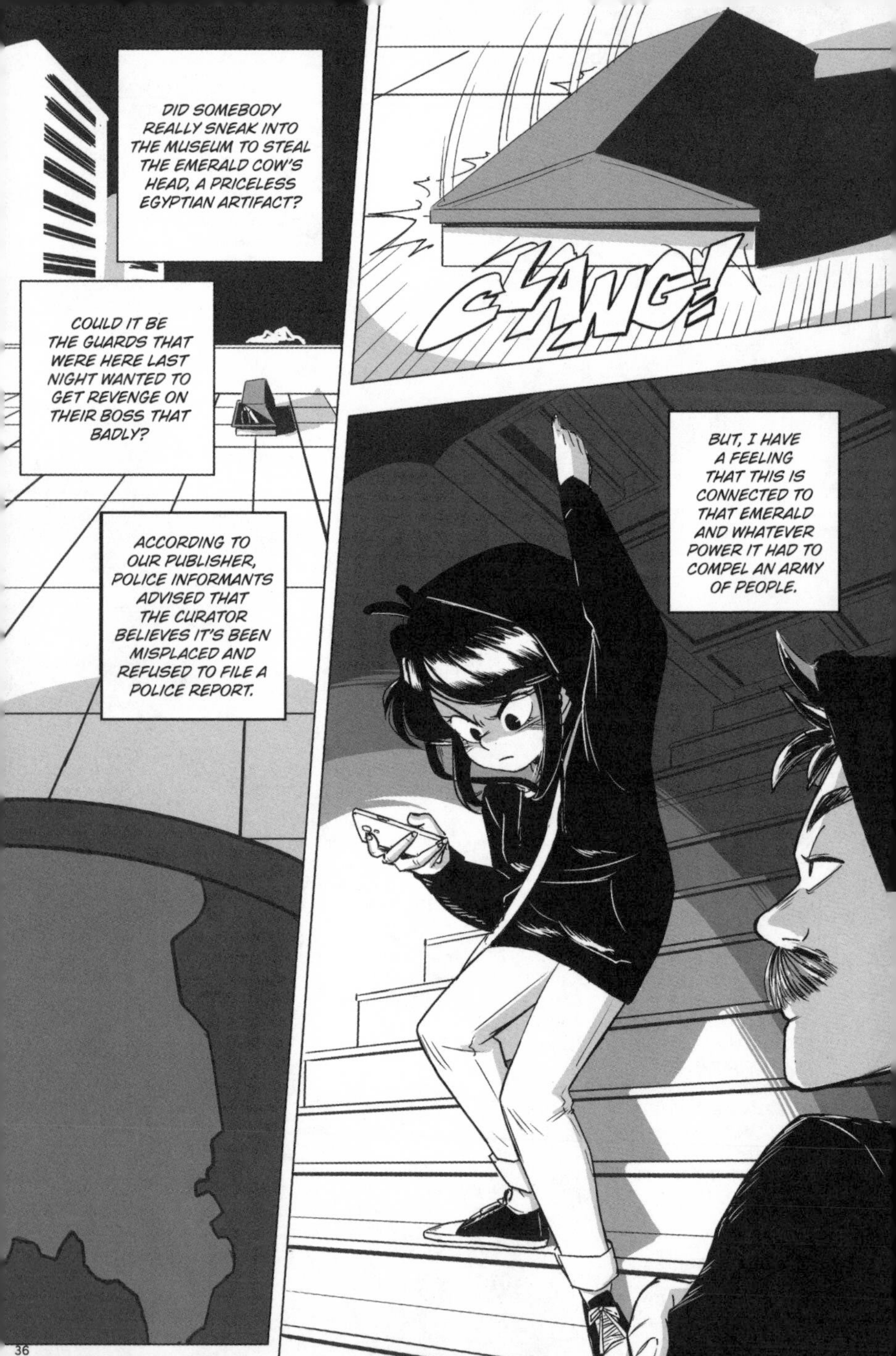
DID SOMEBODY REALLY SNEAK INTO THE MUSEUM TO STEAL THE EMERALD COW'S HEAD, A PRICELESS EGYPTIAN ARTIFACT?
COULD IT BE THE GUARDS THAT WERE HERE LAST NIGHT WANTED TO GET REVENGE ON THEIR BOSS THAT BADLY?
ACCORDING TO OUR PUBLISHER, POLICE INFORMANTS ADVISED THAT THE CURATOR BELIEVES IT'S BEEN MISPLACED AND REFUSED TO FILE A POLICE REPORT.
CLANG!
BUT, I HAVE A FEELING THAT THIS IS CONNECTED TO THAT EMERALD AND WHATEVER POWER IT HAD TO COMPEL AN ARMY OF PEOPLE.

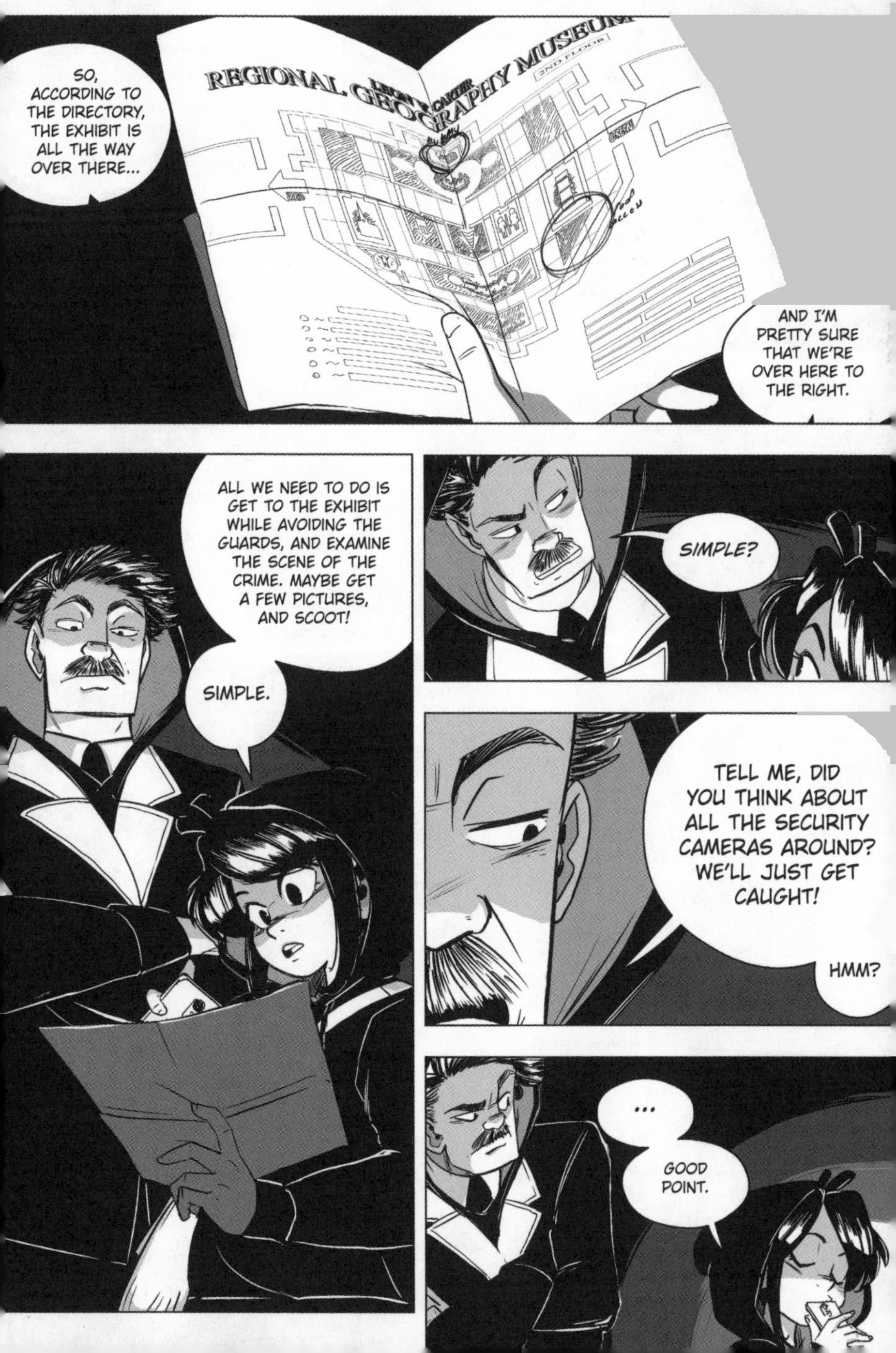
SO, ACCORDING TO THE DIRECTORY, THE EXHIBIT IS ALL THE WAY OVER THERE...
REGIONAL GEOGRAPHY MUSEUM
2ND FLOOR
AND I'M PRETTY SURE THAT WE'RE OVER HERE TO THE RIGHT.
ALL WE NEED TO DO IS GET TO THE EXHIBIT WHILE AVOIDING THE GUARDS, AND EXAMINE THE SCENE OF THE CRIME. MAYBE GET A FEW PICTURES, AND SCOOT!
SIMPLE.
SIMPLE?
TELL ME, DID YOU THINK ABOUT ALL THE SECURITY CAMERAS AROUND? WE'LL JUST GET CAUGHT!
HMM?
...
GOOD POINT.

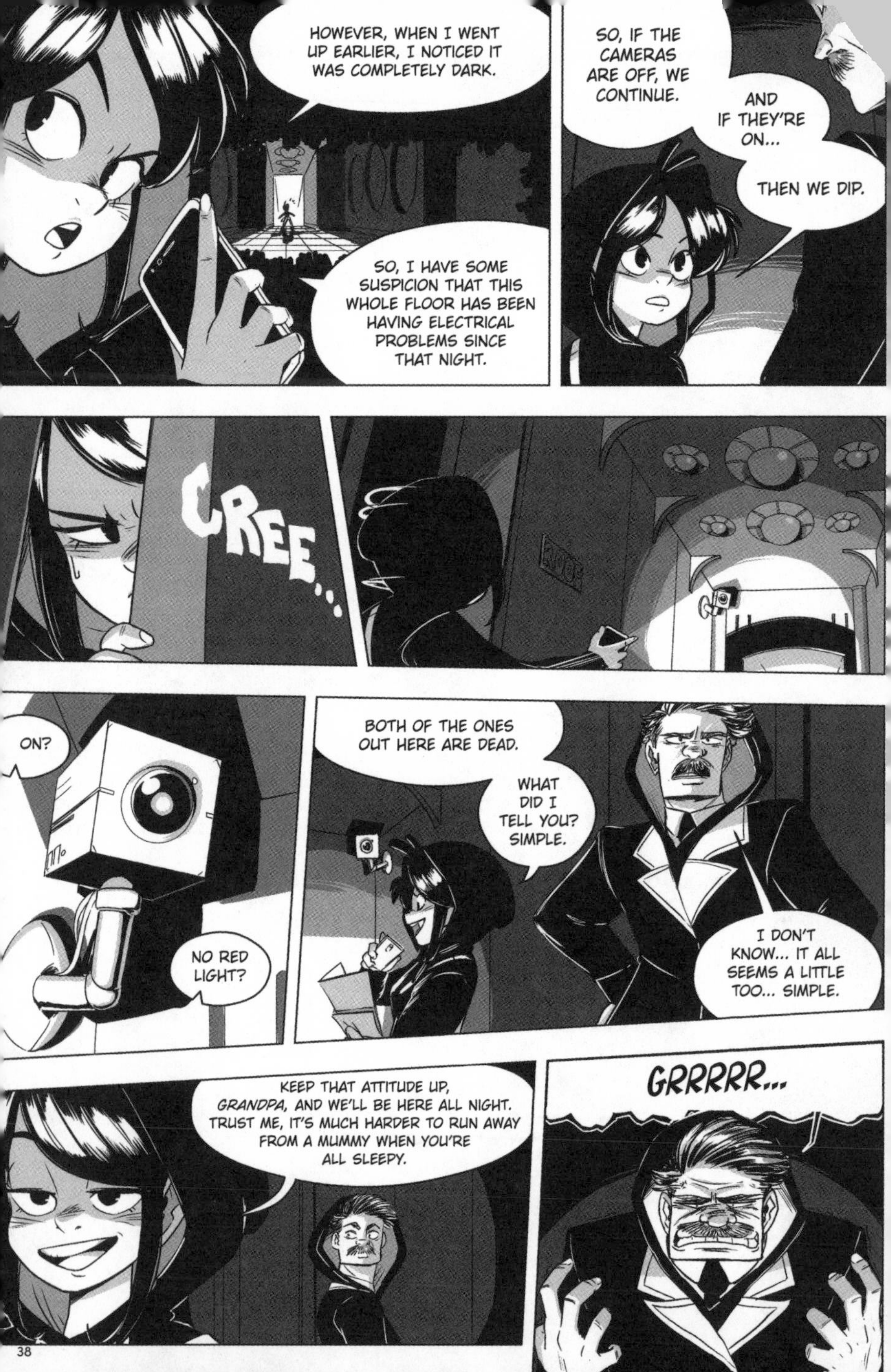
HOWEVER, WHEN I WENT UP EARLIER, I NOTICED IT WAS COMPLETELY DARK.
SO, I HAVE SOME SUSPICION THAT THIS WHOLE FLOOR HAS BEEN HAVING ELECTRICAL PROBLEMS SINCE THAT NIGHT.
SO, IF THE CAMERAS ARE OFF, WE CONTINUE.
AND IF THEY'RE ON...
THEN WE DIP.
CREE...
ROOF
ON?
NO RED LIGHT?
BOTH OF THE ONES OUT HERE ARE DEAD.
WHAT DID I TELL YOU? SIMPLE.
I DON'T KNOW... IT ALL SEEMS A LITTLE TOO... SIMPLE.
KEEP THAT ATTITUDE UP, *GRANDPA*, AND WE'LL BE HERE ALL NIGHT. TRUST ME, IT'S MUCH HARDER TO RUN AWAY FROM A MUMMY WHEN YOU'RE ALL SLEEPY.
GRRRRR...

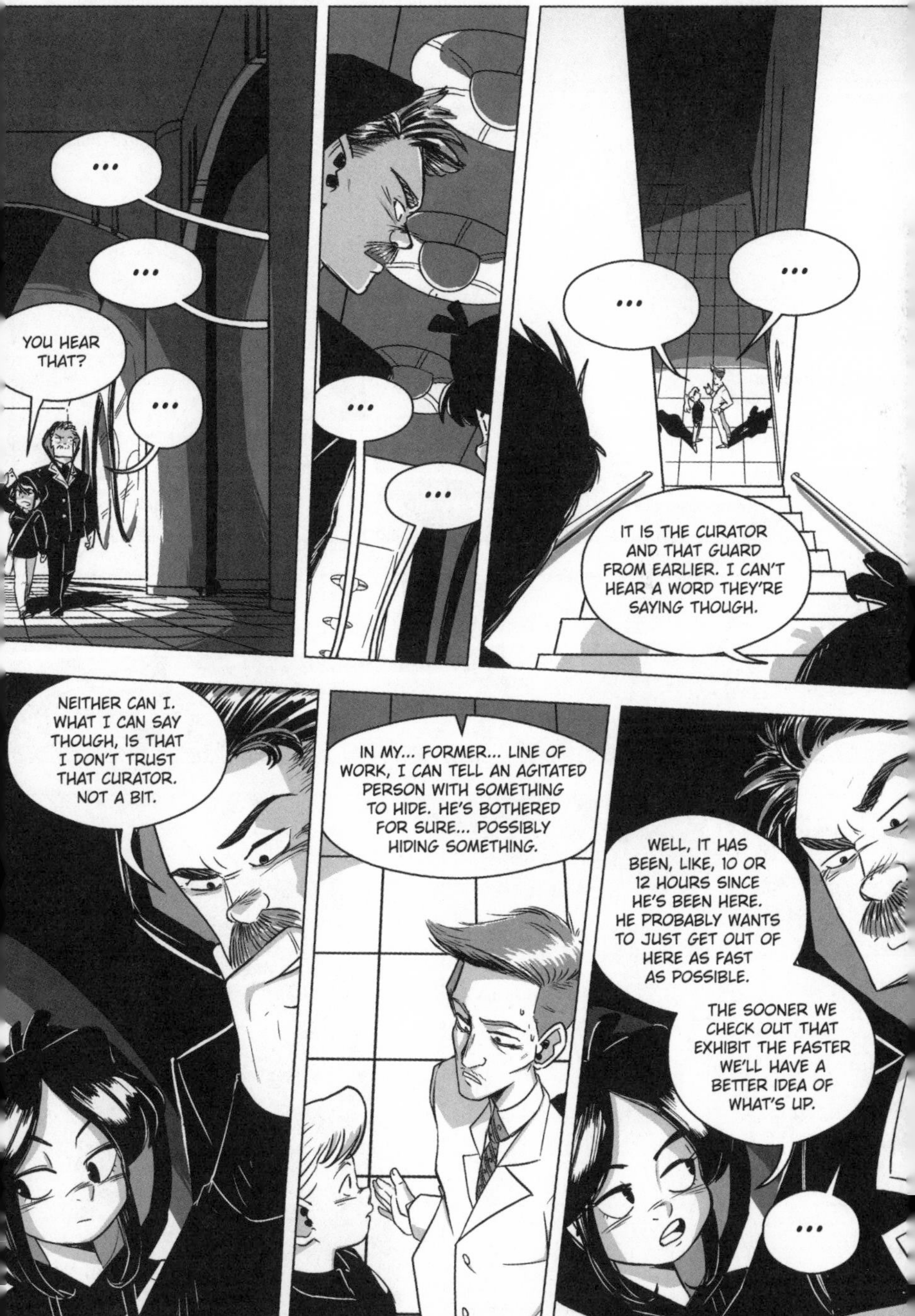
...
...
YOU HEAR THAT?
...
...
...
...
...
IT IS THE CURATOR AND THAT GUARD FROM EARLIER. I CAN'T HEAR A WORD THEY'RE SAYING THOUGH.
NEITHER CAN I. WHAT I CAN SAY THOUGH, IS THAT I DON'T TRUST THAT CURATOR. NOT A BIT.
IN MY... FORMER... LINE OF WORK, I CAN TELL AN AGITATED PERSON WITH SOMETHING TO HIDE. HE'S BOTHERED FOR SURE... POSSIBLY HIDING SOMETHING.
WELL, IT HAS BEEN, LIKE, 10 OR 12 HOURS SINCE HE'S BEEN HERE. HE PROBABLY WANTS TO JUST GET OUT OF HERE AS FAST AS POSSIBLE.
THE SOONER WE CHECK OUT THAT EXHIBIT THE FASTER WE'LL HAVE A BETTER IDEA OF WHAT'S UP.
...

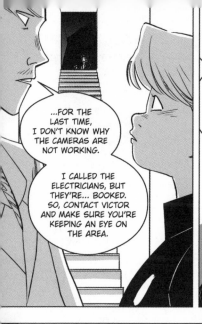

...FOR THE LAST TIME, I DON'T KNOW WHY THE CAMERAS ARE NOT WORKING.

I CALLED THE ELECTRICIANS, BUT THEY'RE... BOOKED. SO, CONTACT VICTOR AND MAKE SURE YOU'RE KEEPING AN EYE ON THE AREA.

A-ARE YOU SURE THAT'S NECESSARY?

I MEAN, I'VE BEEN MAKING SURE THAT NO ONE WENT UP THERE ALL DAY...

AH! I KNOW YOU HAVE, MY DEAR. AND YOU'VE DONE A TERRIFIC JOB!

IT'S JUST IF WE CAN'T FIND THE EMERALD, OUR JOBS WILL BE THREATENED. I JUST NEED ANOTHER HOUR.

SO PLEASE, JUST THIS LAST THING, AND YOU'RE FREE TO GO. I PROMISE.

...

...ALRIGHT.

FINE.

THANK YOU FOR THIS. REALLY APPRECIATE IT. HONESTLY, THANK YOU.

... JEEZ.

JUST GET ME OUT OF THIS DUMP ALREADY...

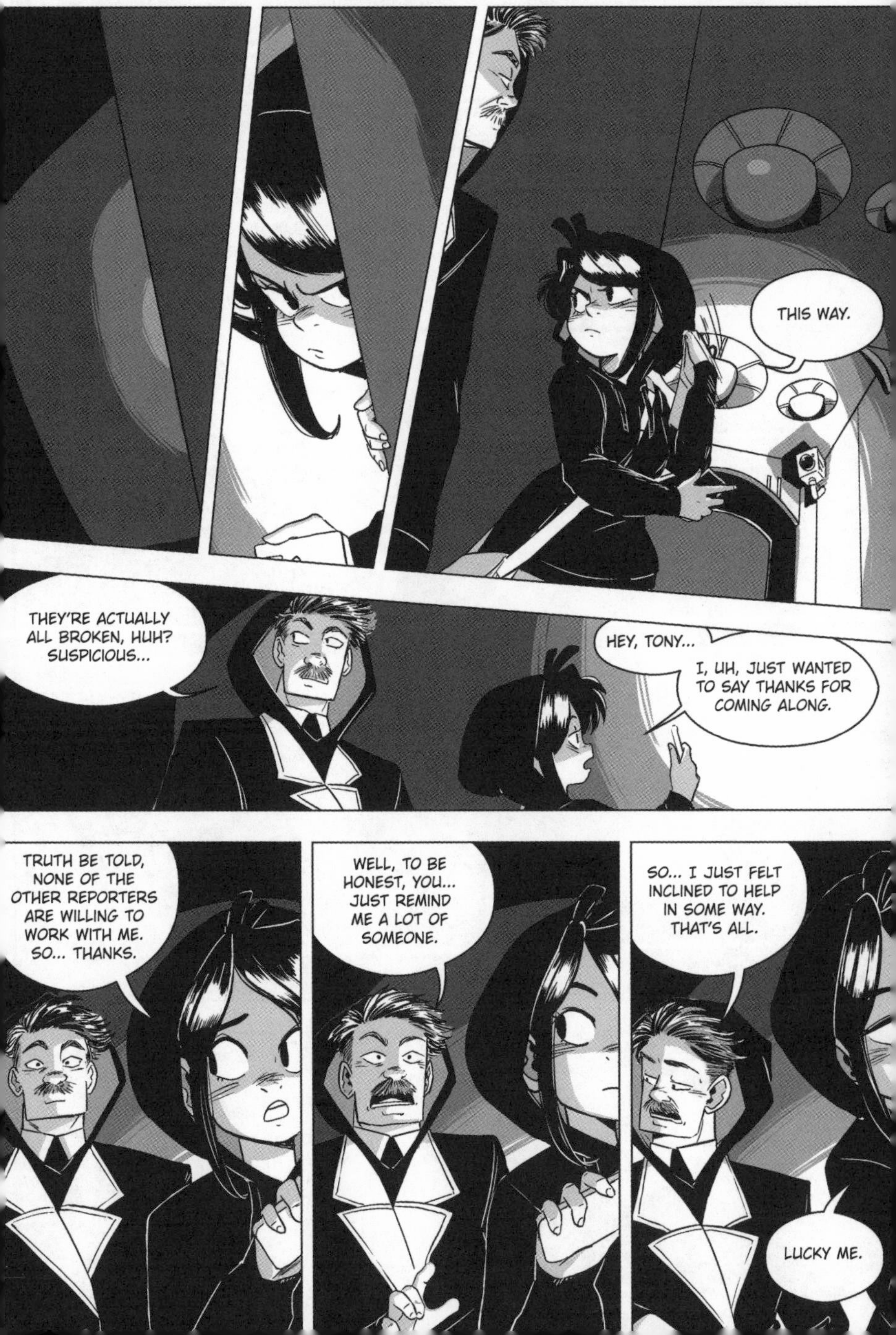
THIS WAY.
THEY'RE ACTUALLY ALL BROKEN, HUH? SUSPICIOUS...
HEY, TONY...
I, UH, JUST WANTED TO SAY THANKS FOR COMING ALONG.
TRUTH BE TOLD, NONE OF THE OTHER REPORTERS ARE WILLING TO WORK WITH ME. SO... THANKS.
WELL, TO BE HONEST, YOU... JUST REMIND ME A LOT OF SOMEONE.
SO... I JUST FELT INCLINED TO HELP IN SOME WAY. THAT'S ALL.
LUCKY ME.

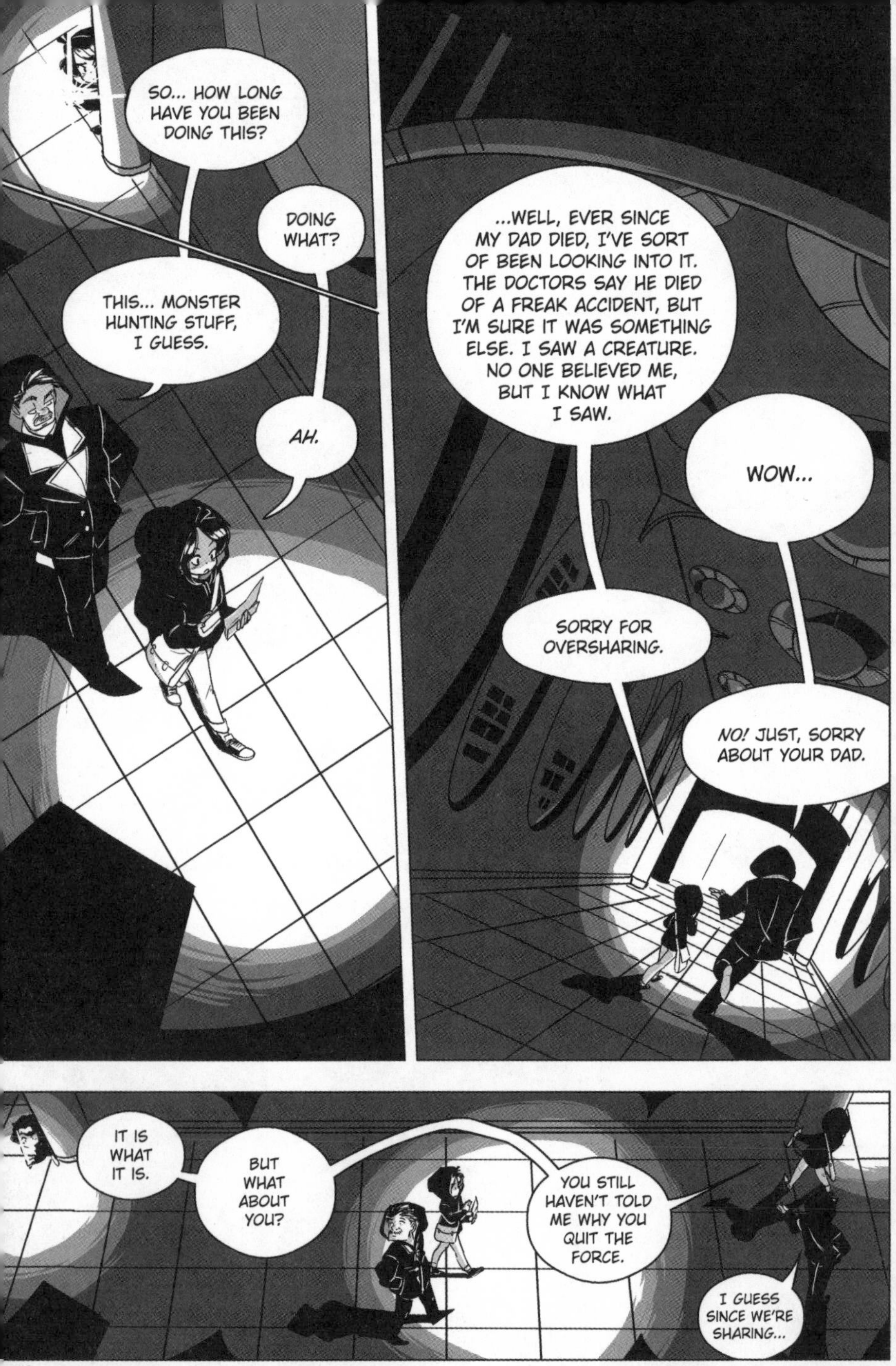
SO... HOW LONG HAVE YOU BEEN DOING THIS?
DOING WHAT?
THIS... MONSTER HUNTING STUFF, I GUESS.
AH.
...WELL, EVER SINCE MY DAD DIED, I'VE SORT OF BEEN LOOKING INTO IT. THE DOCTORS SAY HE DIED OF A FREAK ACCIDENT, BUT I'M SURE IT WAS SOMETHING ELSE. I SAW A CREATURE. NO ONE BELIEVED ME, BUT I KNOW WHAT I SAW.
WOW...
SORRY FOR OVERSHARING.
NO! JUST, SORRY ABOUT YOUR DAD.
IT IS WHAT IT IS.
BUT WHAT ABOUT YOU?
YOU STILL HAVEN'T TOLD ME WHY YOU QUIT THE FORCE.
I GUESS SINCE WE'RE SHARING...

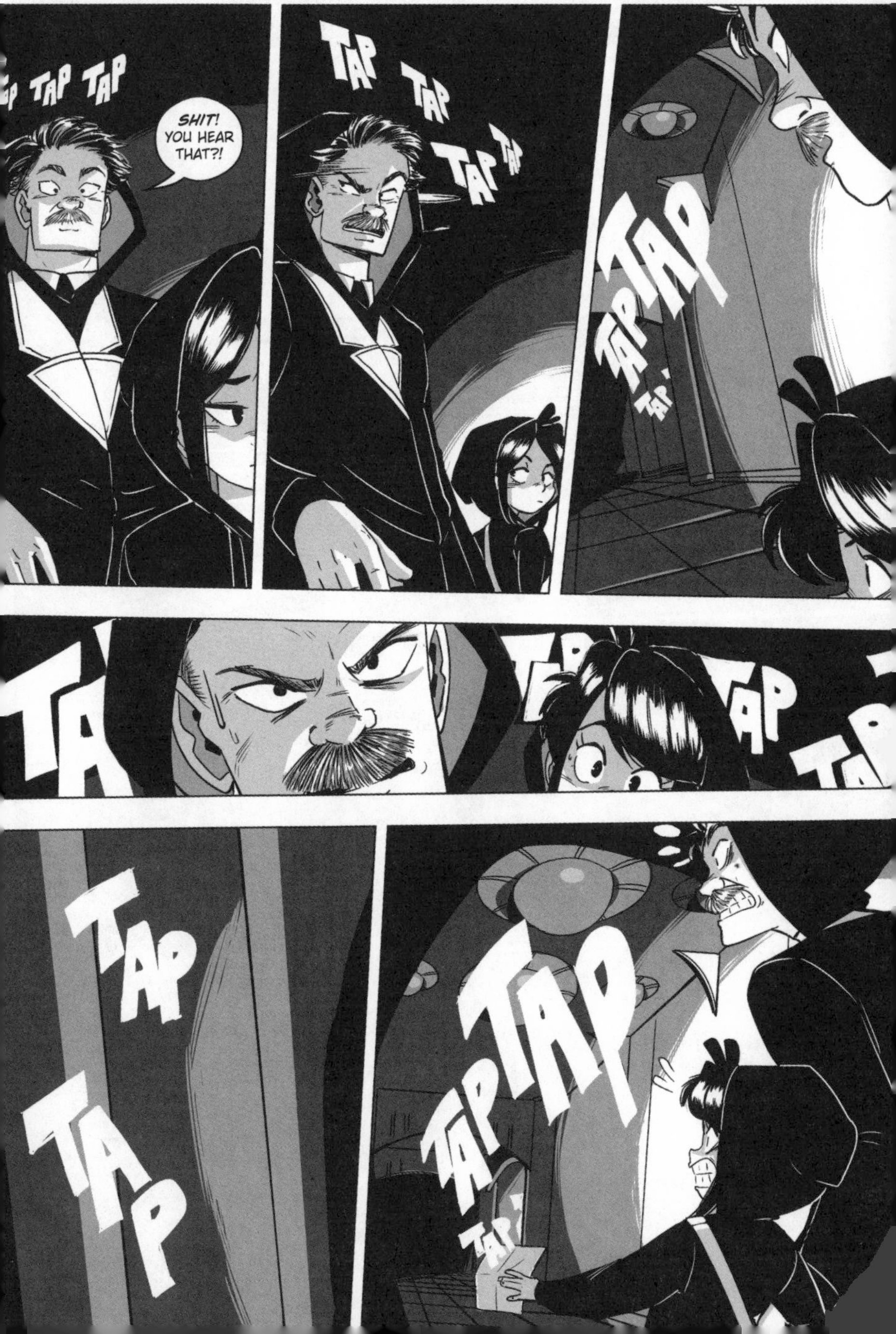
TAP TAP
SHIT! YOU HEAR THAT?!
TAP TAP TAP TAP
TAPTAP
TAP
TAP
TAP
TAP
TAP
TAP
TAP
TAPTAP
TAP

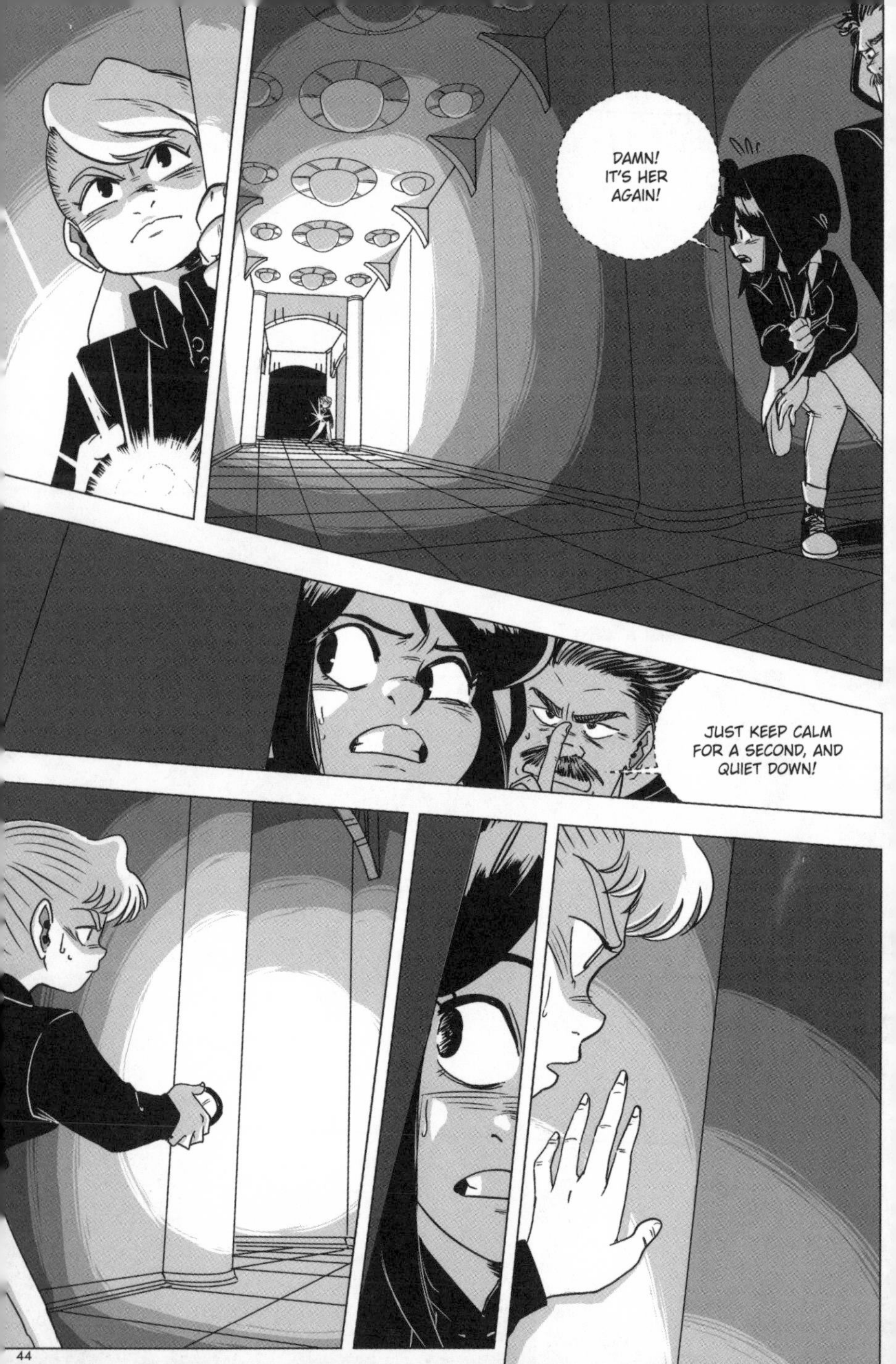
DAMN! IT'S HER AGAIN!
JUST KEEP CALM FOR A SECOND, AND QUIET DOWN!

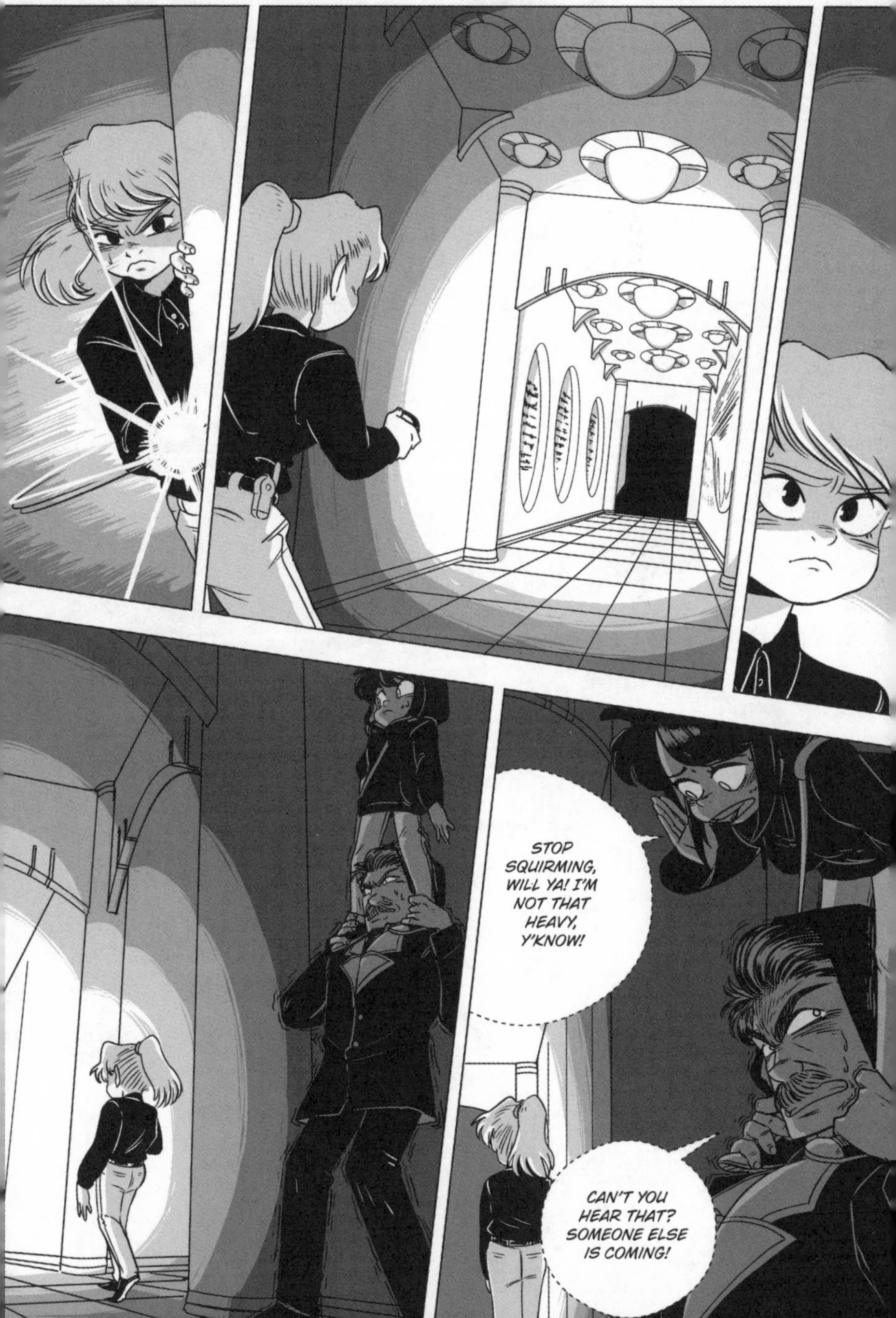
STOP SQUIRMING, WILL YA! I'M NOT THAT HEAVY, Y'KNOW!
CAN'T YOU HEAR THAT? SOMEONE ELSE IS COMING!

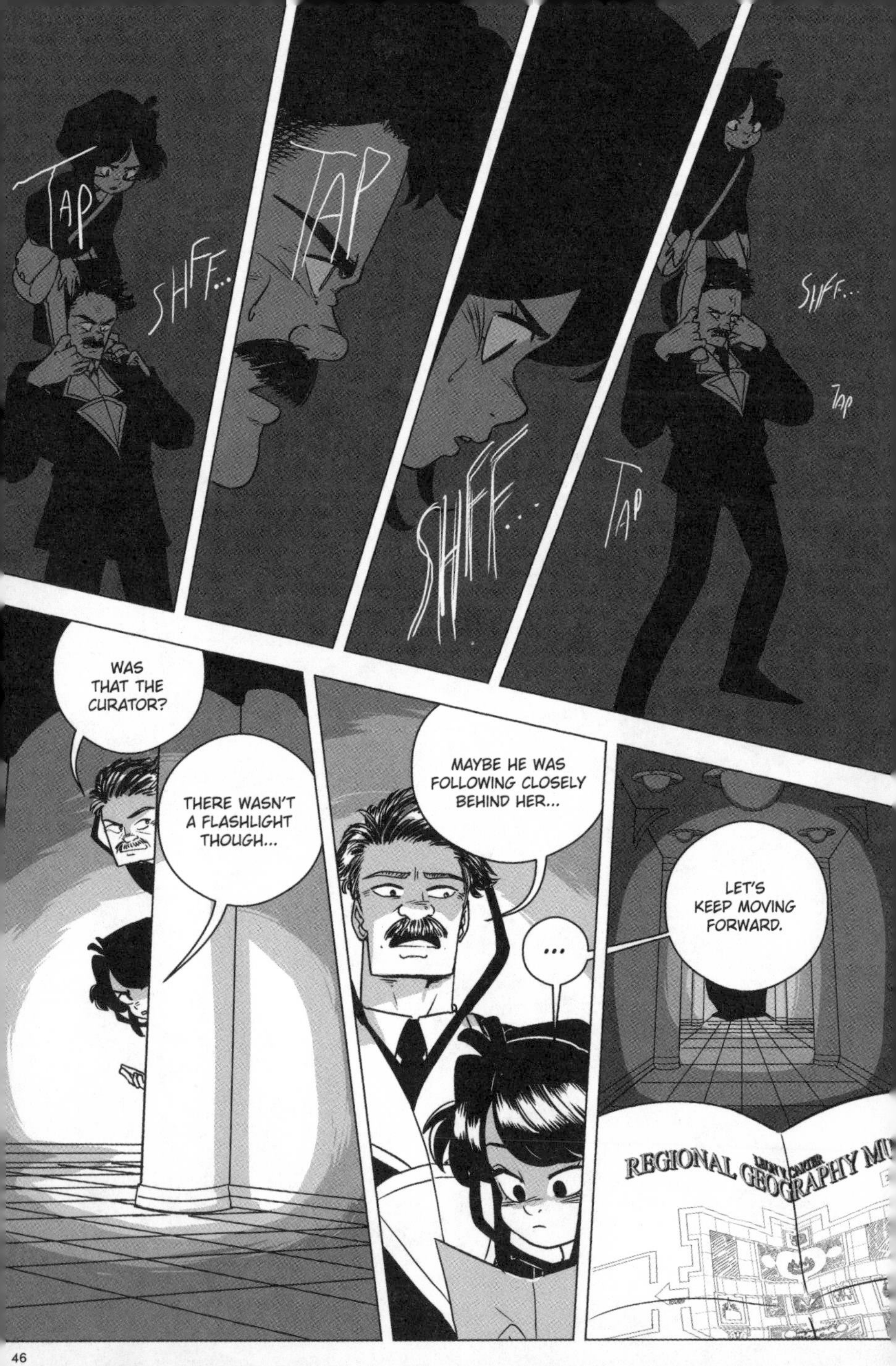

TAP
SHFF...
TAP
SHFF...
SHFF...
TAP
TAP
WAS THAT THE CURATOR?
THERE WASN'T A FLASHLIGHT THOUGH...
MAYBE HE WAS FOLLOWING CLOSELY BEHIND HER...
...
LET'S KEEP MOVING FORWARD.
REGIONAL GEOGRAPHY MU

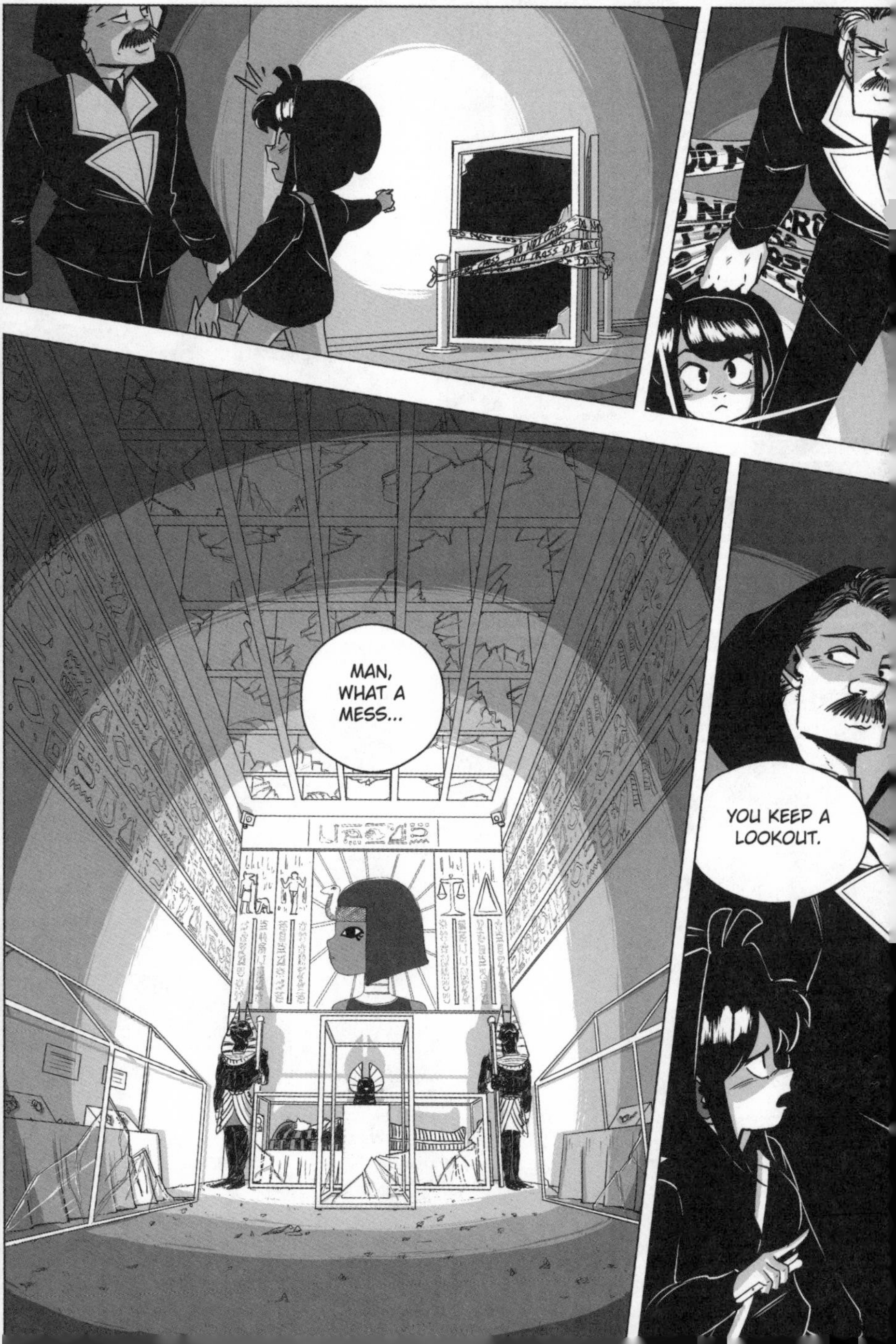
MAN, WHAT A MESS...
YOU KEEP A LOOKOUT.

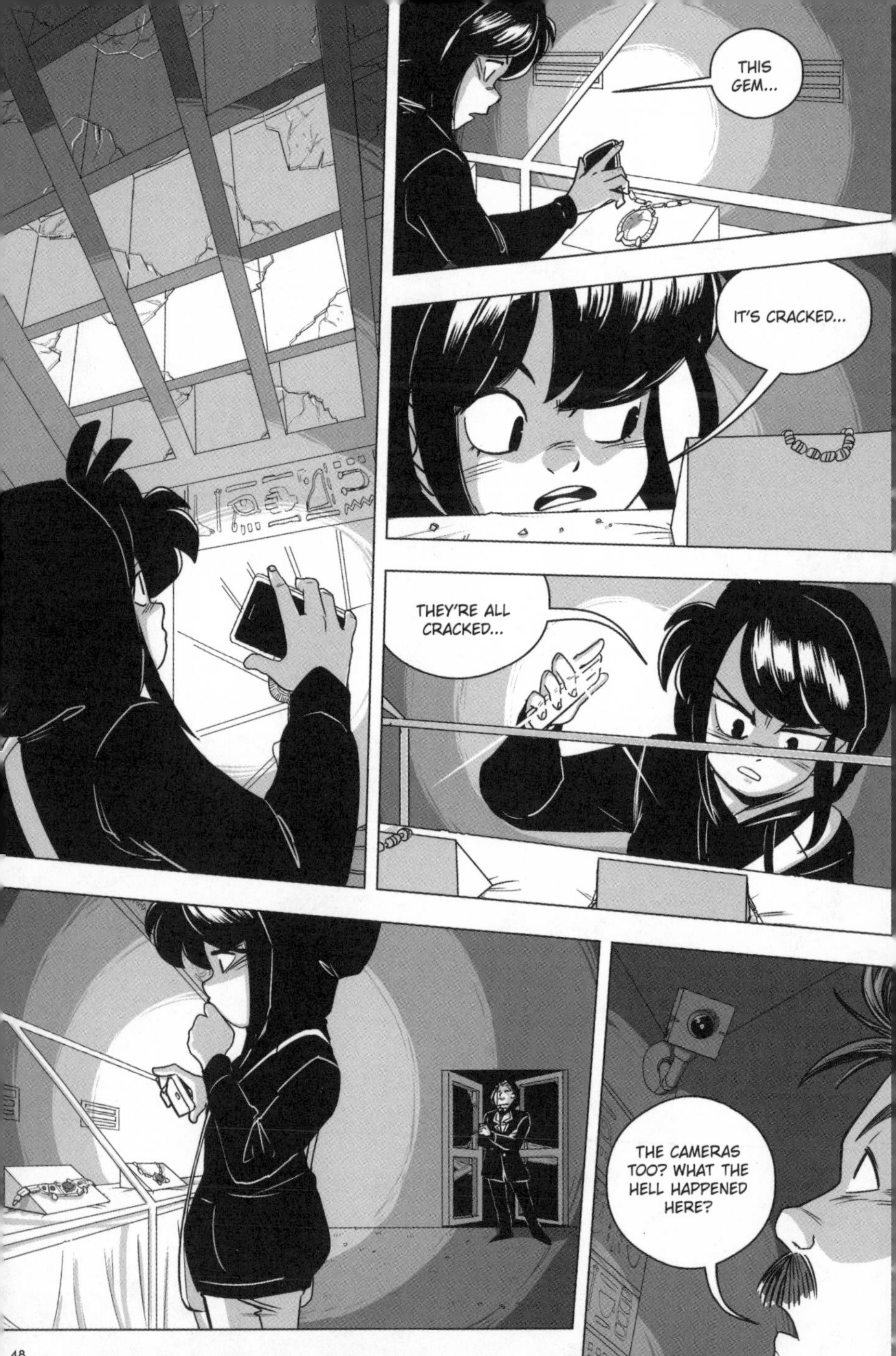
THIS GEM...
IT'S CRACKED...
THEY'RE ALL CRACKED...
THE CAMERAS TOO? WHAT THE HELL HAPPENED HERE?

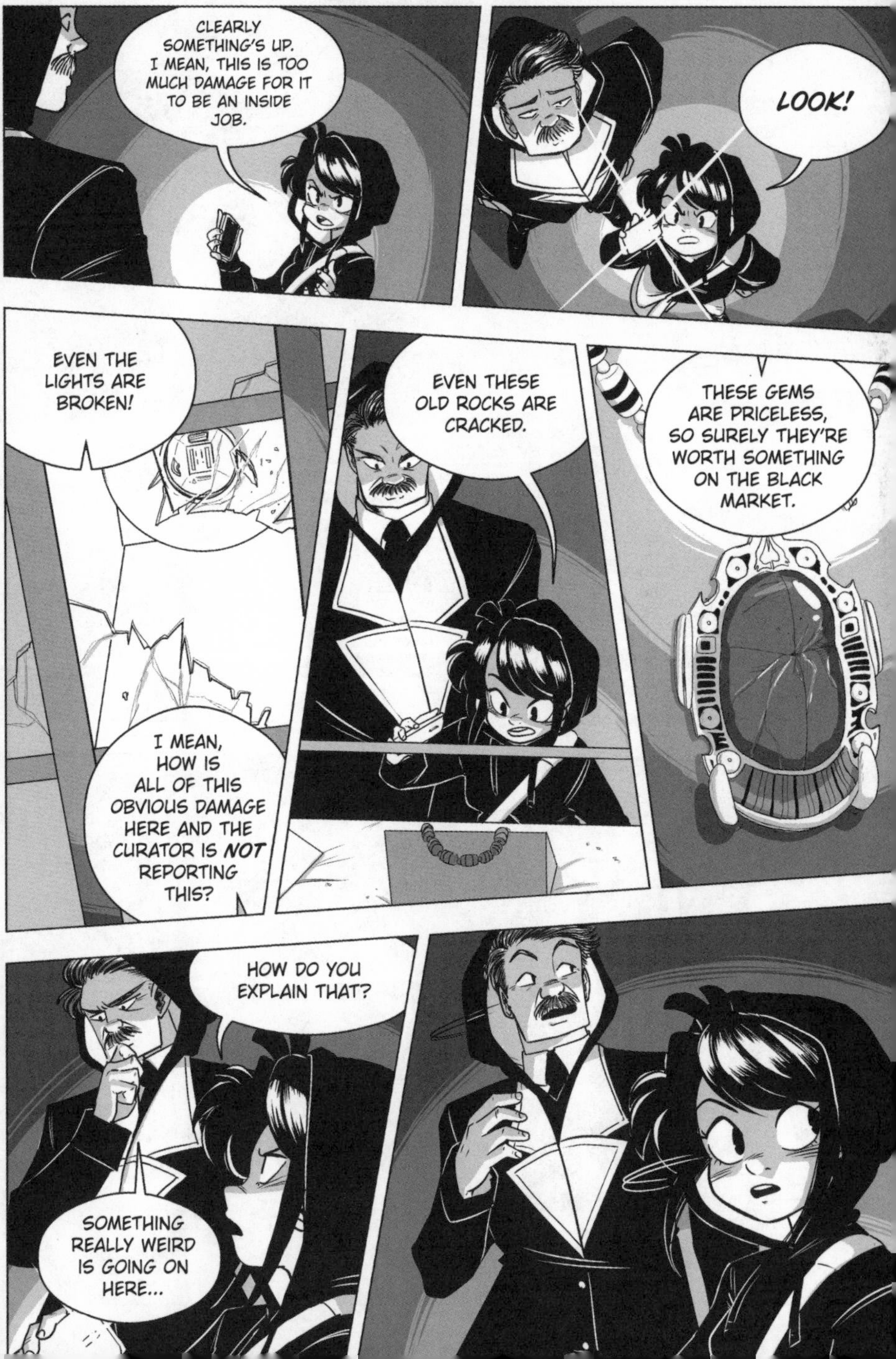

CLEARLY SOMETHING'S UP. I MEAN, THIS IS TOO MUCH DAMAGE FOR IT TO BE AN INSIDE JOB.
LOOK!
EVEN THE LIGHTS ARE BROKEN!
I MEAN, HOW IS ALL OF THIS OBVIOUS DAMAGE HERE AND THE CURATOR IS ***NOT*** REPORTING THIS?
EVEN THESE OLD ROCKS ARE CRACKED.
THESE GEMS ARE PRICELESS, SO SURELY THEY'RE WORTH SOMETHING ON THE BLACK MARKET.
HOW DO YOU EXPLAIN THAT?
SOMETHING REALLY WEIRD IS GOING ON HERE...

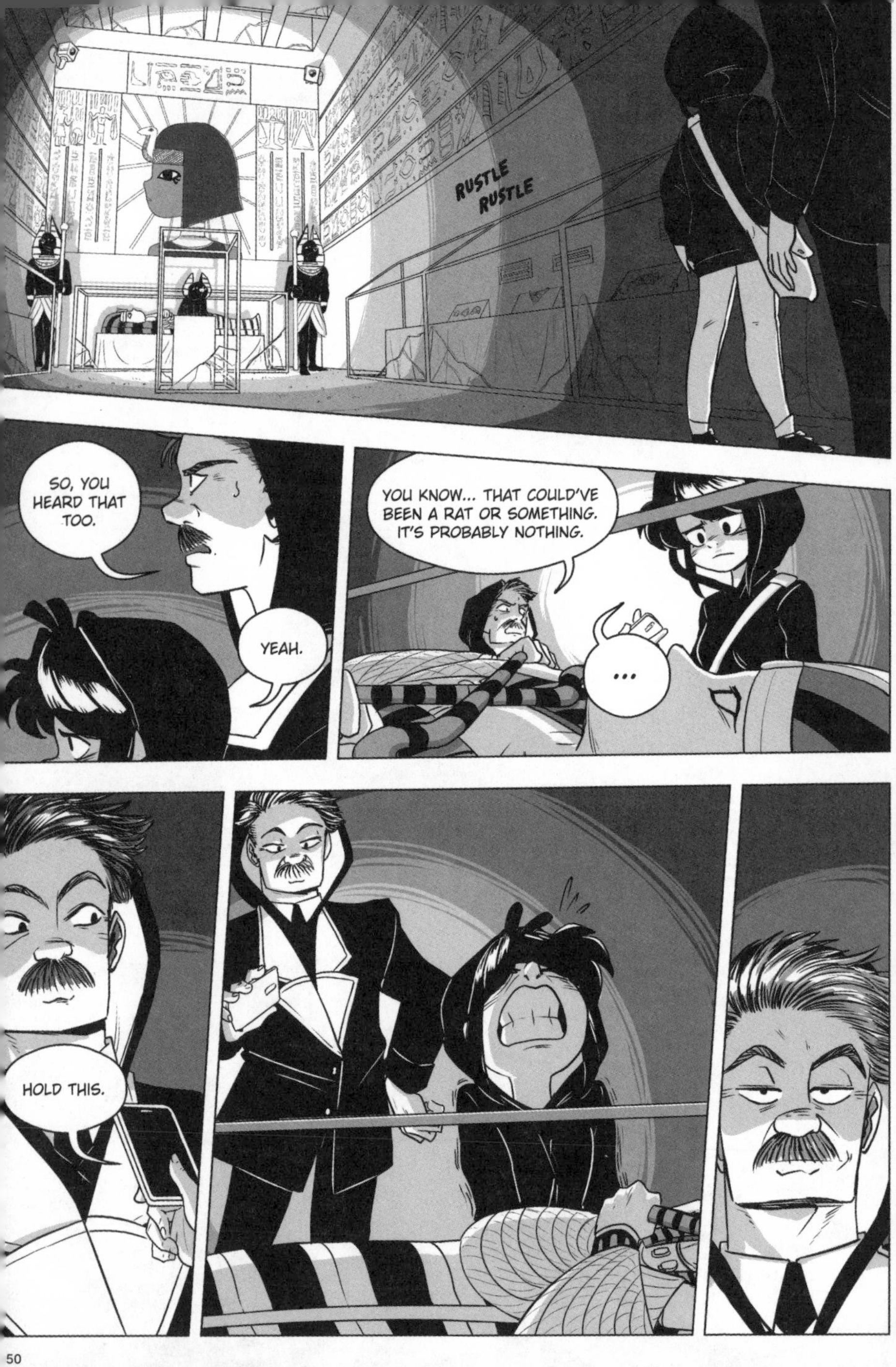
RUSTLE
RUSTLE
SO, YOU HEARD THAT TOO.
YEAH.
YOU KNOW... THAT COULD'VE BEEN A RAT OR SOMETHING. IT'S PROBABLY NOTHING.
...
HOLD THIS.

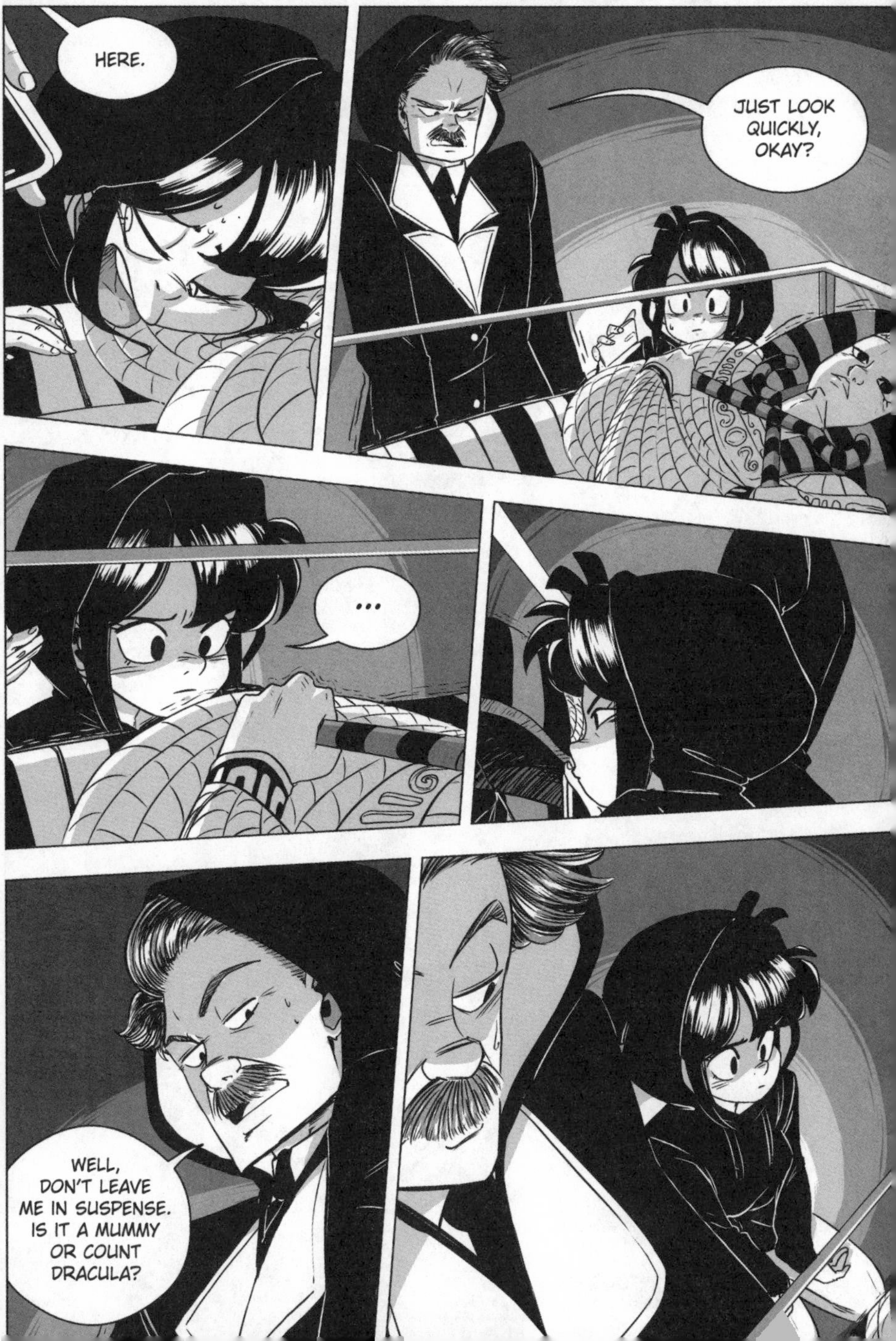
HERE.
JUST LOOK QUICKLY, OKAY?
...
WELL, DON'T LEAVE ME IN SUSPENSE. IS IT A MUMMY OR COUNT DRACULA?

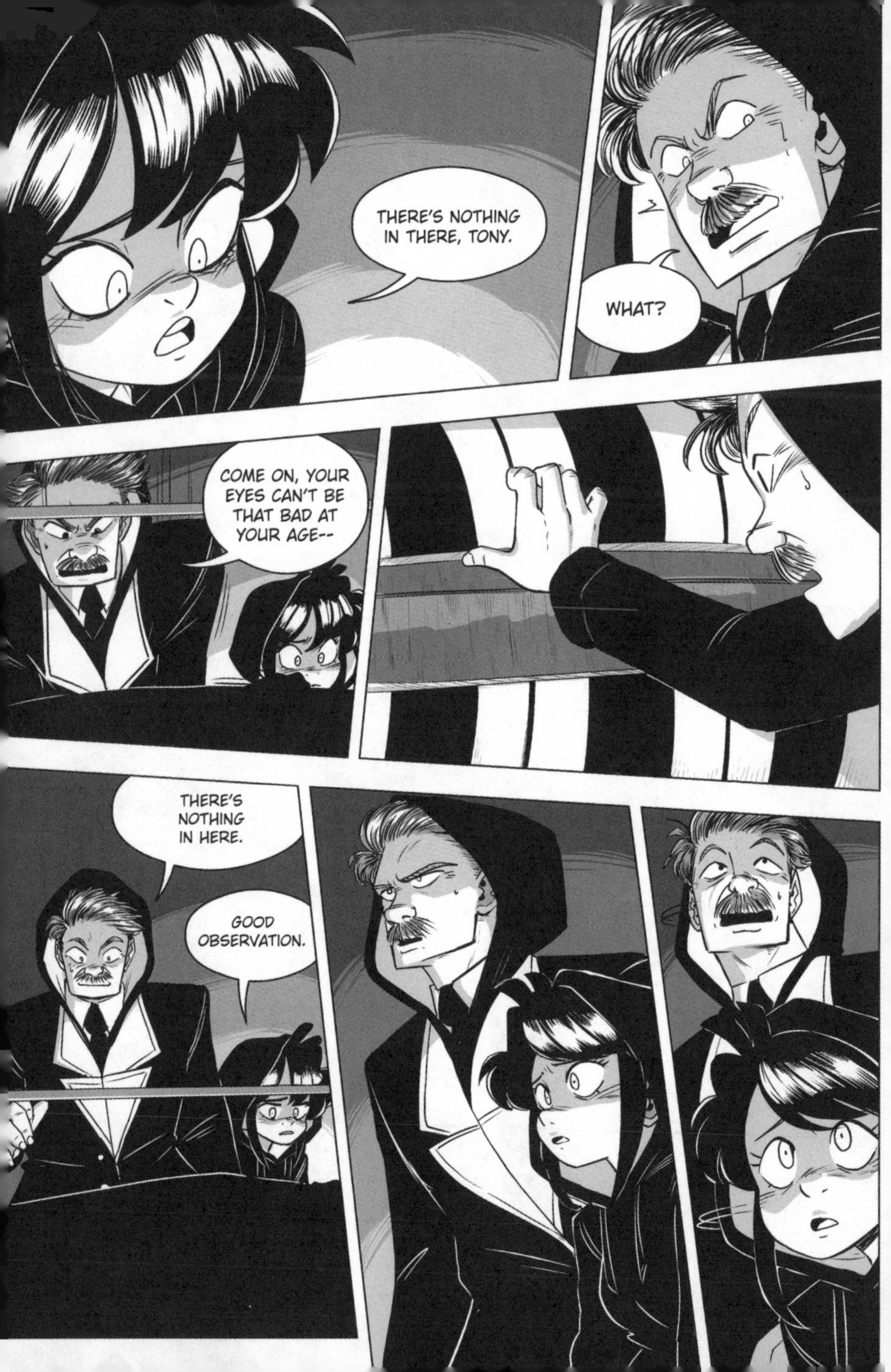
THERE'S NOTHING IN THERE, TONY.
WHAT?
COME ON, YOUR EYES CAN'T BE THAT BAD AT YOUR AGE--
THERE'S NOTHING IN HERE.
GOOD OBSERVATION.

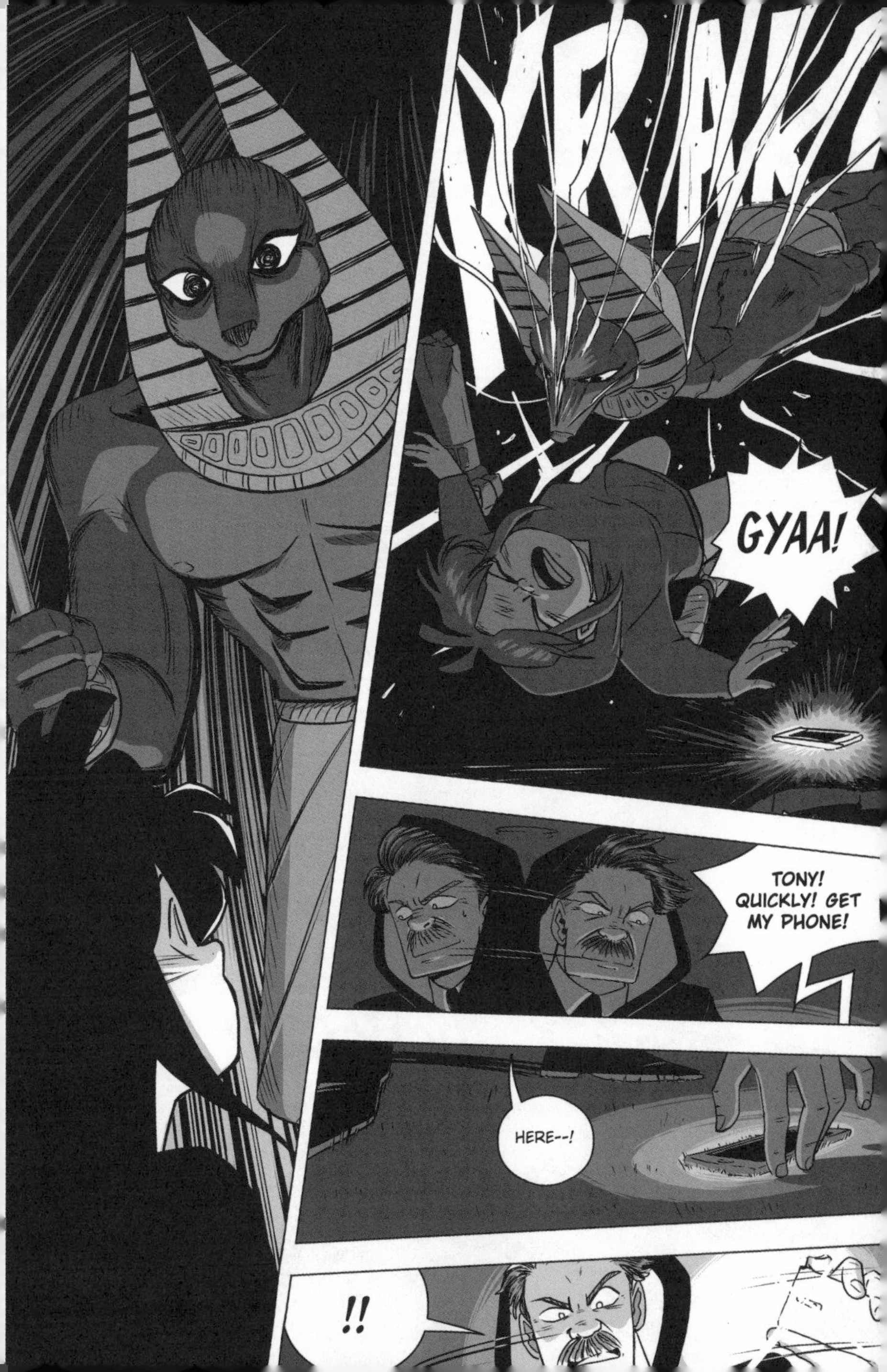
GYAA!
TONY! QUICKLY! GET MY PHONE!
HERE--!
!!

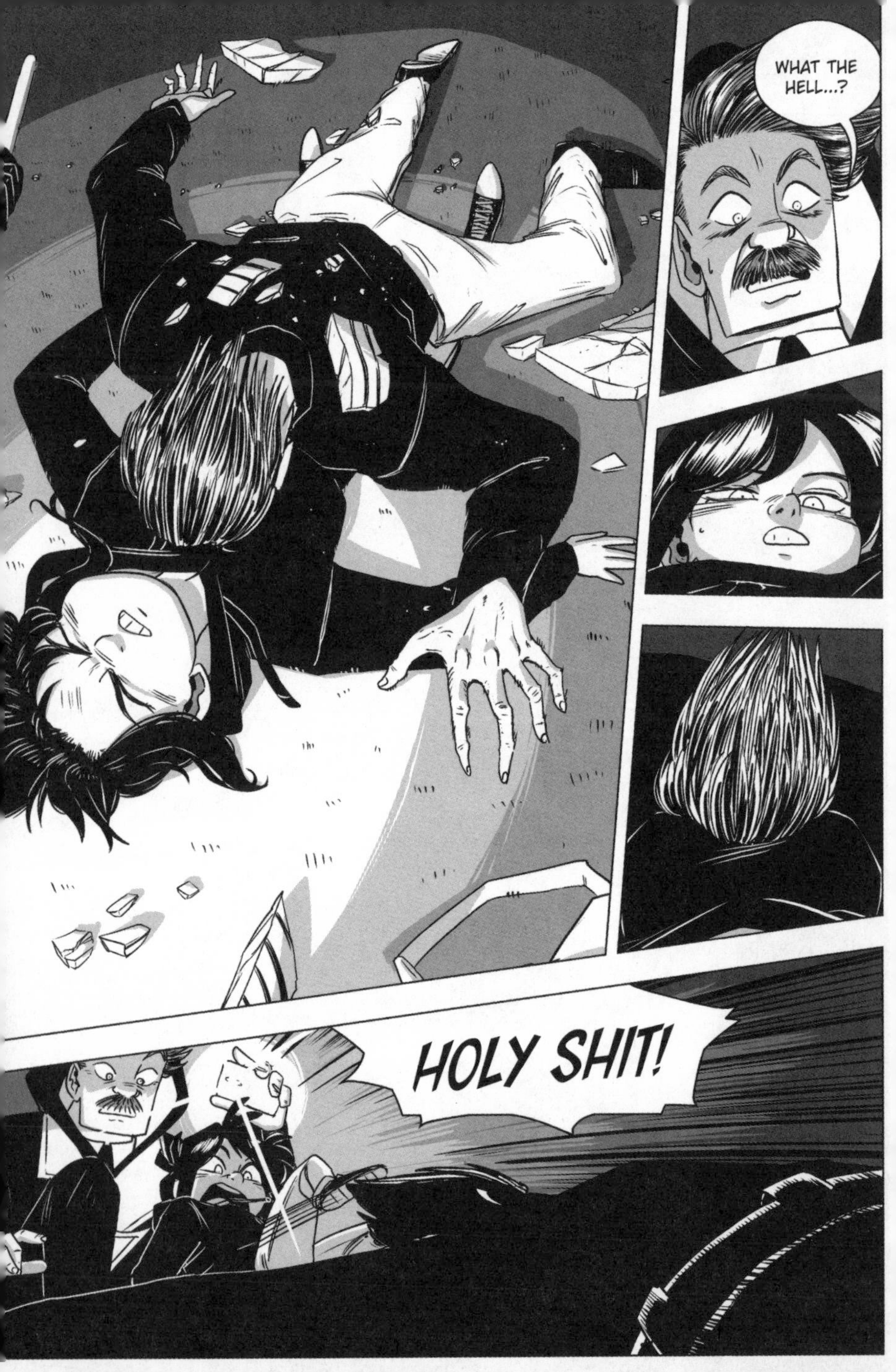
WHAT THE HELL...?
HOLY SHIT!

THAT
WAS IN THE
STATUE?!

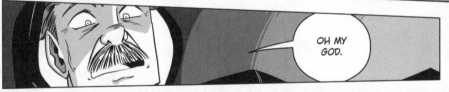

OH MY
GOD.

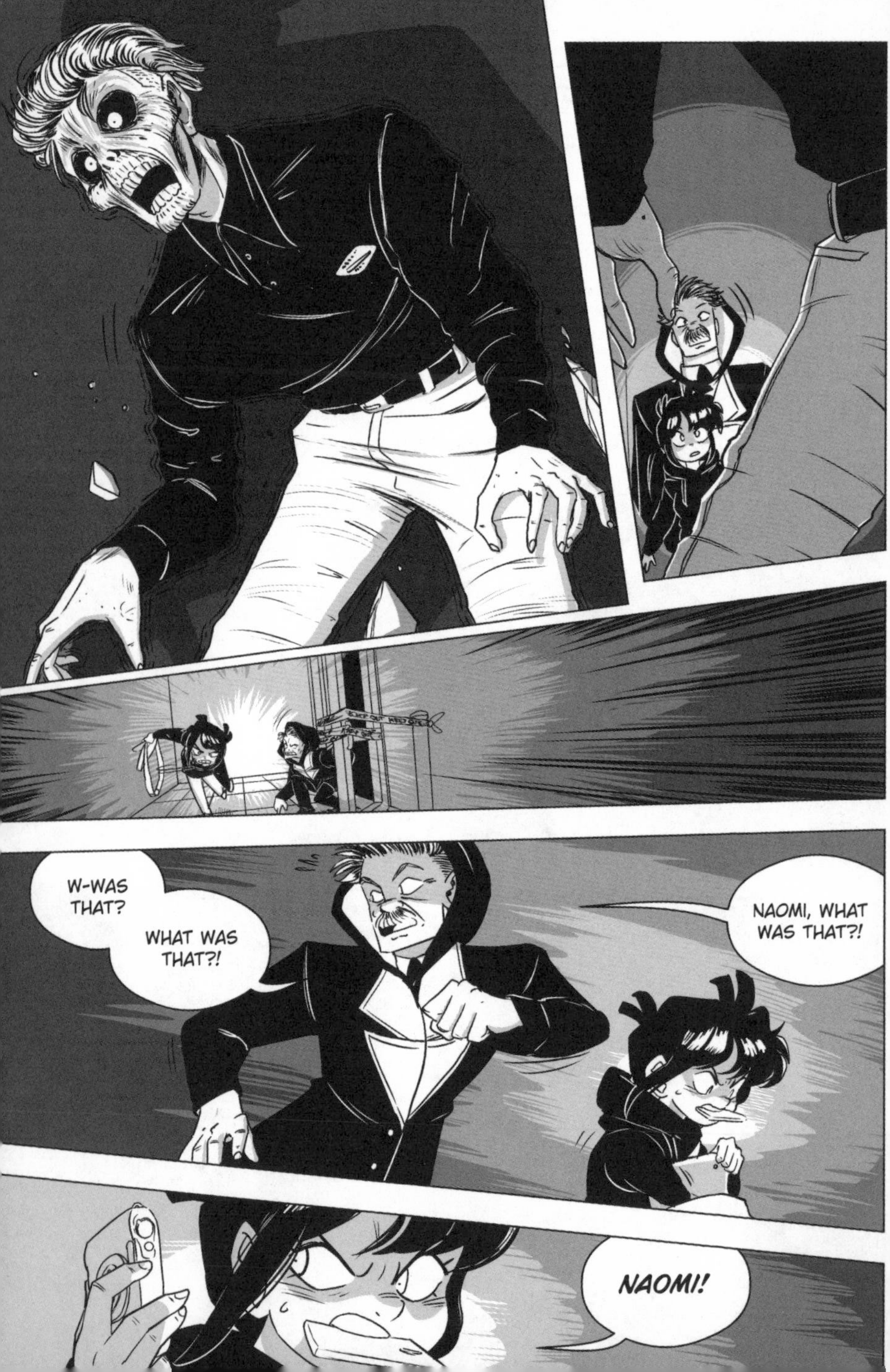
W-WAS THAT?
WHAT WAS THAT?!
NAOMI, WHAT WAS THAT?!
NAOMI!

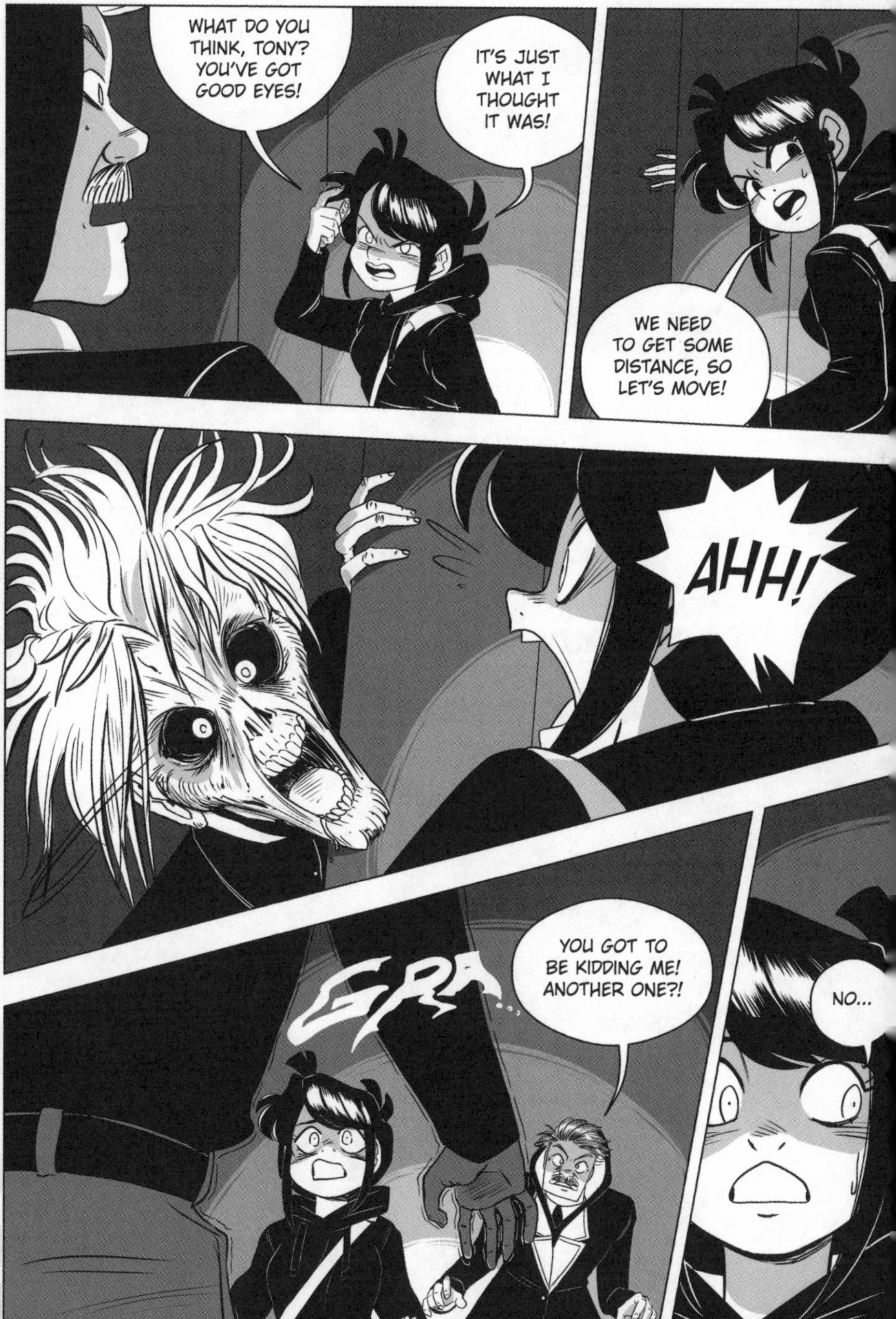
WHAT DO YOU THINK, TONY? YOU'VE GOT GOOD EYES!
IT'S JUST WHAT I THOUGHT IT WAS!
WE NEED TO GET SOME DISTANCE, SO LET'S MOVE!
AHH!
GRR
YOU GOT TO BE KIDDING ME! ANOTHER ONE?!
NO...

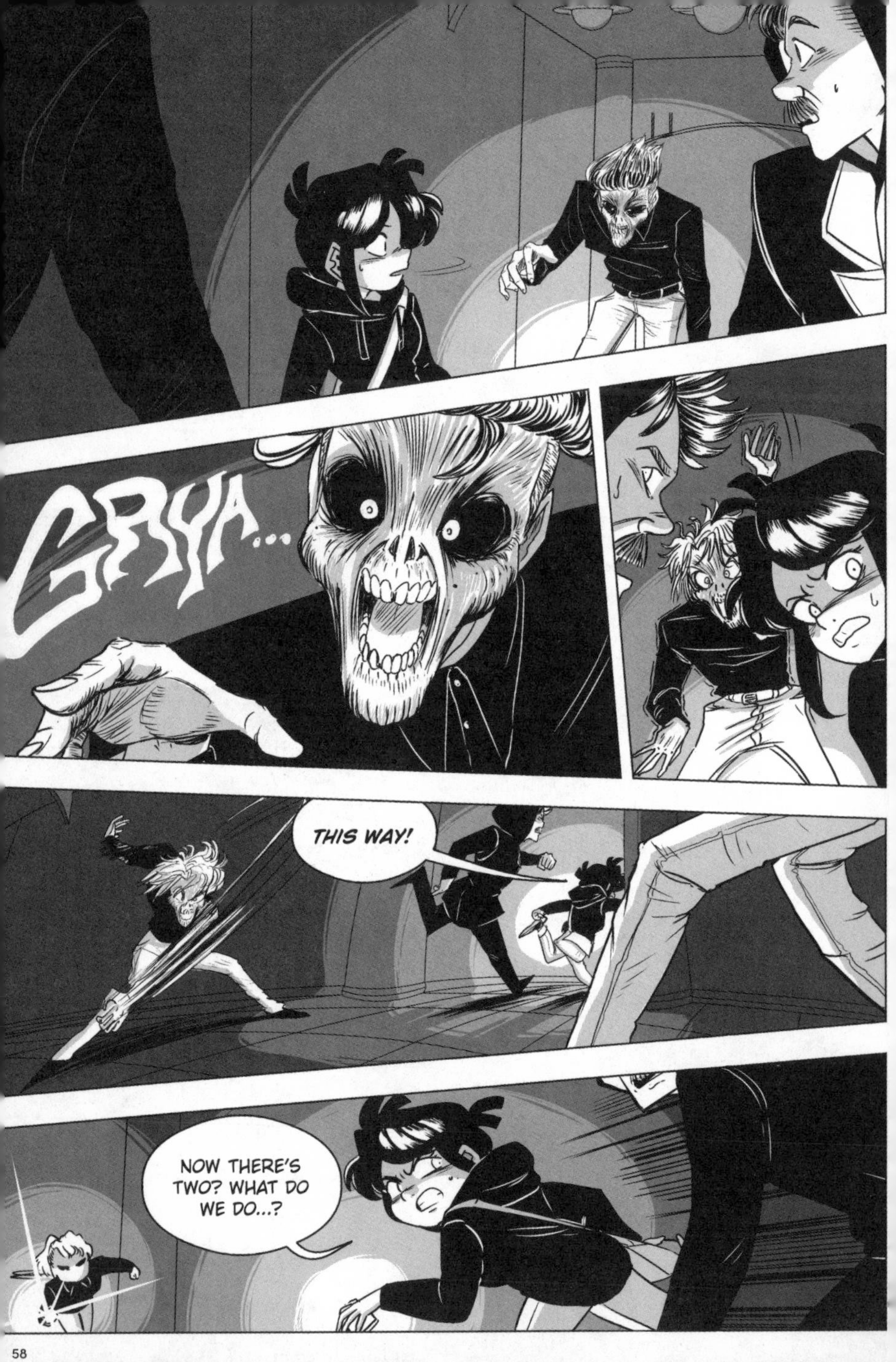
GRYA...
THIS WAY!
NOW THERE'S TWO? WHAT DO WE DO...?

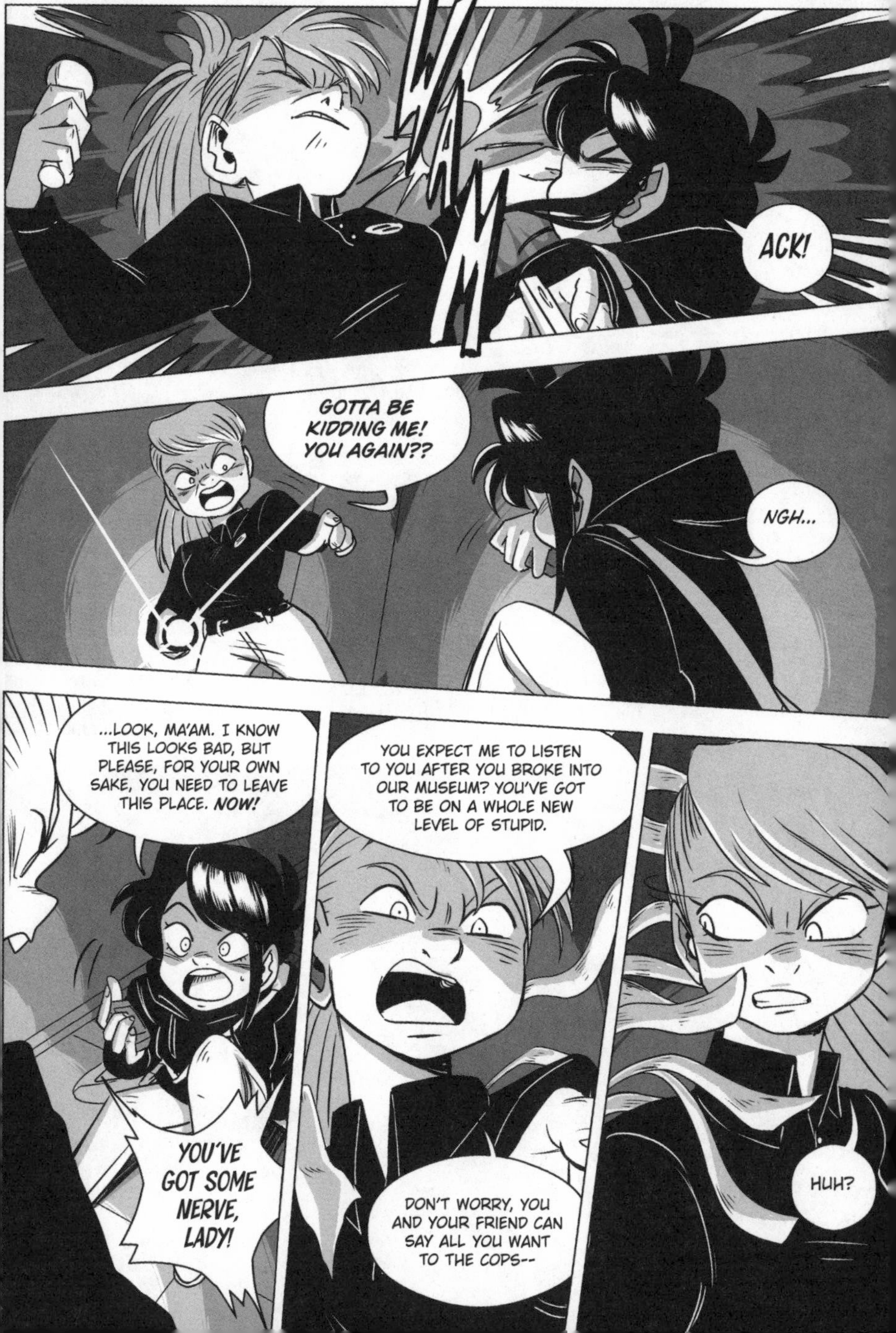
WAM
ACK!
GOTTA BE KIDDING ME! YOU AGAIN??
NGH...
...LOOK, MA'AM. I KNOW THIS LOOKS BAD, BUT PLEASE, FOR YOUR OWN SAKE, YOU NEED TO LEAVE THIS PLACE. NOW!
YOU'VE GOT SOME NERVE, LADY!
YOU EXPECT ME TO LISTEN TO YOU AFTER YOU BROKE INTO OUR MUSEUM? YOU'VE GOT TO BE ON A WHOLE NEW LEVEL OF STUPID.
DON'T WORRY, YOU AND YOUR FRIEND CAN SAY ALL YOU WANT TO THE COPS--
HUH?

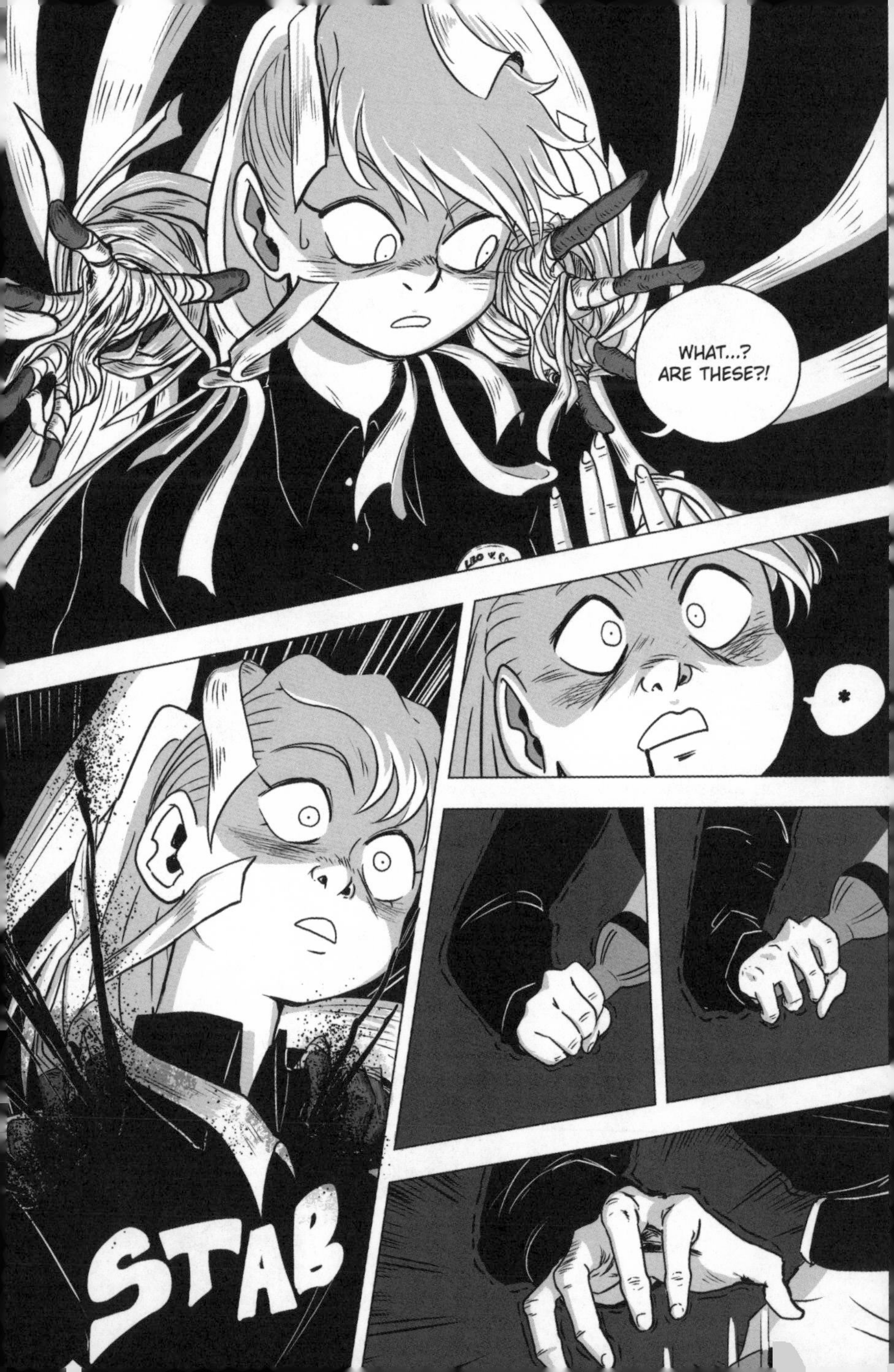
WHAT...?
ARE THESE?!
STAB
*

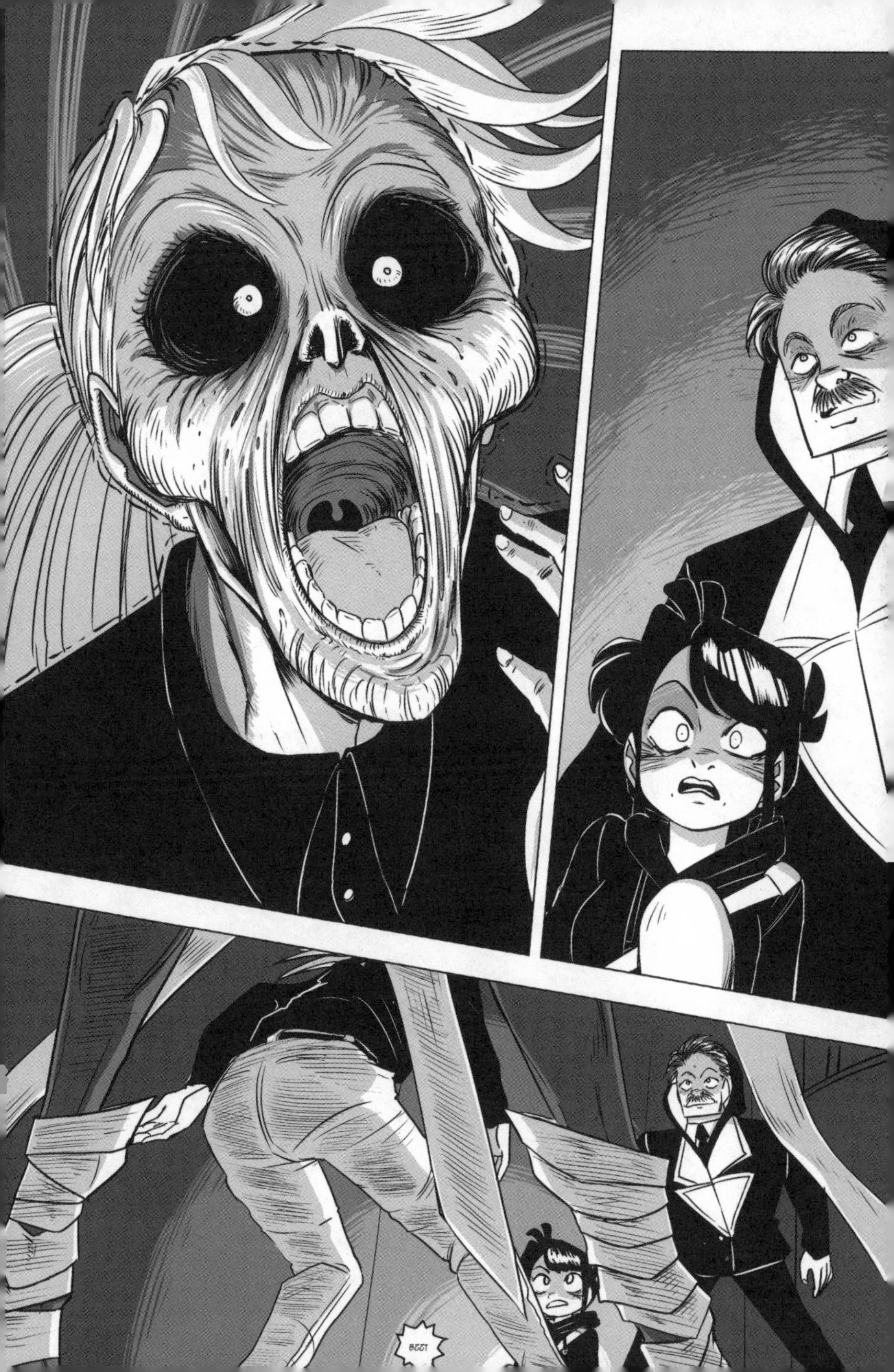

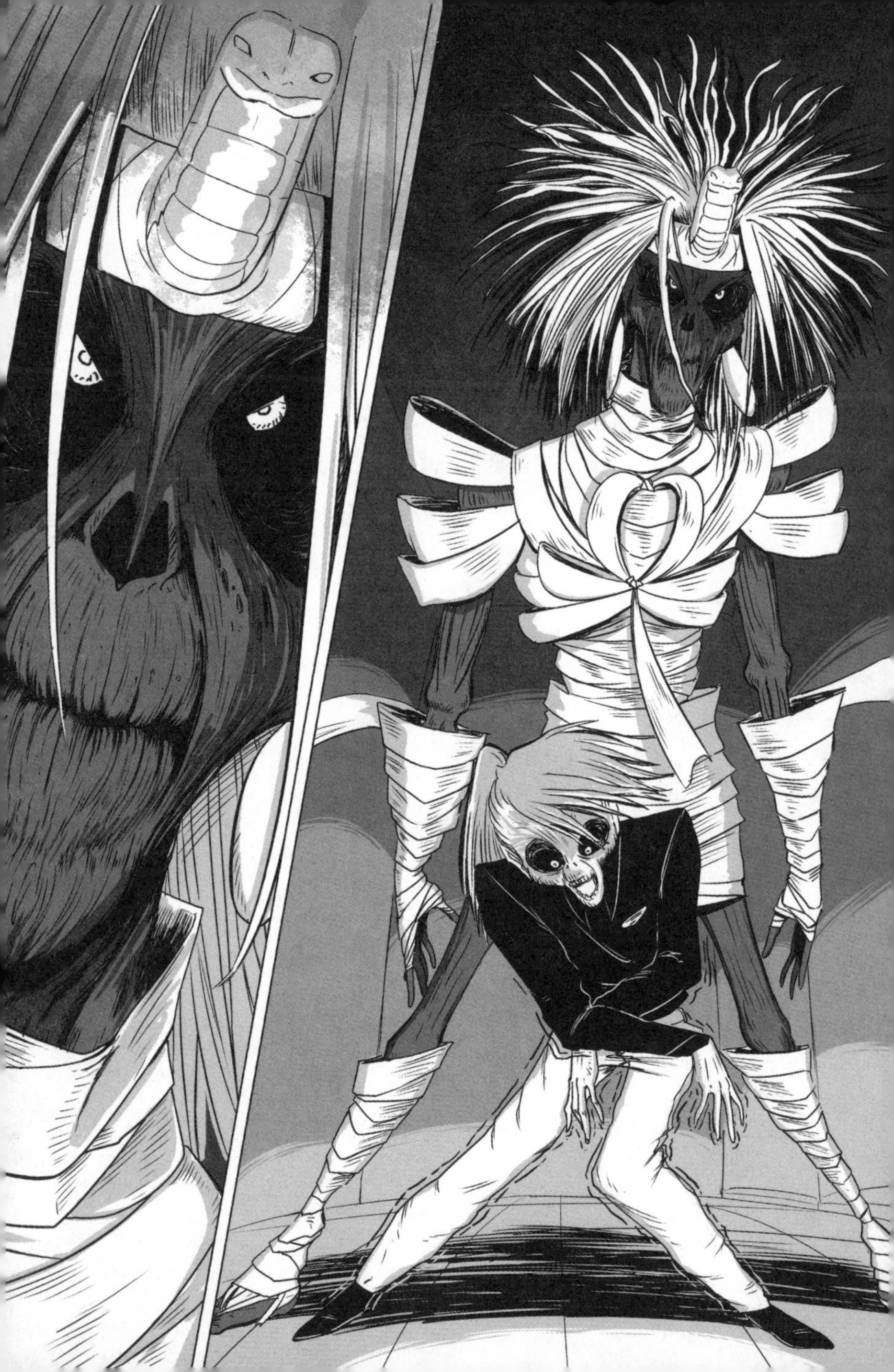

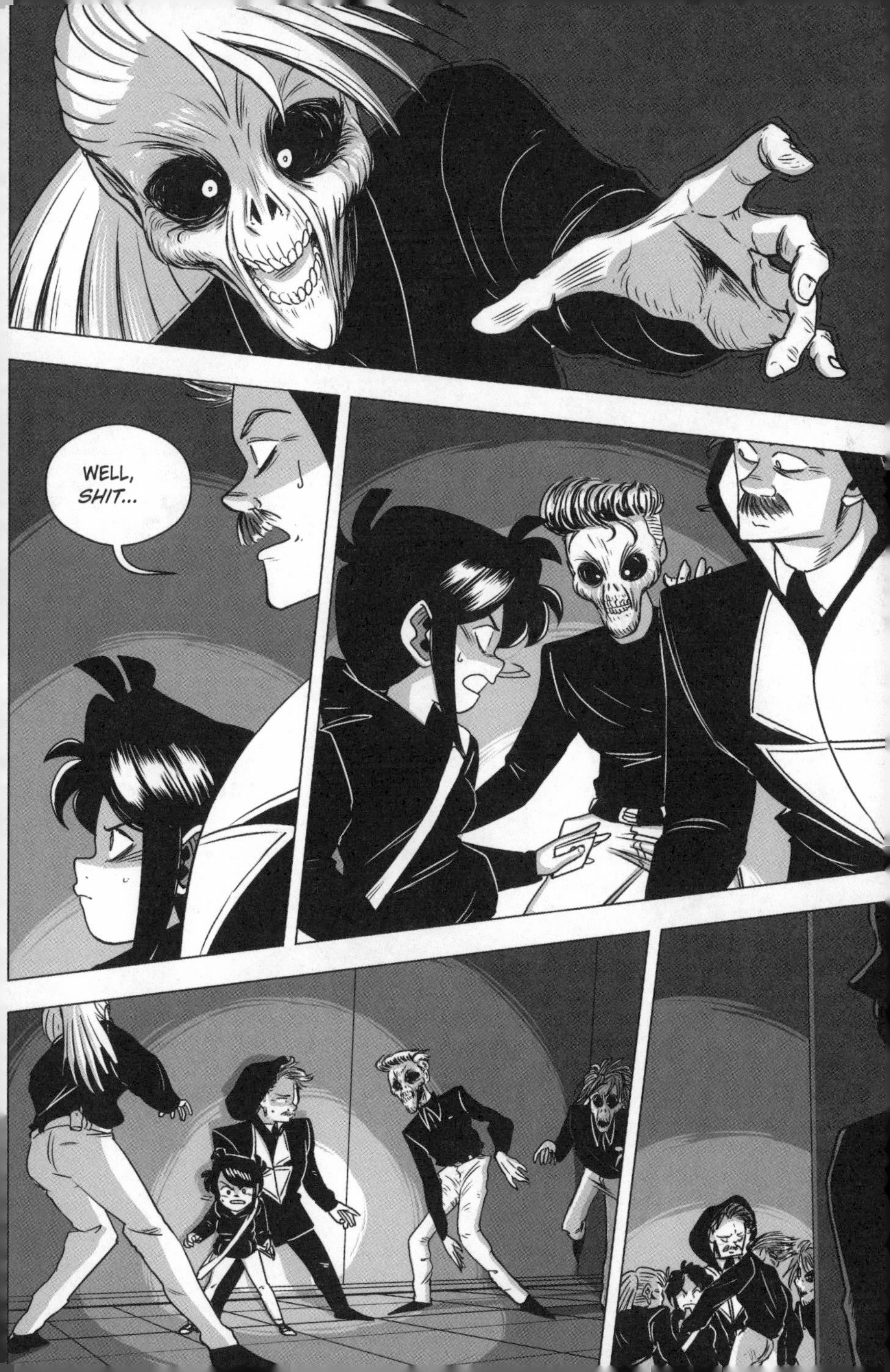
WELL, SHIT...

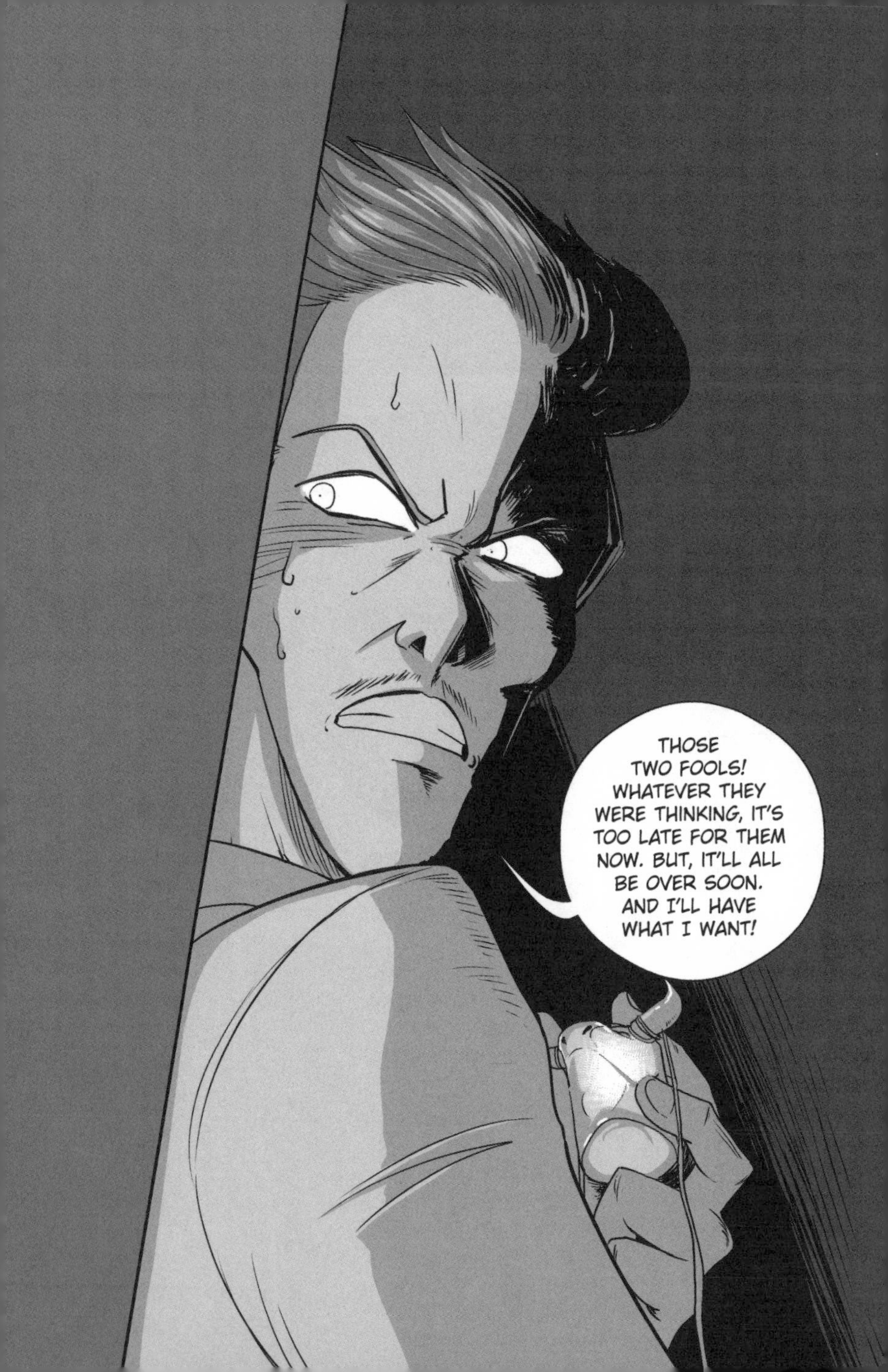
THOSE TWO FOOLS! WHATEVER THEY WERE THINKING, IT'S TOO LATE FOR THEM NOW. BUT, IT'LL ALL BE OVER SOON. AND I'LL HAVE WHAT I WANT!

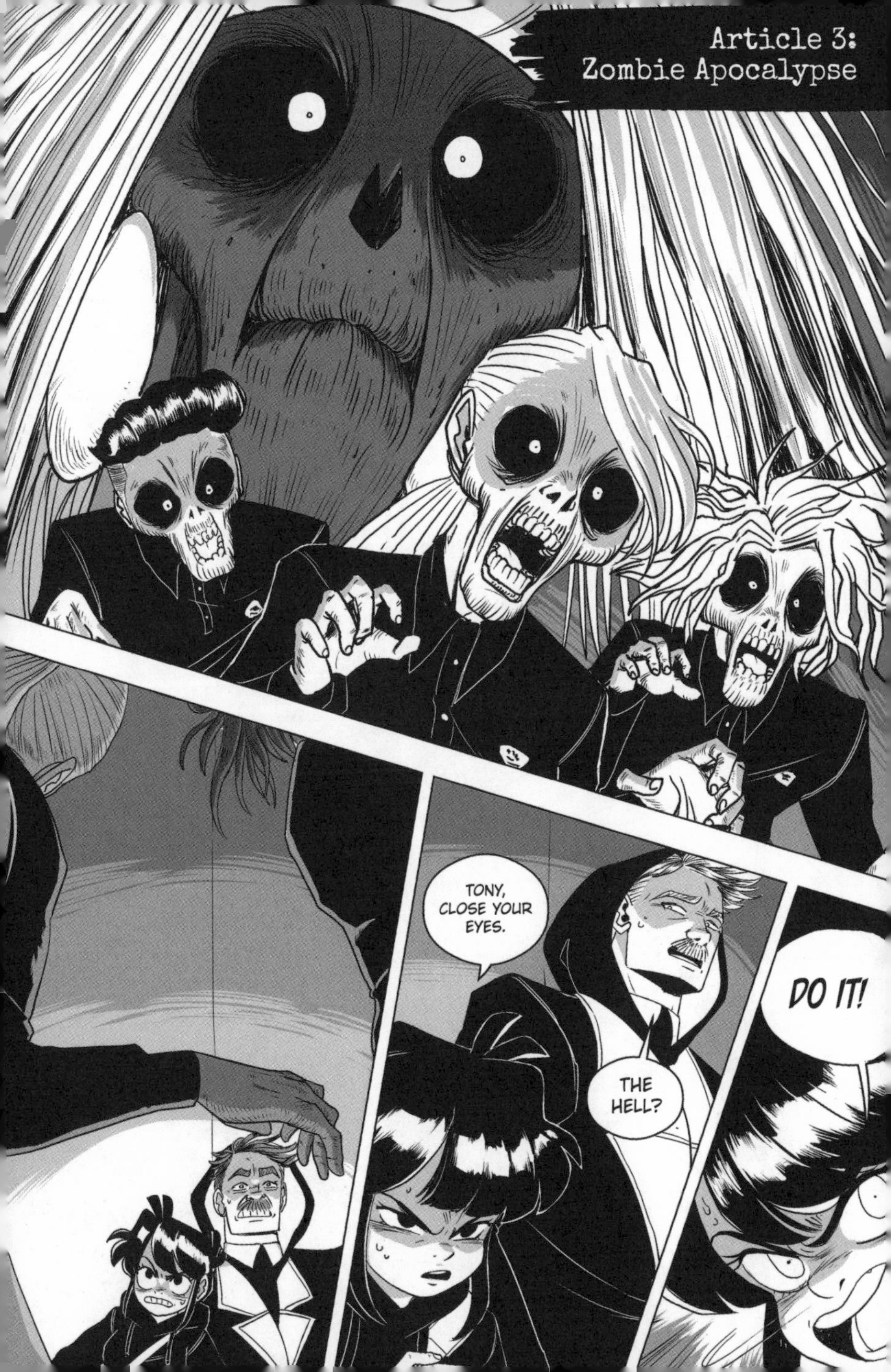
Article 3:
Zombie Apocalypse
TONY, CLOSE YOUR EYES.
THE HELL?
DO IT!

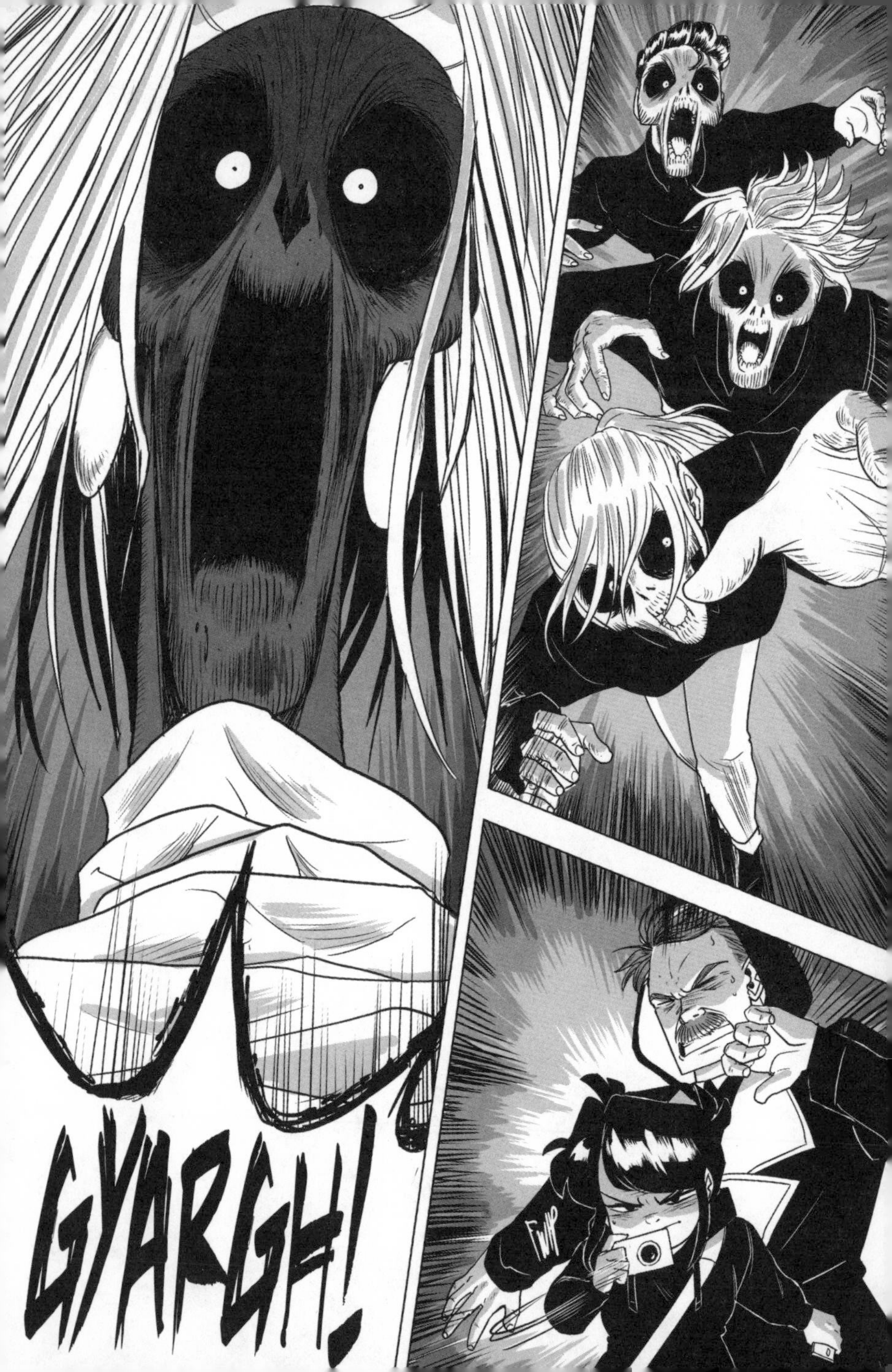
GYARGH!
FWIP

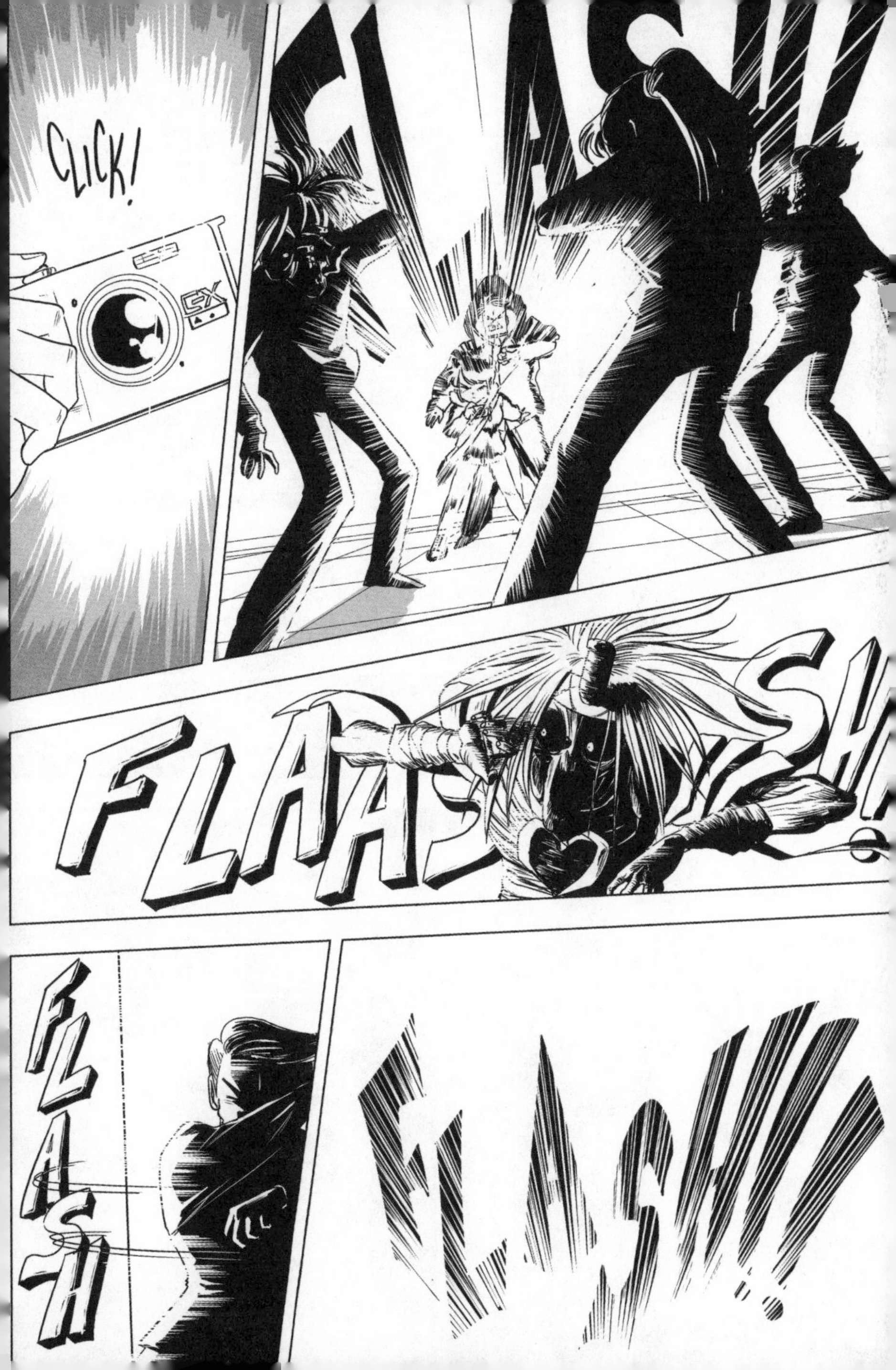
CLICK!
CX
FLASH
FLASH!
FLASH
FLASH!!

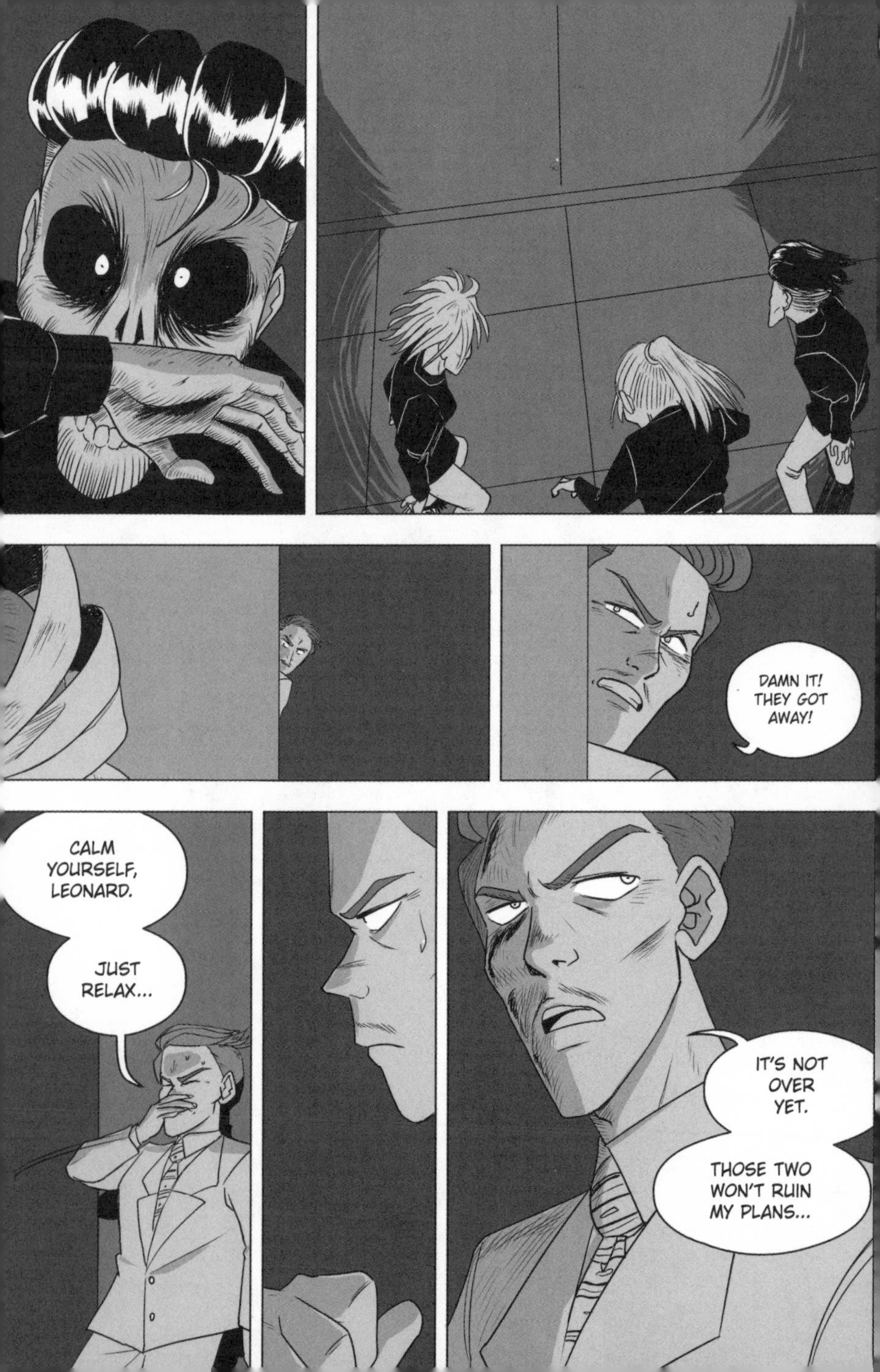
DAMN IT! THEY GOT AWAY!
CALM YOURSELF, LEONARD.
JUST RELAX...
IT'S NOT OVER YET.
THOSE TWO WON'T RUIN MY PLANS...

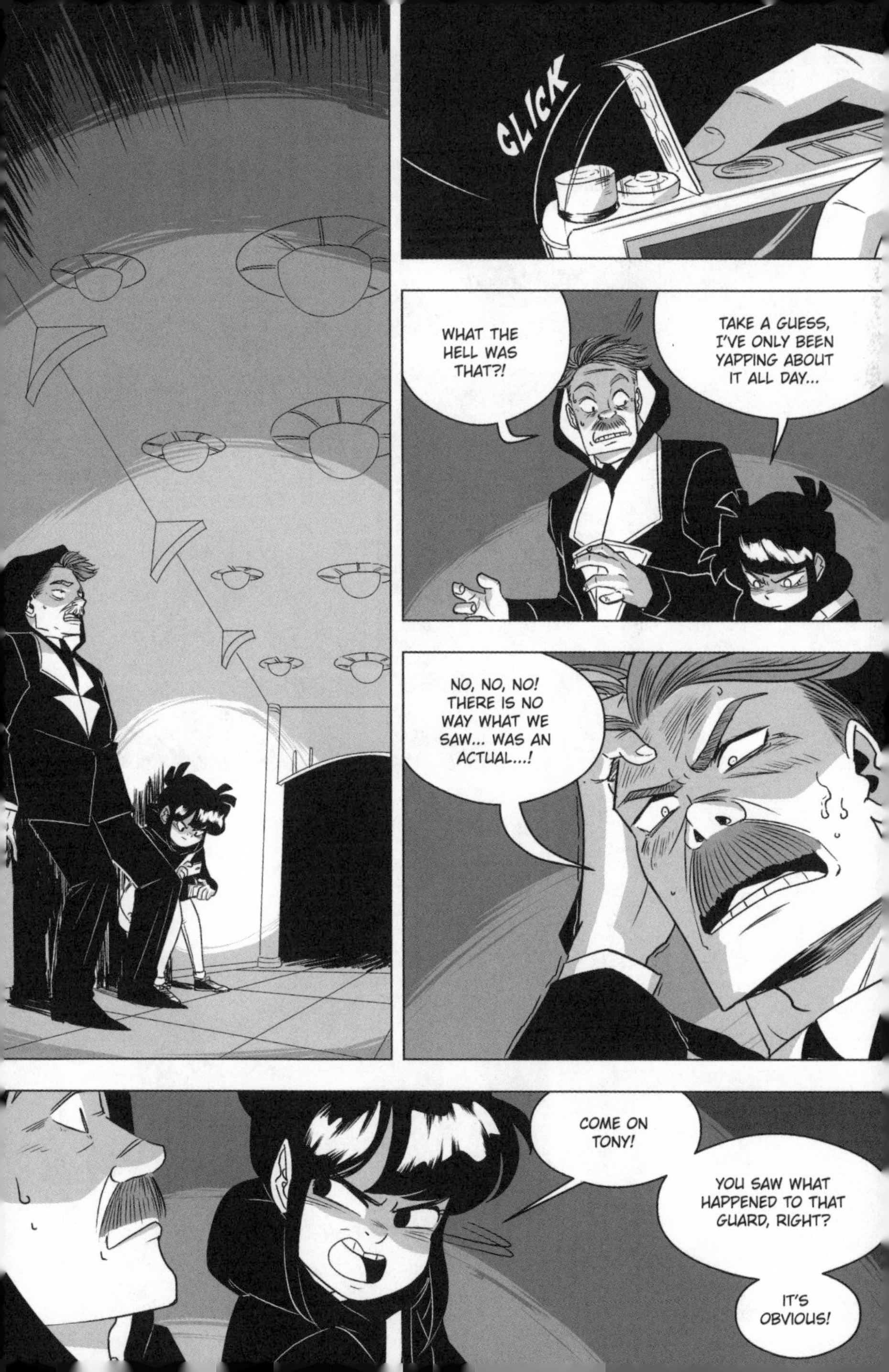
CLICK
WHAT THE HELL WAS THAT?!
TAKE A GUESS, I'VE ONLY BEEN YAPPING ABOUT IT ALL DAY...
NO, NO, NO! THERE IS NO WAY WHAT WE SAW... WAS AN ACTUAL...!
COME ON TONY!
YOU SAW WHAT HAPPENED TO THAT GUARD, RIGHT?
IT'S OBVIOUS!

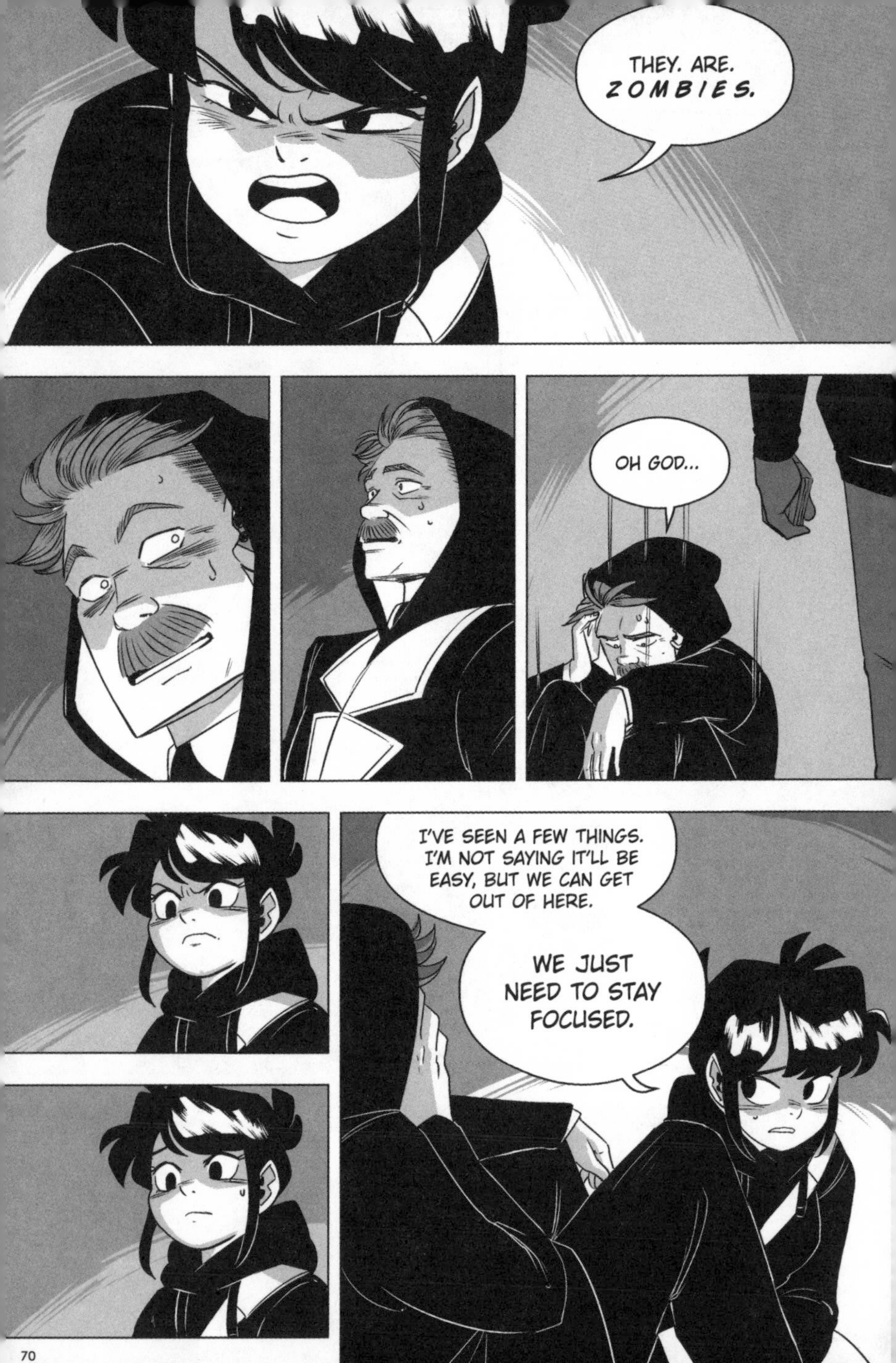
THEY. ARE. ZOMBIES.
OH GOD...
I'VE SEEN A FEW THINGS. I'M NOT SAYING IT'LL BE EASY, BUT WE CAN GET OUT OF HERE.
WE JUST NEED TO STAY FOCUSED.

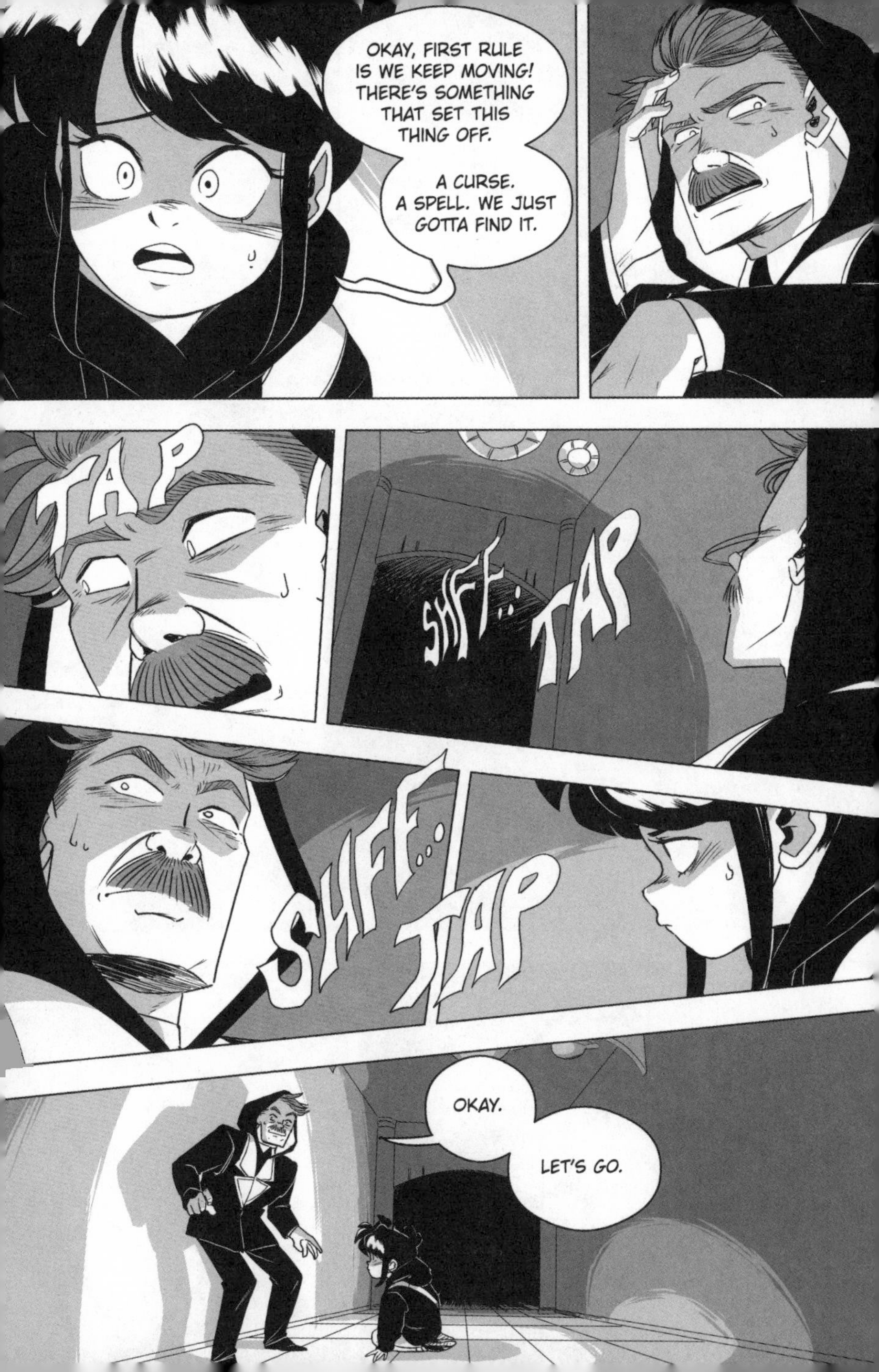
OKAY, FIRST RULE IS WE KEEP MOVING! THERE'S SOMETHING THAT SET THIS THING OFF.
A CURSE. A SPELL. WE JUST GOTTA FIND IT.
TAP
SHFF.. TAP
SHFF... TAP
OKAY.
LET'S GO.

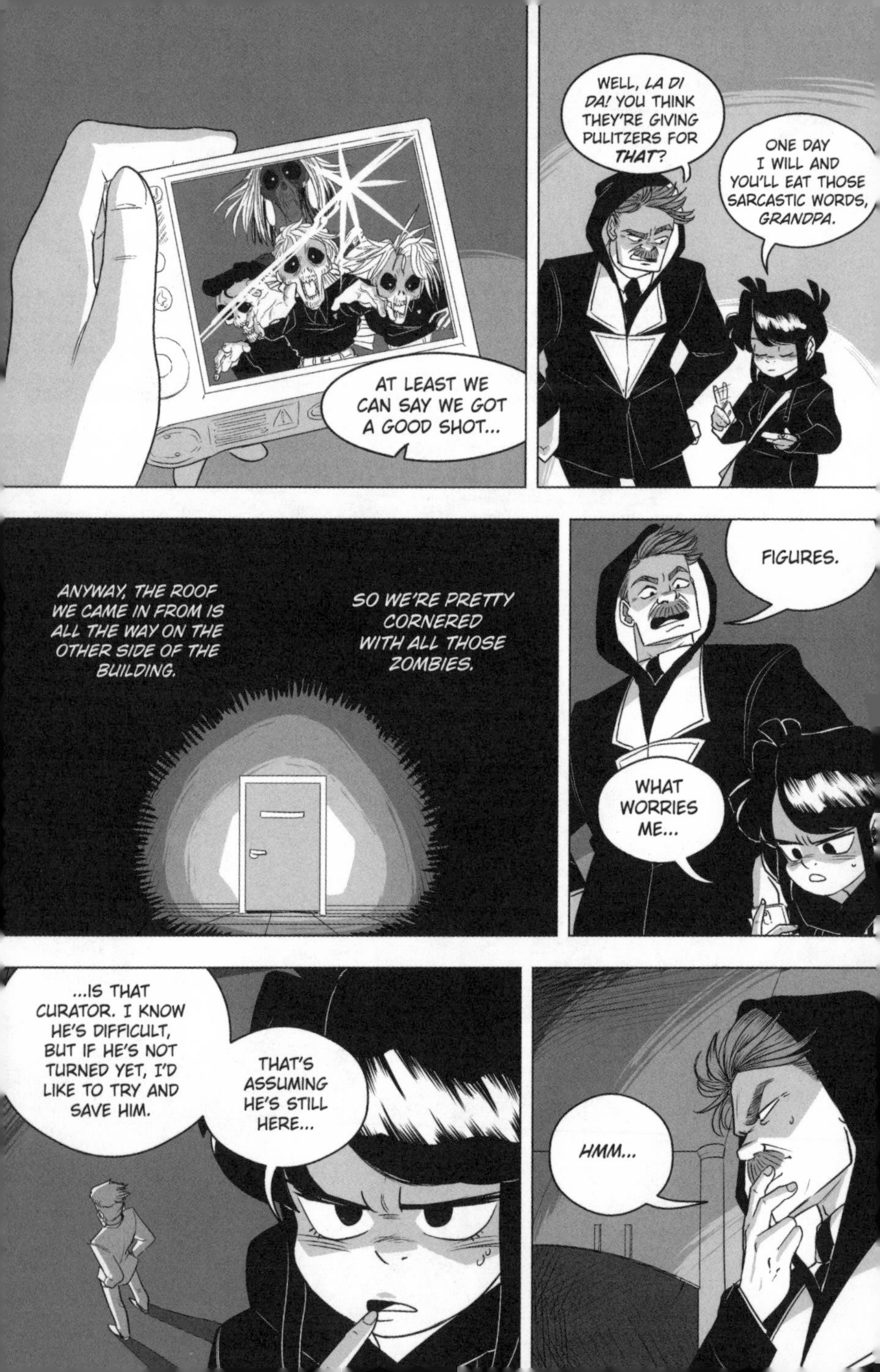
AT LEAST WE CAN SAY WE GOT A GOOD SHOT...
WELL, *LA DI DA!* YOU THINK THEY'RE GIVING PULITZERS FOR ***THAT***?
ONE DAY I WILL AND YOU'LL EAT THOSE SARCASTIC WORDS, *GRANDPA.*
ANYWAY, THE ROOF WE CAME IN FROM IS ALL THE WAY ON THE OTHER SIDE OF THE BUILDING.
SO WE'RE PRETTY CORNERED WITH ALL THOSE ZOMBIES.
FIGURES.
WHAT WORRIES ME...
...IS THAT CURATOR. I KNOW HE'S DIFFICULT, BUT IF HE'S NOT TURNED YET, I'D LIKE TO TRY AND SAVE HIM.
THAT'S ASSUMING HE'S STILL HERE...
HMM...

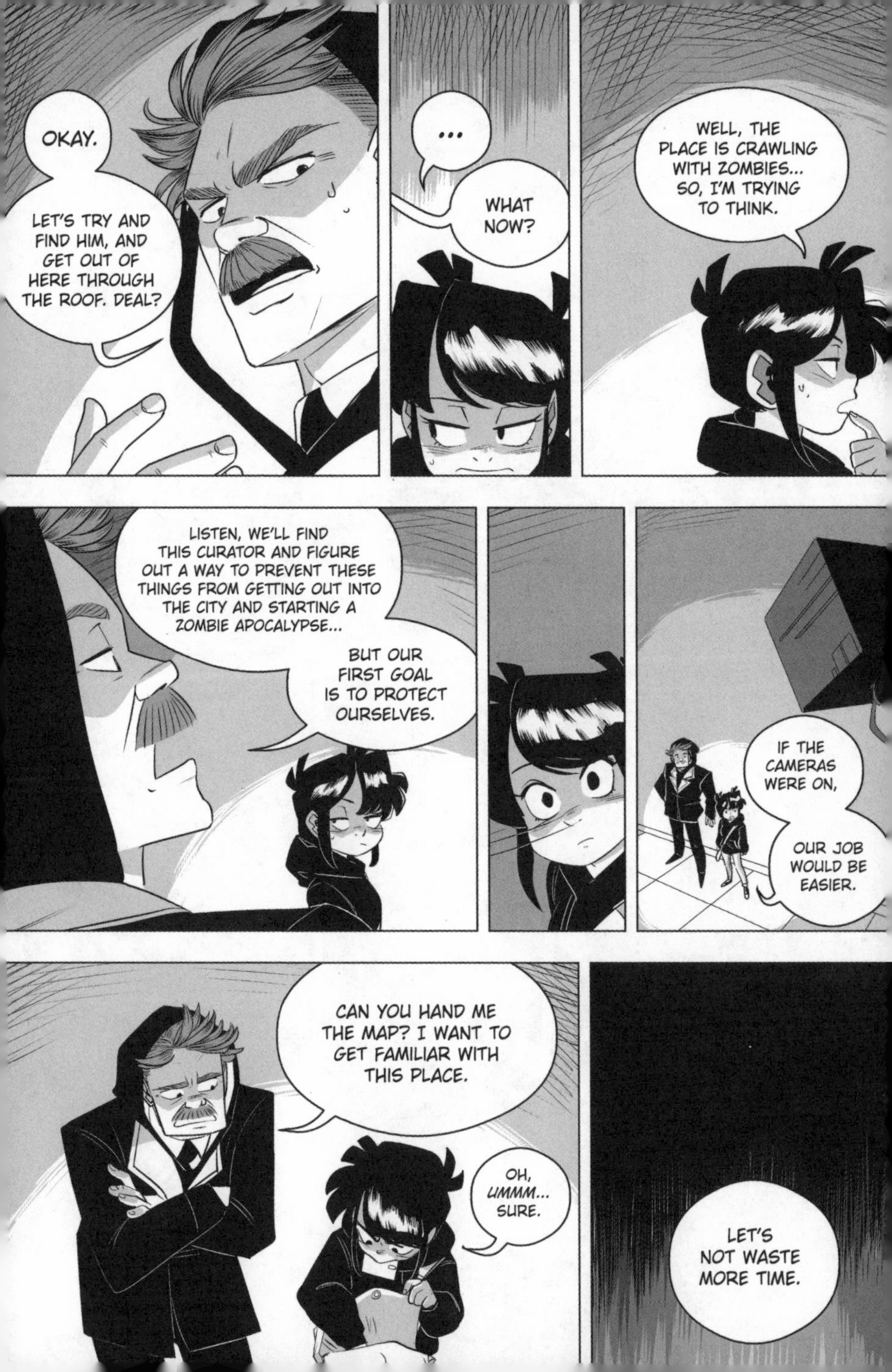
OKAY.
LET'S TRY AND FIND HIM, AND GET OUT OF HERE THROUGH THE ROOF. DEAL?
...
WHAT NOW?
WELL, THE PLACE IS CRAWLING WITH ZOMBIES... SO, I'M TRYING TO THINK.
LISTEN, WE'LL FIND THIS CURATOR AND FIGURE OUT A WAY TO PREVENT THESE THINGS FROM GETTING OUT INTO THE CITY AND STARTING A ZOMBIE APOCALYPSE...
BUT OUR FIRST GOAL IS TO PROTECT OURSELVES.
IF THE CAMERAS WERE ON,
OUR JOB WOULD BE EASIER.
CAN YOU HAND ME THE MAP? I WANT TO GET FAMILIAR WITH THIS PLACE.
OH, UMMM... SURE.
LET'S NOT WASTE MORE TIME.

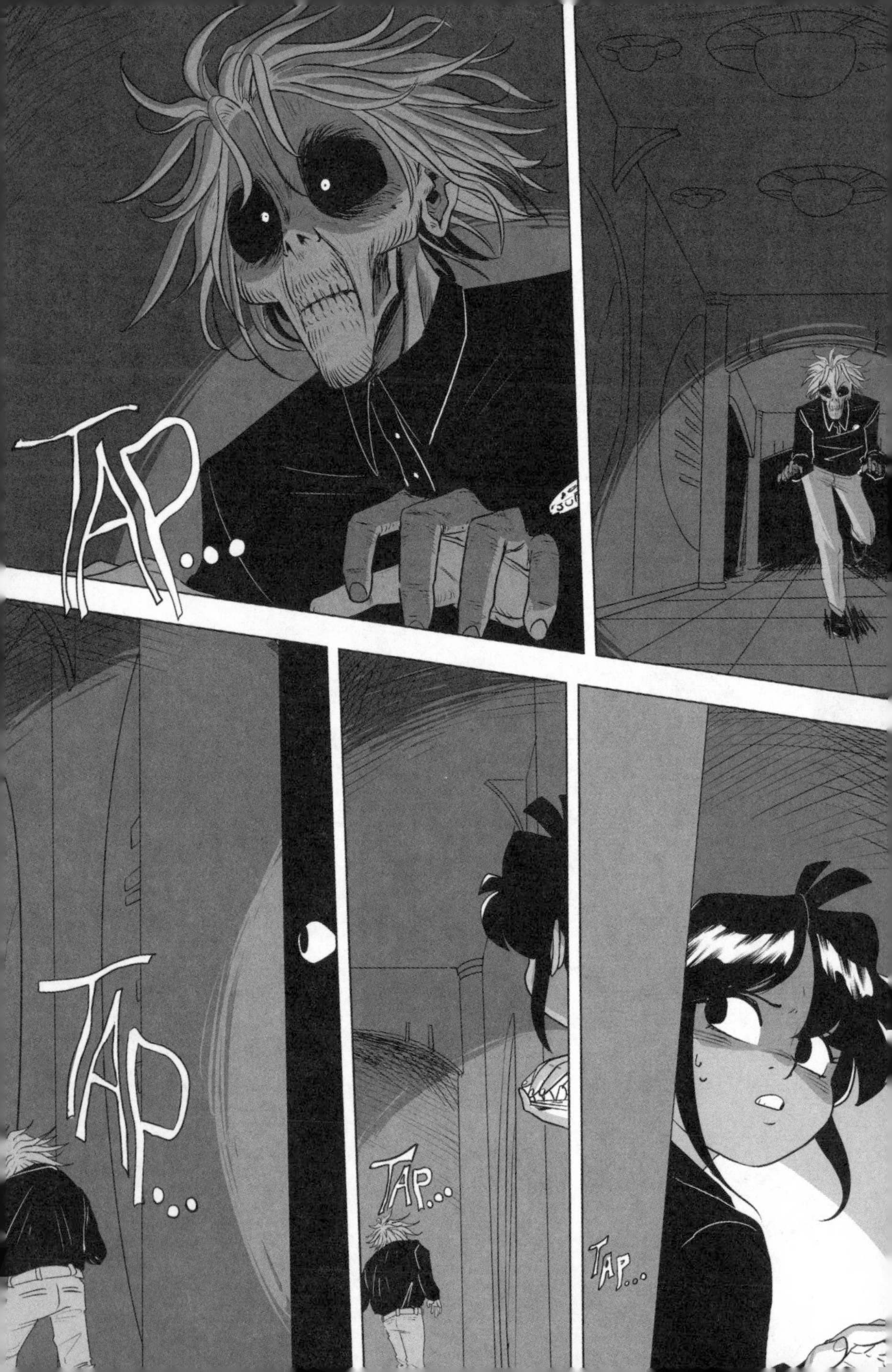
TAP...
TAP...
TAP...
TAP...

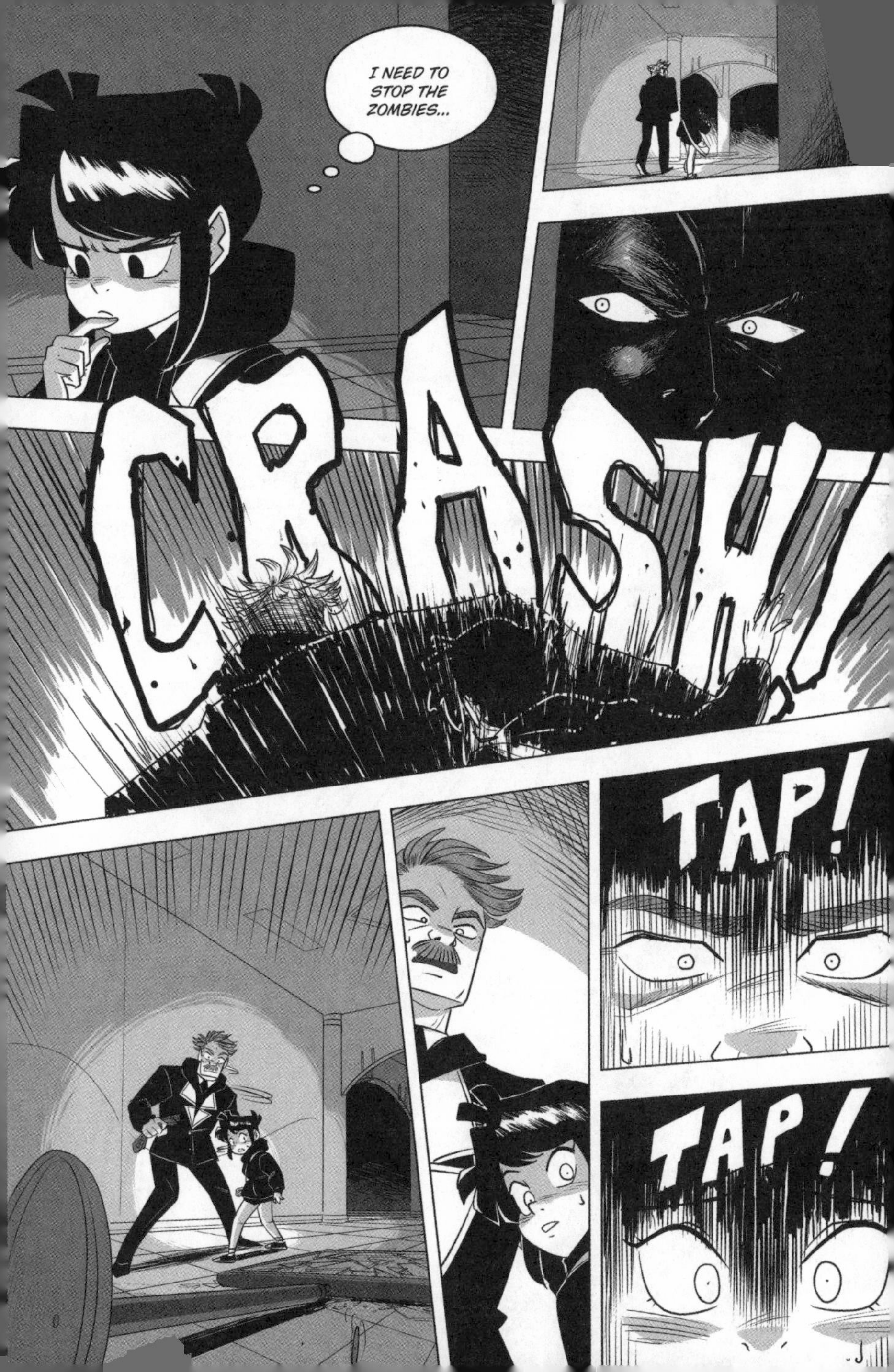
I NEED TO STOP THE ZOMBIES...
CRASH!
TAP!
TAP!

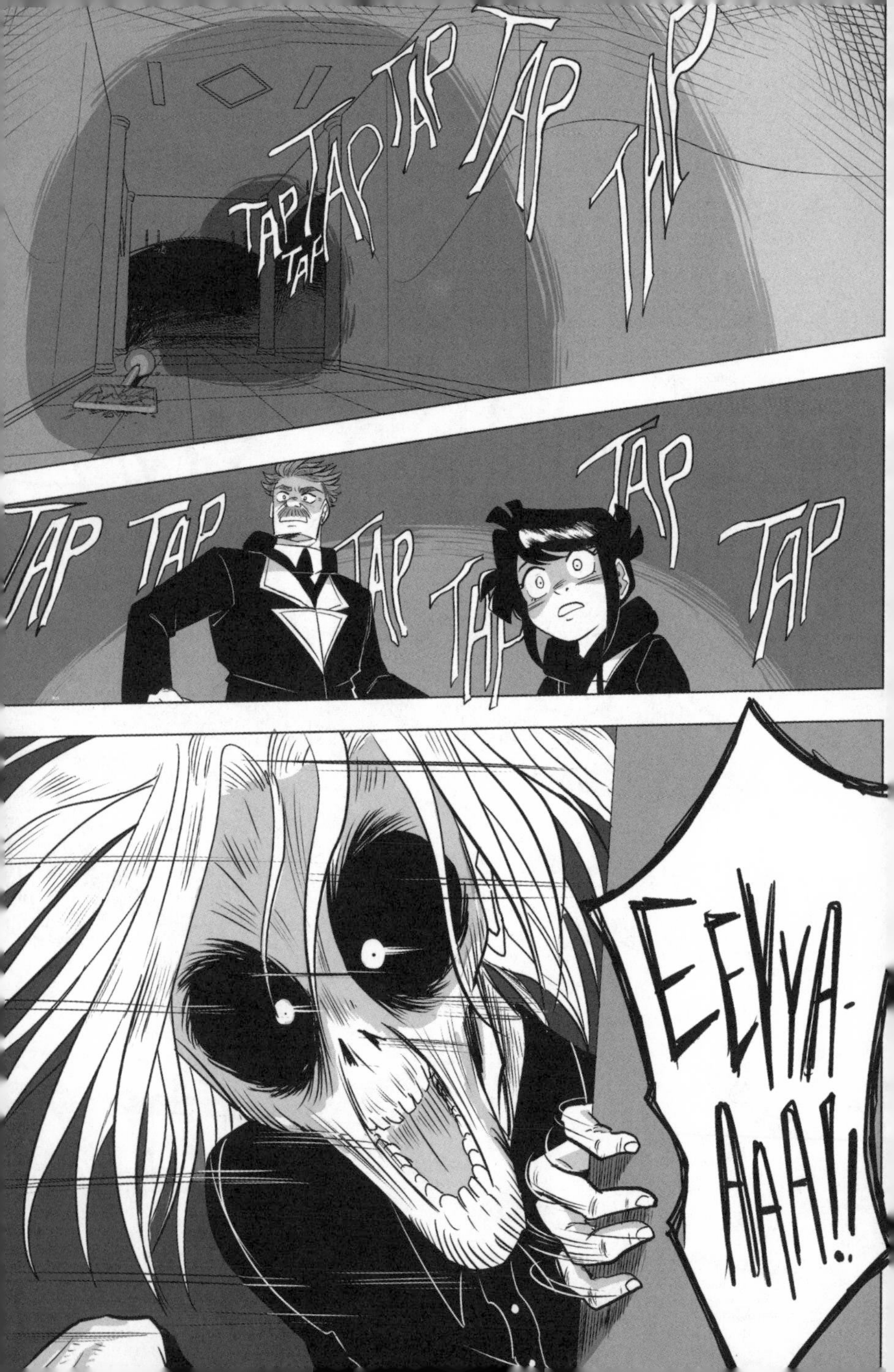
TAP TAP TAP TAP TAP TAP TAP
TAP TAP TAP TAP TAP TAP
EEYAA-AAA!!

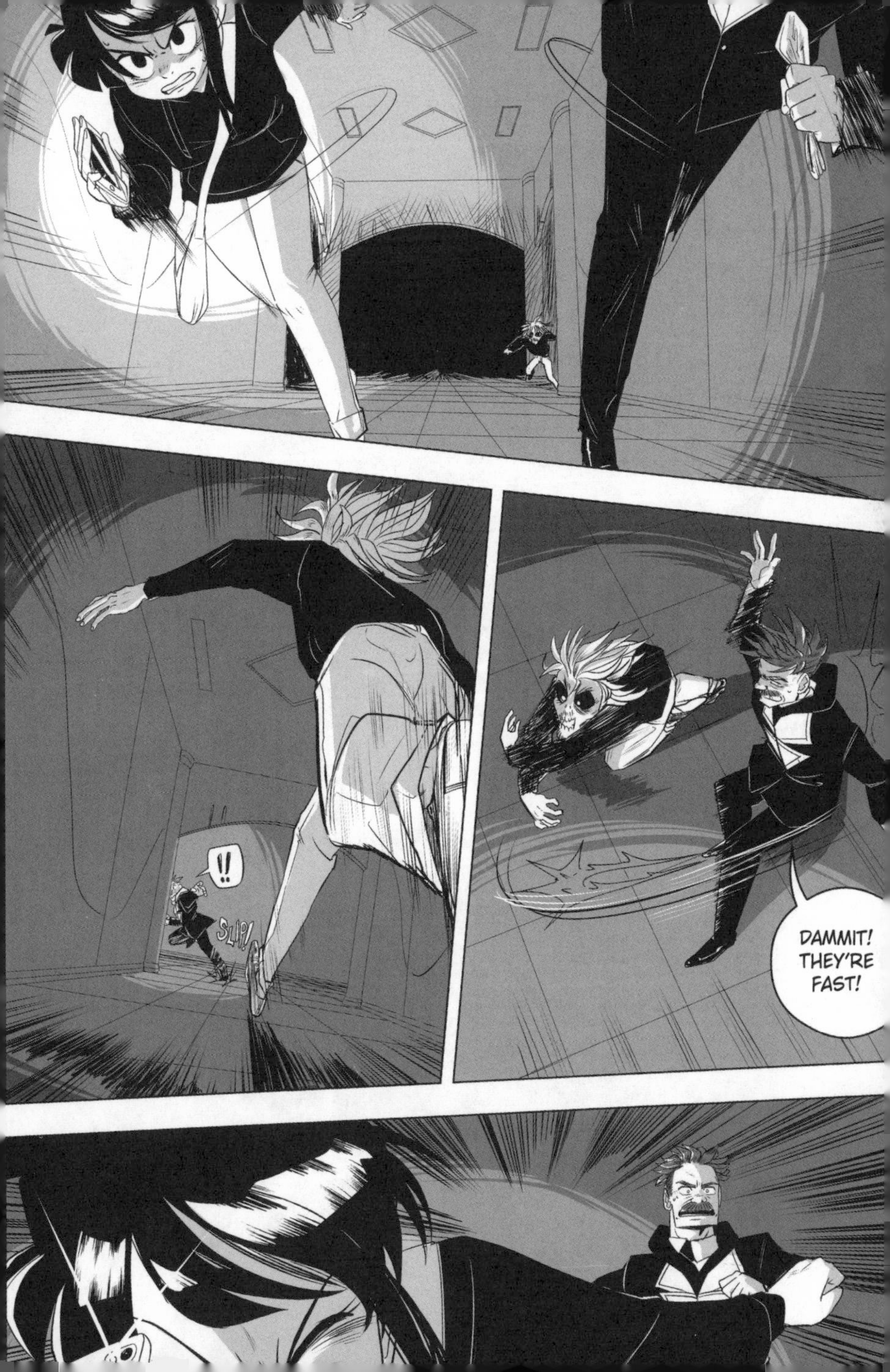
!!
SLIP!
DAMMIT! THEY'RE FAST!

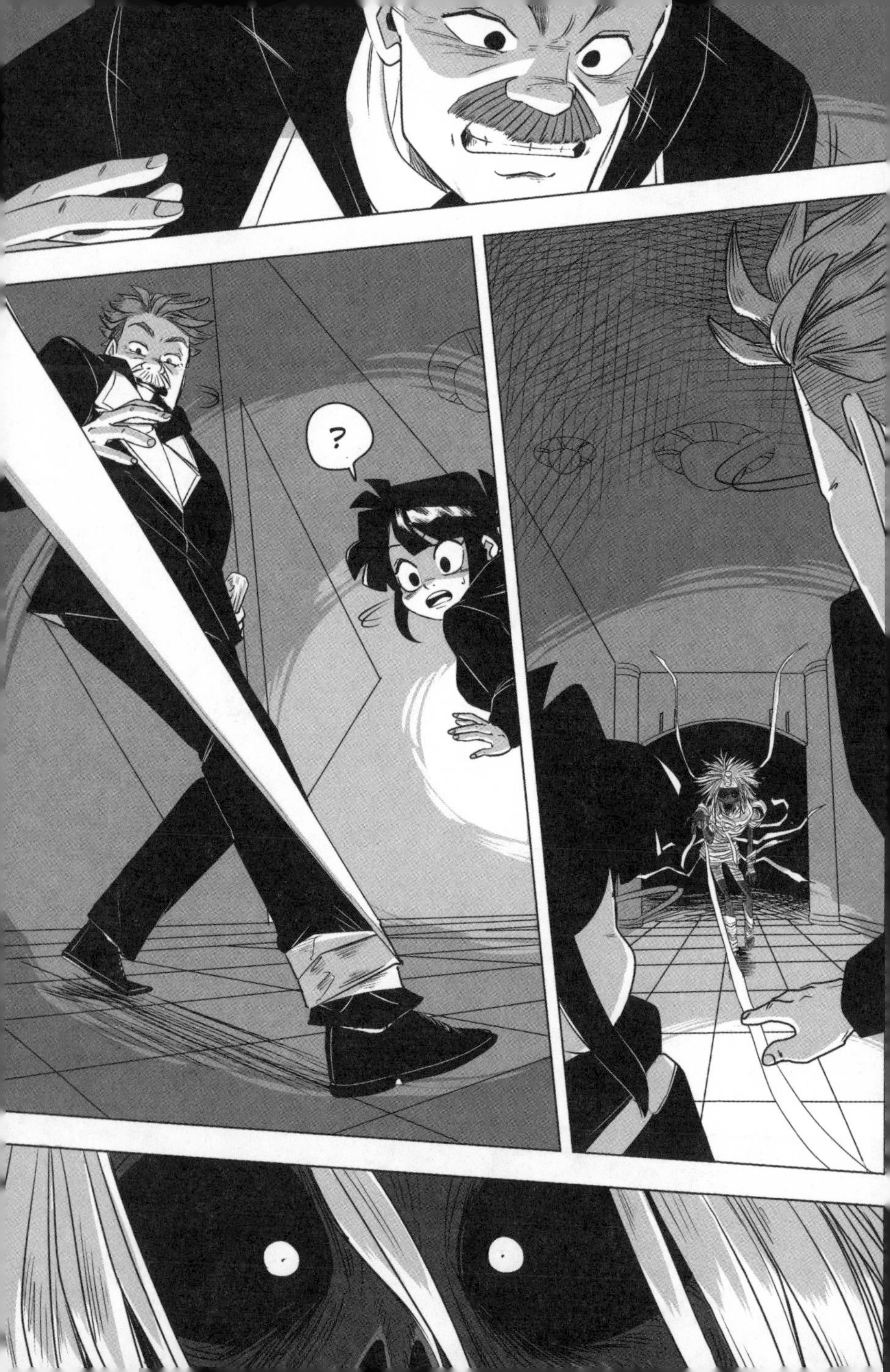
?

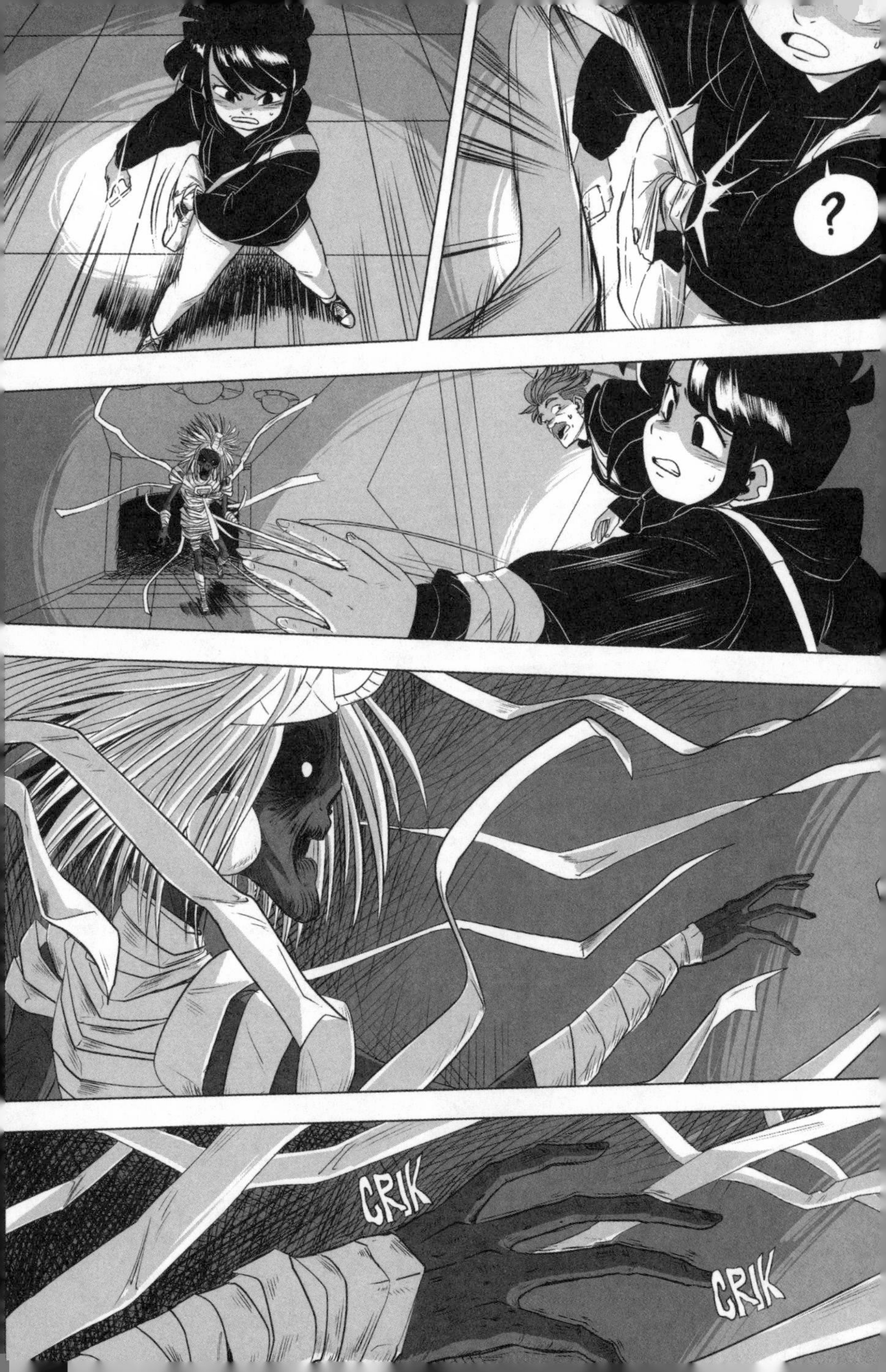
?
CRIK
CRIK

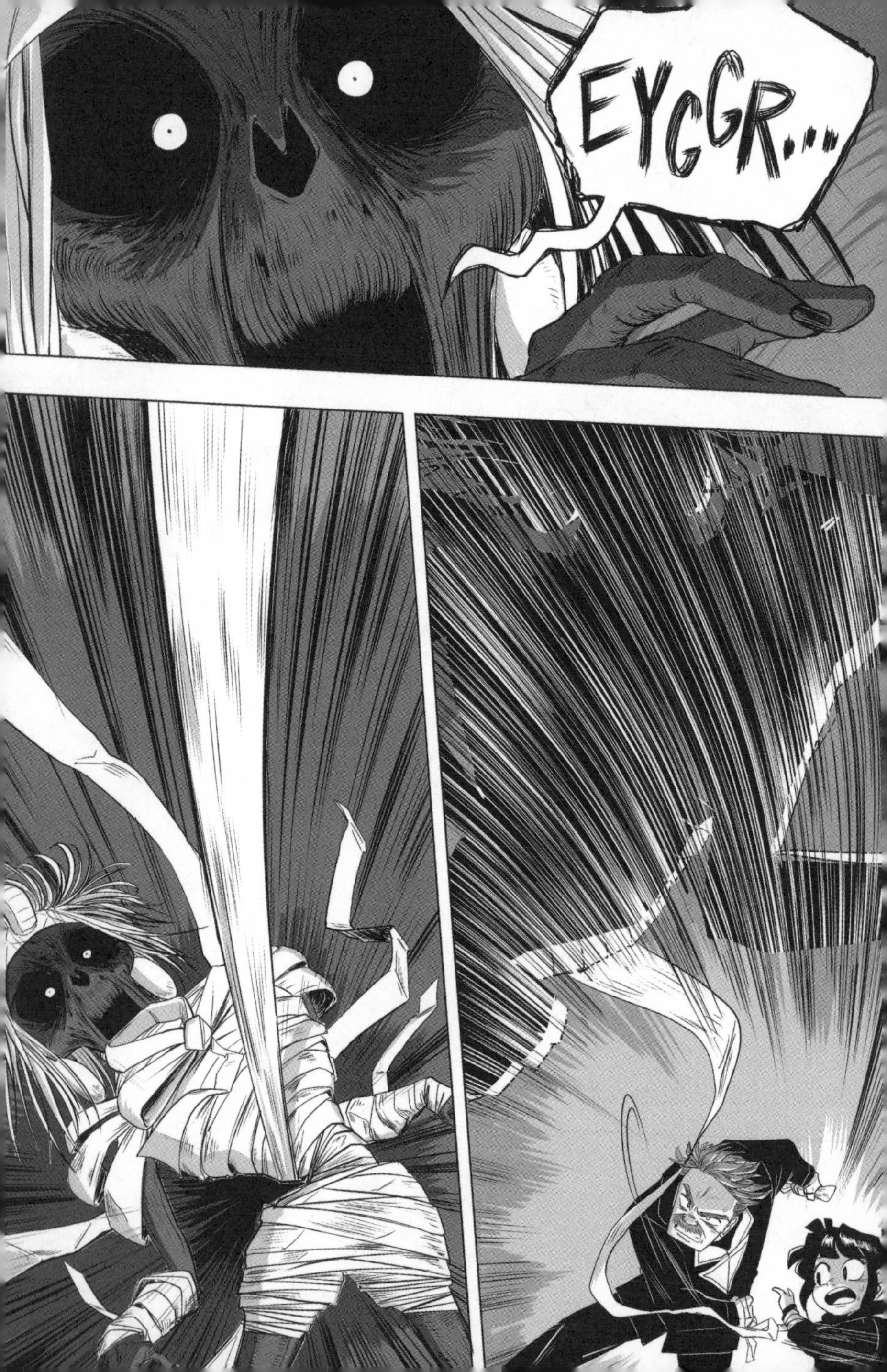
EYGGR...

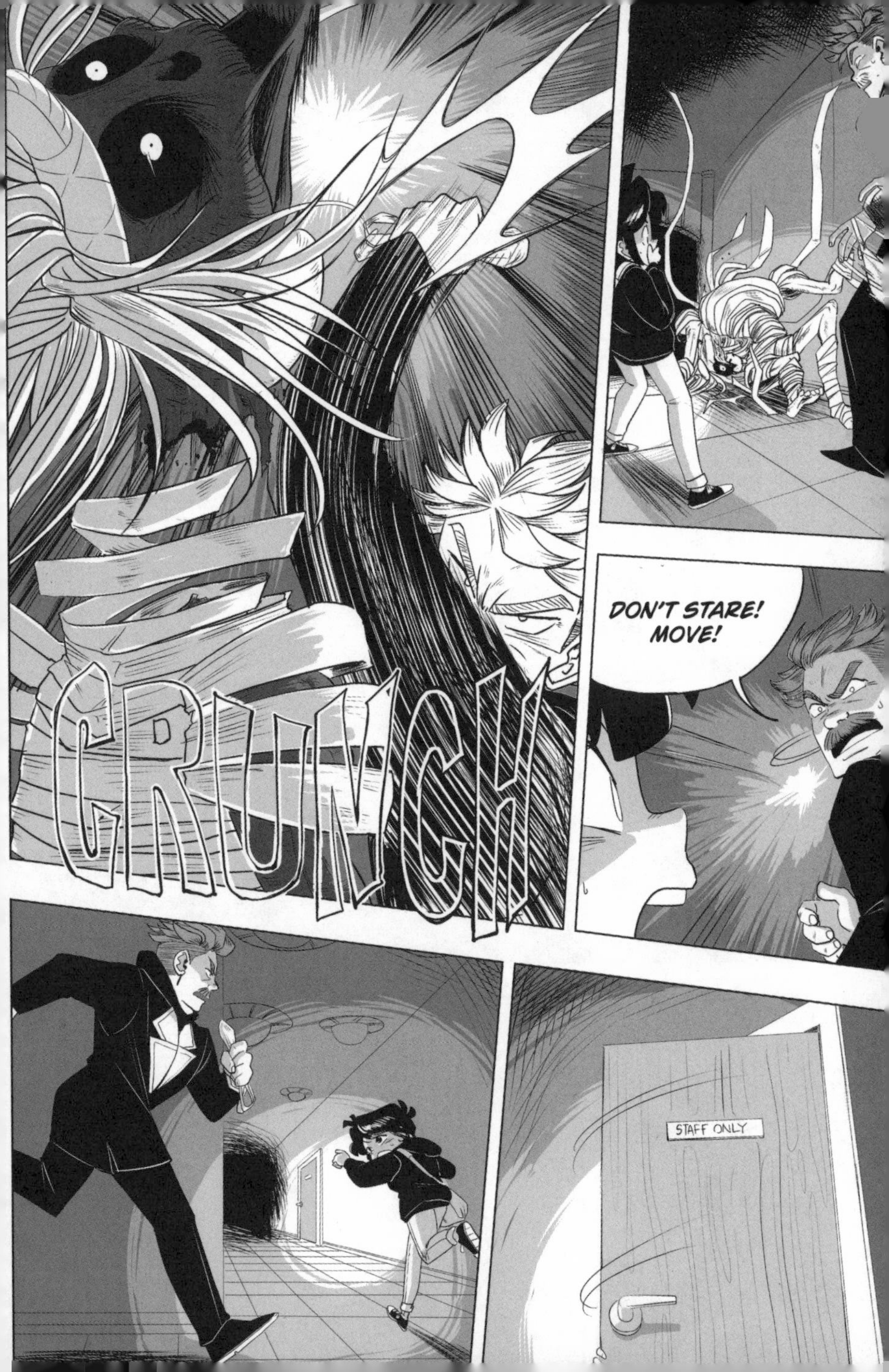
CRUNCH
DON'T STARE! MOVE!
STAFF ONLY

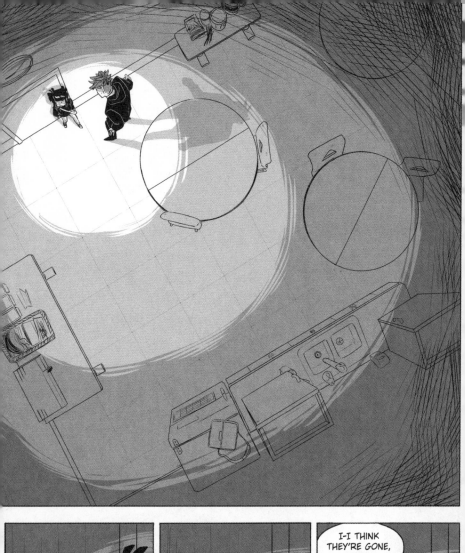

I-I THINK THEY'RE GONE, TONY.

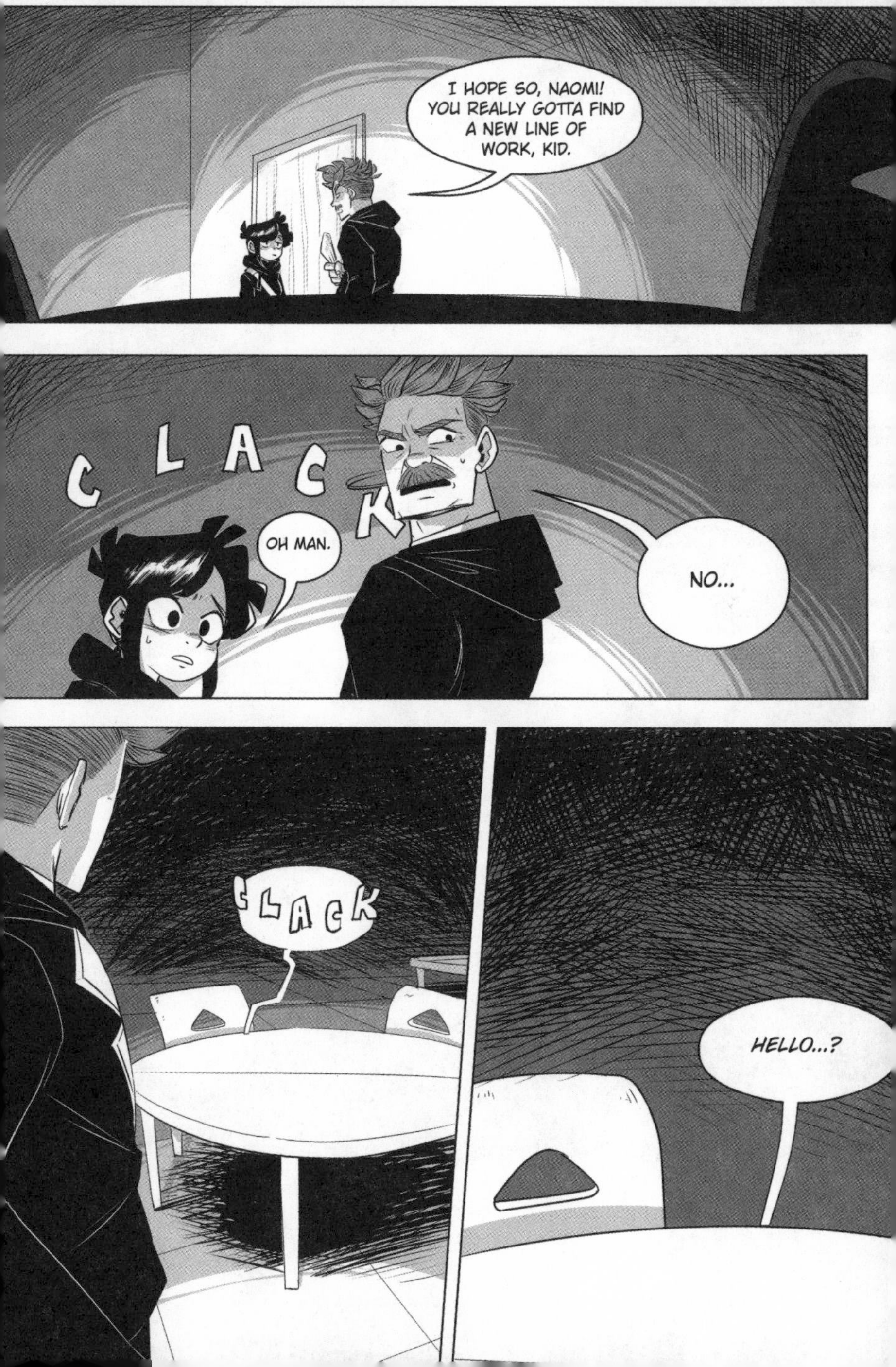
I HOPE SO, NAOMI! YOU REALLY GOTTA FIND A NEW LINE OF WORK, KID.
CLACK
OH MAN.
NO...
CLACK
HELLO...?

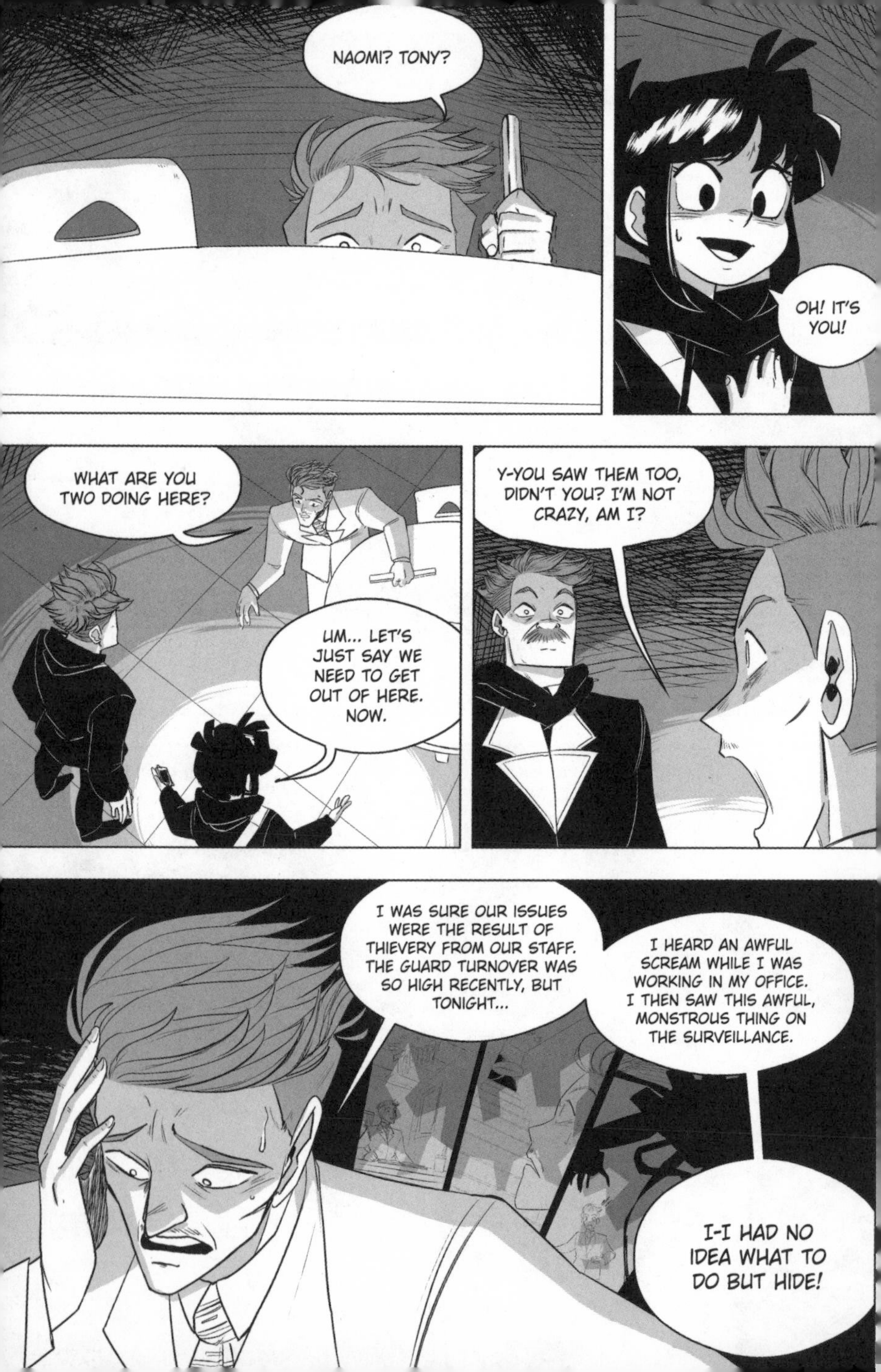
NAOMI? TONY?
OH! IT'S YOU!
WHAT ARE YOU TWO DOING HERE?
UM... LET'S JUST SAY WE NEED TO GET OUT OF HERE. NOW.
Y-YOU SAW THEM TOO, DIDN'T YOU? I'M NOT CRAZY, AM I?
I WAS SURE OUR ISSUES WERE THE RESULT OF THIEVERY FROM OUR STAFF. THE GUARD TURNOVER WAS SO HIGH RECENTLY, BUT TONIGHT...
I HEARD AN AWFUL SCREAM WHILE I WAS WORKING IN MY OFFICE. I THEN SAW THIS AWFUL, MONSTROUS THING ON THE SURVEILLANCE.
I-I HAD NO IDEA WHAT TO DO BUT HIDE!

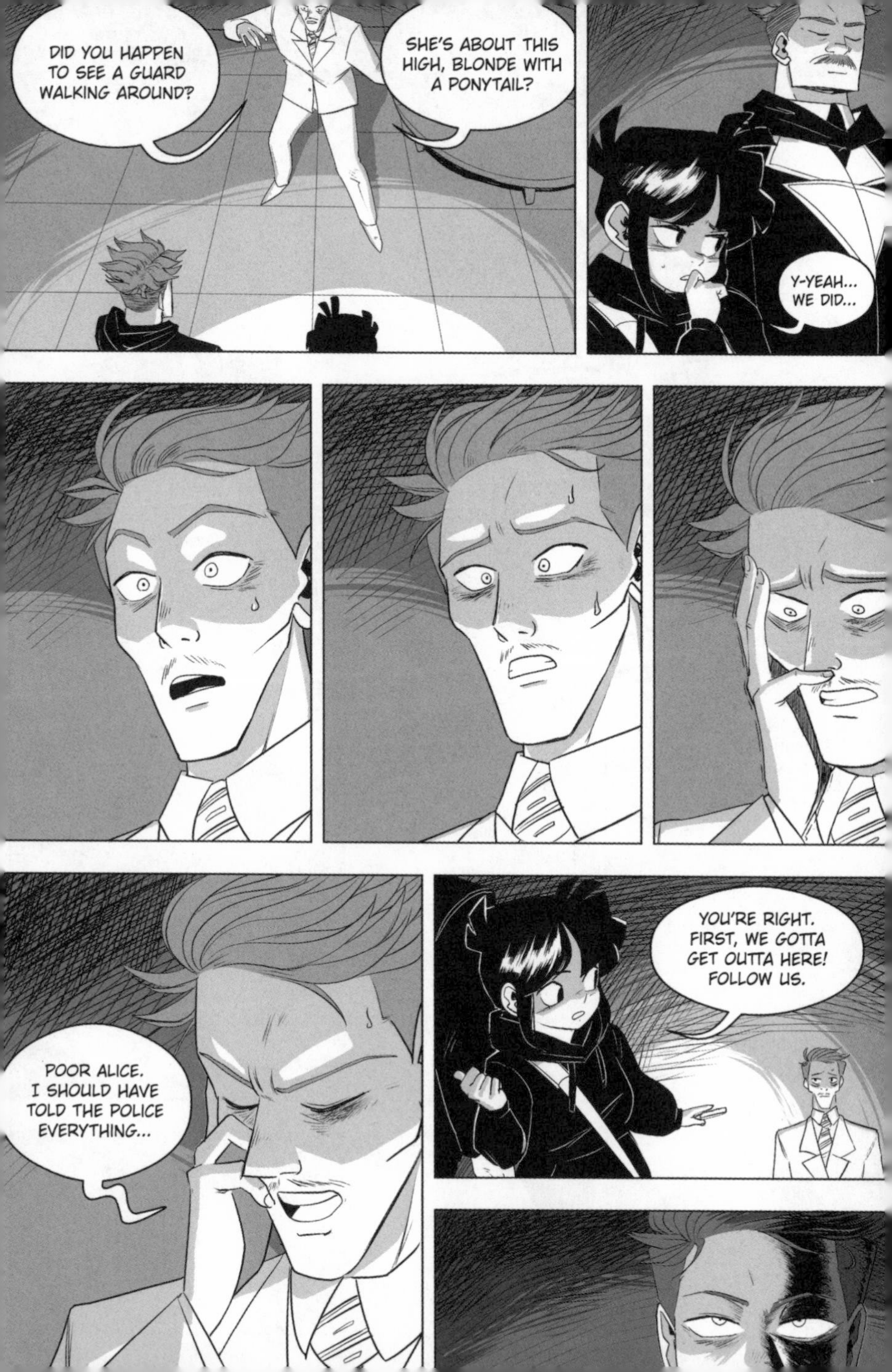
DID YOU HAPPEN TO SEE A GUARD WALKING AROUND?
SHE'S ABOUT THIS HIGH, BLONDE WITH A PONYTAIL?
Y-YEAH... WE DID...
POOR ALICE. I SHOULD HAVE TOLD THE POLICE EVERYTHING...
YOU'RE RIGHT. FIRST, WE GOTTA GET OUTTA HERE! FOLLOW US.

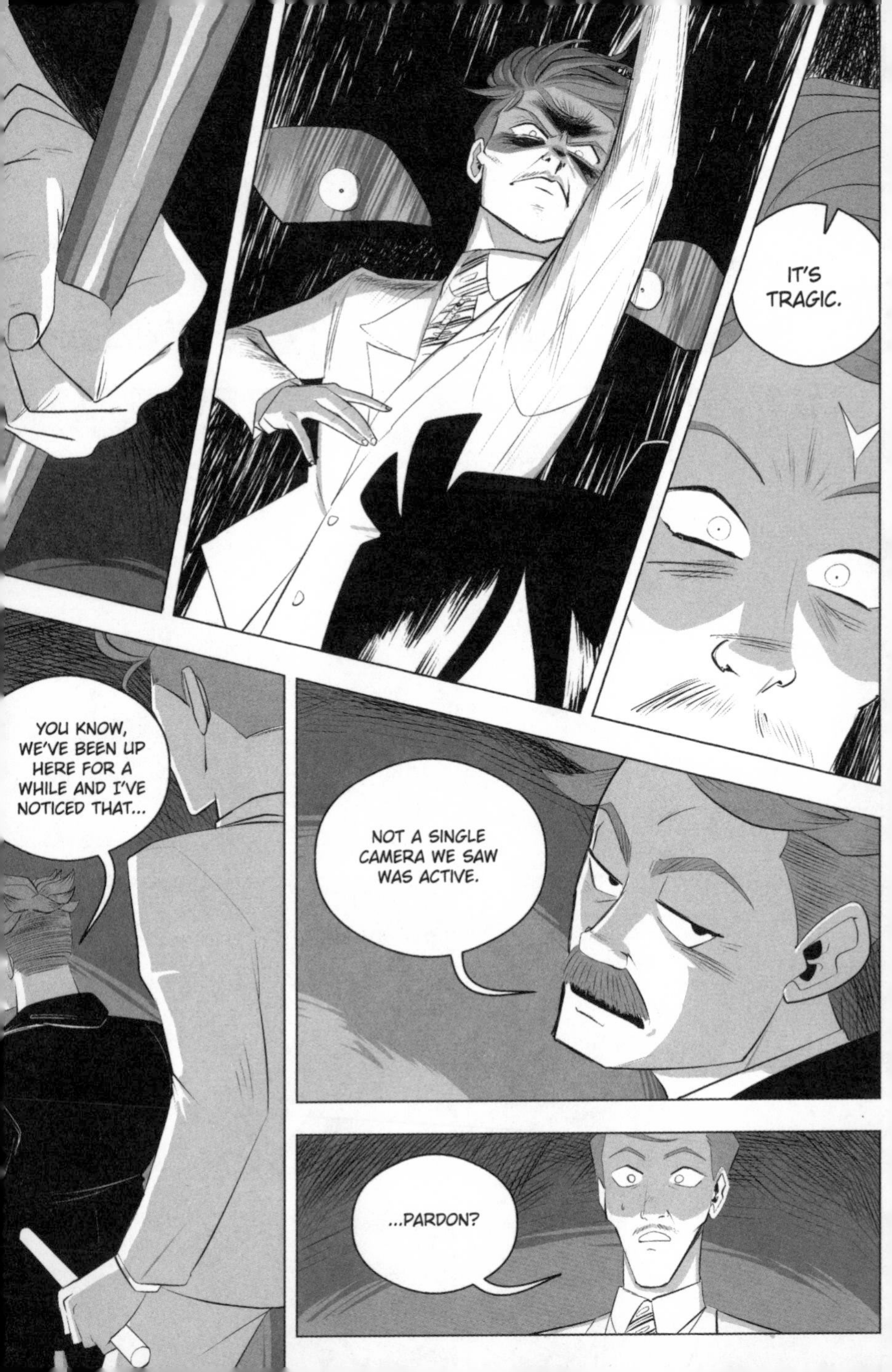
IT'S TRAGIC.
YOU KNOW, WE'VE BEEN UP HERE FOR A WHILE AND I'VE NOTICED THAT...
NOT A SINGLE CAMERA WE SAW WAS ACTIVE.
...PARDON?

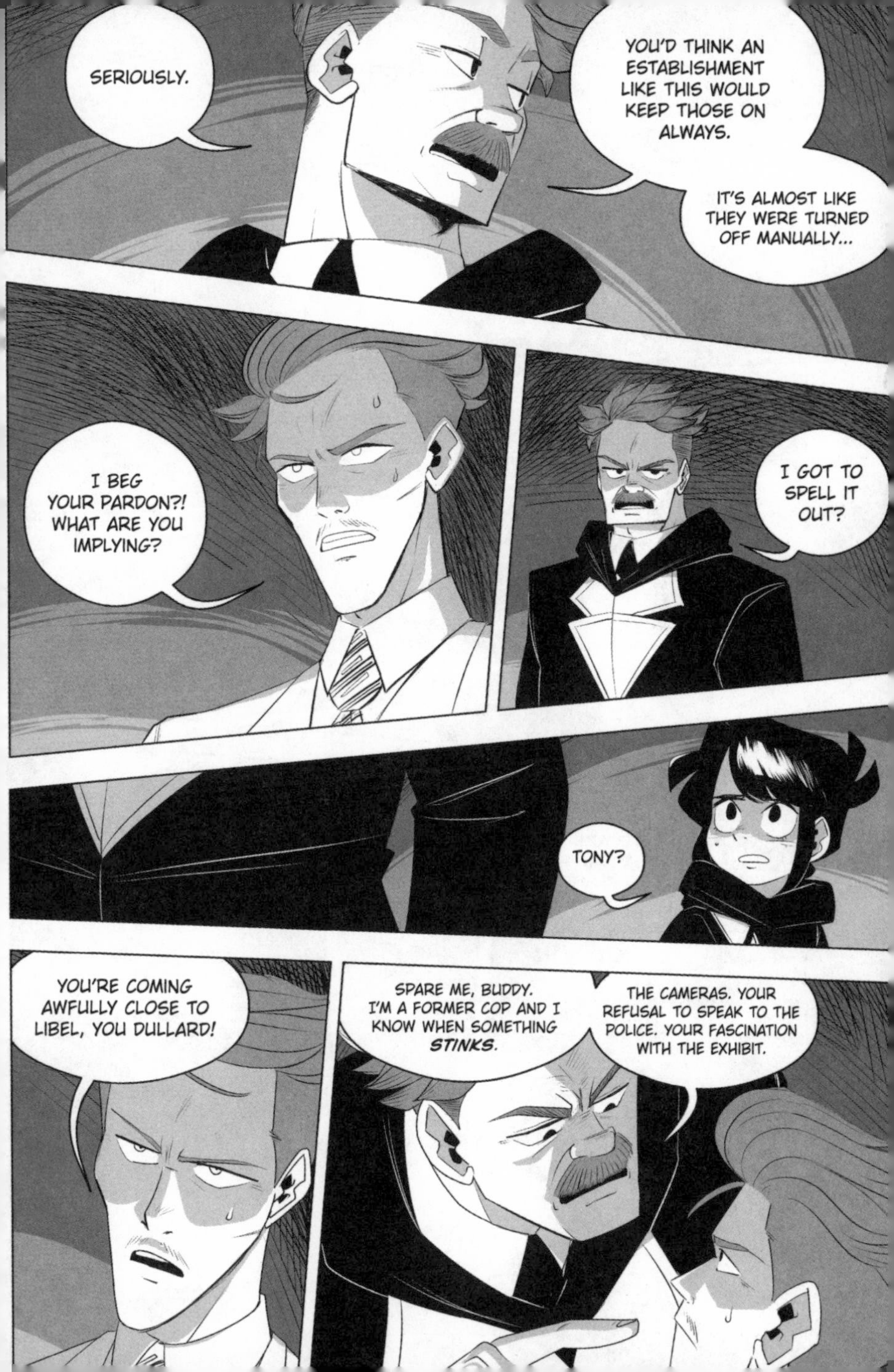
SERIOUSLY.
YOU'D THINK AN ESTABLISHMENT LIKE THIS WOULD KEEP THOSE ON ALWAYS.
IT'S ALMOST LIKE THEY WERE TURNED OFF MANUALLY...
I BEG YOUR PARDON?! WHAT ARE YOU IMPLYING?
I GOT TO SPELL IT OUT?
TONY?
YOU'RE COMING AWFULLY CLOSE TO LIBEL, YOU DULLARD!
SPARE ME, BUDDY. I'M A FORMER COP AND I KNOW WHEN SOMETHING *STINKS*.
THE CAMERAS. YOUR REFUSAL TO SPEAK TO THE POLICE. YOUR FASCINATION WITH THE EXHIBIT.

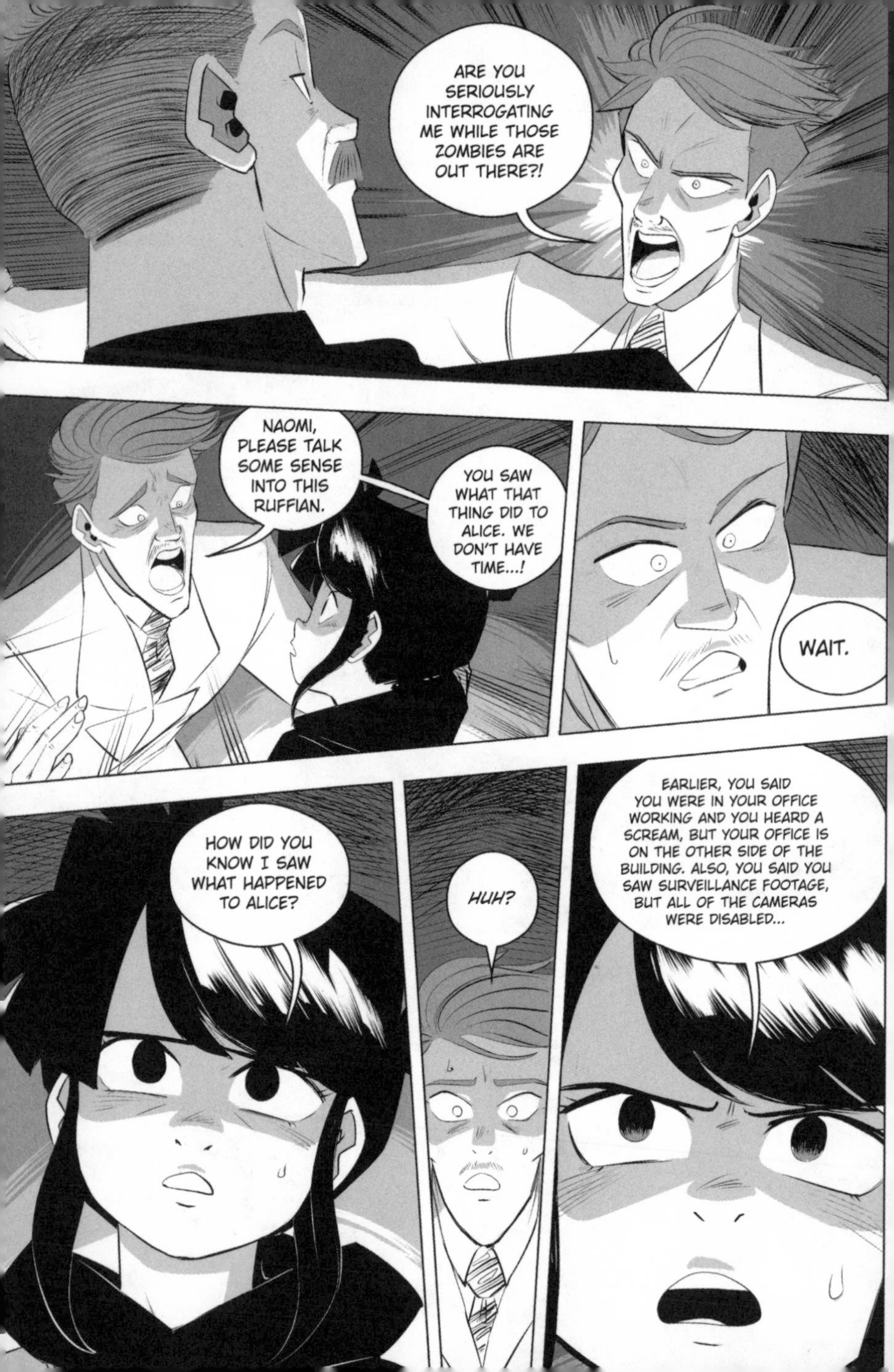
ARE YOU SERIOUSLY INTERROGATING ME WHILE THOSE ZOMBIES ARE OUT THERE?!
NAOMI, PLEASE TALK SOME SENSE INTO THIS RUFFIAN.
YOU SAW WHAT THAT THING DID TO ALICE. WE DON'T HAVE TIME...!
WAIT.
HOW DID YOU KNOW I SAW WHAT HAPPENED TO ALICE?
HUH?
EARLIER, YOU SAID YOU WERE IN YOUR OFFICE WORKING AND YOU HEARD A SCREAM, BUT YOUR OFFICE IS ON THE OTHER SIDE OF THE BUILDING. ALSO, YOU SAID YOU SAW SURVEILLANCE FOOTAGE, BUT ALL OF THE CAMERAS WERE DISABLED...

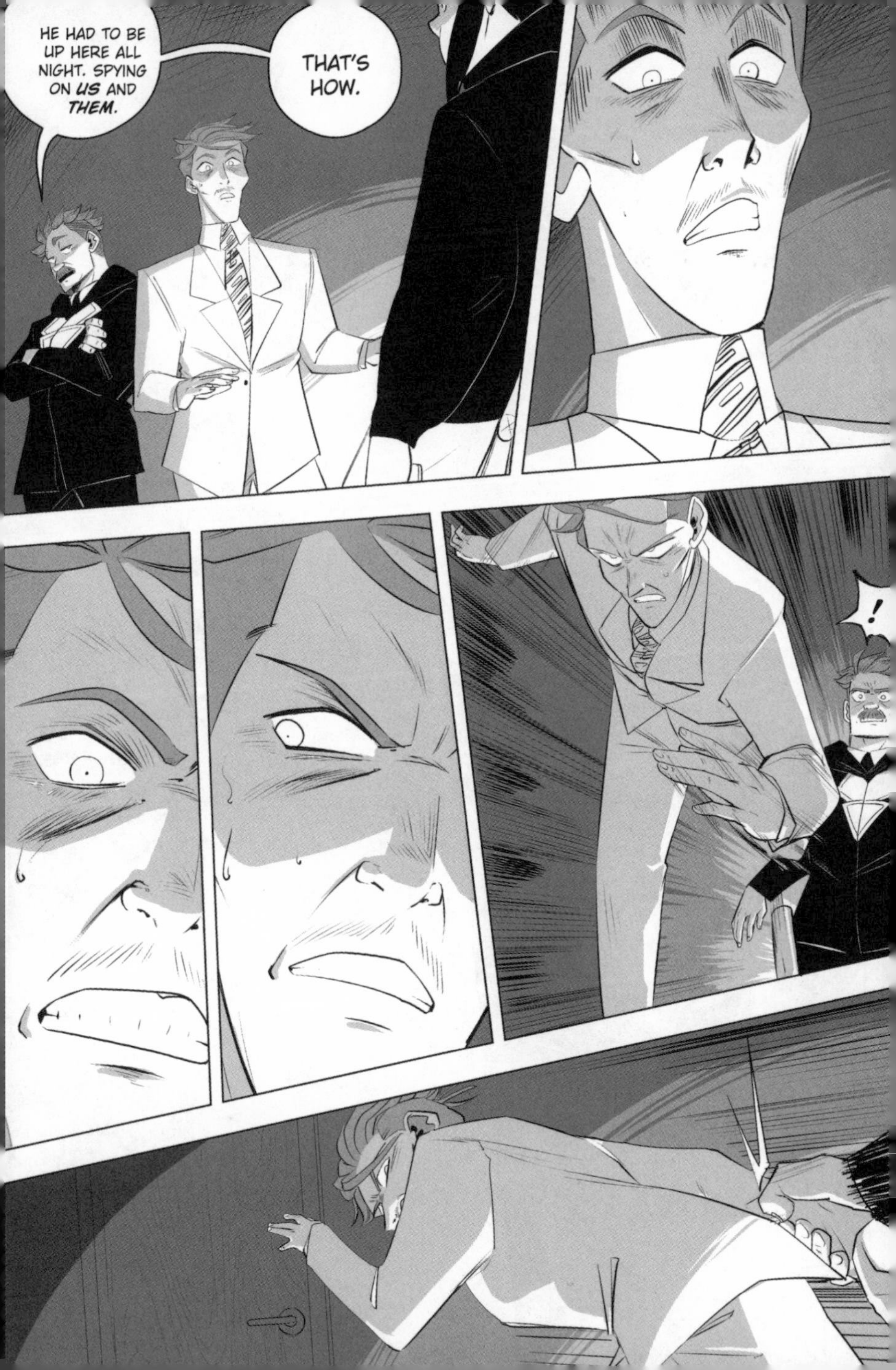
HE HAD TO BE UP HERE ALL NIGHT. SPYING ON *US* AND *THEM*.
THAT'S HOW.
!

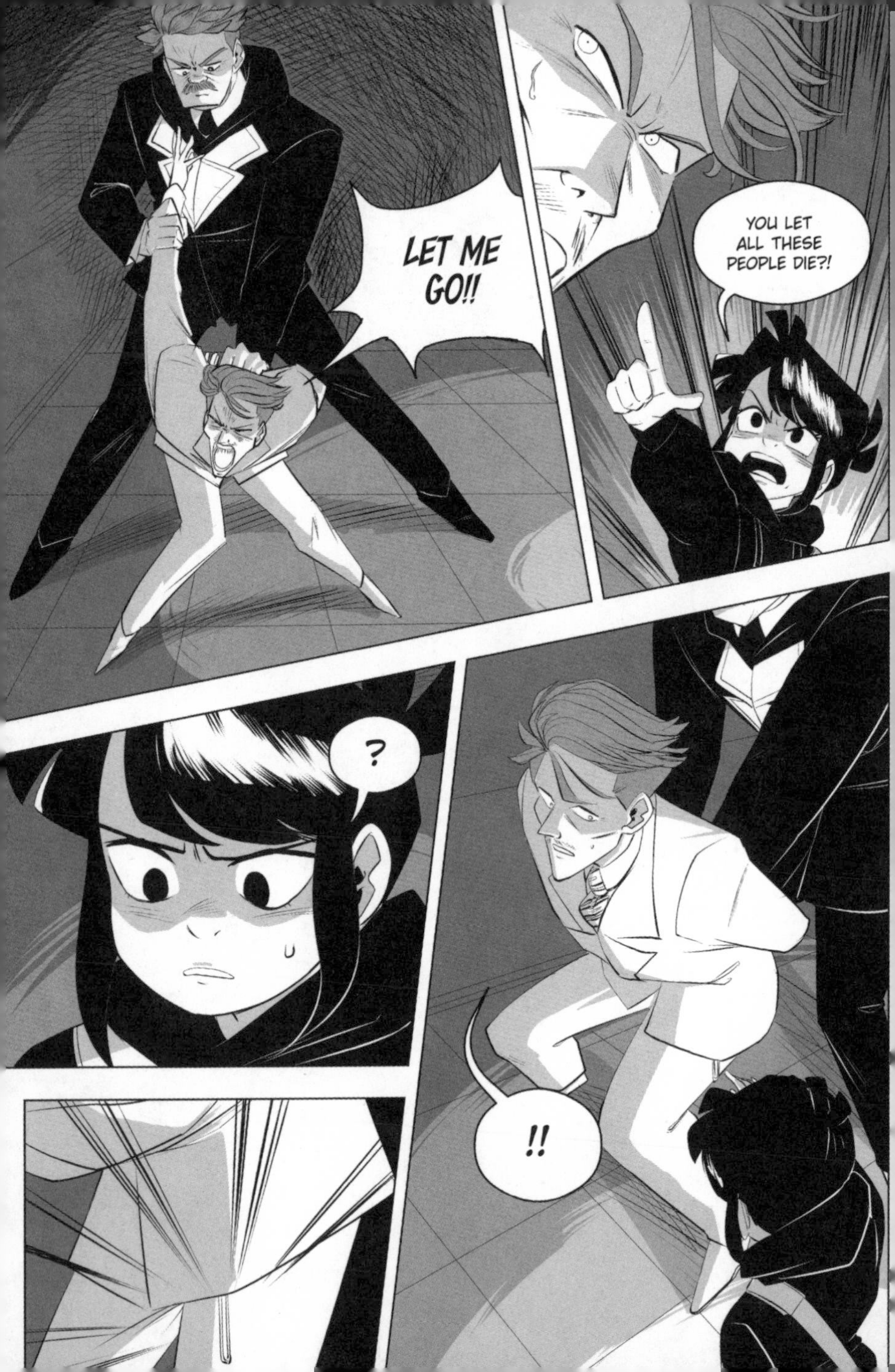
LET ME GO!!
YOU LET ALL THESE PEOPLE DIE?!
?
!!

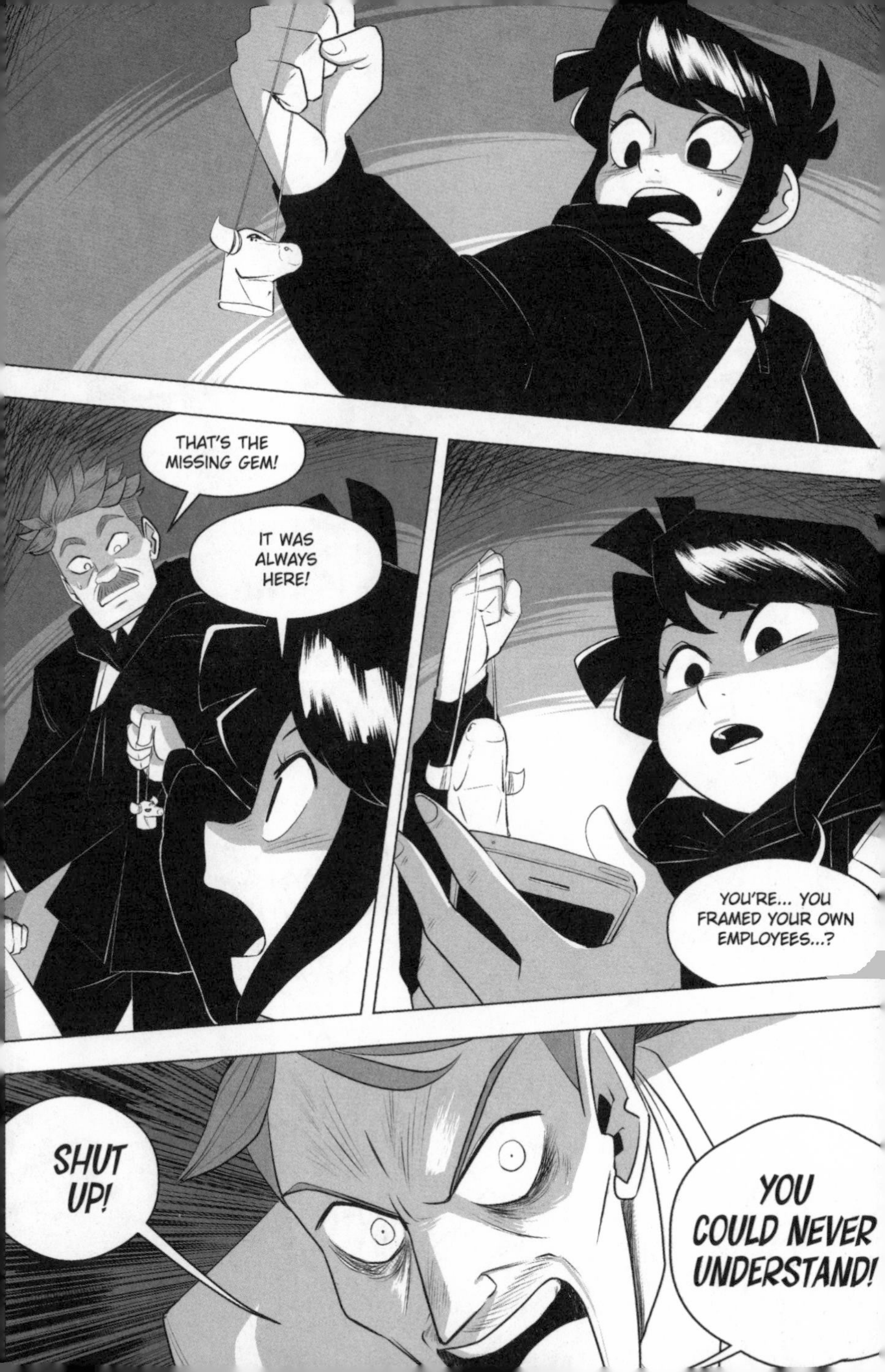
THAT'S THE MISSING GEM!
IT WAS ALWAYS HERE!
YOU'RE... YOU FRAMED YOUR OWN EMPLOYEES...?
SHUT UP!
YOU COULD NEVER UNDERSTAND!

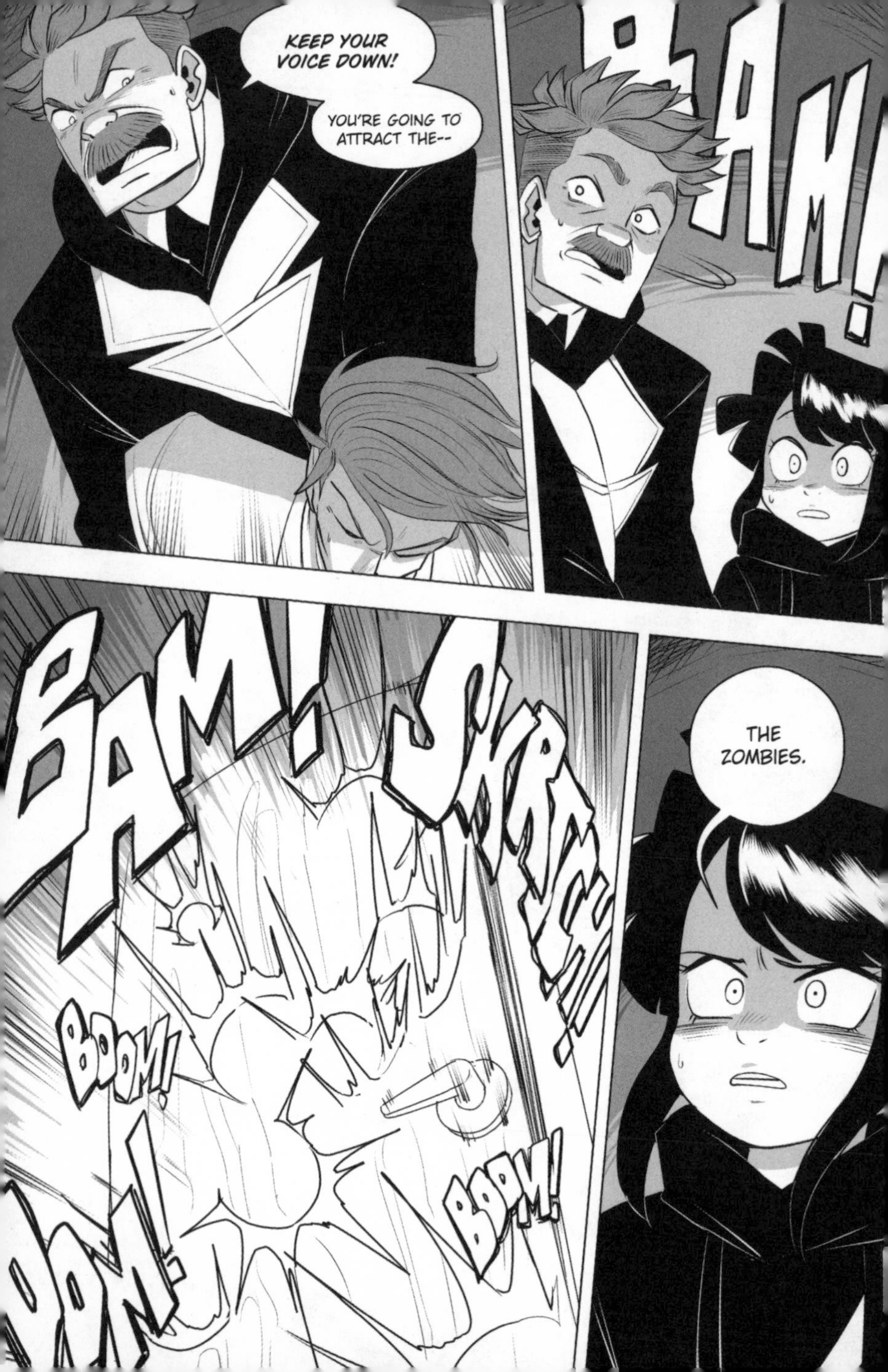
KEEP YOUR VOICE DOWN!
YOU'RE GOING TO ATTRACT THE--
BAM!
BOOM!
BOOM!
THE ZOMBIES.

Article 4: Dawn of the Dead

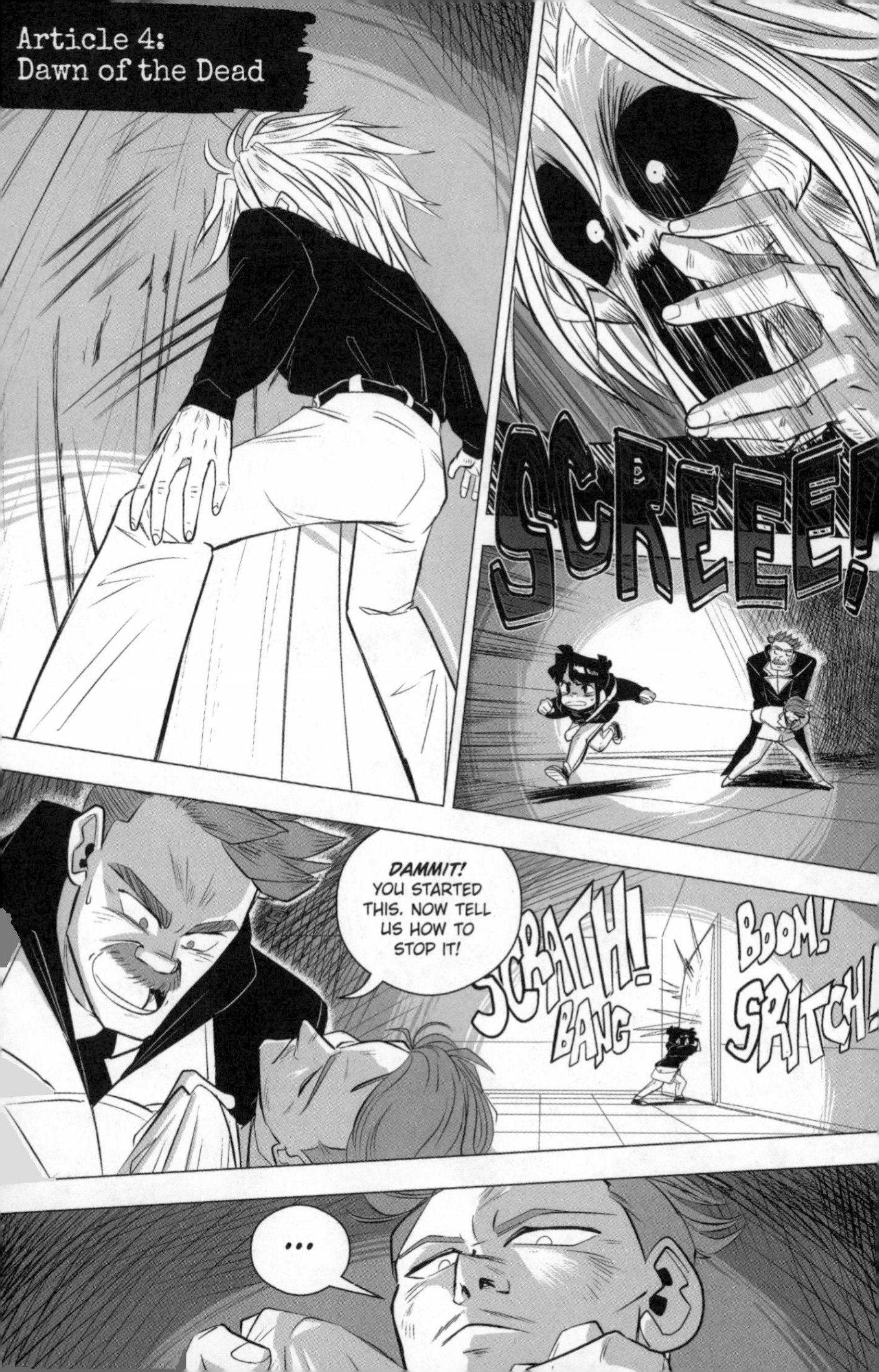
SCREEE!
DAMMIT! YOU STARTED THIS. NOW TELL US HOW TO STOP IT!
SCRATH!
BANG
BOOM!
SRITCH!
...

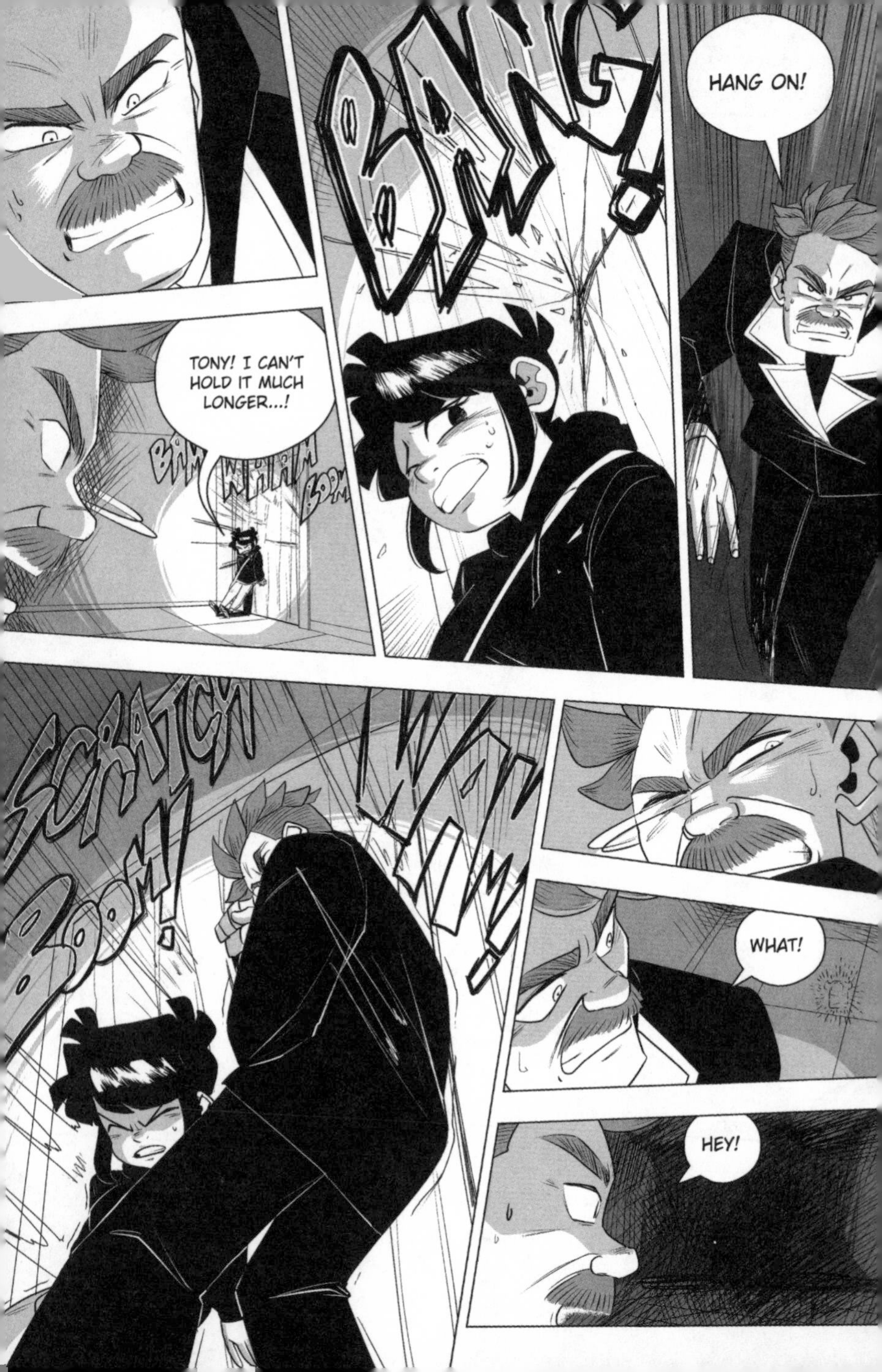
BANG!
HANG ON!
TONY! I CAN'T HOLD IT MUCH LONGER...!
BAM
WHAM
BOOM
SCRATCH
BOOM!
WHAM!
WHAT!
HEY!

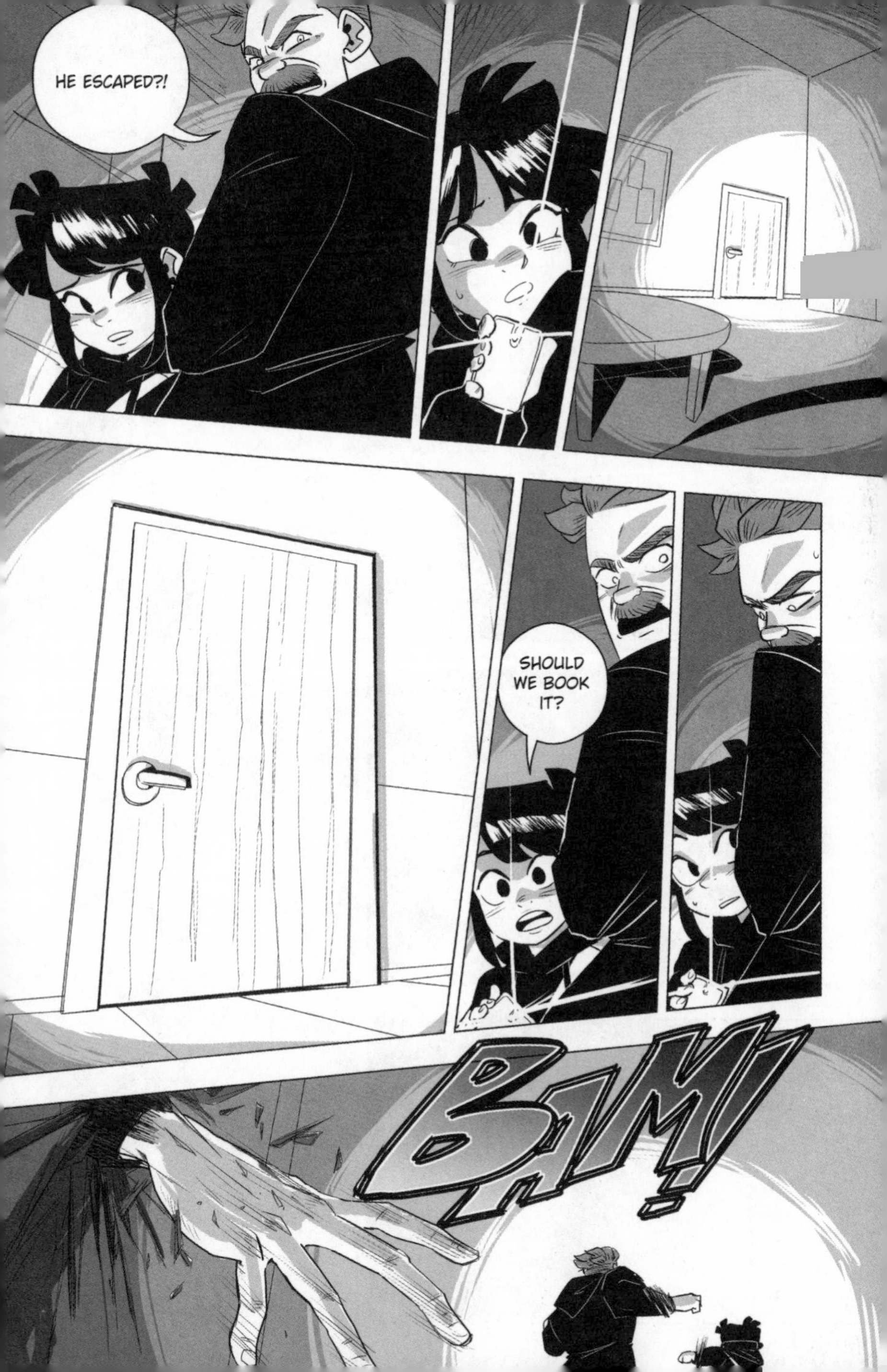
HE ESCAPED?!
SHOULD WE BOOK IT?
BAM!

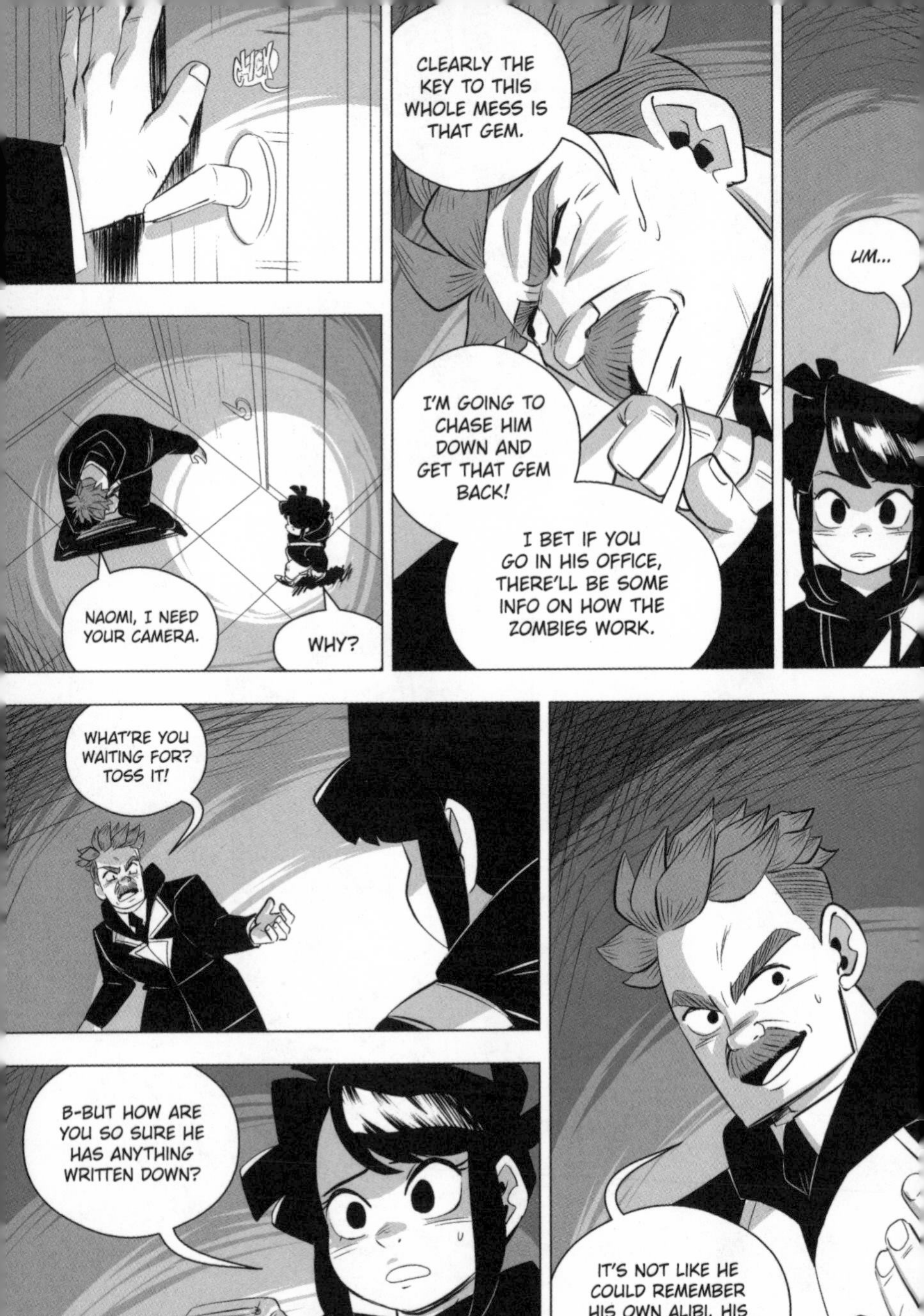
CLICK
NAOMI, I NEED YOUR CAMERA.
WHY?
CLEARLY THE KEY TO THIS WHOLE MESS IS THAT GEM.
I'M GOING TO CHASE HIM DOWN AND GET THAT GEM BACK!
I BET IF YOU GO IN HIS OFFICE, THERE'LL BE SOME INFO ON HOW THE ZOMBIES WORK.
UM...
WHAT'RE YOU WAITING FOR? TOSS IT!
B-BUT HOW ARE YOU SO SURE HE HAS ANYTHING WRITTEN DOWN?
IT'S NOT LIKE HE COULD REMEMBER HIS OWN ALIBI. HIS BAD MEMORY IS A SAFE BET.

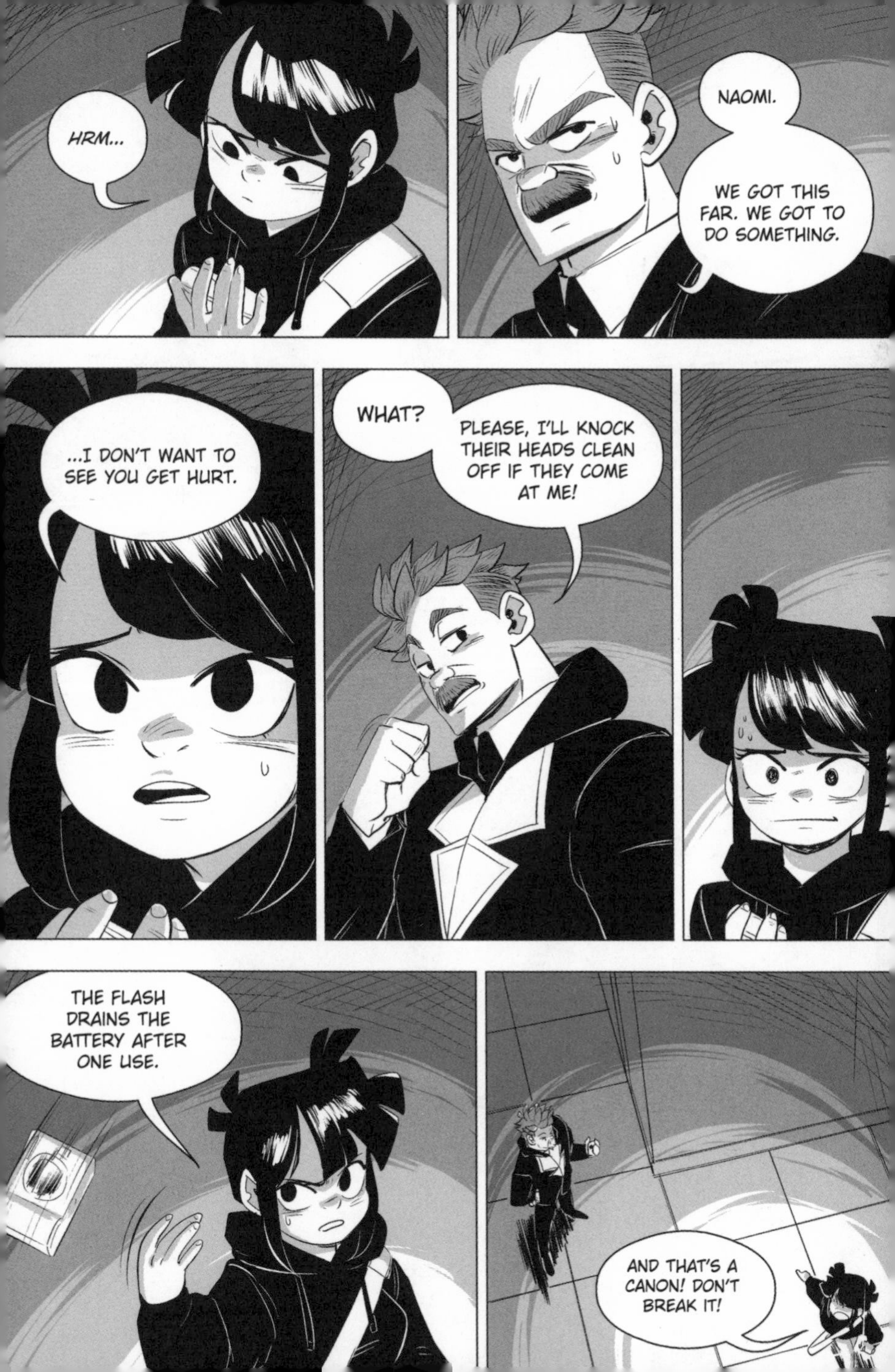
HRM...
NAOMI.
WE GOT THIS FAR. WE GOT TO DO SOMETHING.
...I DON'T WANT TO SEE YOU GET HURT.
WHAT?
PLEASE, I'LL KNOCK THEIR HEADS CLEAN OFF IF THEY COME AT ME!
THE FLASH DRAINS THE BATTERY AFTER ONE USE.
AND THAT'S A CANON! DON'T BREAK IT!

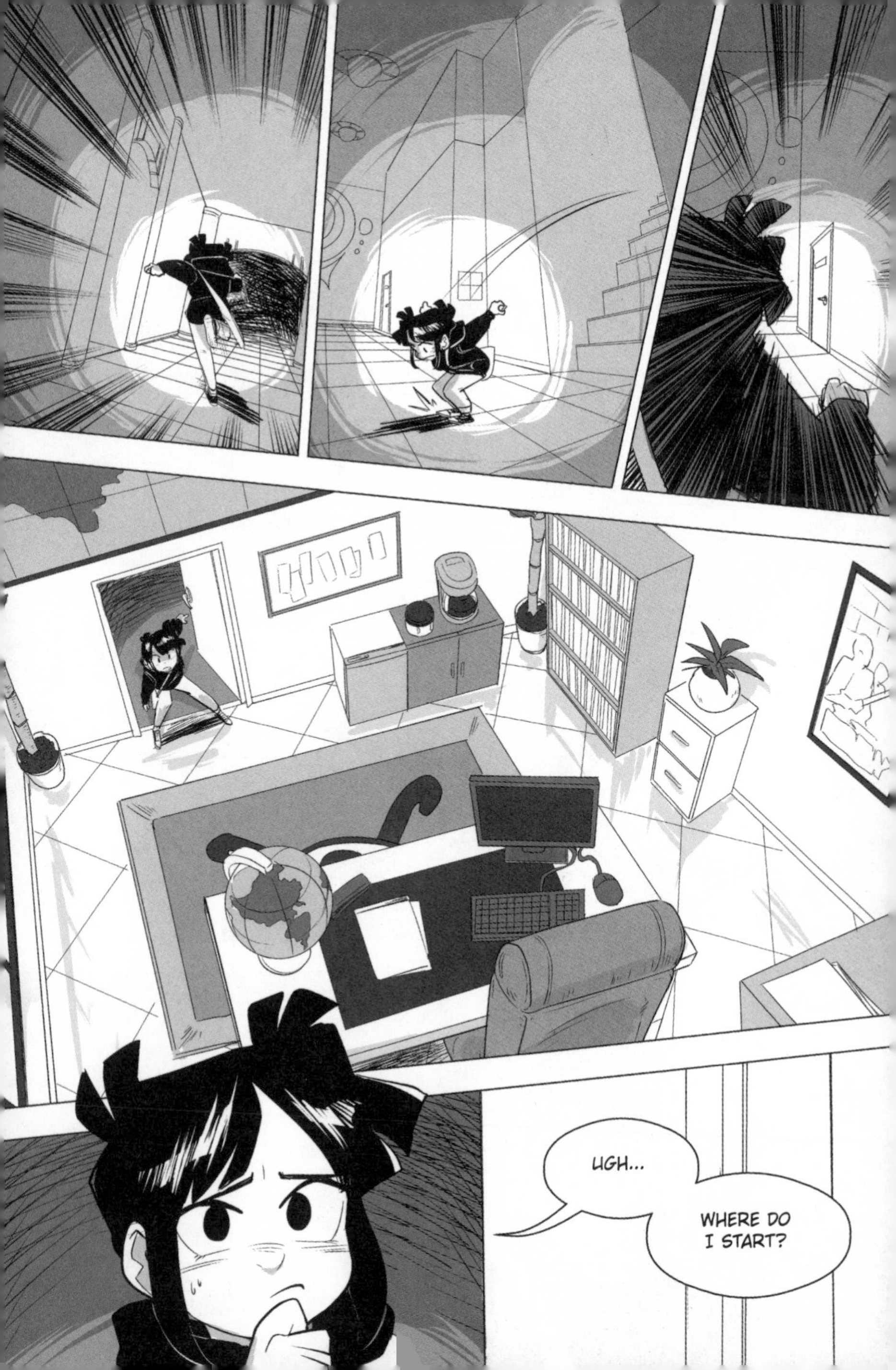
UGH...
WHERE DO I START?

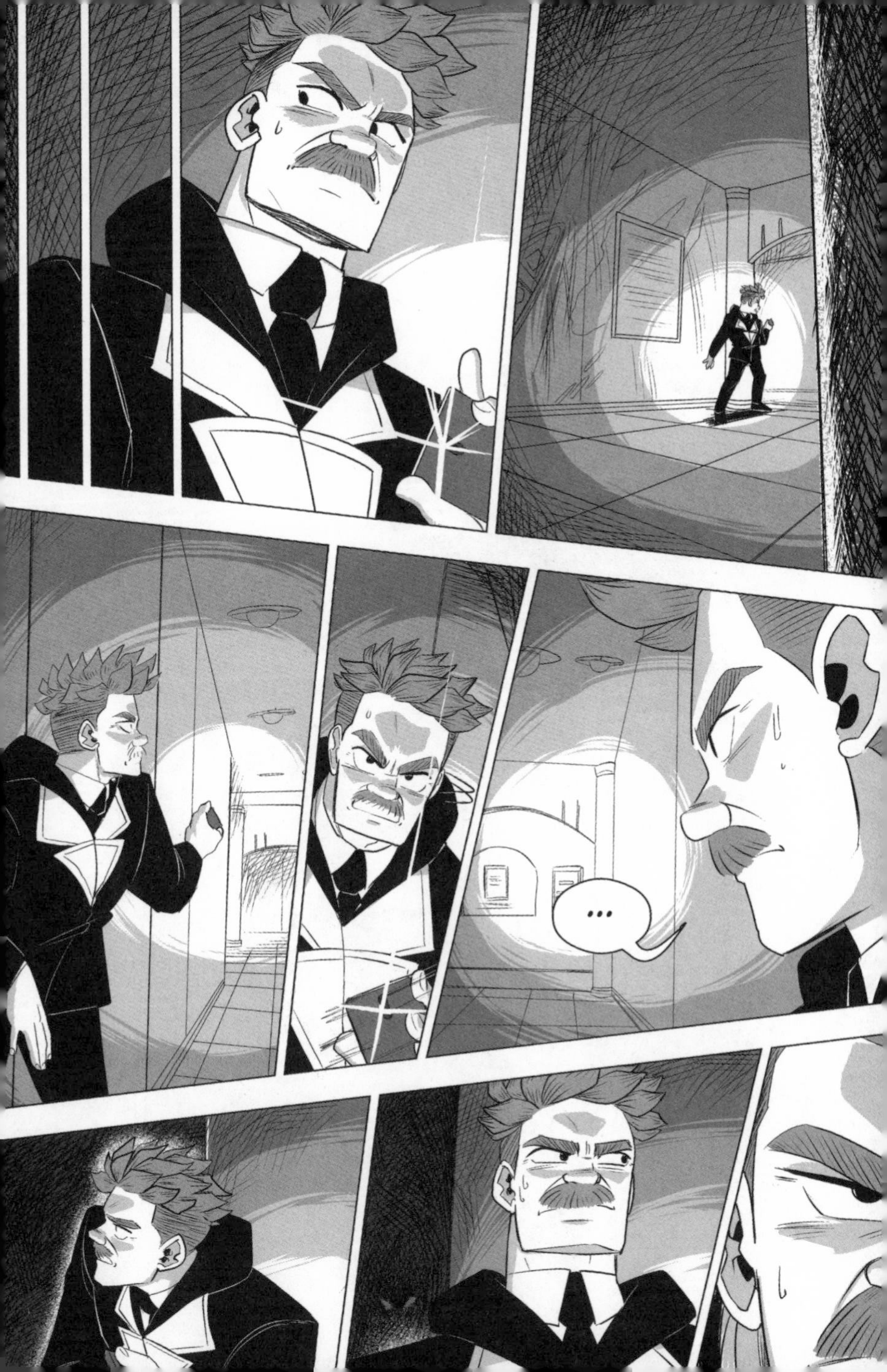
...

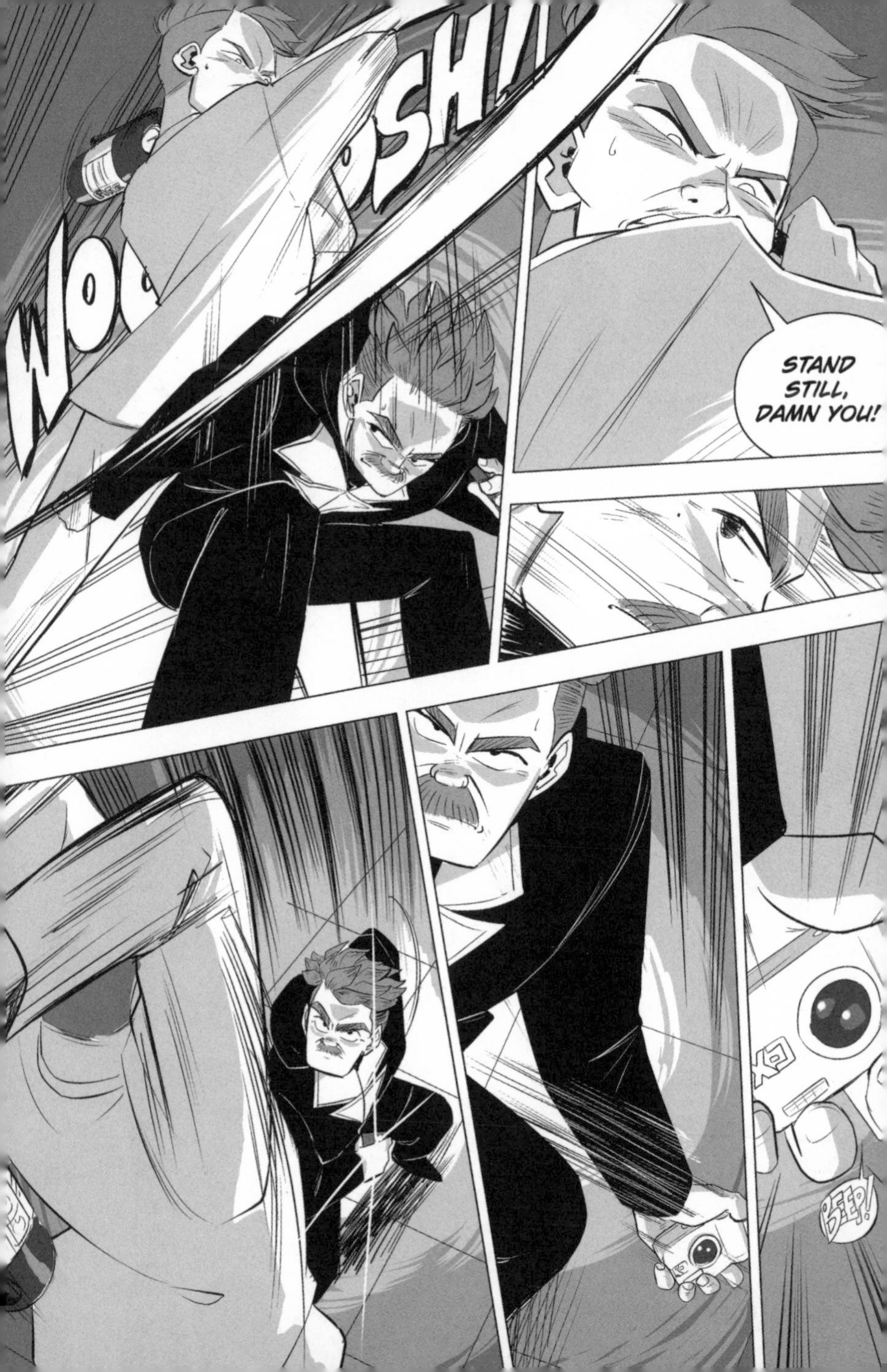
WOO
SH
STAND STILL, DAMN YOU!
BEEP!

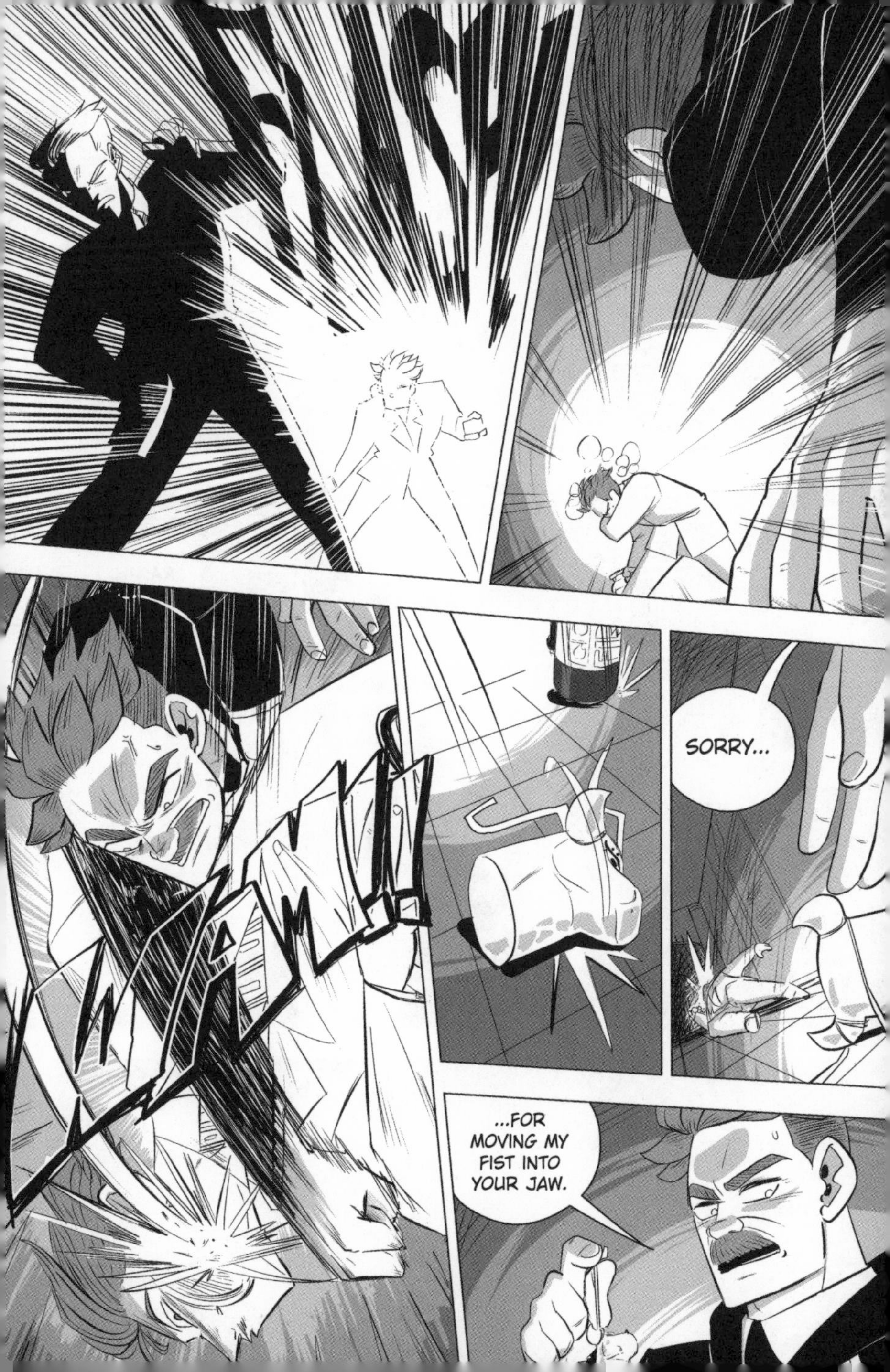
SORRY...
...FOR MOVING MY FIST INTO YOUR JAW.

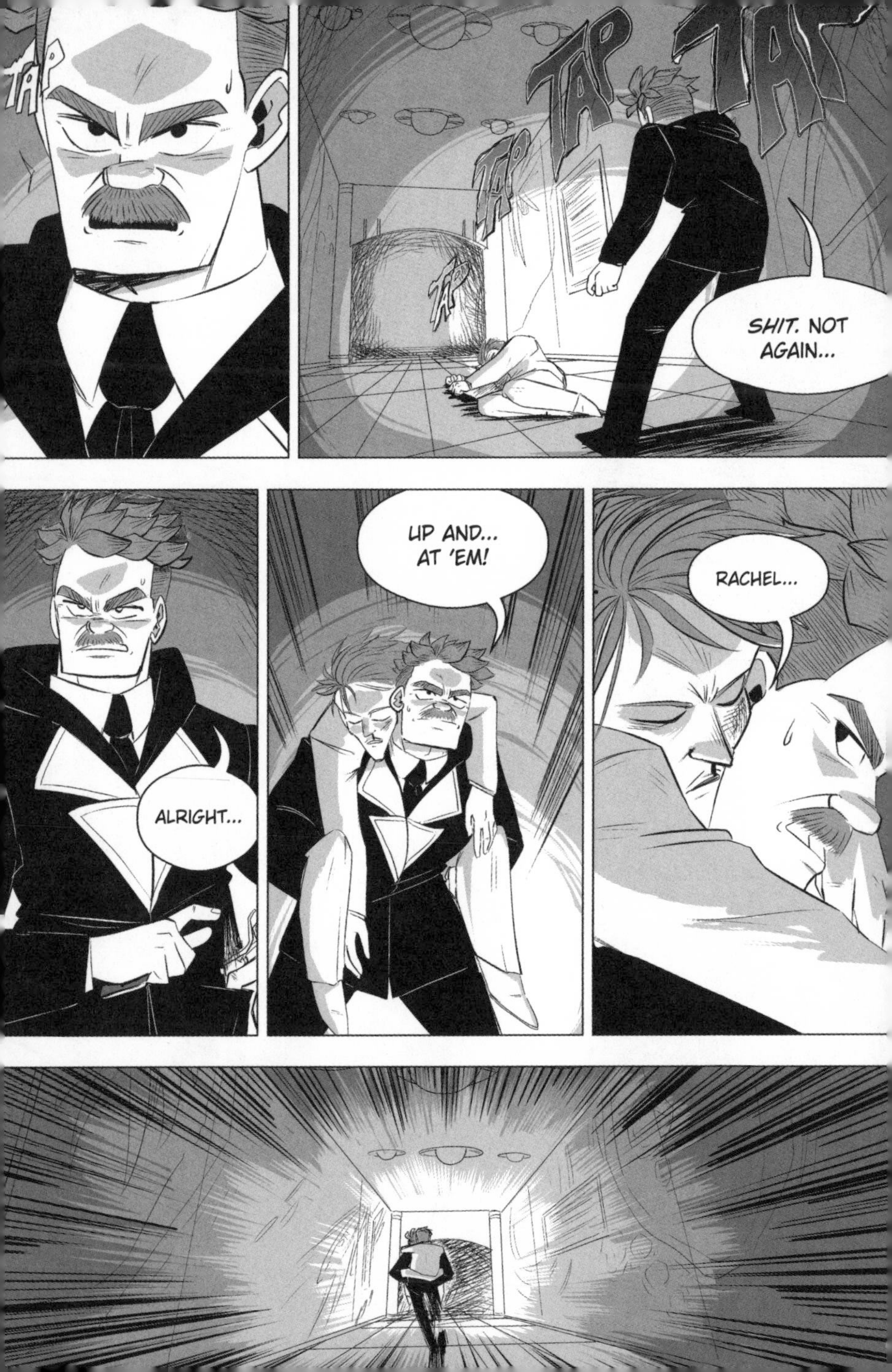
TAP
TAP
TAP
TAP
TAP
SHIT. NOT AGAIN...
ALRIGHT...
UP AND... AT 'EM!
RACHEL...

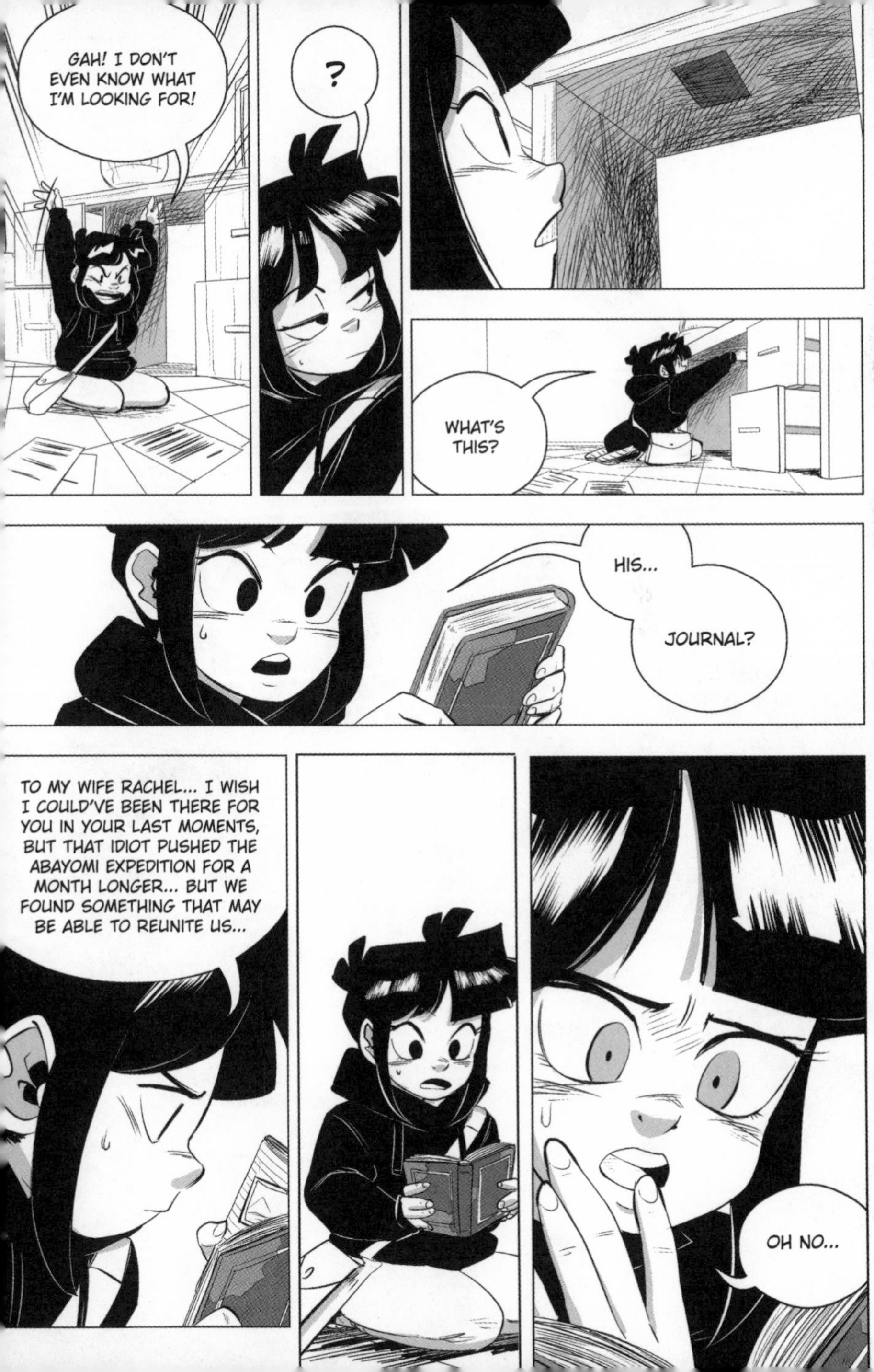
GAH! I DON'T EVEN KNOW WHAT I'M LOOKING FOR!
?
WHAT'S THIS?
HIS...
JOURNAL?
TO MY WIFE RACHEL... I WISH I COULD'VE BEEN THERE FOR YOU IN YOUR LAST MOMENTS, BUT THAT IDIOT PUSHED THE ABAYOMI EXPEDITION FOR A MONTH LONGER... BUT WE FOUND SOMETHING THAT MAY BE ABLE TO REUNITE US...
OH NO...

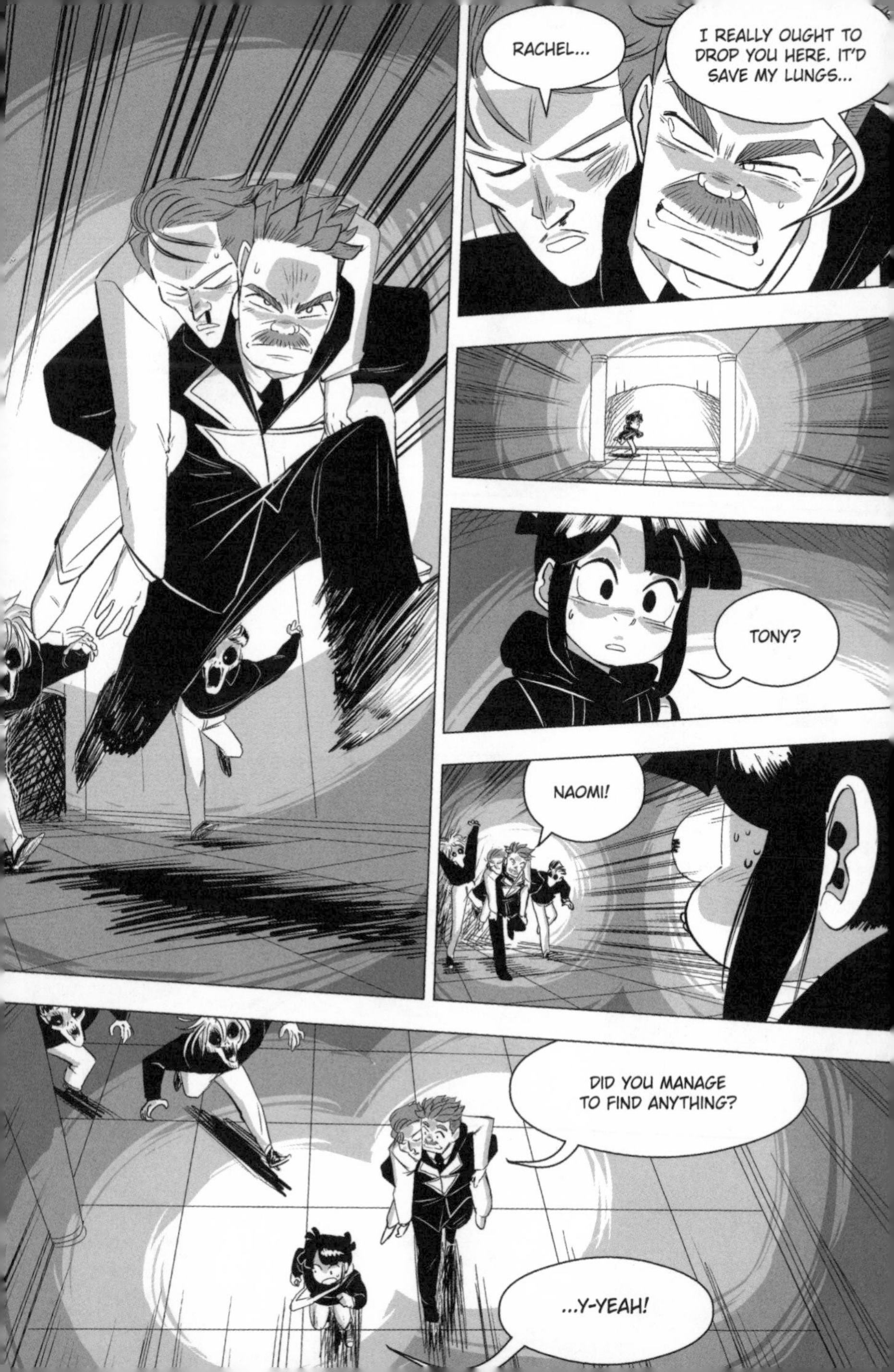
RACHEL...
I REALLY OUGHT TO DROP YOU HERE. IT'D SAVE MY LUNGS...
TONY?
NAOMI!
DID YOU MANAGE TO FIND ANYTHING?
...Y-YEAH!

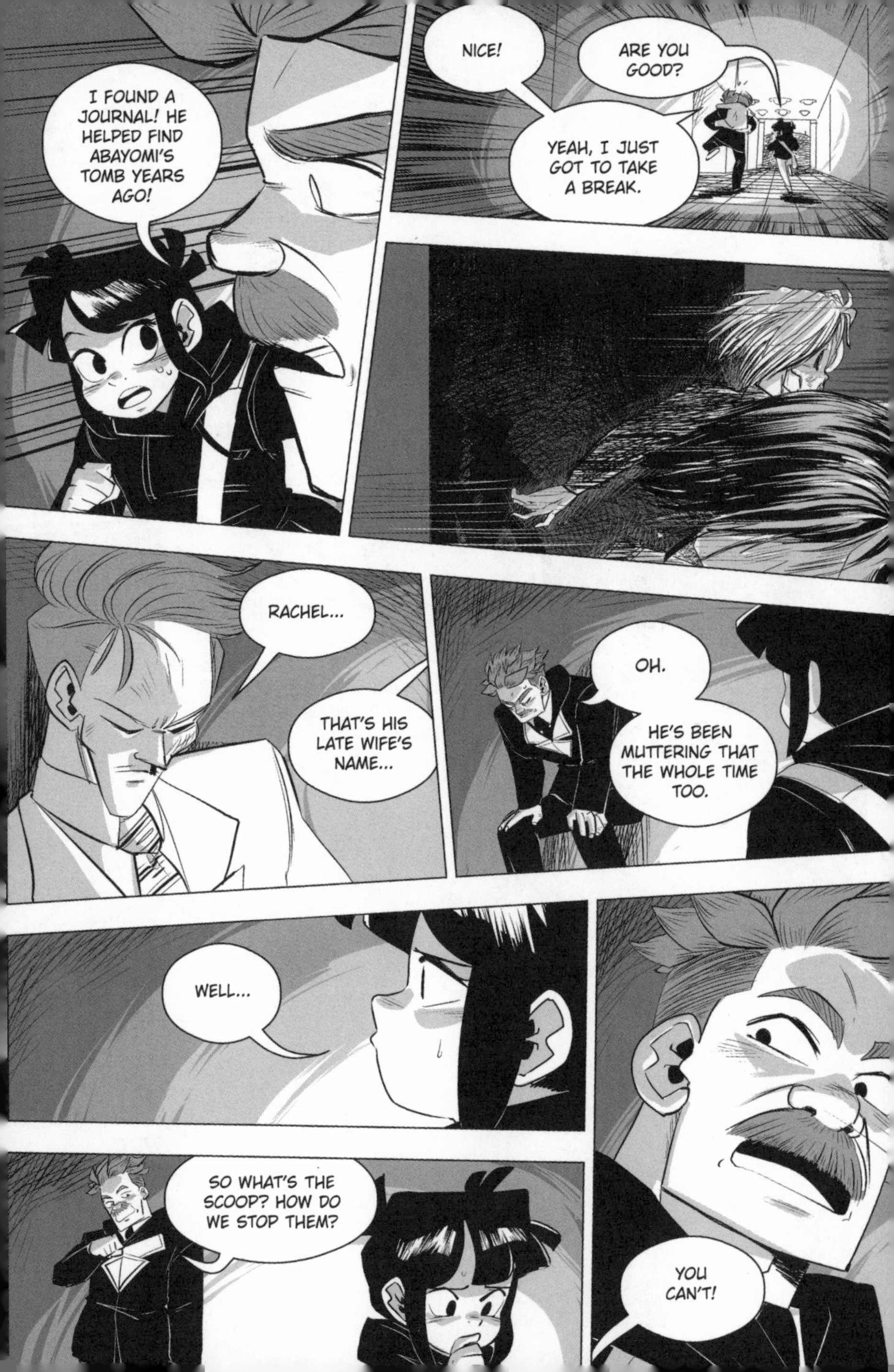
I FOUND A JOURNAL! HE HELPED FIND ABAYOMI'S TOMB YEARS AGO!
NICE!
ARE YOU GOOD?
YEAH, I JUST GOT TO TAKE A BREAK.
RACHEL...
THAT'S HIS LATE WIFE'S NAME...
OH.
HE'S BEEN MUTTERING THAT THE WHOLE TIME TOO.
WELL...
SO WHAT'S THE SCOOP? HOW DO WE STOP THEM?
YOU CAN'T!

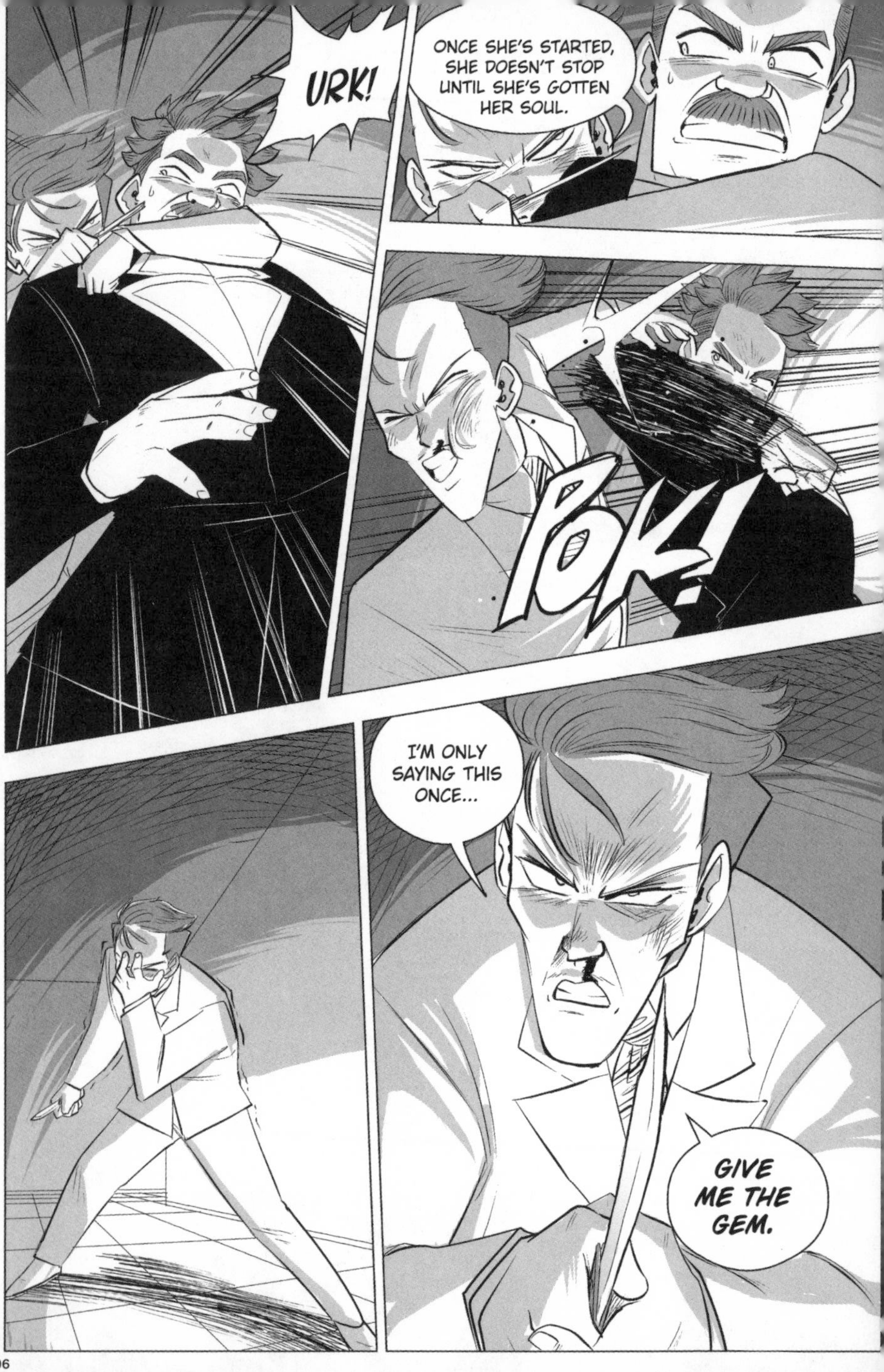
URK!
ONCE SHE'S STARTED, SHE DOESN'T STOP UNTIL SHE'S GOTTEN HER SOUL.
POK!
I'M ONLY SAYING THIS ONCE...
GIVE ME THE GEM.

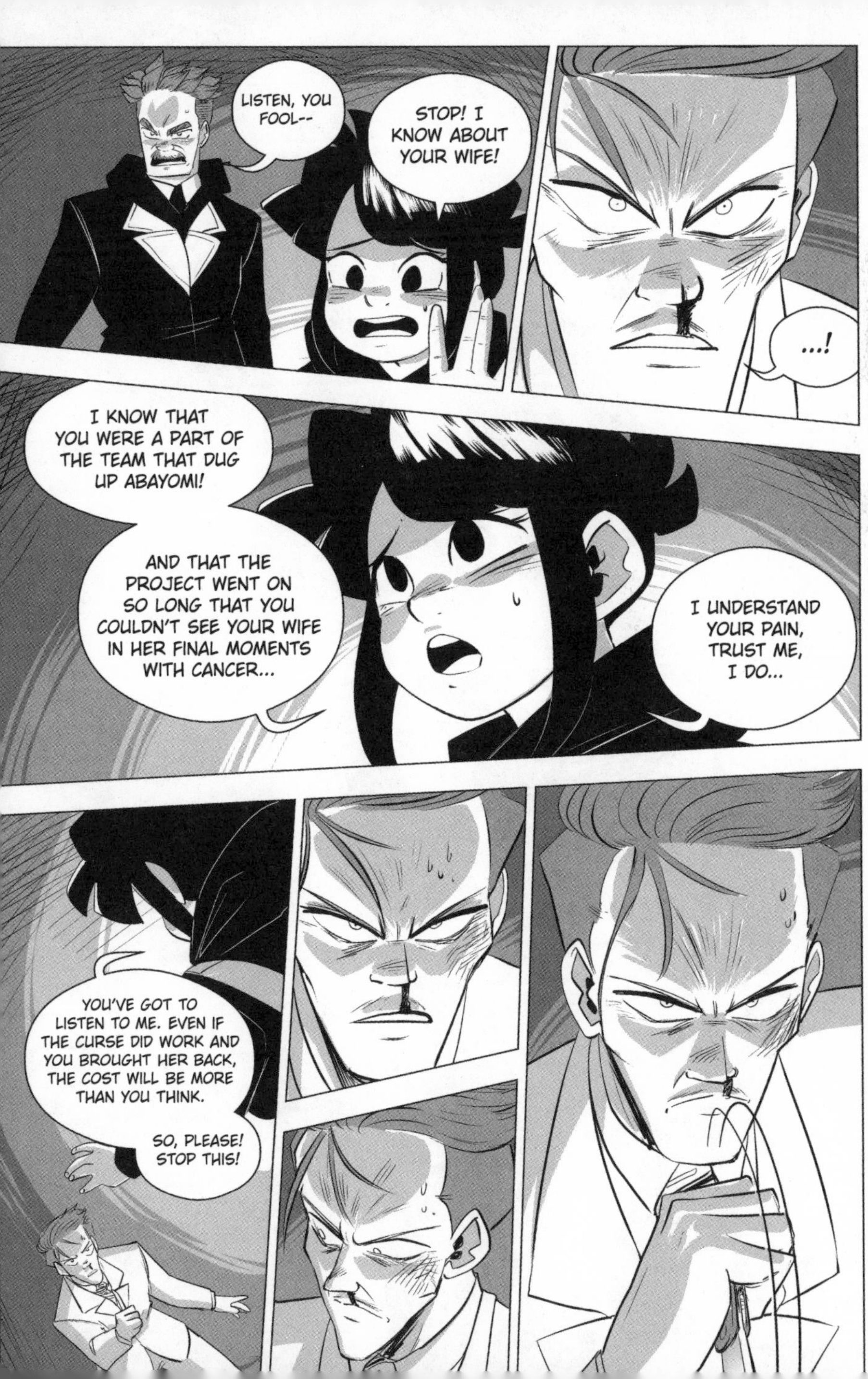
LISTEN, YOU FOOL--
STOP! I KNOW ABOUT YOUR WIFE!
...!
I KNOW THAT YOU WERE A PART OF THE TEAM THAT DUG UP ABAYOMI!
AND THAT THE PROJECT WENT ON SO LONG THAT YOU COULDN'T SEE YOUR WIFE IN HER FINAL MOMENTS WITH CANCER...
I UNDERSTAND YOUR PAIN, TRUST ME, I DO...
YOU'VE GOT TO LISTEN TO ME. EVEN IF THE CURSE DID WORK AND YOU BROUGHT HER BACK, THE COST WILL BE MORE THAN YOU THINK.
SO, PLEASE! STOP THIS!

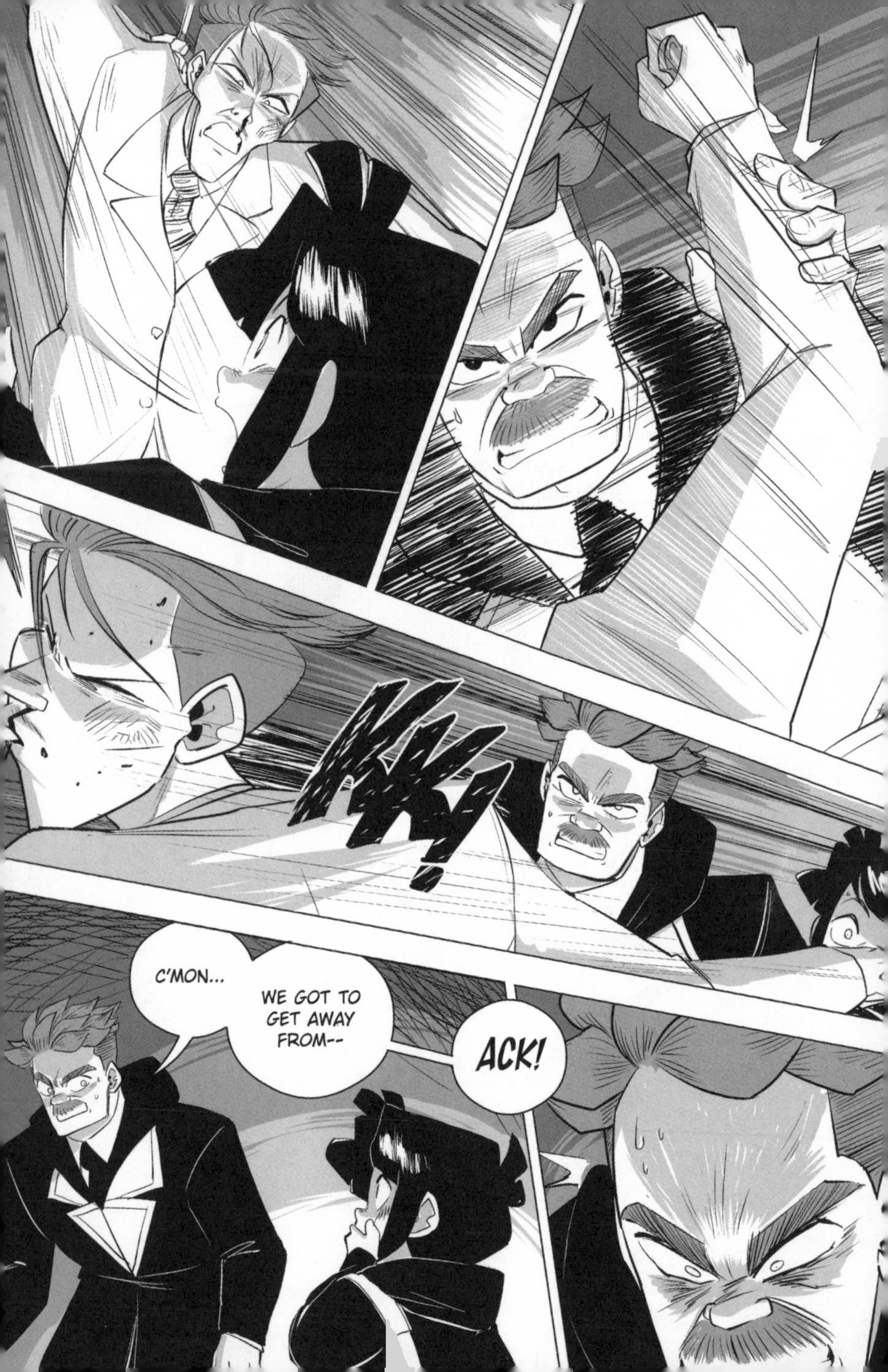
WK!
C'MON...
WE GOT TO GET AWAY FROM--
ACK!

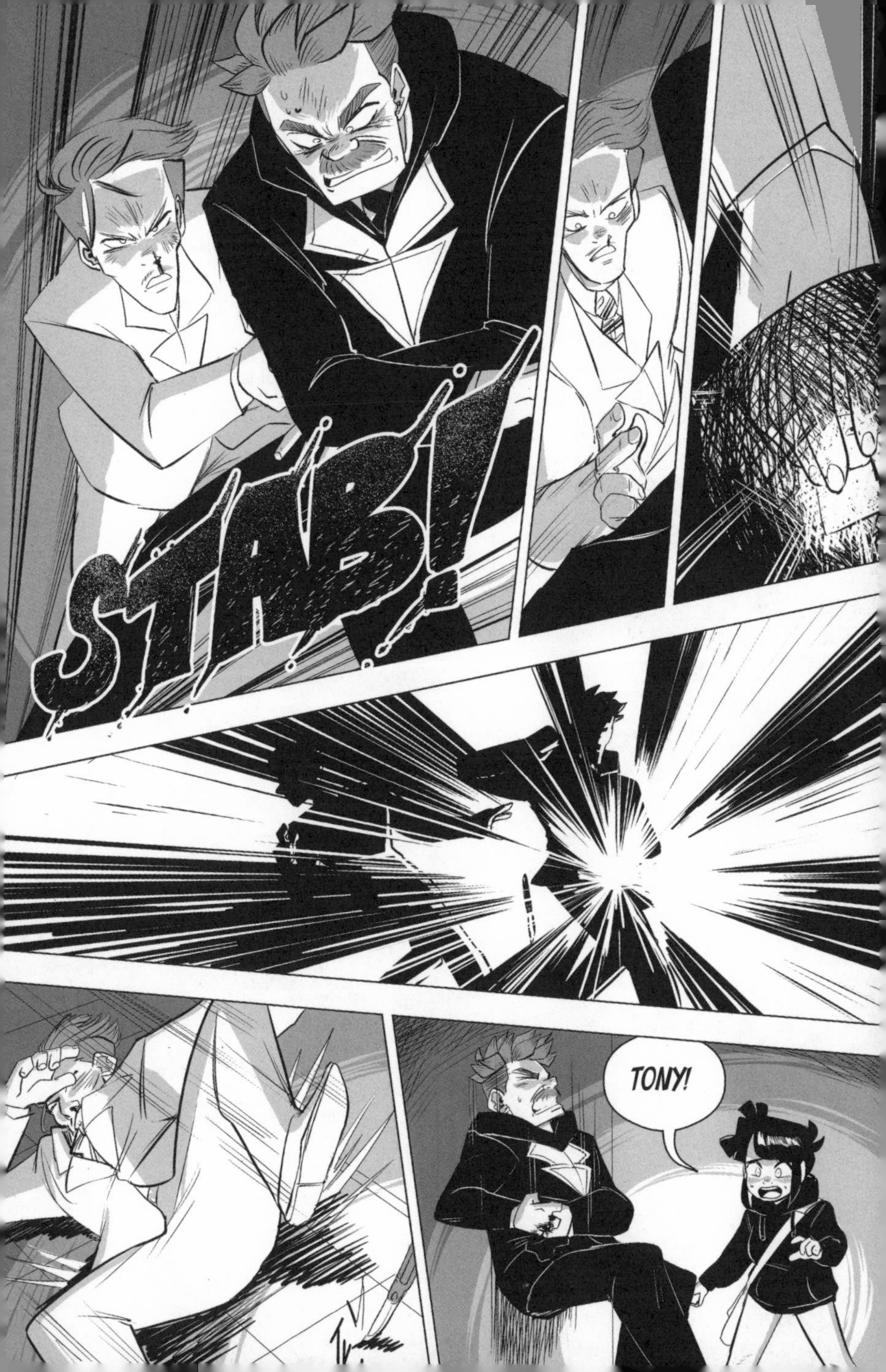
STAB!
TONY!

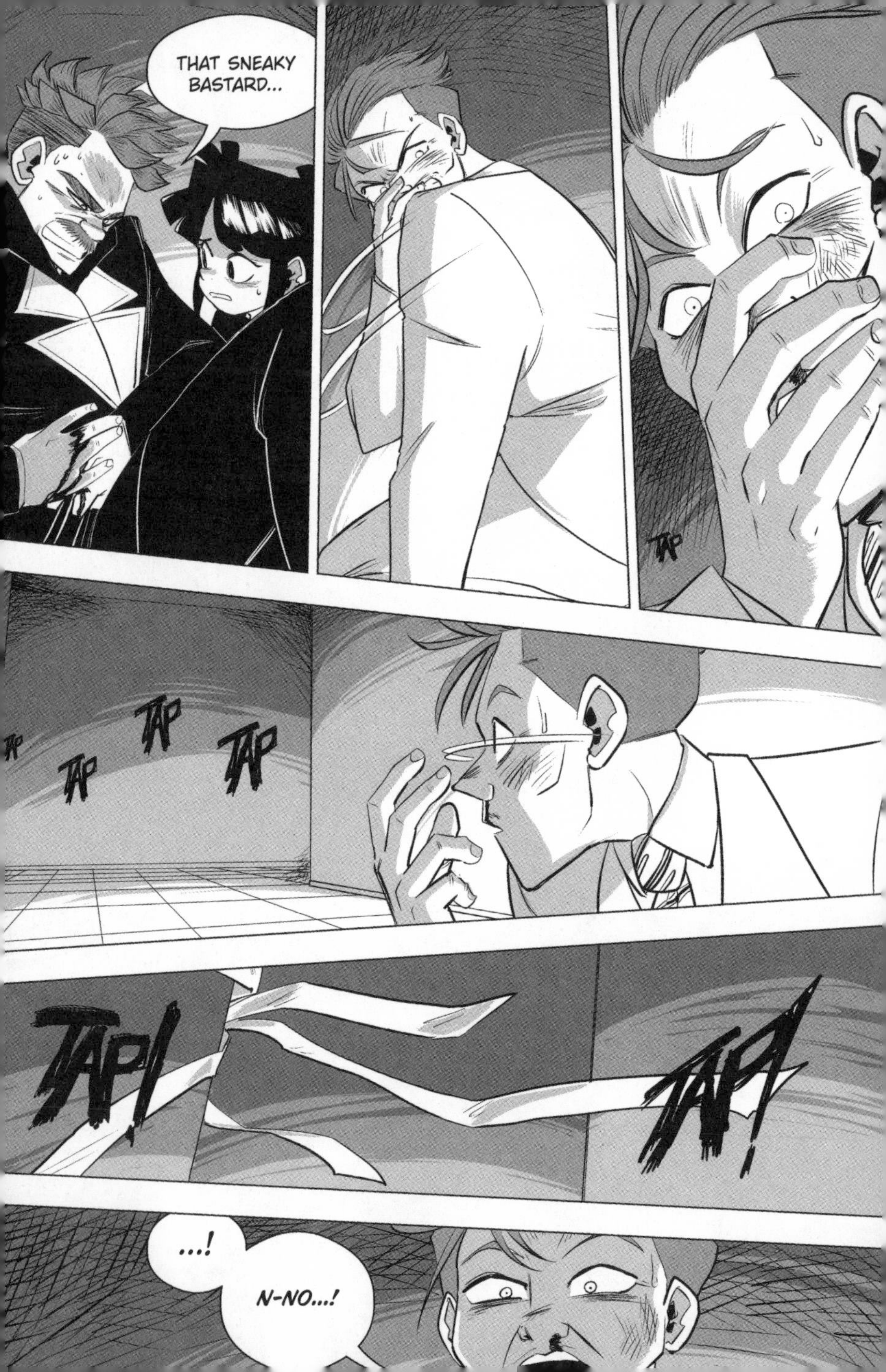
THAT SNEAKY BASTARD...
TAP
TAP
TAP
TAP
TAP
TAP!
TAP!
...!
N-NO...!

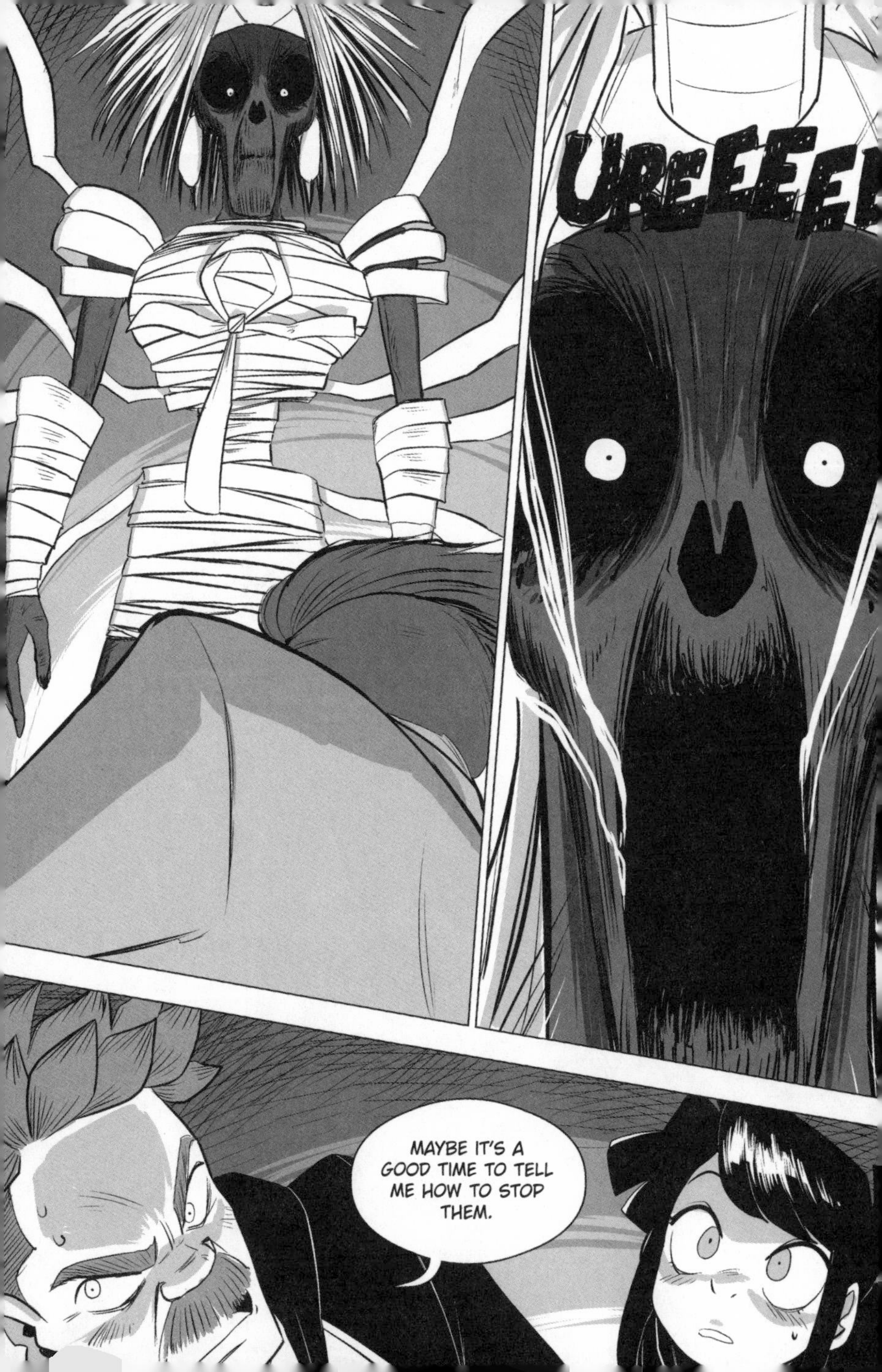
UREEEE
MAYBE IT'S A GOOD TIME TO TELL ME HOW TO STOP THEM.

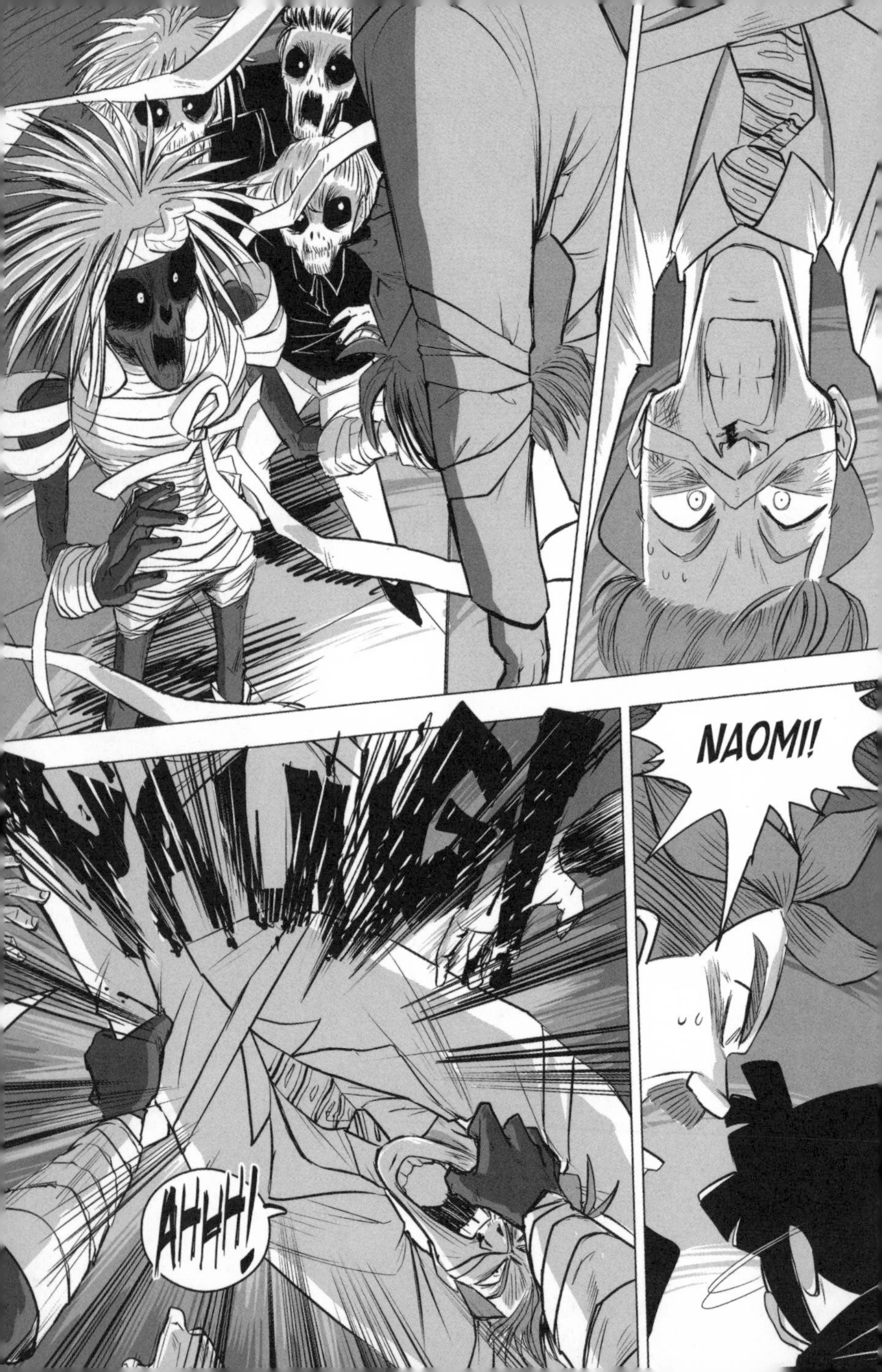
AHHH!
NAOMI!

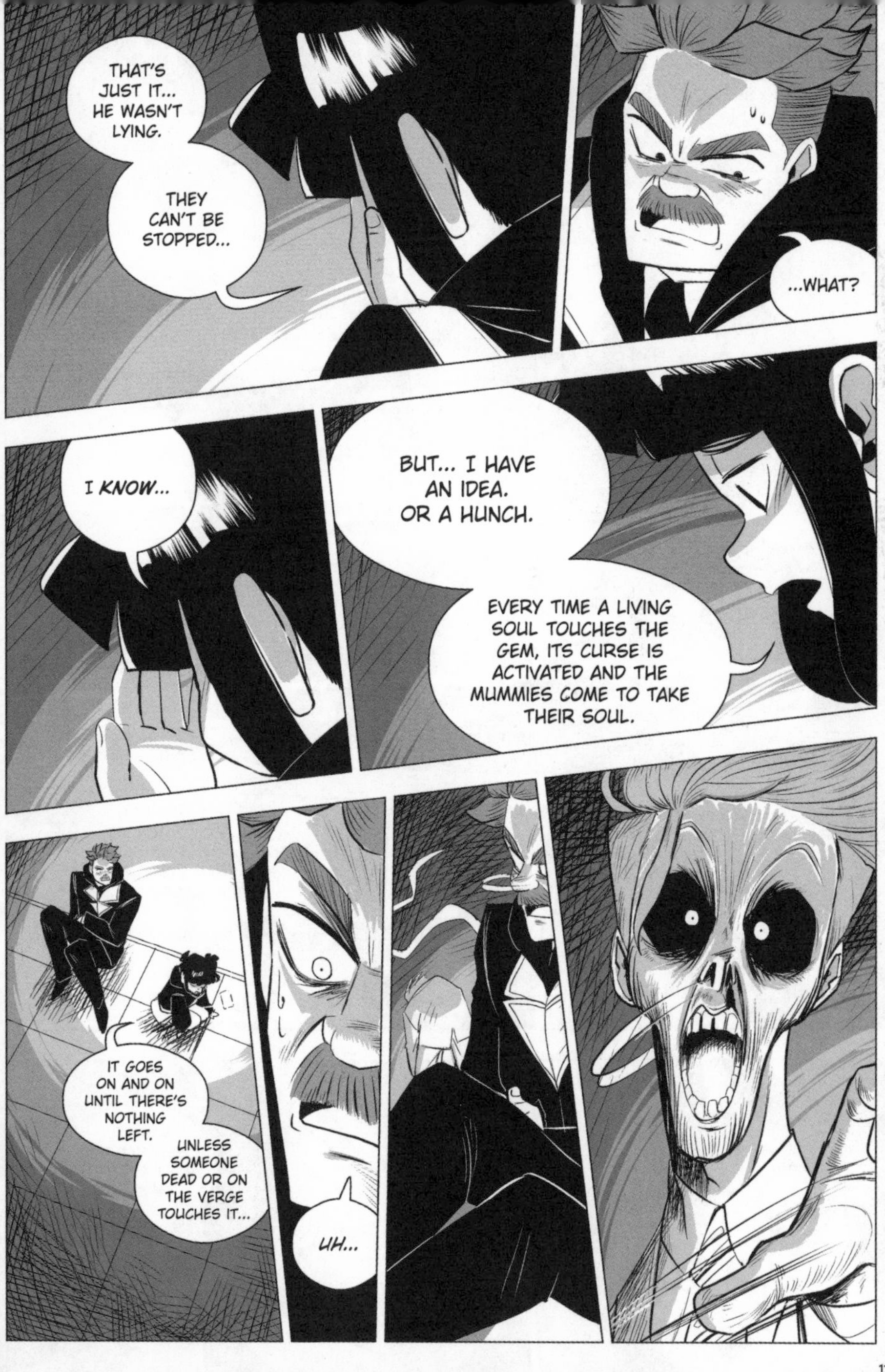

THAT'S JUST IT... HE WASN'T LYING.
THEY CAN'T BE STOPPED...
...WHAT?
I KNOW...
BUT... I HAVE AN IDEA. OR A HUNCH.
EVERY TIME A LIVING SOUL TOUCHES THE GEM, ITS CURSE IS ACTIVATED AND THE MUMMIES COME TO TAKE THEIR SOUL.
IT GOES ON AND ON UNTIL THERE'S NOTHING LEFT.
UNLESS SOMEONE DEAD OR ON THE VERGE TOUCHES IT...
UH...

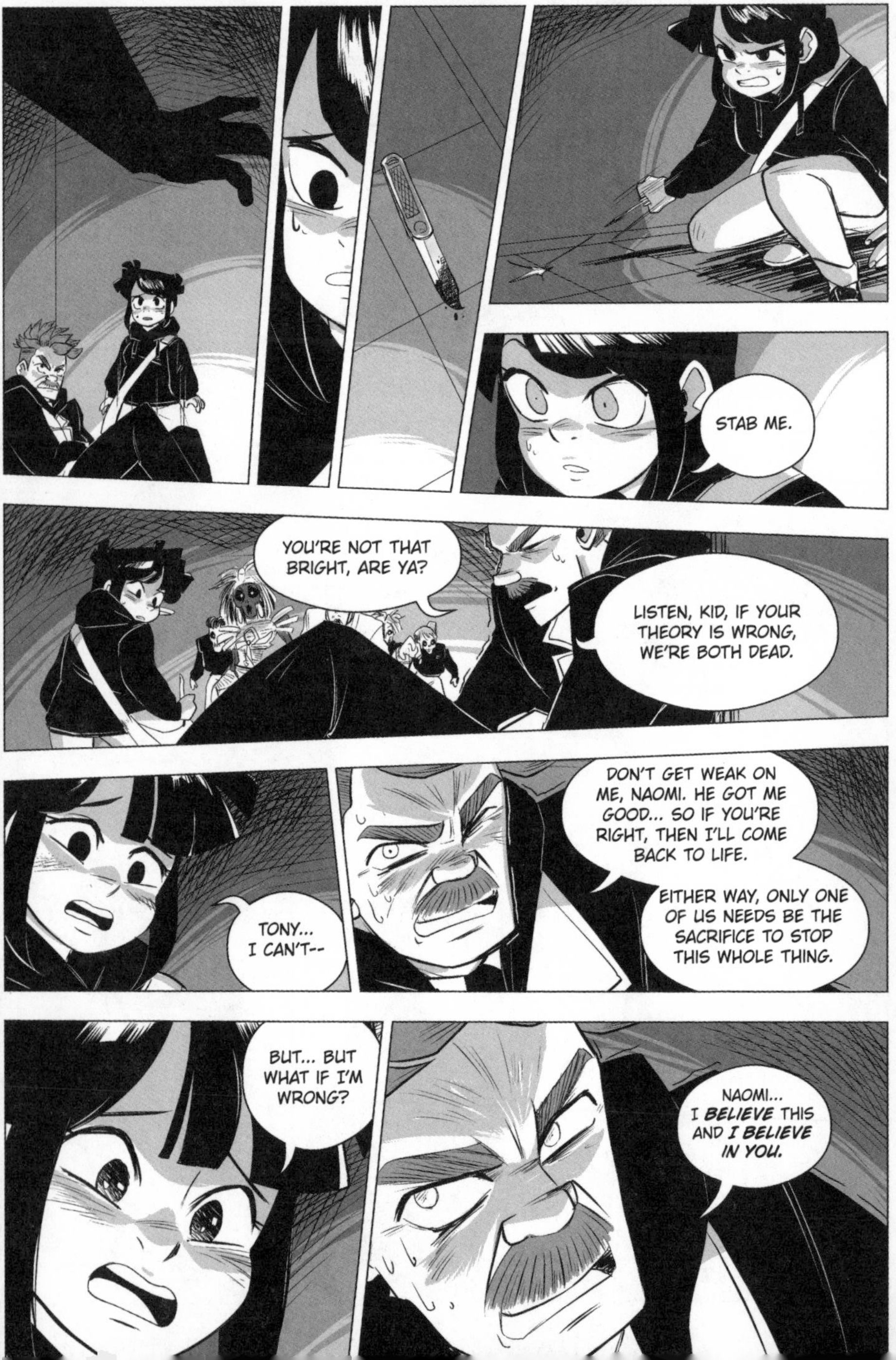
STAB ME.
YOU'RE NOT THAT BRIGHT, ARE YA?
LISTEN, KID, IF YOUR THEORY IS WRONG, WE'RE BOTH DEAD.
TONY... I CAN'T--
DON'T GET WEAK ON ME, NAOMI. HE GOT ME GOOD... SO IF YOU'RE RIGHT, THEN I'LL COME BACK TO LIFE.
EITHER WAY, ONLY ONE OF US NEEDS BE THE SACRIFICE TO STOP THIS WHOLE THING.
BUT... BUT WHAT IF I'M WRONG?
NAOMI... I ***BELIEVE*** THIS AND ***I BELIEVE IN YOU.***

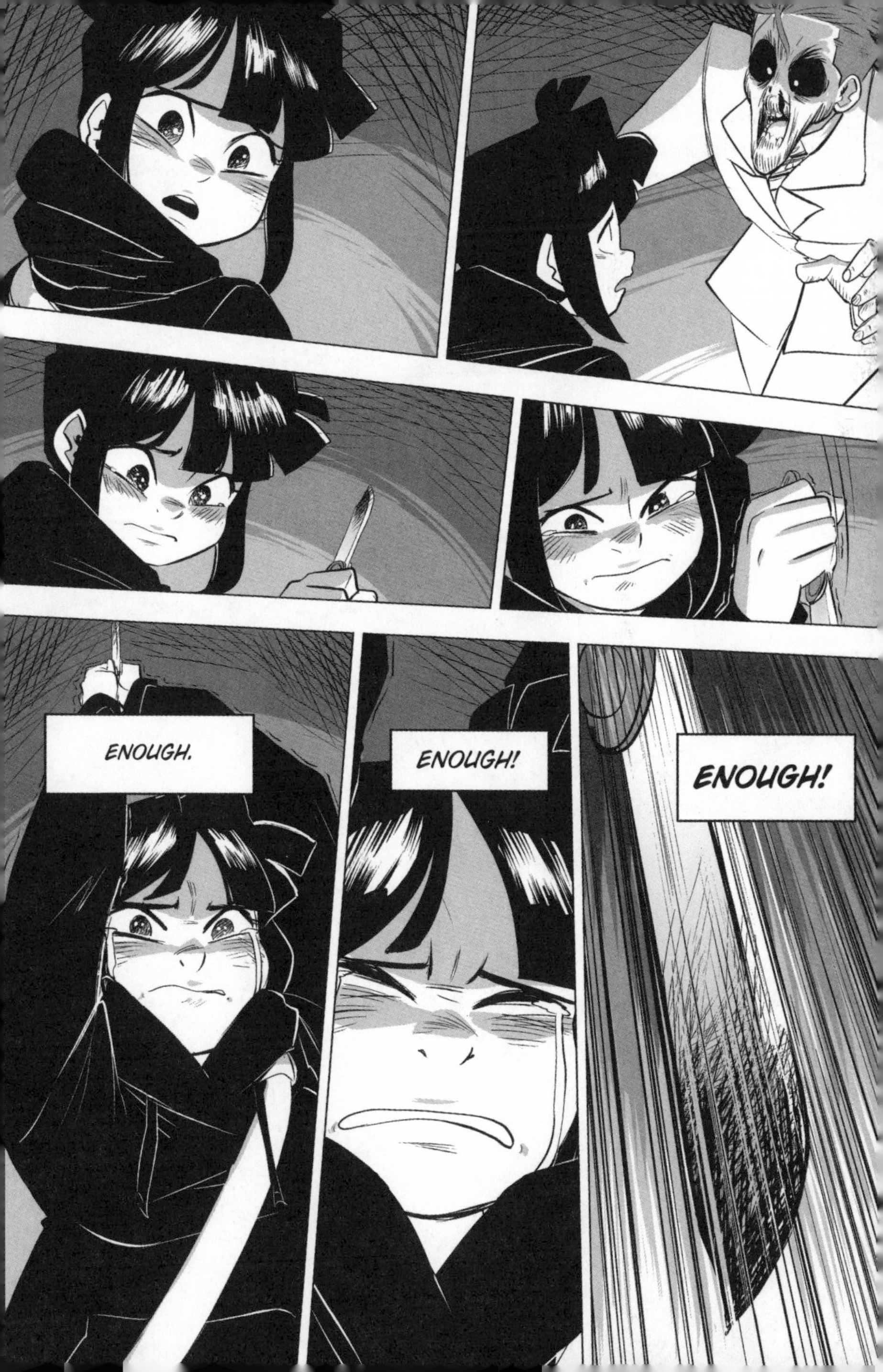
ENOUGH.
ENOUGH!
ENOUGH!

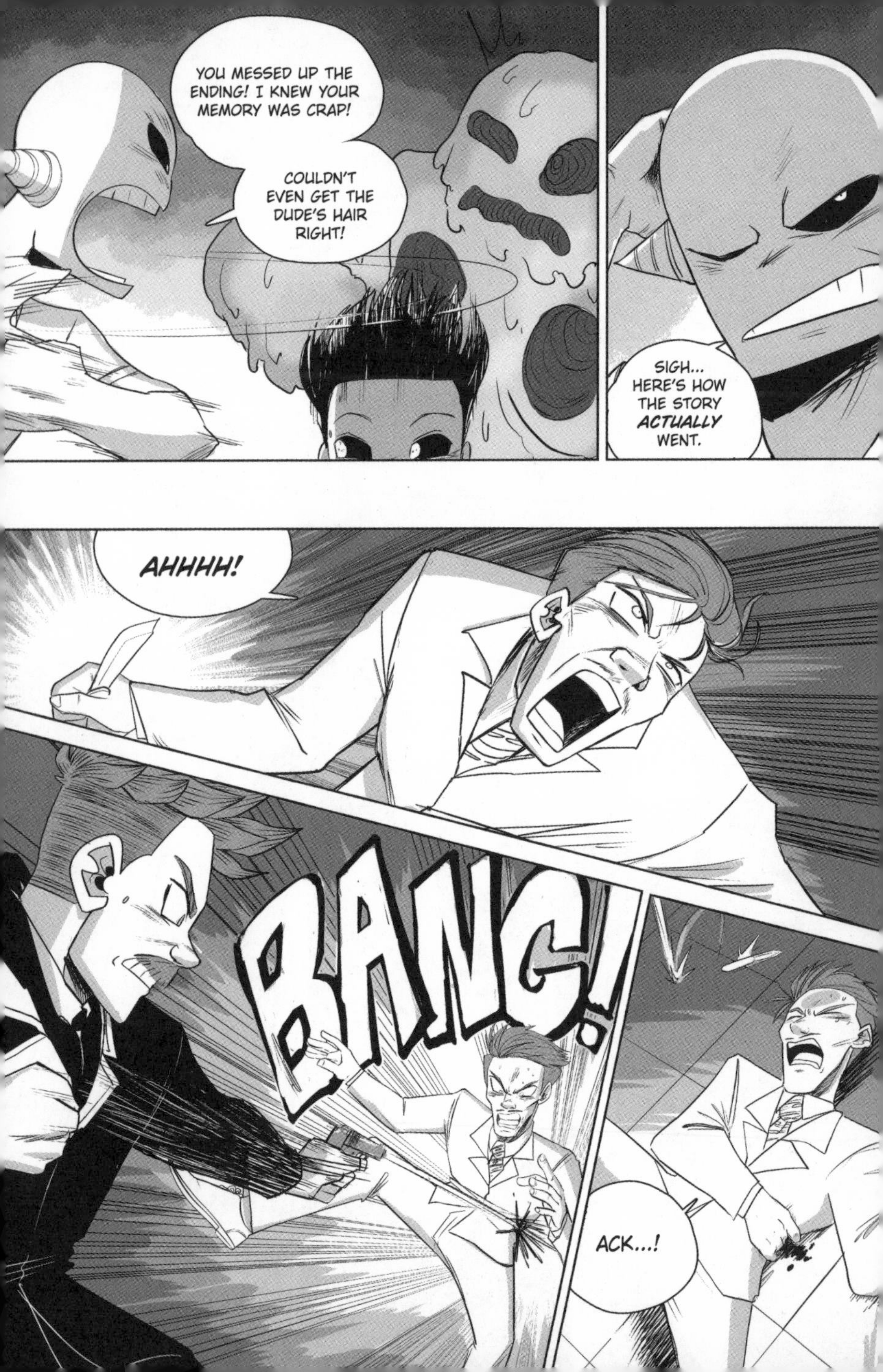

YOU MESSED UP THE ENDING! I KNEW YOUR MEMORY WAS CRAP!
COULDN'T EVEN GET THE DUDE'S HAIR RIGHT!
SIGH... HERE'S HOW THE STORY ***ACTUALLY*** WENT.
AHHHH!
BANG!
ACK...!

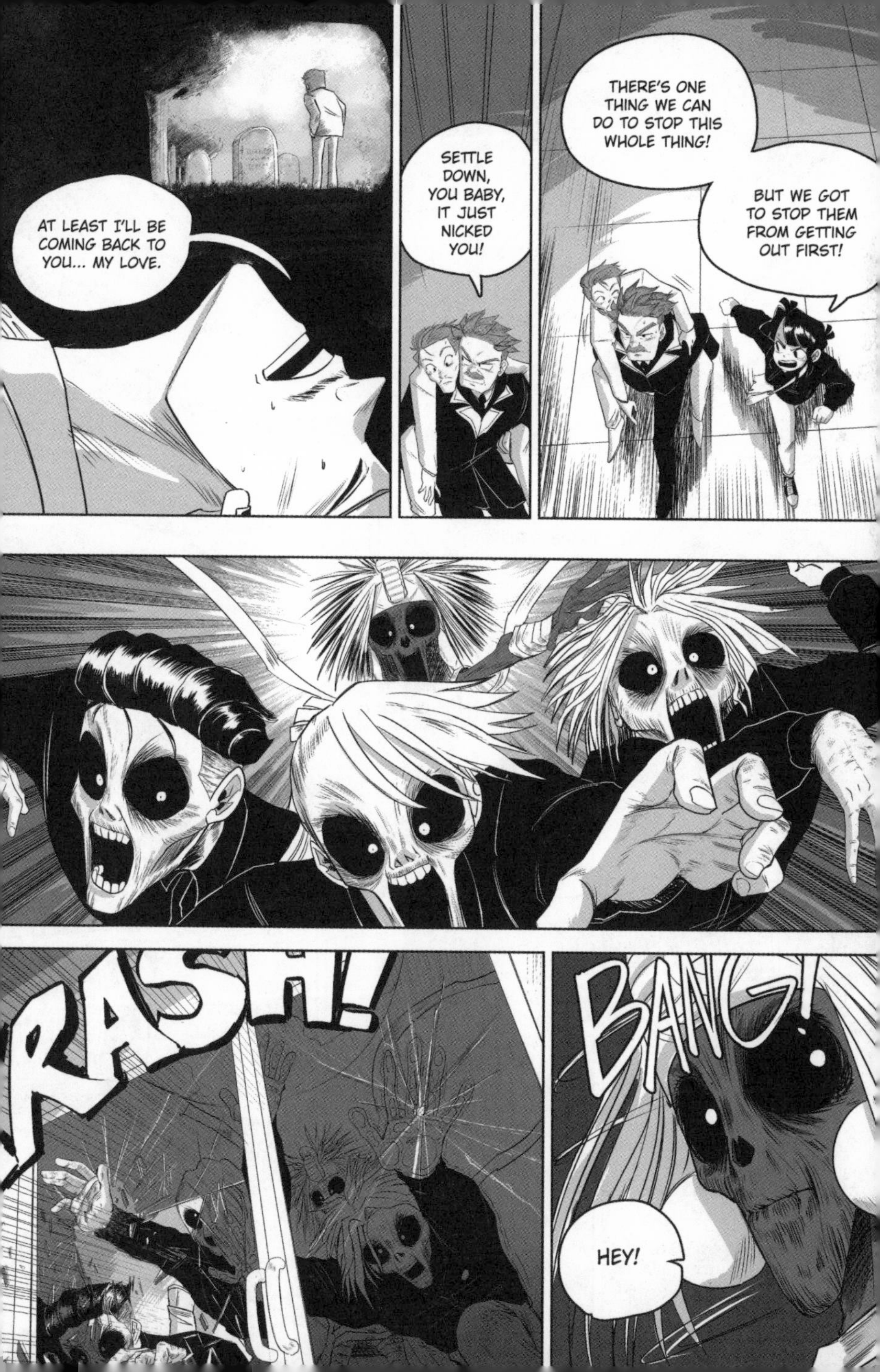
AT LEAST I'LL BE COMING BACK TO YOU... MY LOVE.
SETTLE DOWN, YOU BABY, IT JUST NICKED YOU!
THERE'S ONE THING WE CAN DO TO STOP THIS WHOLE THING!
BUT WE GOT TO STOP THEM FROM GETTING OUT FIRST!
RASH!
BANG!
HEY!

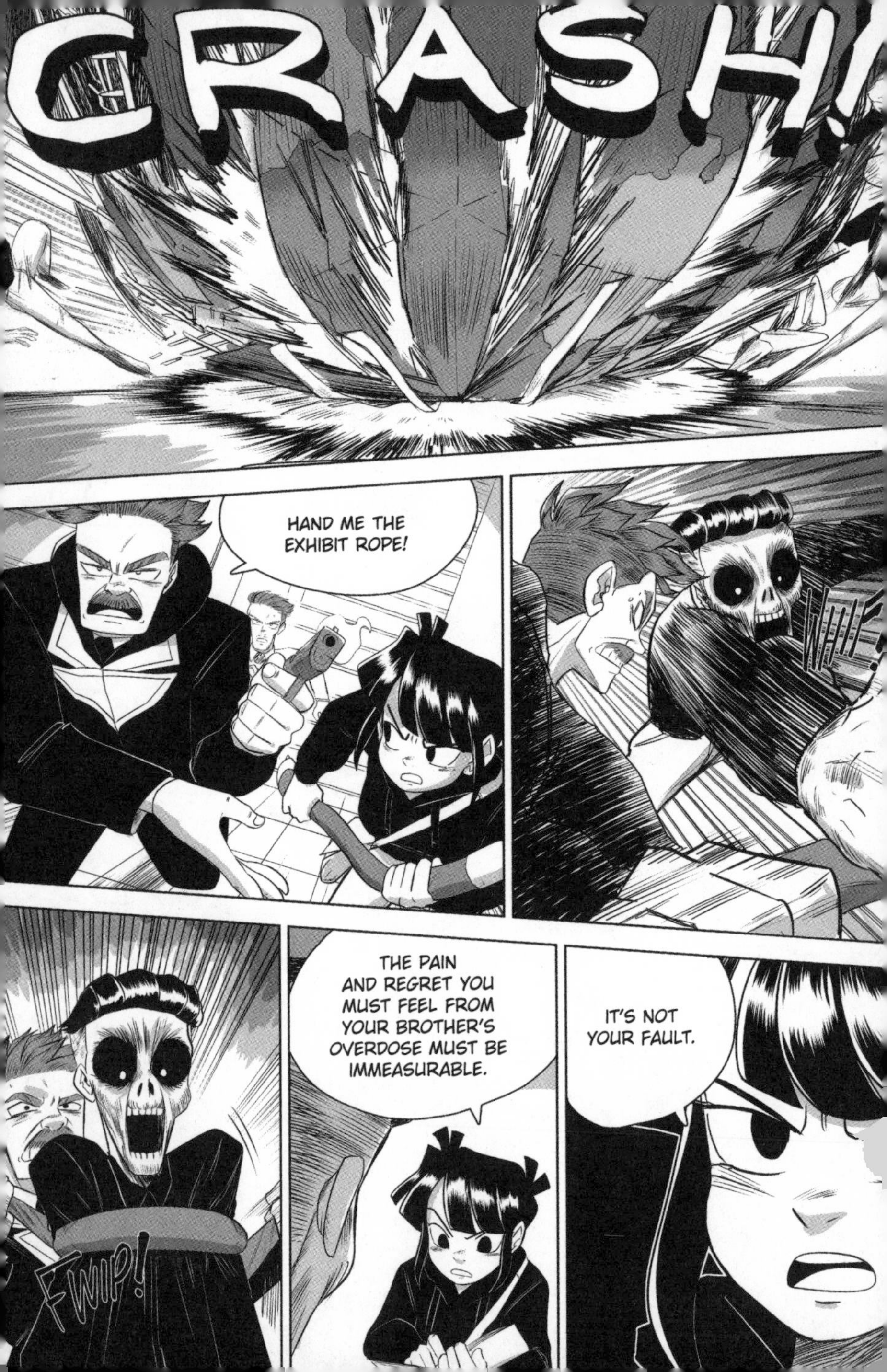
CRASH!!
HAND ME THE EXHIBIT ROPE!
WHIF!
FWIP!
THE PAIN AND REGRET YOU MUST FEEL FROM YOUR BROTHER'S OVERDOSE MUST BE IMMEASURABLE.
IT'S NOT YOUR FAULT.

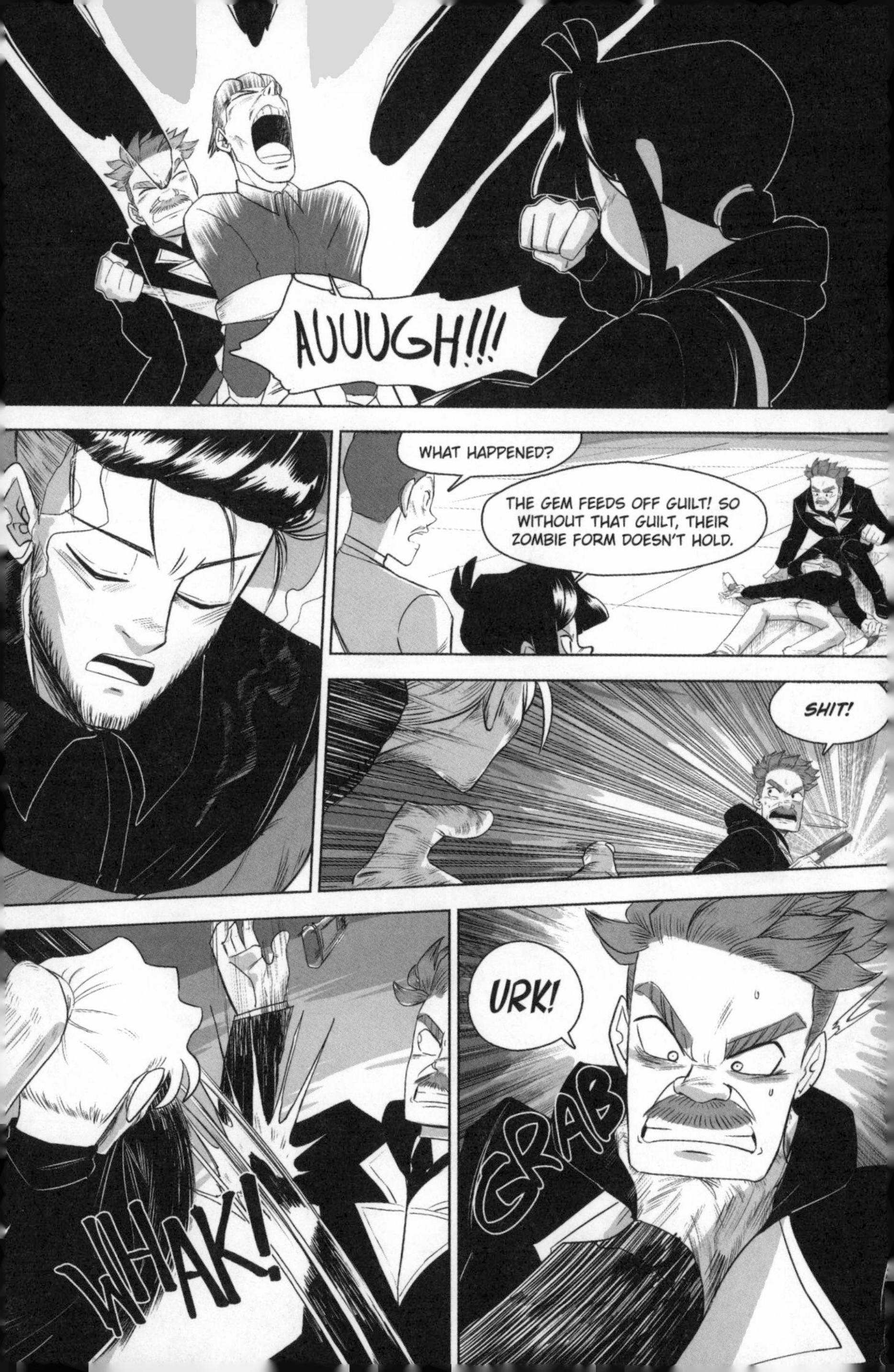
AUUUGH!!!
WHAT HAPPENED?
THE GEM FEEDS OFF GUILT! SO WITHOUT THAT GUILT, THEIR ZOMBIE FORM DOESN'T HOLD.
SHIT!
WHAK!
URK!
GRAB

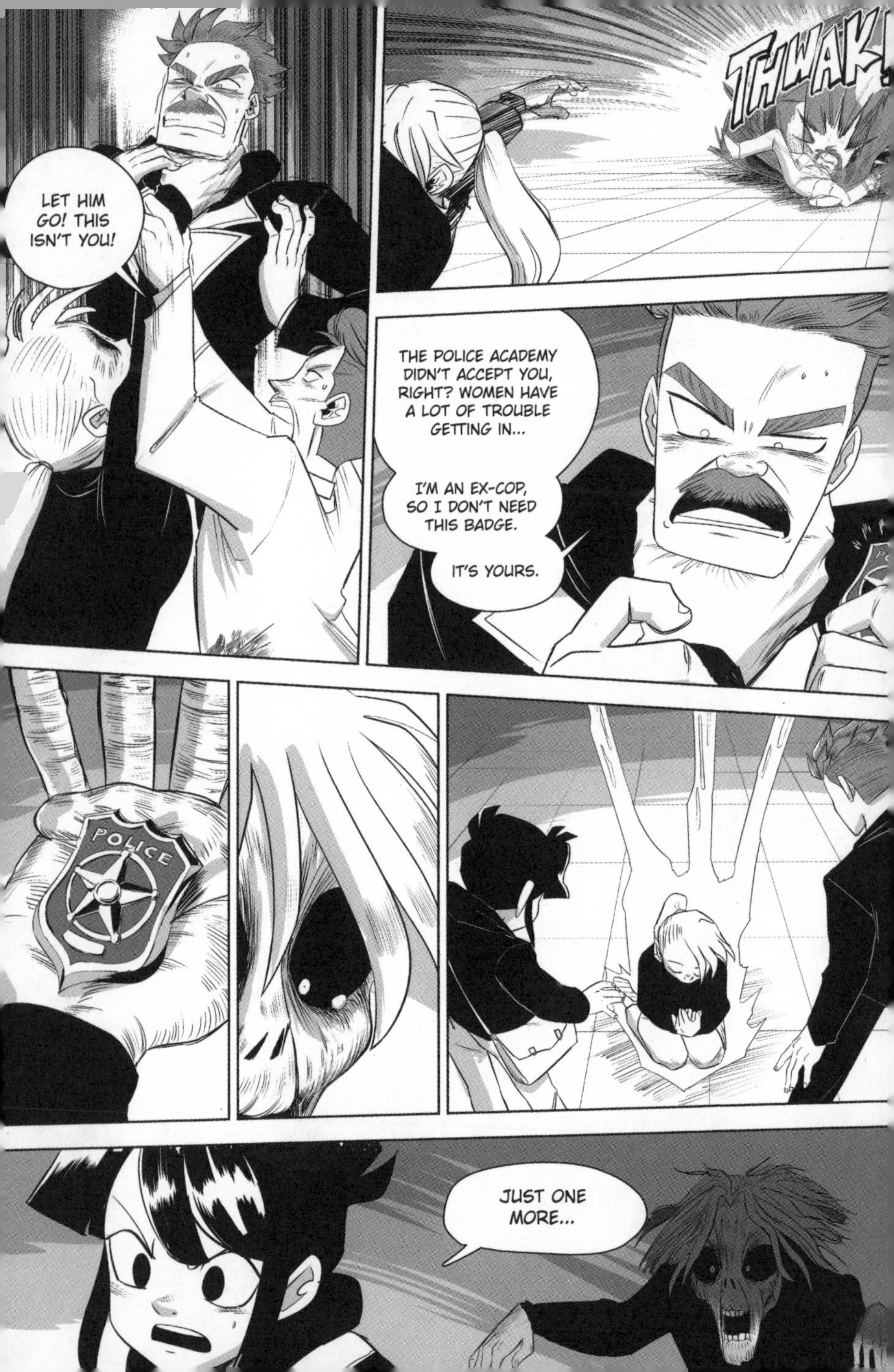
LET HIM GO! THIS ISN'T YOU!
THWAK!
THE POLICE ACADEMY DIDN'T ACCEPT YOU, RIGHT? WOMEN HAVE A LOT OF TROUBLE GETTING IN...
I'M AN EX-COP, SO I DON'T NEED THIS BADGE.
IT'S YOURS.
POLICE
JUST ONE MORE...

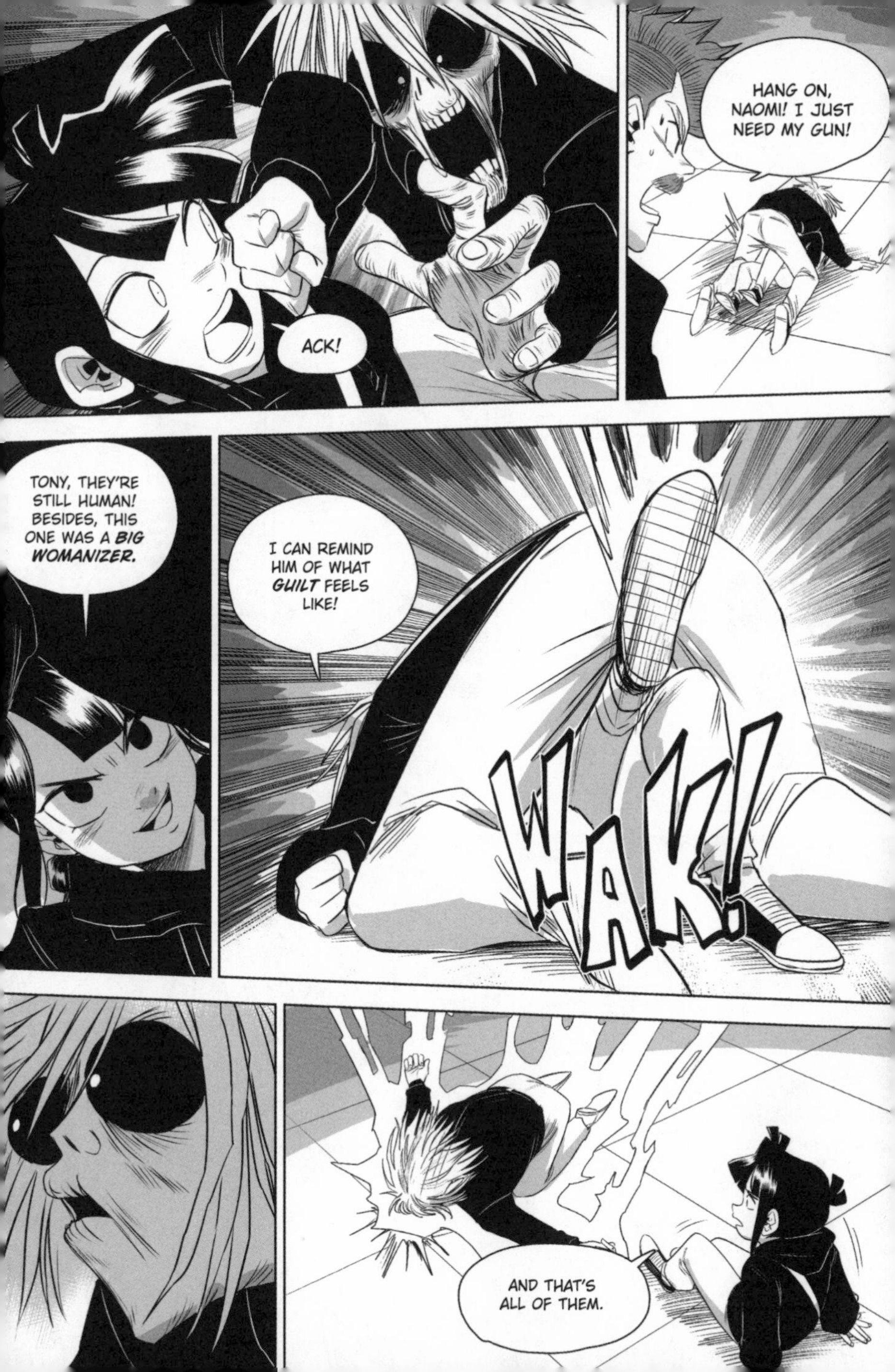
ACK!
HANG ON, NAOMI! I JUST NEED MY GUN!
TONY, THEY'RE STILL HUMAN! BESIDES, THIS ONE WAS A ***BIG WOMANIZER.***
I CAN REMIND HIM OF WHAT ***GUILT*** FEELS LIKE!
WAK!
AND THAT'S ALL OF THEM.

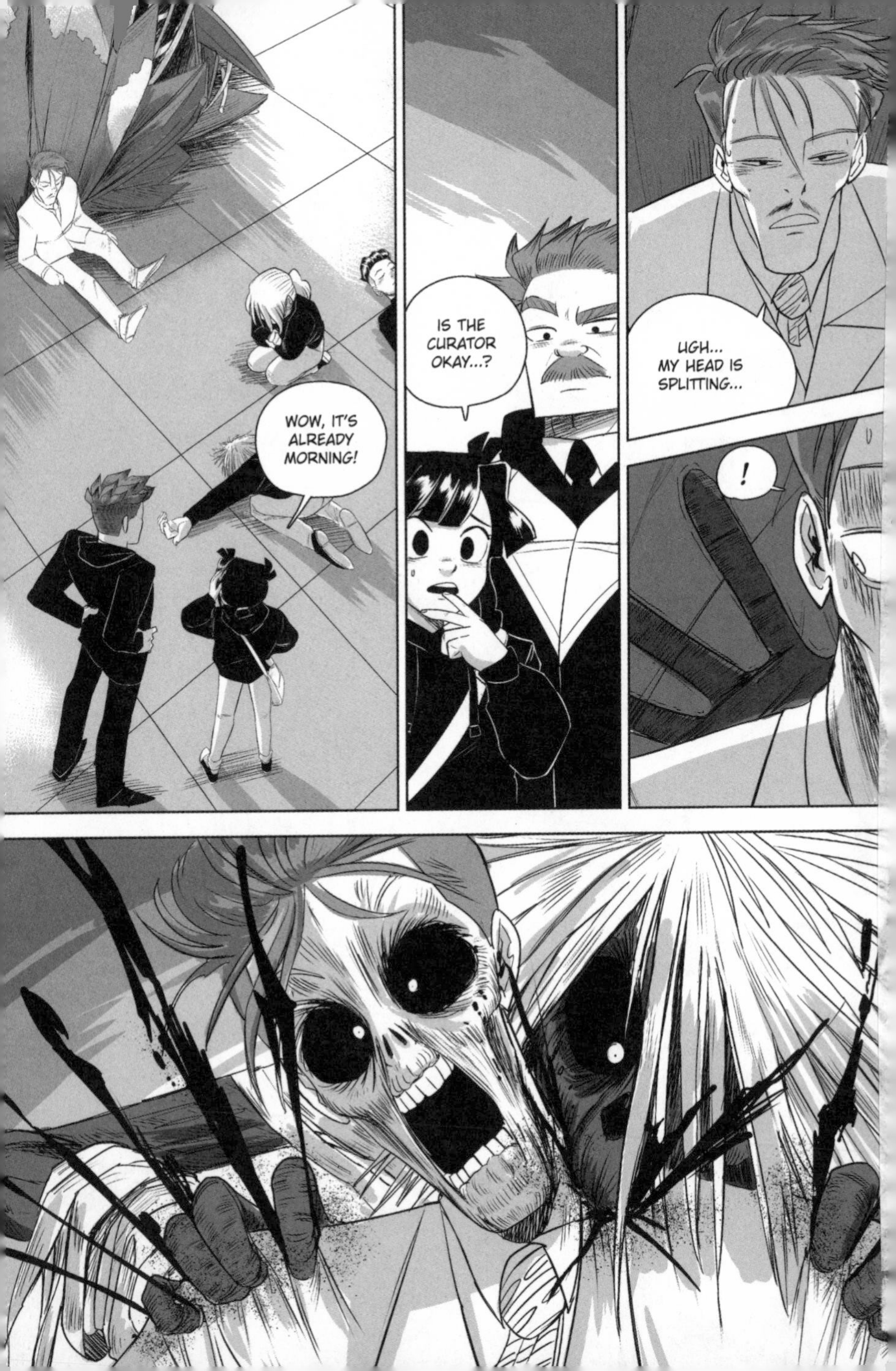
WOW, IT'S ALREADY MORNING!
IS THE CURATOR OKAY...?
UGH... MY HEAD IS SPLITTING...
!

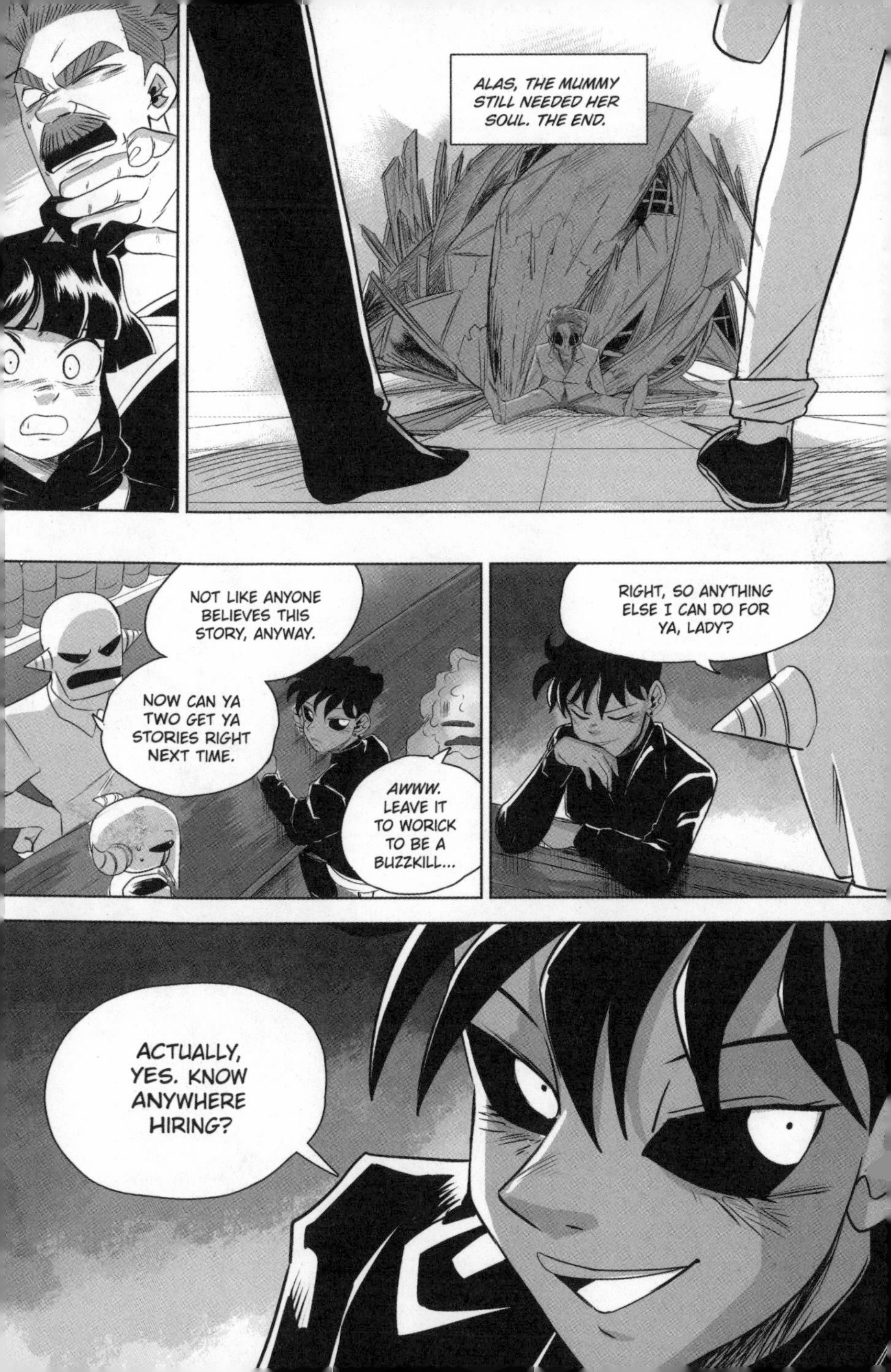
ALAS, THE MUMMY STILL NEEDED HER SOUL. THE END.
NOT LIKE ANYONE BELIEVES THIS STORY, ANYWAY.
NOW CAN YA TWO GET YA STORIES RIGHT NEXT TIME.
AWWW. LEAVE IT TO WORICK TO BE A BUZZKILL...
RIGHT, SO ANYTHING ELSE I CAN DO FOR YA, LADY?
ACTUALLY, YES. KNOW ANYWHERE HIRING?

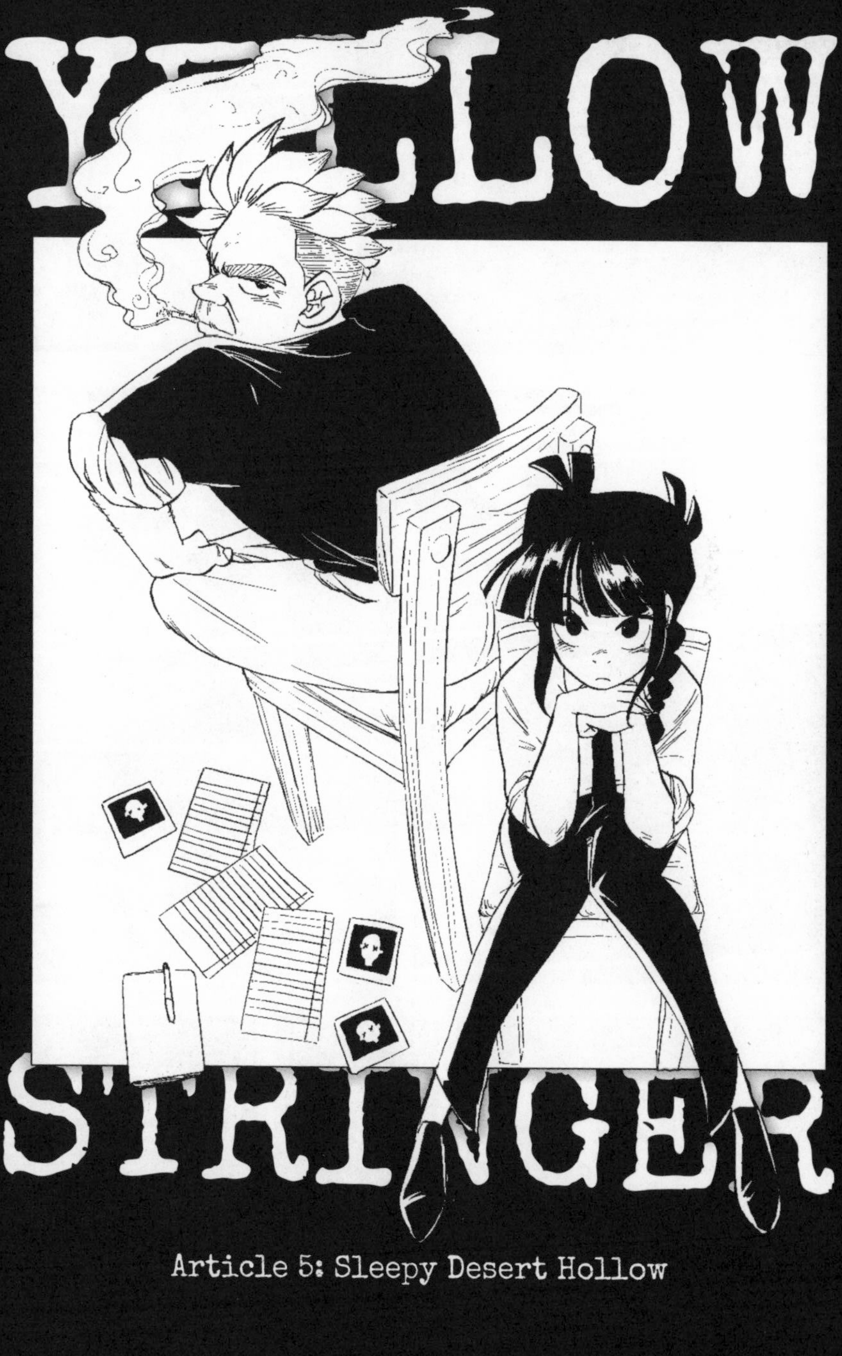
YELLOW
STRINGER

Article 5: Sleepy Desert Hollow

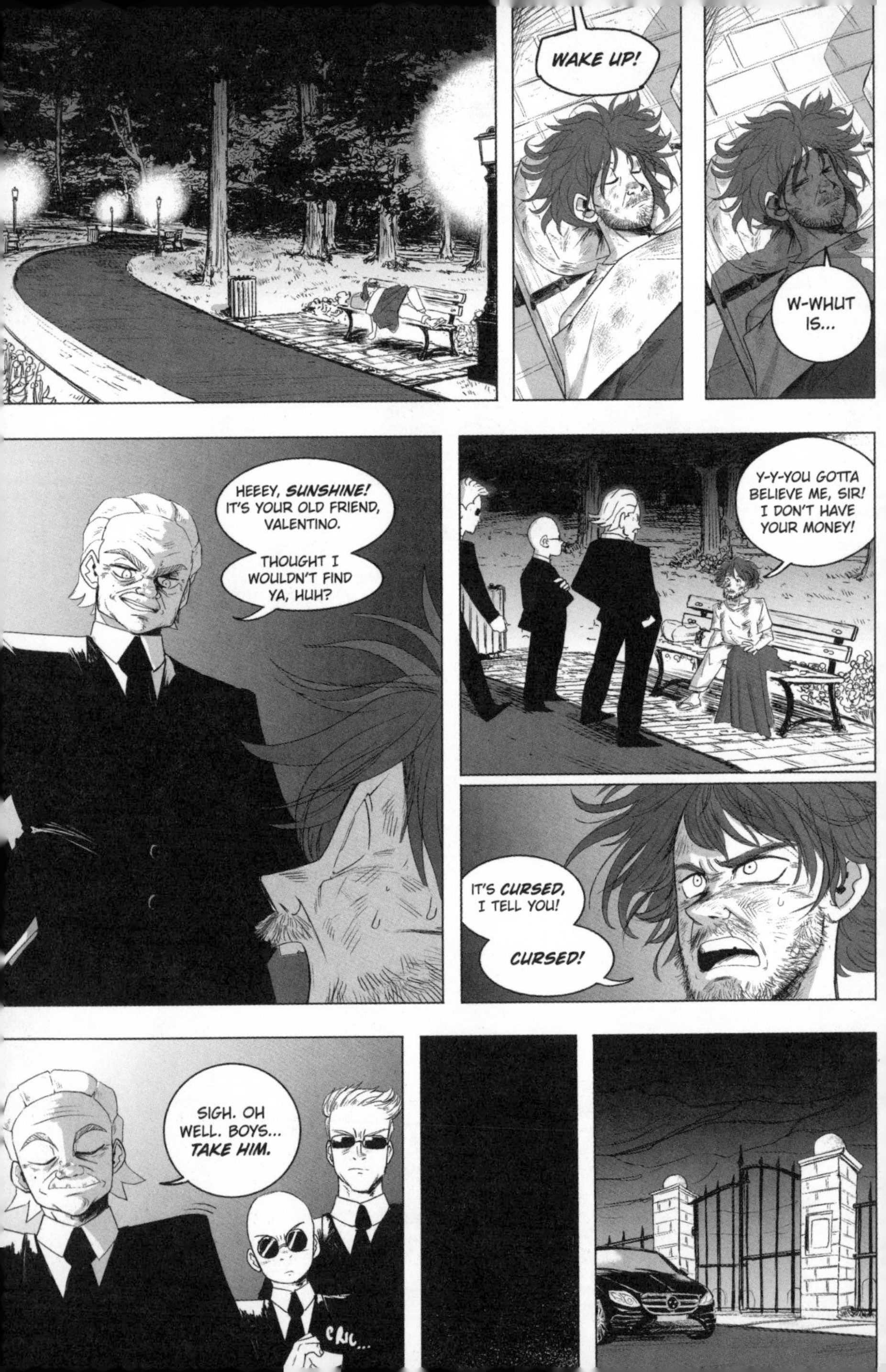
WAKE UP!
W-WHUT IS...
HEEEY, SUNSHINE! IT'S YOUR OLD FRIEND, VALENTINO.
THOUGHT I WOULDN'T FIND YA, HUH?
Y-Y-YOU GOTTA BELIEVE ME, SIR! I DON'T HAVE YOUR MONEY!
IT'S CURSED, I TELL YOU!
CURSED!
SIGH. OH WELL. BOYS... TAKE HIM.
CRIC...

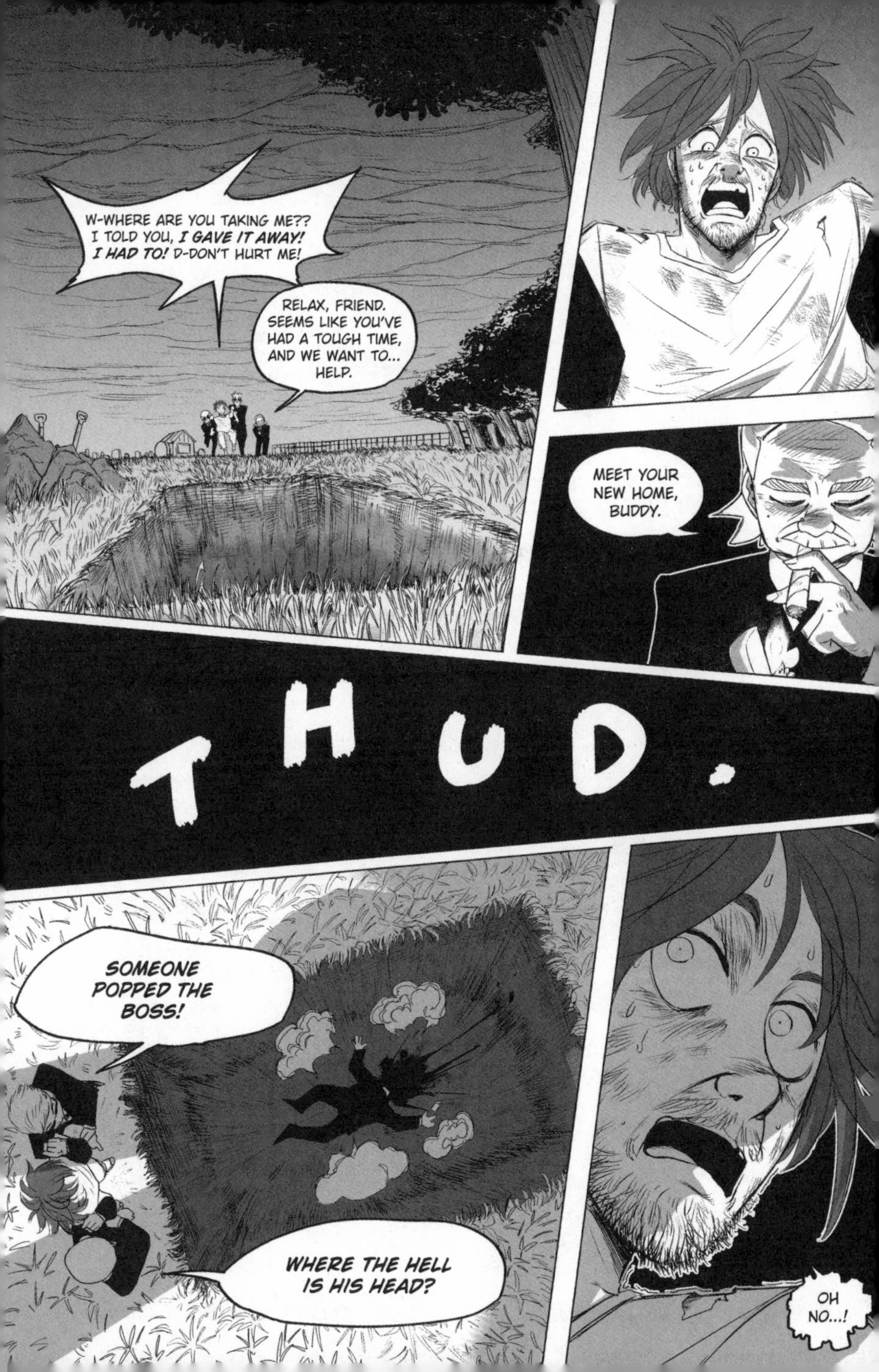
W-WHERE ARE YOU TAKING ME?? I TOLD YOU, *I GAVE IT AWAY! I HAD TO!* D-DON'T HURT ME!
RELAX, FRIEND. SEEMS LIKE YOU'VE HAD A TOUGH TIME, AND WE WANT TO... HELP.
MEET YOUR NEW HOME, BUDDY.
THUD.
SOMEONE POPPED THE BOSS!
WHERE THE HELL IS HIS HEAD?
OH NO...!

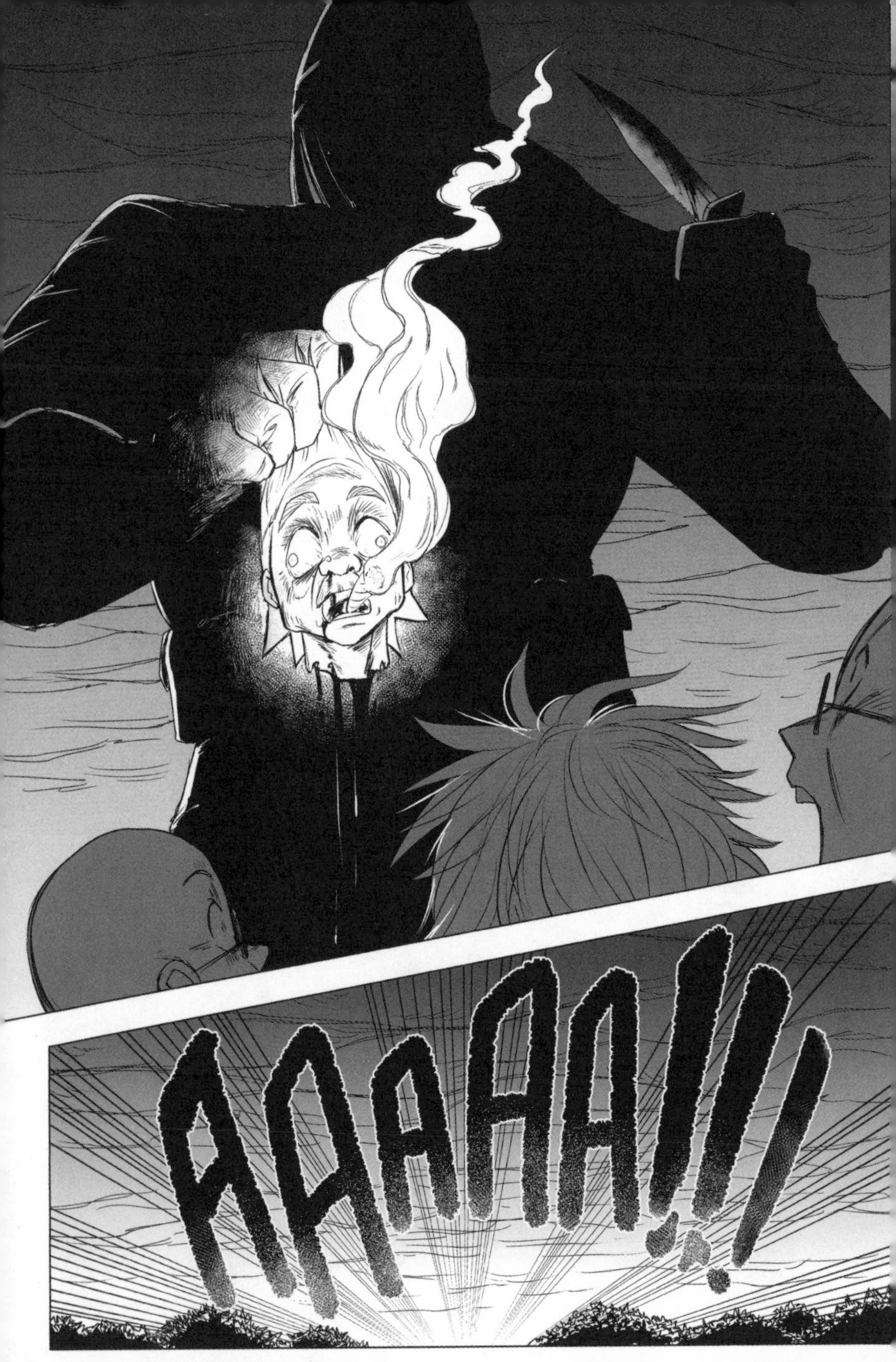
AAAAA!!!

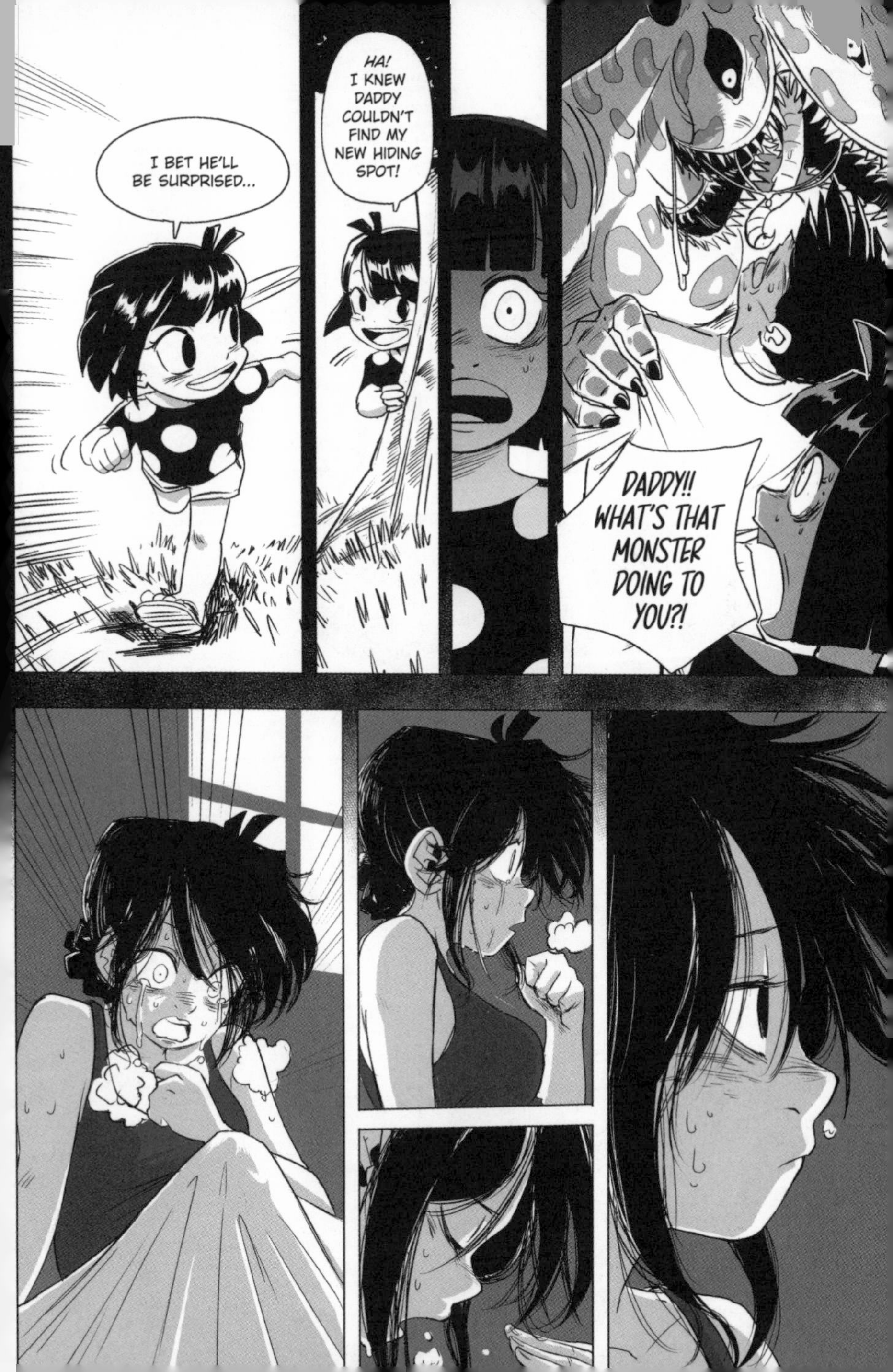
I BET HE'LL BE SURPRISED...
HA! I KNEW DADDY COULDN'T FIND MY NEW HIDING SPOT!
DADDY!! WHAT'S THAT MONSTER DOING TO YOU?!

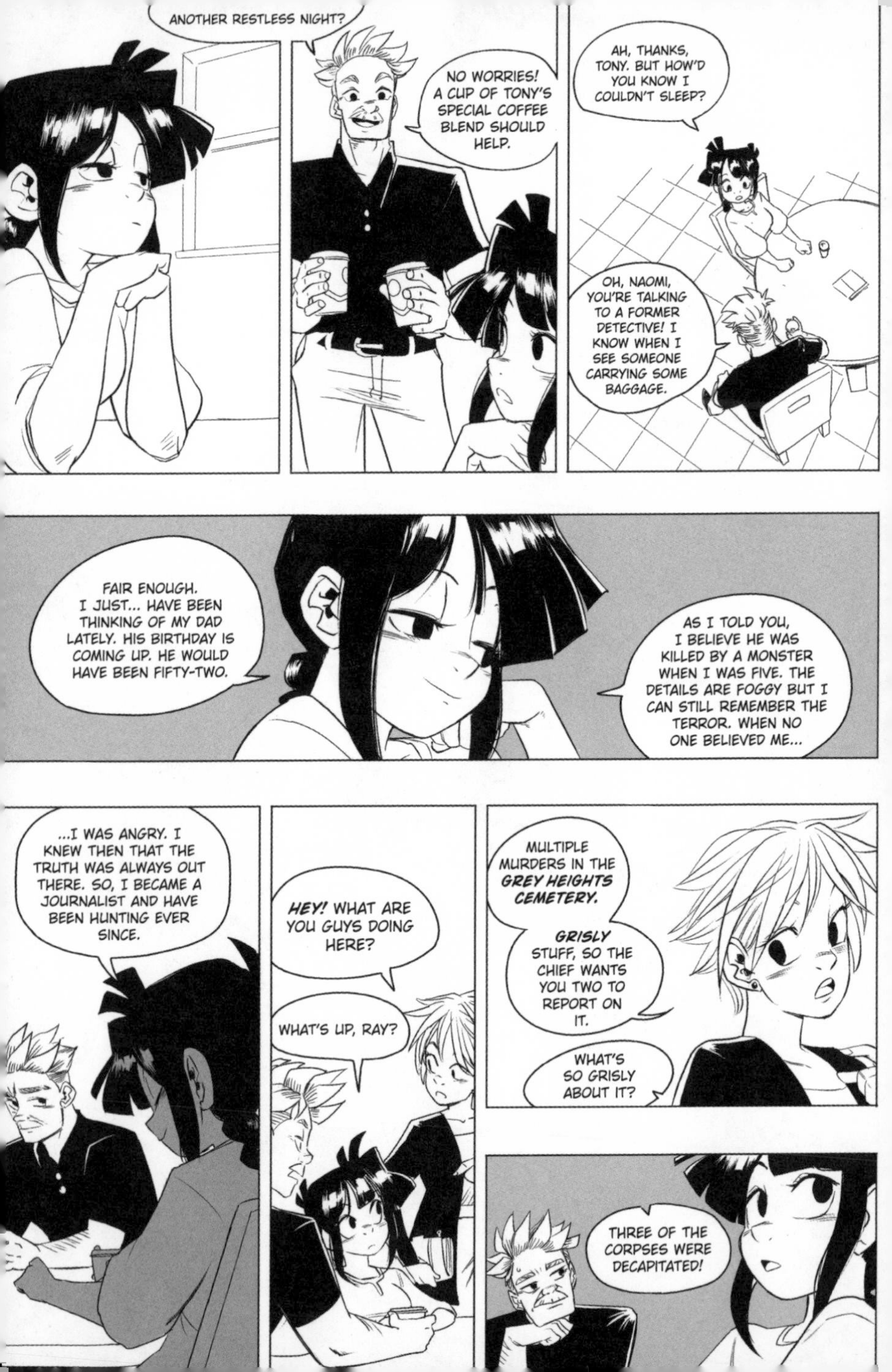
ANOTHER RESTLESS NIGHT?
NO WORRIES! A CUP OF TONY'S SPECIAL COFFEE BLEND SHOULD HELP.
AH, THANKS, TONY. BUT HOW'D YOU KNOW I COULDN'T SLEEP?
OH, NAOMI, YOU'RE TALKING TO A FORMER DETECTIVE! I KNOW WHEN I SEE SOMEONE CARRYING SOME BAGGAGE.
FAIR ENOUGH. I JUST... HAVE BEEN THINKING OF MY DAD LATELY. HIS BIRTHDAY IS COMING UP. HE WOULD HAVE BEEN FIFTY-TWO.
AS I TOLD YOU, I BELIEVE HE WAS KILLED BY A MONSTER WHEN I WAS FIVE. THE DETAILS ARE FOGGY BUT I CAN STILL REMEMBER THE TERROR. WHEN NO ONE BELIEVED ME...
...I WAS ANGRY. I KNEW THEN THAT THE TRUTH WAS ALWAYS OUT THERE. SO, I BECAME A JOURNALIST AND HAVE BEEN HUNTING EVER SINCE.
HEY! WHAT ARE YOU GUYS DOING HERE?
WHAT'S UP, RAY?
MULTIPLE MURDERS IN THE GREY HEIGHTS CEMETERY.
GRISLY STUFF, SO THE CHIEF WANTS YOU TWO TO REPORT ON IT.
WHAT'S SO GRISLY ABOUT IT?
THREE OF THE CORPSES WERE DECAPITATED!

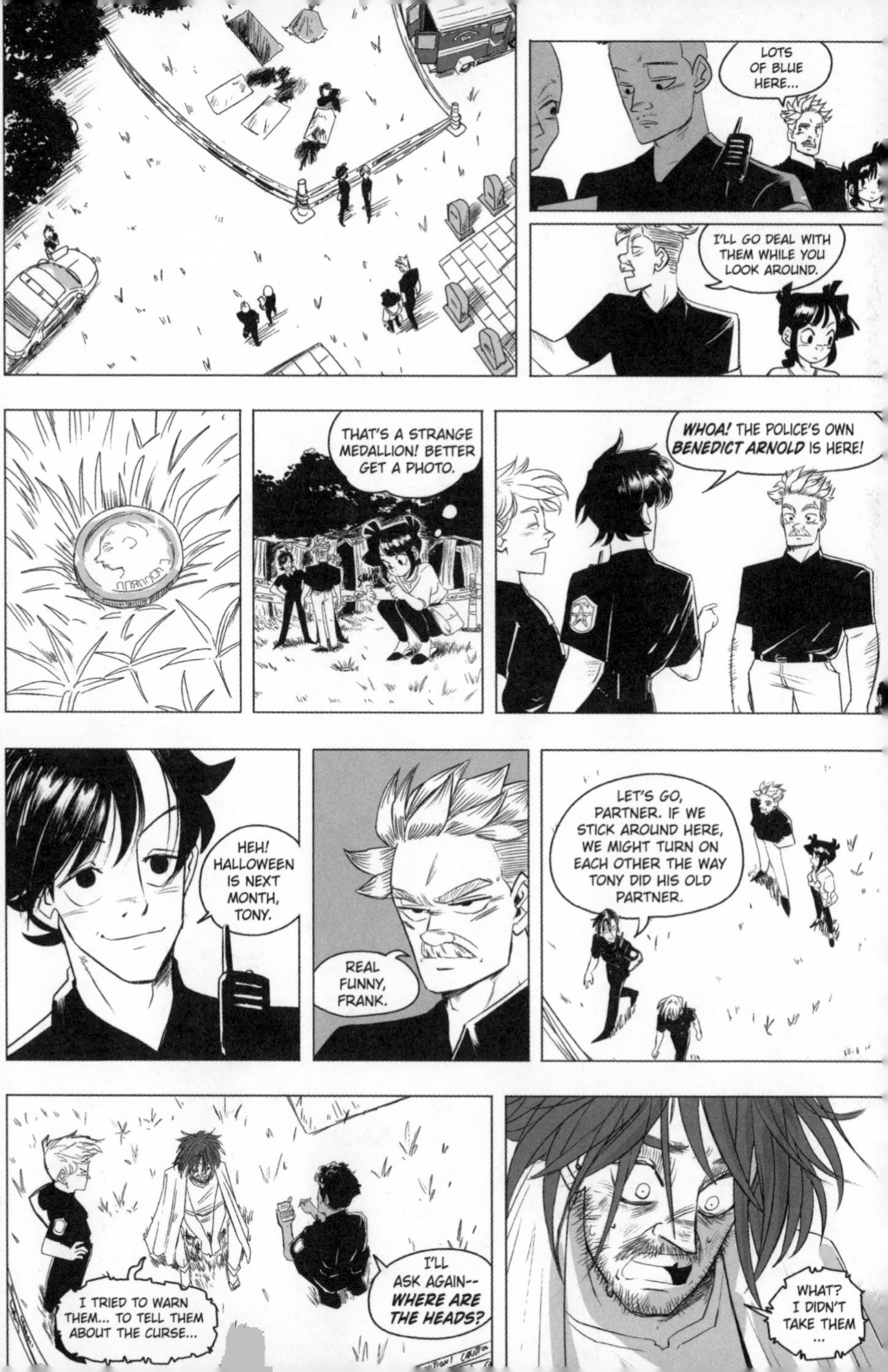
LOTS OF BLUE HERE...
I'LL GO DEAL WITH THEM WHILE YOU LOOK AROUND.
THAT'S A STRANGE MEDALLION! BETTER GET A PHOTO.
SNAP
WHOA! THE POLICE'S OWN BENEDICT ARNOLD IS HERE!
HEH! HALLOWEEN IS NEXT MONTH, TONY.
REAL FUNNY, FRANK.
LET'S GO, PARTNER. IF WE STICK AROUND HERE, WE MIGHT TURN ON EACH OTHER THE WAY TONY DID HIS OLD PARTNER.
I TRIED TO WARN THEM... TO TELL THEM ABOUT THE CURSE...
I'LL ASK AGAIN-- WHERE ARE THE HEADS?
WHAT? I DIDN'T TAKE THEM ...

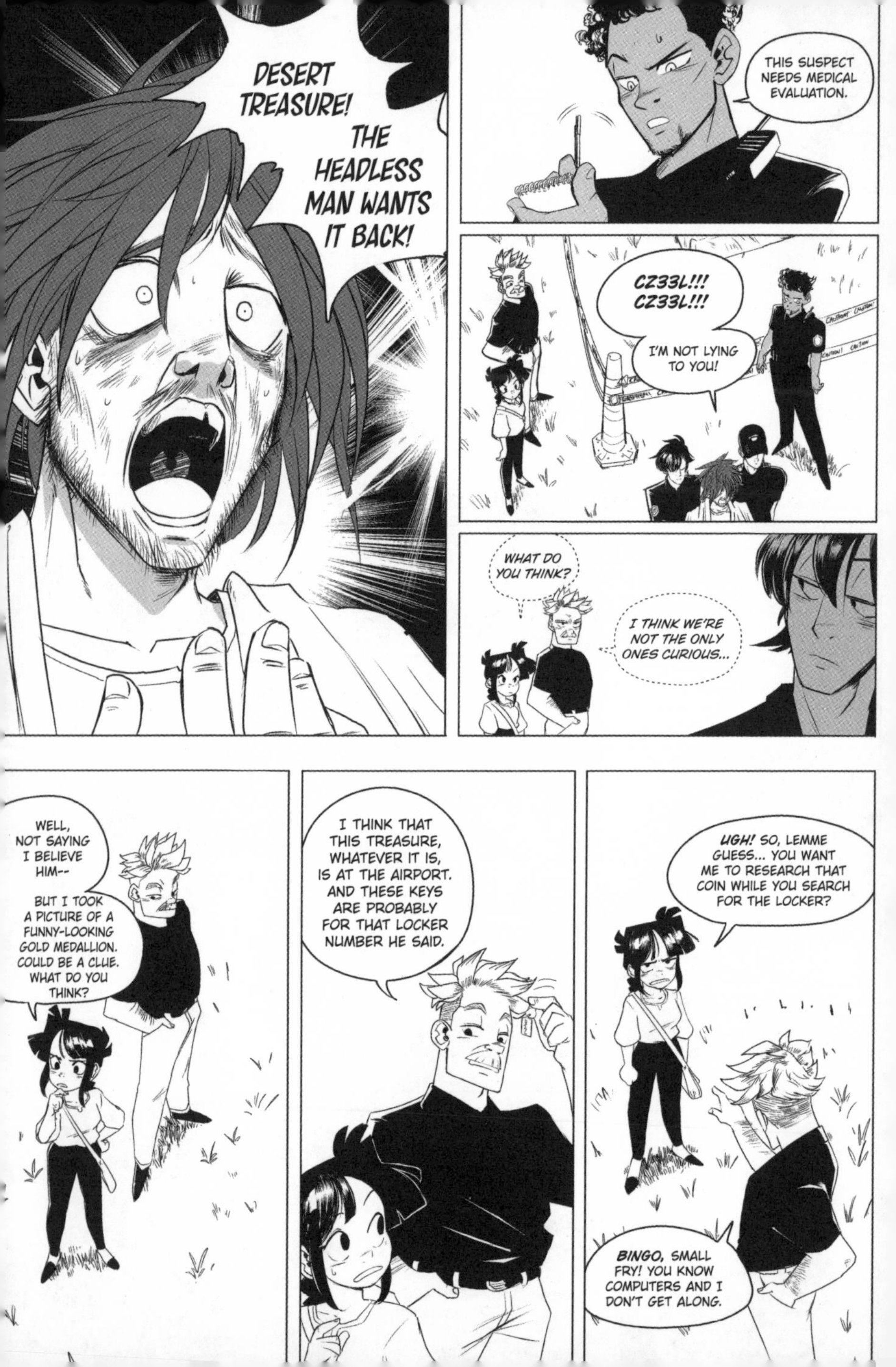
DESERT TREASURE!
THE HEADLESS MAN WANTS IT BACK!
THIS SUSPECT NEEDS MEDICAL EVALUATION.
CZ33L!!! CZ33L!!!
I'M NOT LYING TO YOU!
WHAT DO YOU THINK?
I THINK WE'RE NOT THE ONLY ONES CURIOUS...
WELL, NOT SAYING I BELIEVE HIM--
BUT I TOOK A PICTURE OF A FUNNY-LOOKING GOLD MEDALLION. COULD BE A CLUE. WHAT DO YOU THINK?
I THINK THAT THIS TREASURE, WHATEVER IT IS, IS AT THE AIRPORT. AND THESE KEYS ARE PROBABLY FOR THAT LOCKER NUMBER HE SAID.
UGH! SO, LEMME GUESS... YOU WANT ME TO RESEARCH THAT COIN WHILE YOU SEARCH FOR THE LOCKER?
BINGO, SMALL FRY! YOU KNOW COMPUTERS AND I DON'T GET ALONG.

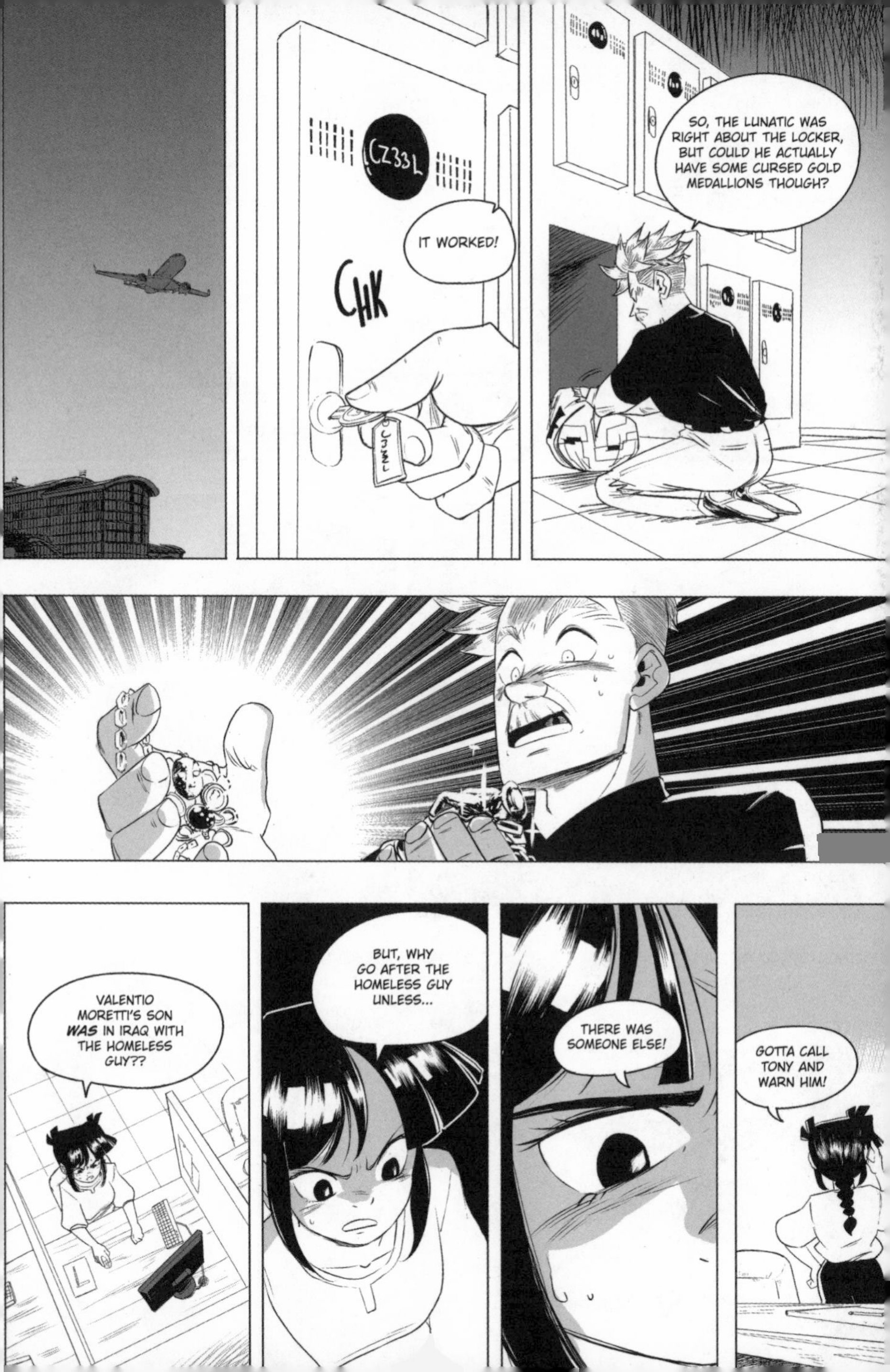
IT WORKED!
CHK
SO, THE LUNATIC WAS RIGHT ABOUT THE LOCKER, BUT COULD HE ACTUALLY HAVE SOME CURSED GOLD MEDALLIONS THOUGH?
VALENTIO MORETTI'S SON **WAS** IN IRAQ WITH THE HOMELESS GUY??
BUT, WHY GO AFTER THE HOMELESS GUY UNLESS...
THERE WAS SOMEONE ELSE!
GOTTA CALL TONY AND WARN HIM!

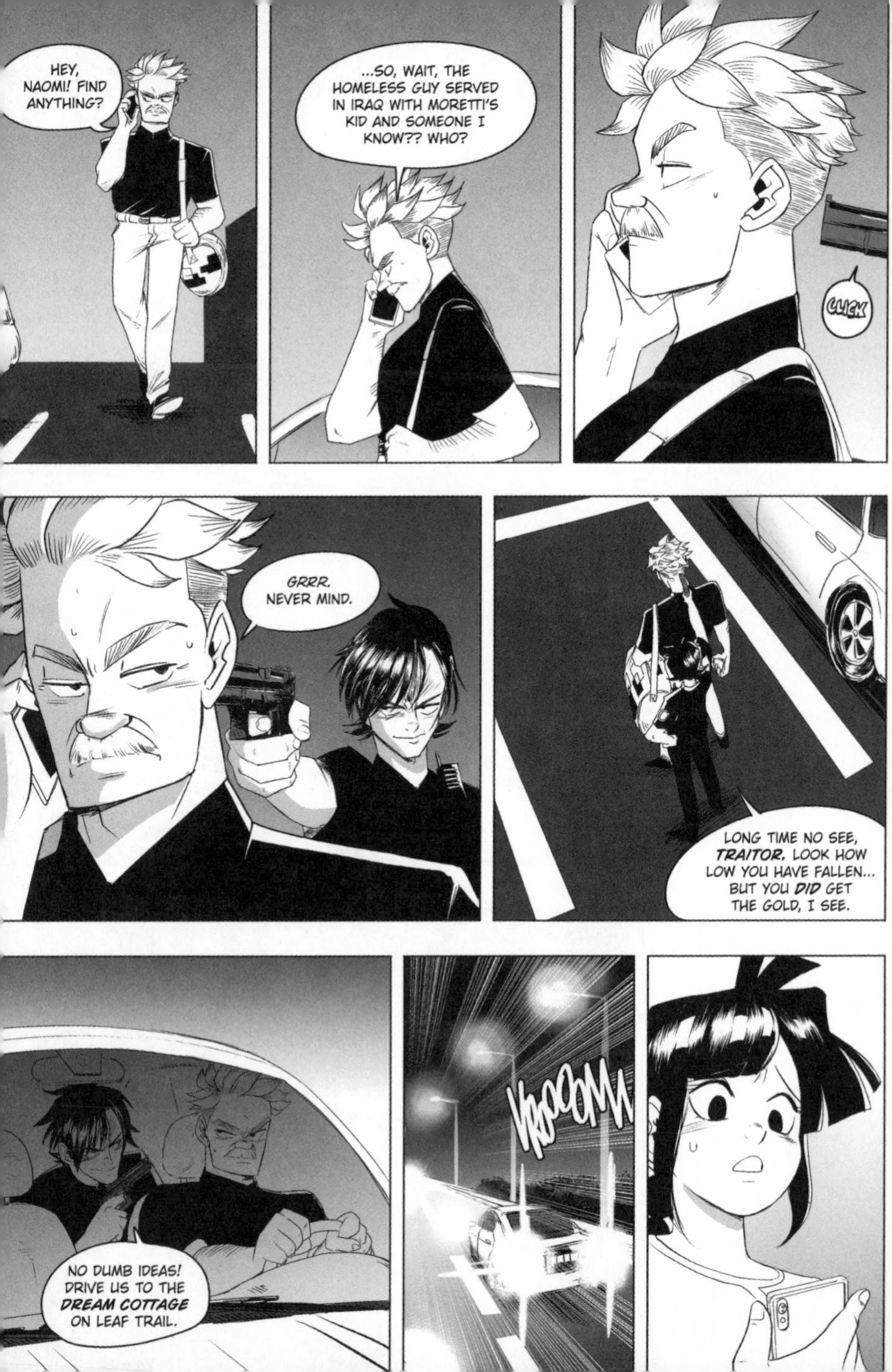
HEY, NAOMI! FIND ANYTHING?
...SO, WAIT, THE HOMELESS GUY SERVED IN IRAQ WITH MORETTI'S KID AND SOMEONE I KNOW?? WHO?
CLICK
GRRR. NEVER MIND.
LONG TIME NO SEE, TRAITOR. LOOK HOW LOW YOU HAVE FALLEN... BUT YOU DID GET THE GOLD, I SEE.
NO DUMB IDEAS! DRIVE US TO THE DREAM COTTAGE ON LEAF TRAIL.
VROOOM

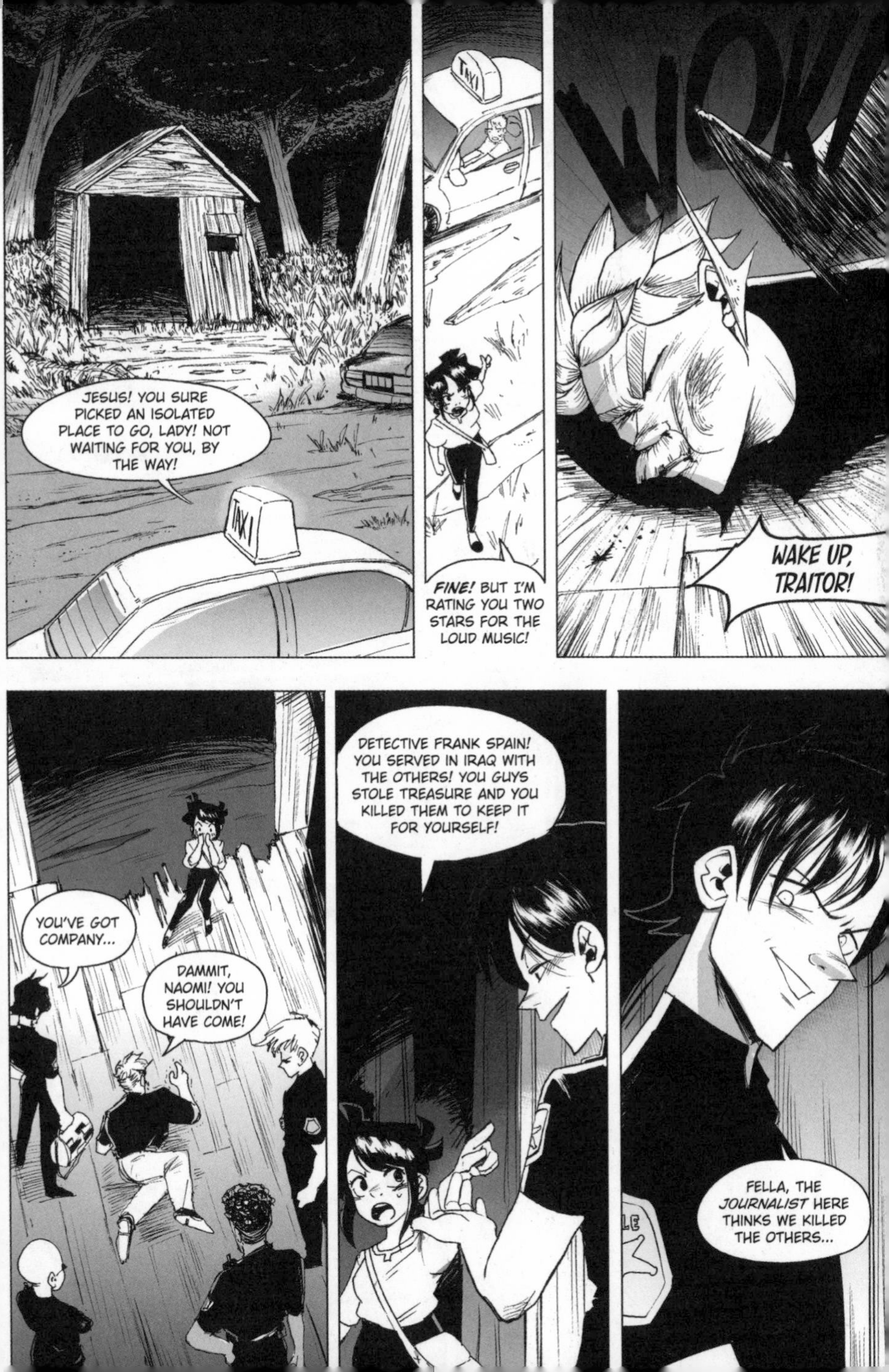
JESUS! YOU SURE PICKED AN ISOLATED PLACE TO GO, LADY! NOT WAITING FOR YOU, BY THE WAY!
FINE! BUT I'M RATING YOU TWO STARS FOR THE LOUD MUSIC!
WAKE UP, TRAITOR!
YOU'VE GOT COMPANY...
DAMMIT, NAOMI! YOU SHOULDN'T HAVE COME!
DETECTIVE FRANK SPAIN! YOU SERVED IN IRAQ WITH THE OTHERS! YOU GUYS STOLE TREASURE AND YOU KILLED THEM TO KEEP IT FOR YOURSELF!
FELLA, THE *JOURNALIST* HERE THINKS WE KILLED THE OTHERS...

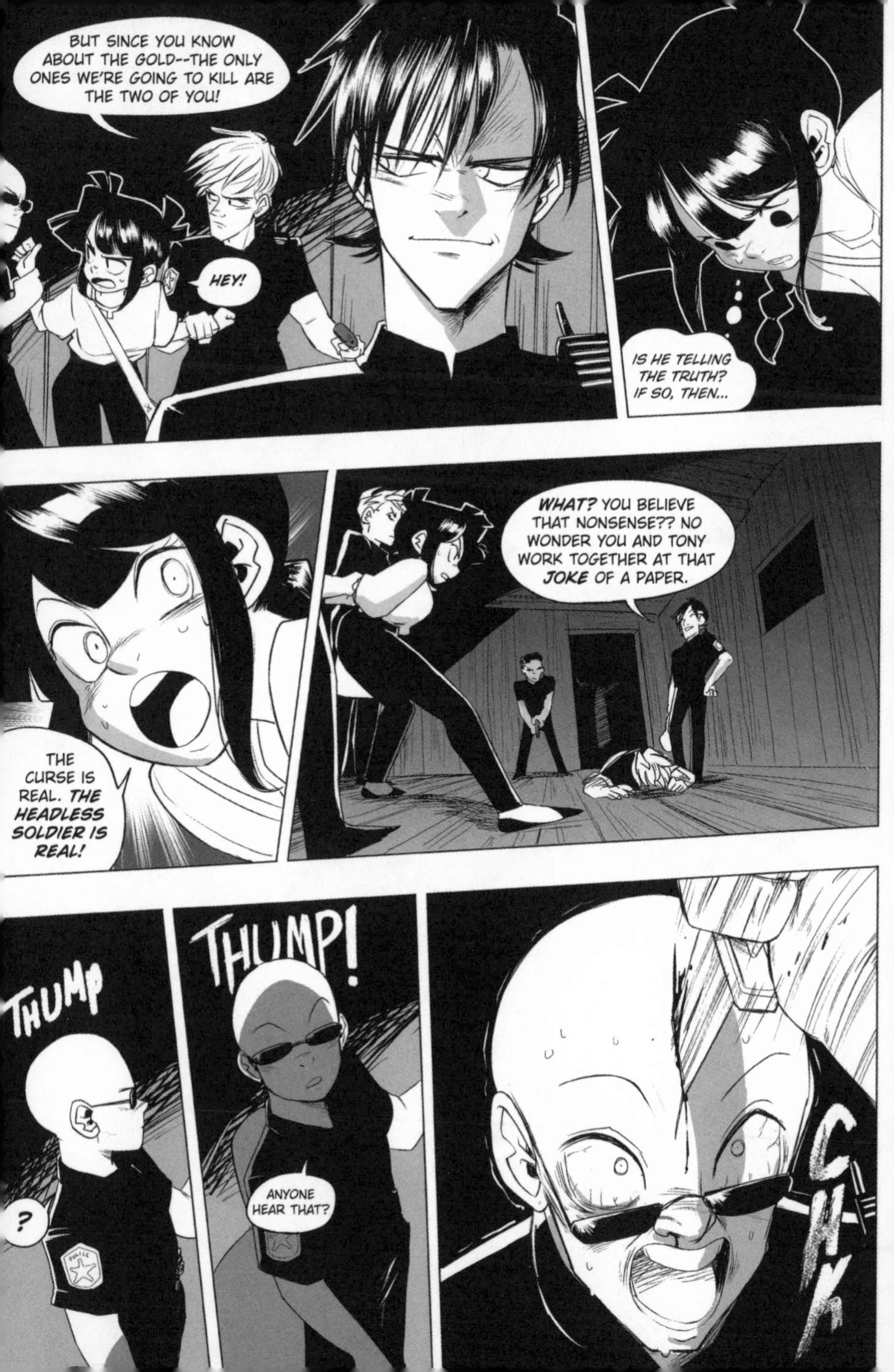
BUT SINCE YOU KNOW ABOUT THE GOLD--THE ONLY ONES WE'RE GOING TO KILL ARE THE TWO OF YOU!
HEY!
IS HE TELLING THE TRUTH? IF SO, THEN...
THE CURSE IS REAL. *THE HEADLESS SOLDIER IS REAL!*
WHAT? YOU BELIEVE THAT NONSENSE?? NO WONDER YOU AND TONY WORK TOGETHER AT THAT ***JOKE*** OF A PAPER.
THUMP
?
THUMP!
ANYONE HEAR THAT?

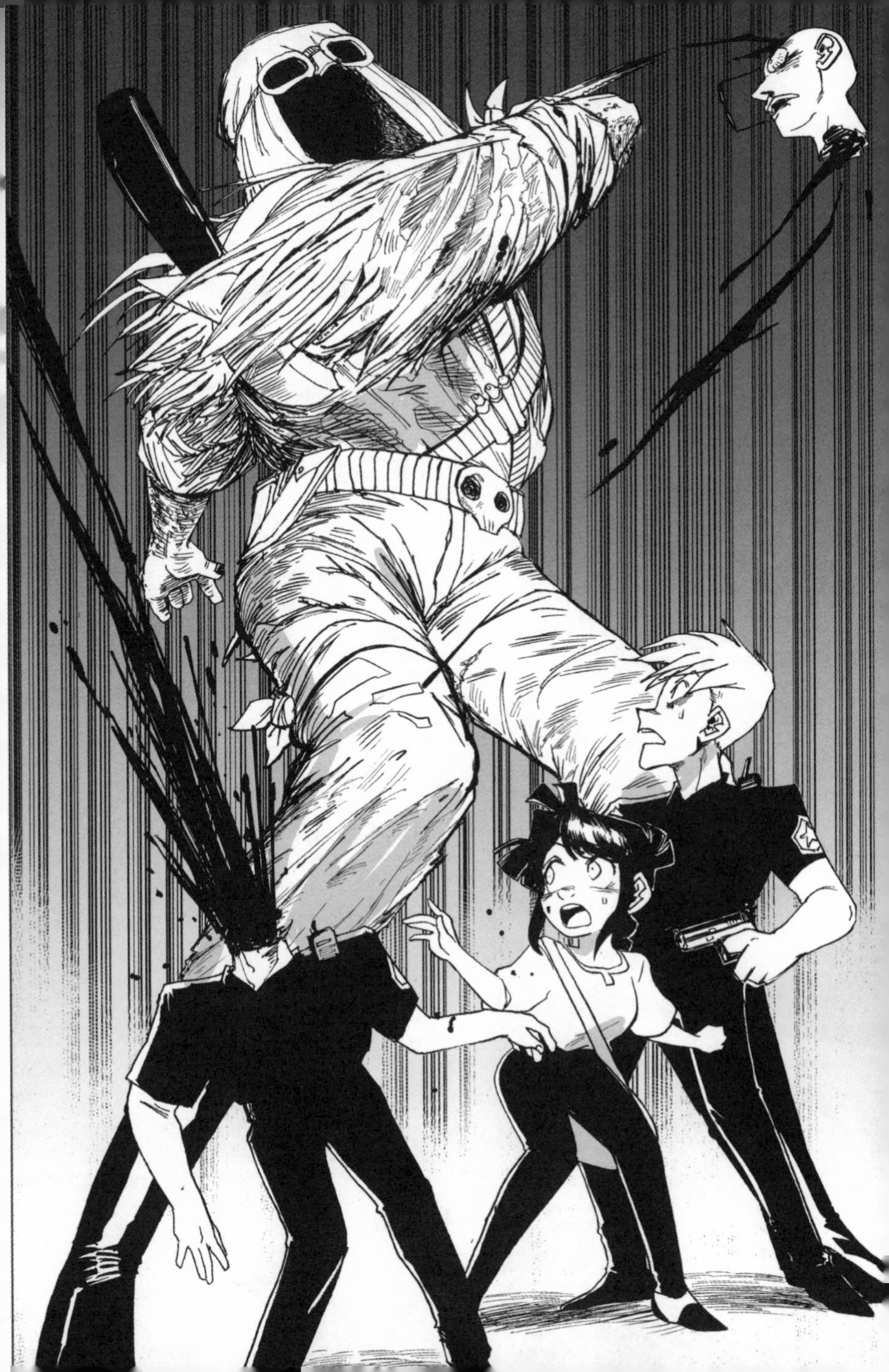

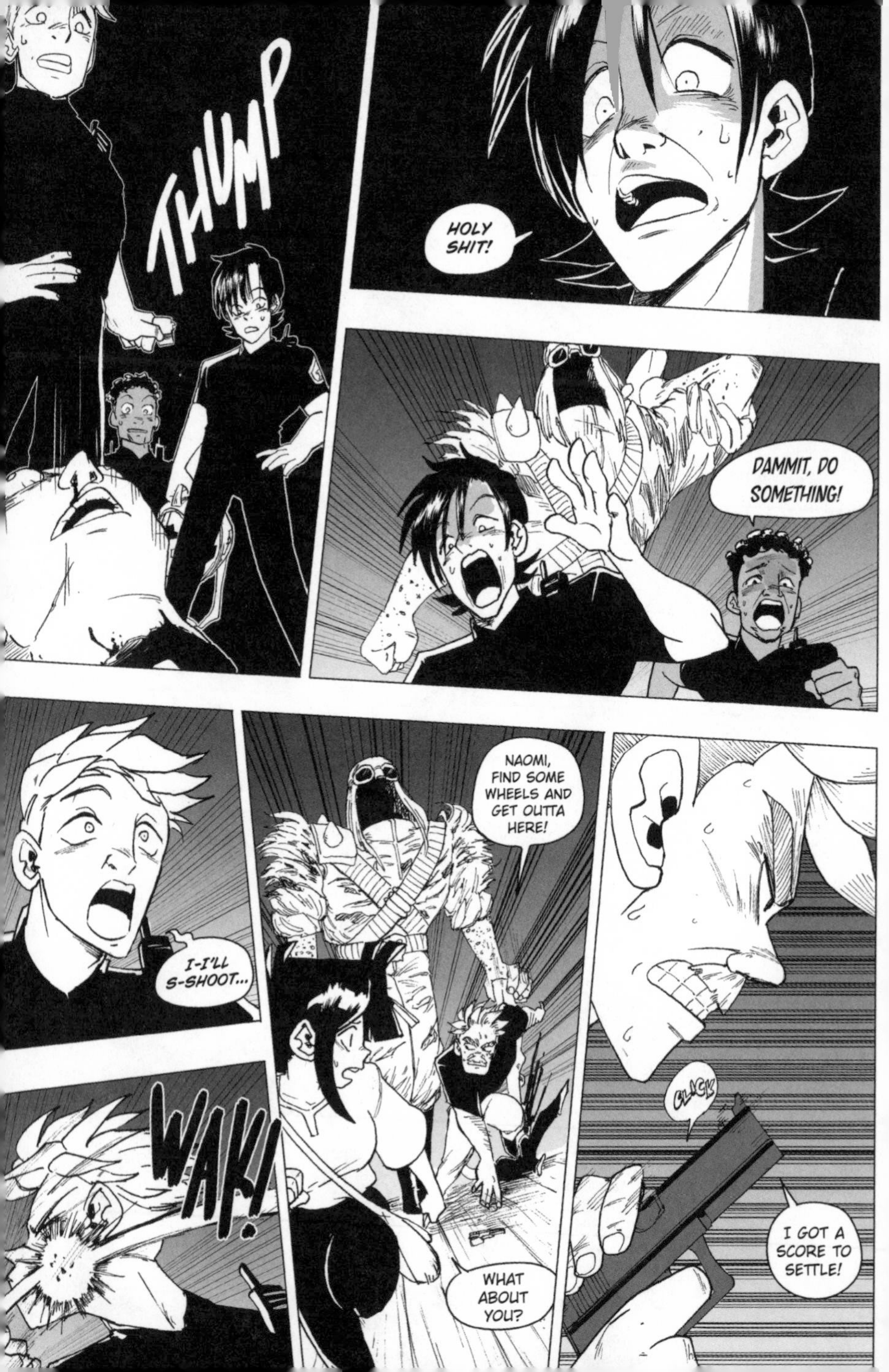
THUMP
HOLY SHIT!
DAMMIT, DO SOMETHING!
I-I'LL S-SHOOT...
WAK!
NAOMI, FIND SOME WHEELS AND GET OUTTA HERE!
WHAT ABOUT YOU?
CLICK
I GOT A SCORE TO SETTLE!

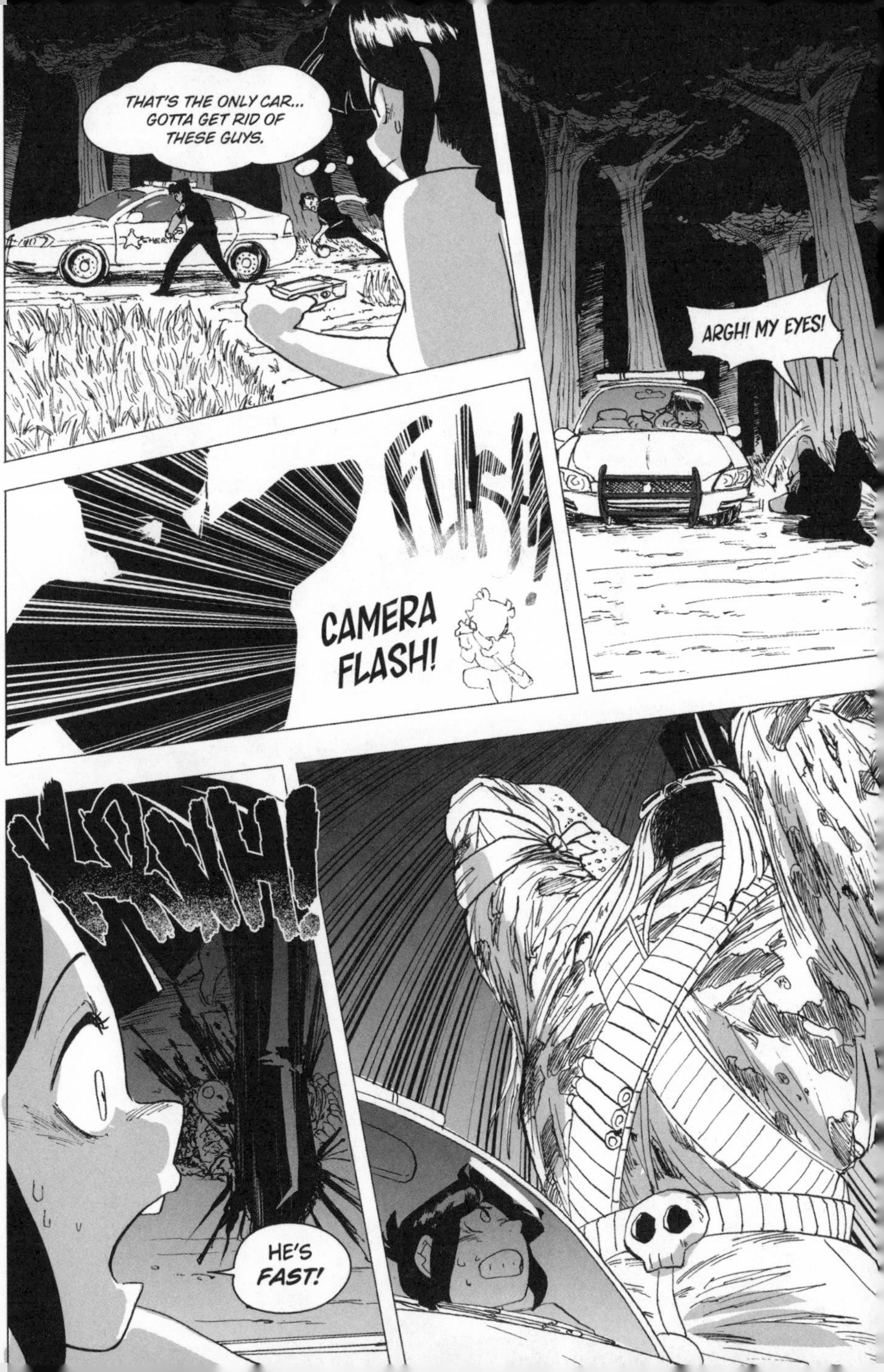
THAT'S THE ONLY CAR... GOTTA GET RID OF THESE GUYS.
ARGH! MY EYES!
FLISH!
CAMERA FLASH!
KRNH!
HE'S FAST!

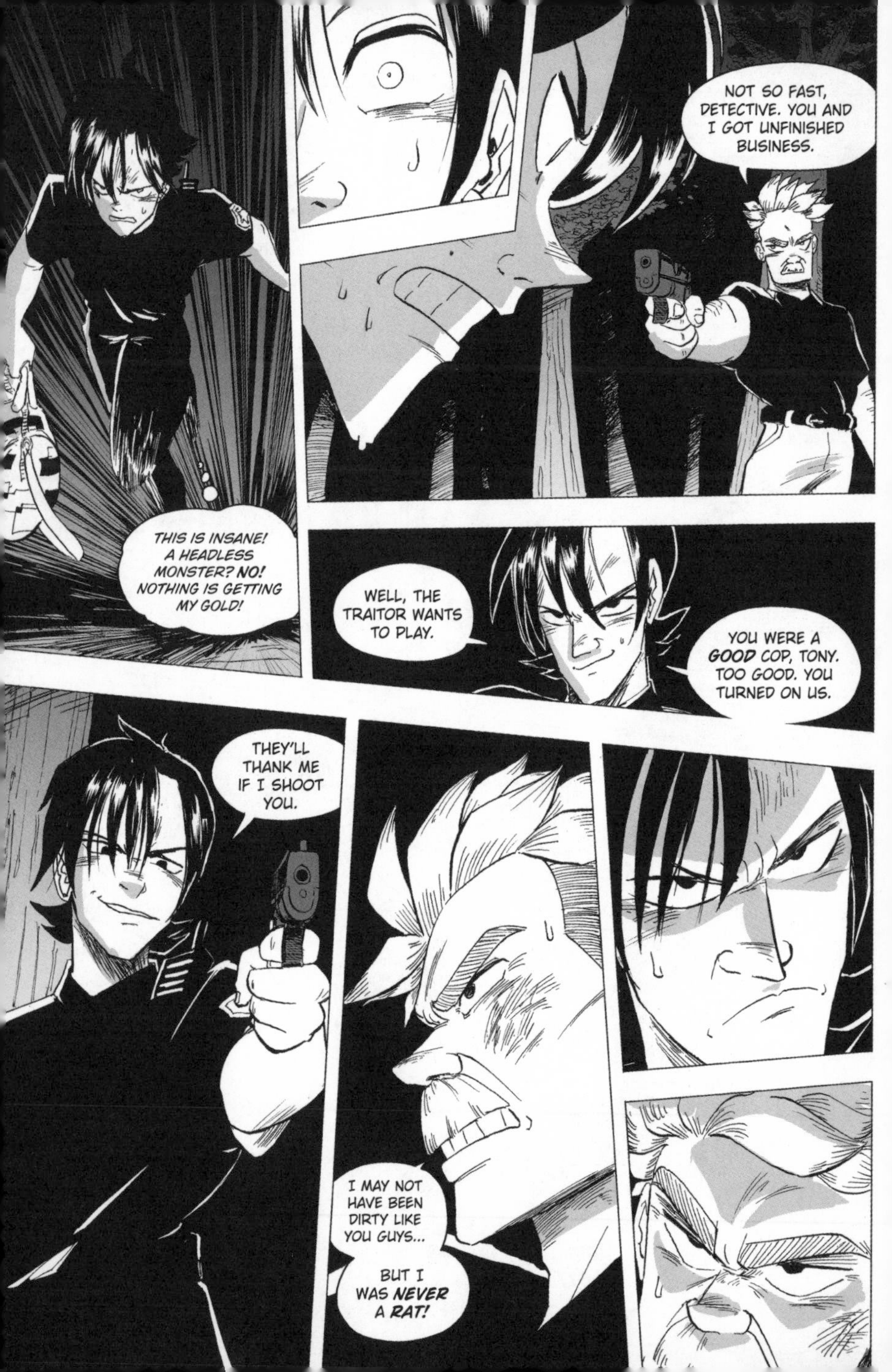
THIS IS INSANE! A HEADLESS MONSTER? NO! NOTHING IS GETTING MY GOLD!
NOT SO FAST, DETECTIVE. YOU AND I GOT UNFINISHED BUSINESS.
WELL, THE TRAITOR WANTS TO PLAY.
YOU WERE A GOOD COP, TONY. TOO GOOD. YOU TURNED ON US.
THEY'LL THANK ME IF I SHOOT YOU.
I MAY NOT HAVE BEEN DIRTY LIKE YOU GUYS...
BUT I WAS NEVER A RAT!

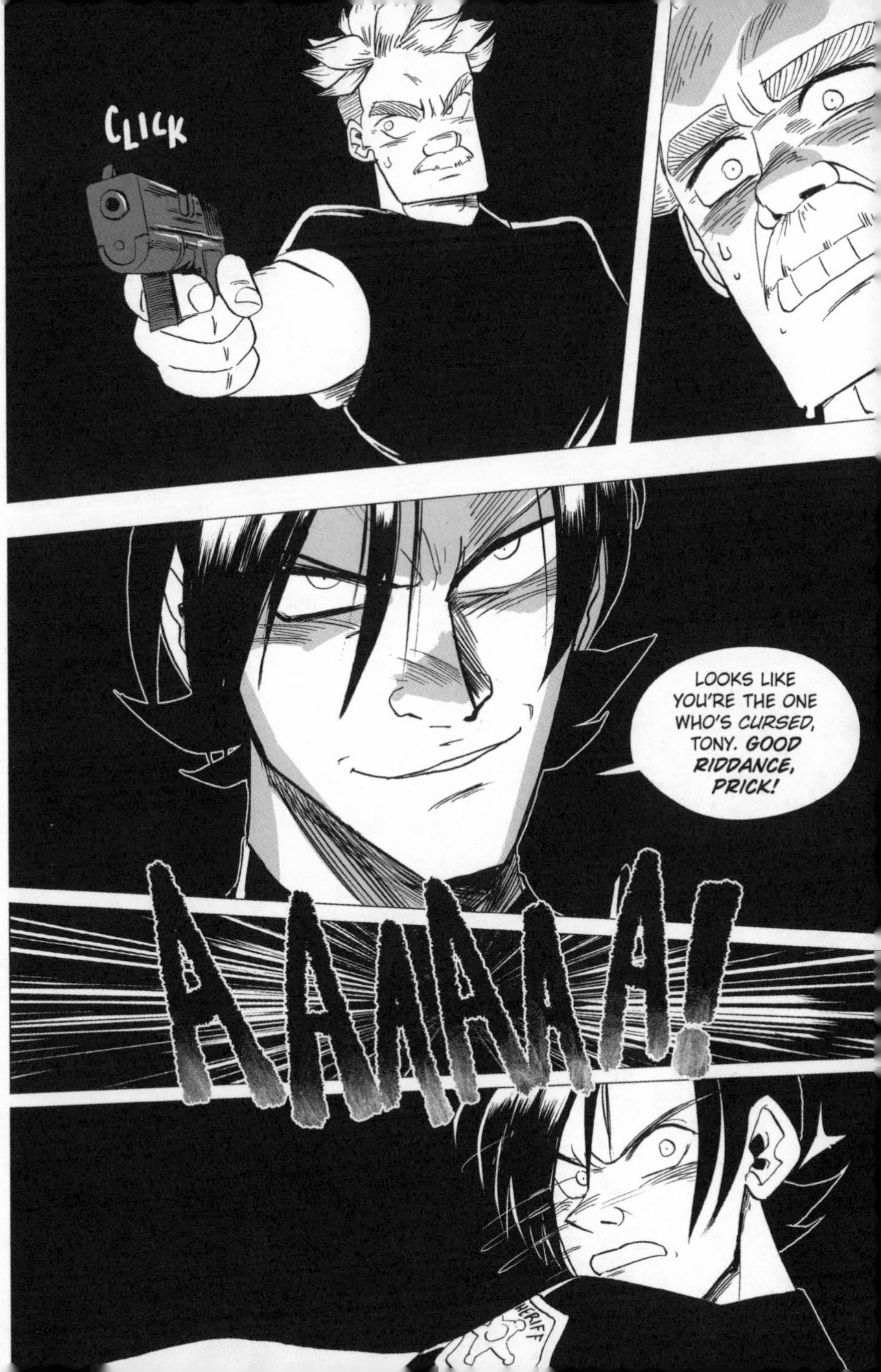
CLICK
LOOKS LIKE YOU'RE THE ONE WHO'S *CURSED*, TONY. ***GOOD RIDDANCE, PRICK!***
AAAAAAA!
SHERIFF

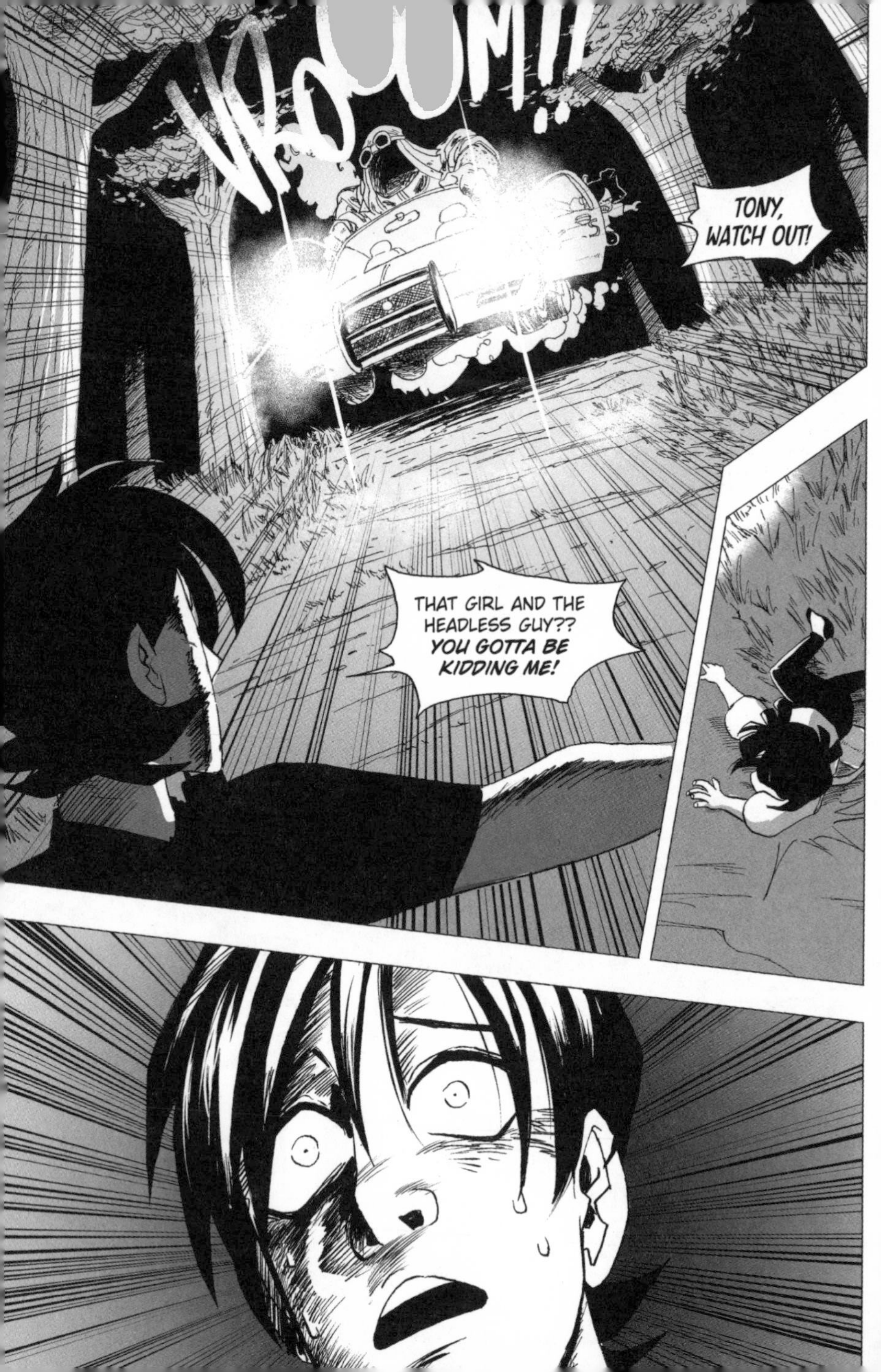
VROOOM!!
TONY, WATCH OUT!
THAT GIRL AND THE HEADLESS GUY?? YOU GOTTA BE KIDDING ME!

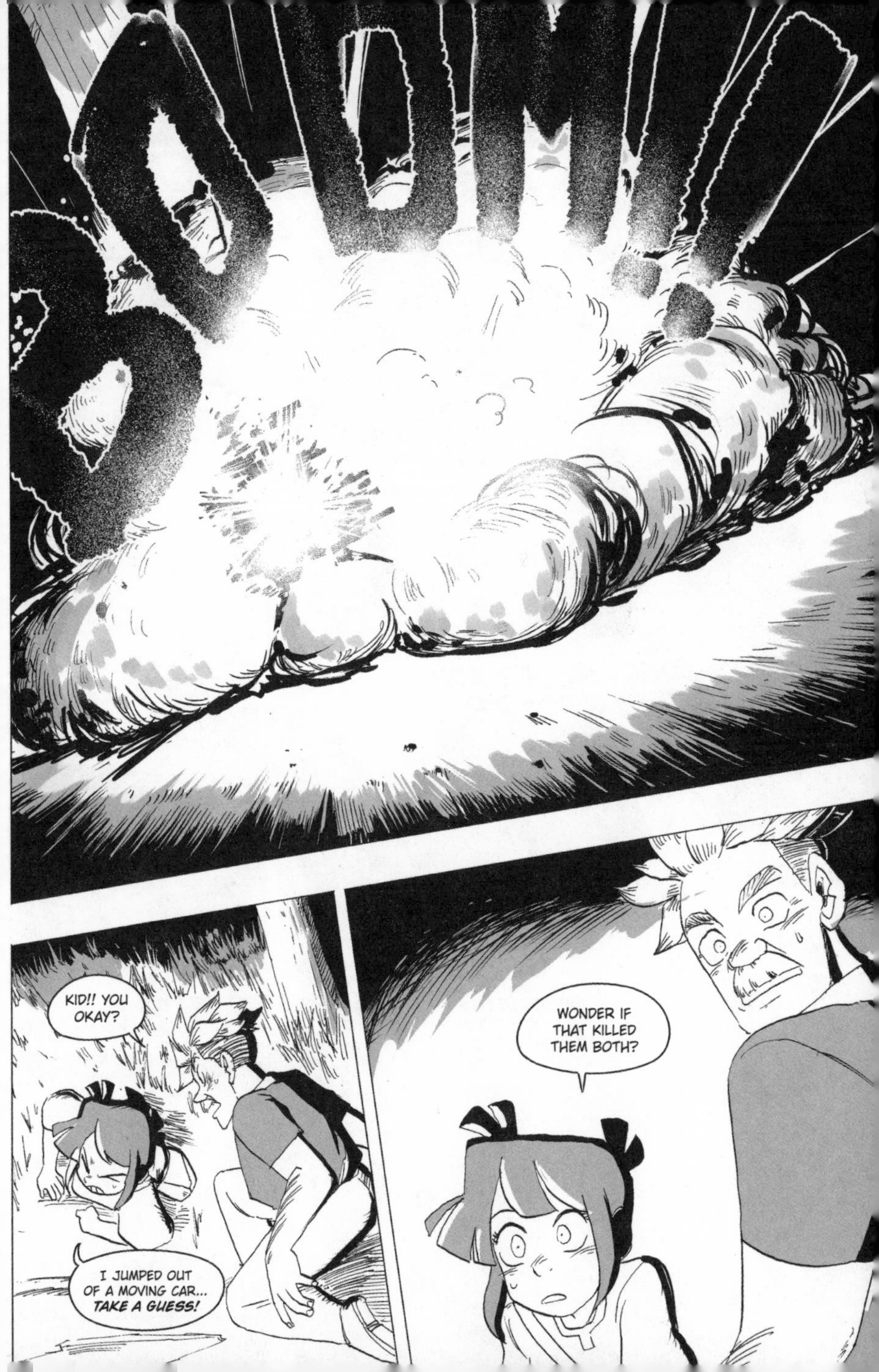
KID!! YOU OKAY?
I JUMPED OUT OF A MOVING CAR... **TAKE A GUESS!**
WONDER IF THAT KILLED THEM BOTH?

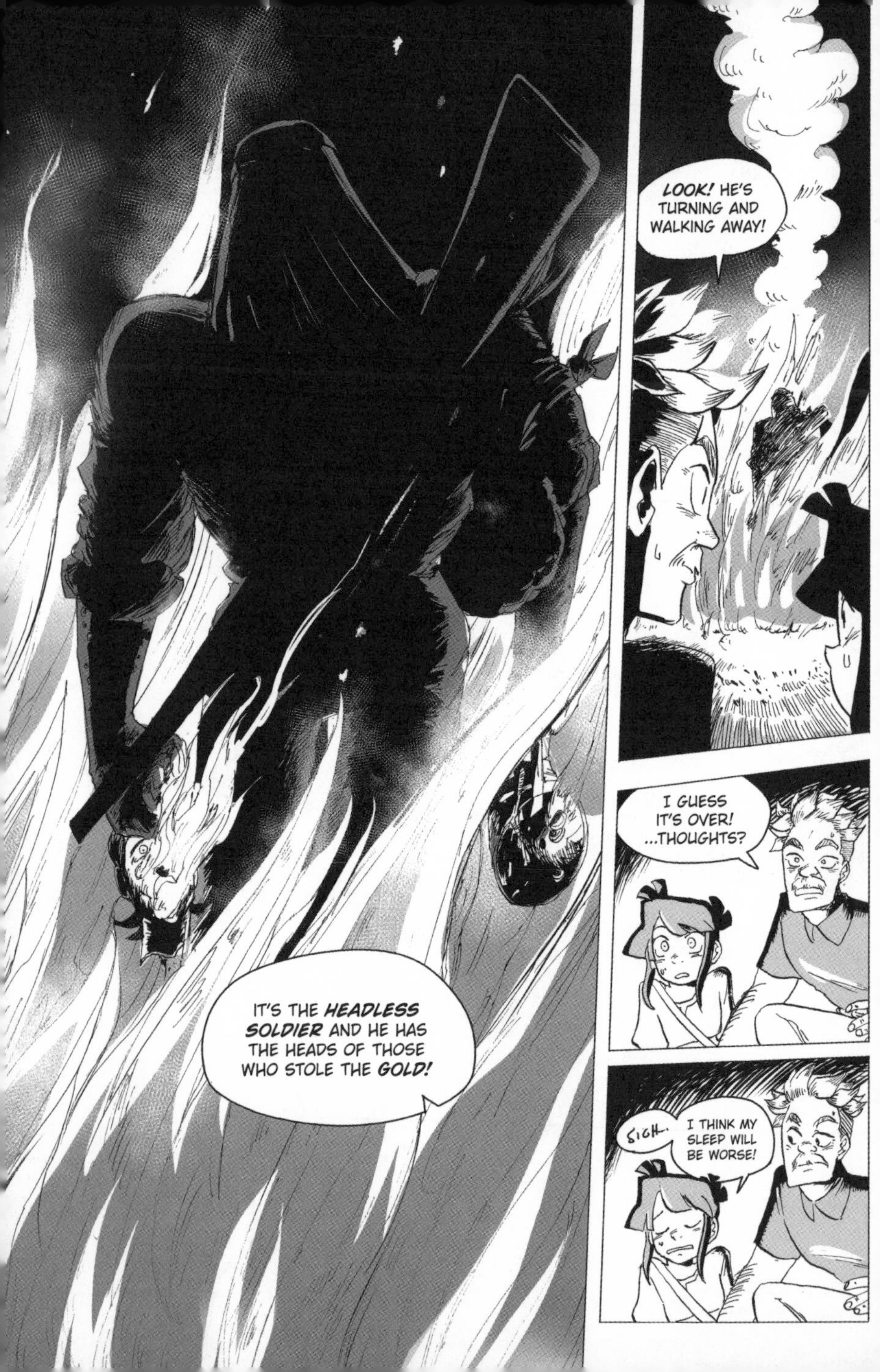
IT'S THE HEADLESS SOLDIER AND HE HAS THE HEADS OF THOSE WHO STOLE THE GOLD!
LOOK! HE'S TURNING AND WALKING AWAY!
I GUESS IT'S OVER! ...THOUGHTS?
SIGH.
I THINK MY SLEEP WILL BE WORSE!

YELLOW

STRINGER

Article 6: Meet-Cute

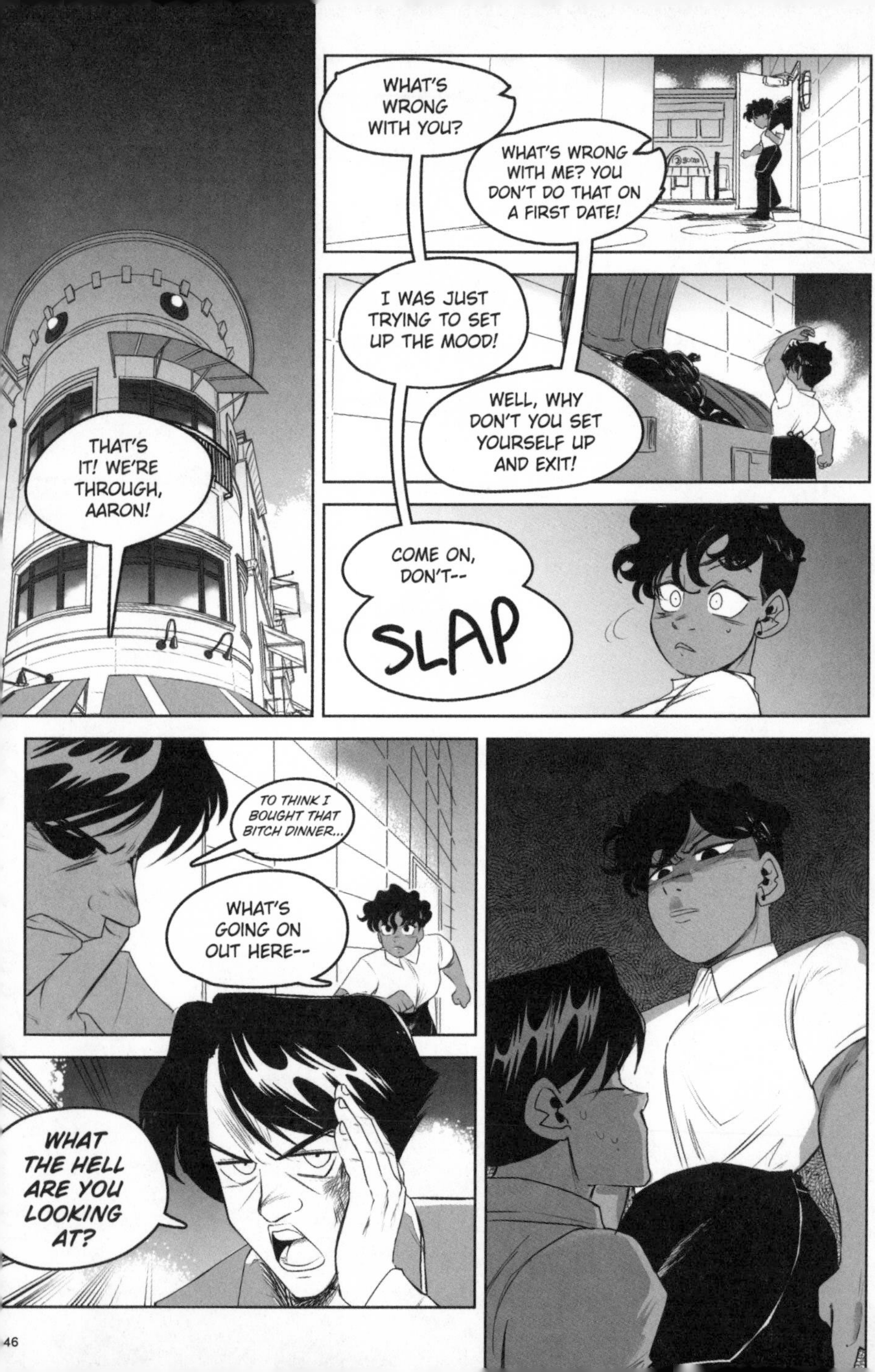
THAT'S IT! WE'RE THROUGH, AARON!
WHAT'S WRONG WITH YOU?
WHAT'S WRONG WITH ME? YOU DON'T DO THAT ON A FIRST DATE!
I WAS JUST TRYING TO SET UP THE MOOD!
WELL, WHY DON'T YOU SET YOURSELF UP AND EXIT!
COME ON, DON'T--
SLAP
TO THINK I BOUGHT THAT BITCH DINNER...
WHAT'S GOING ON OUT HERE--
WHAT THE HELL ARE YOU LOOKING AT?

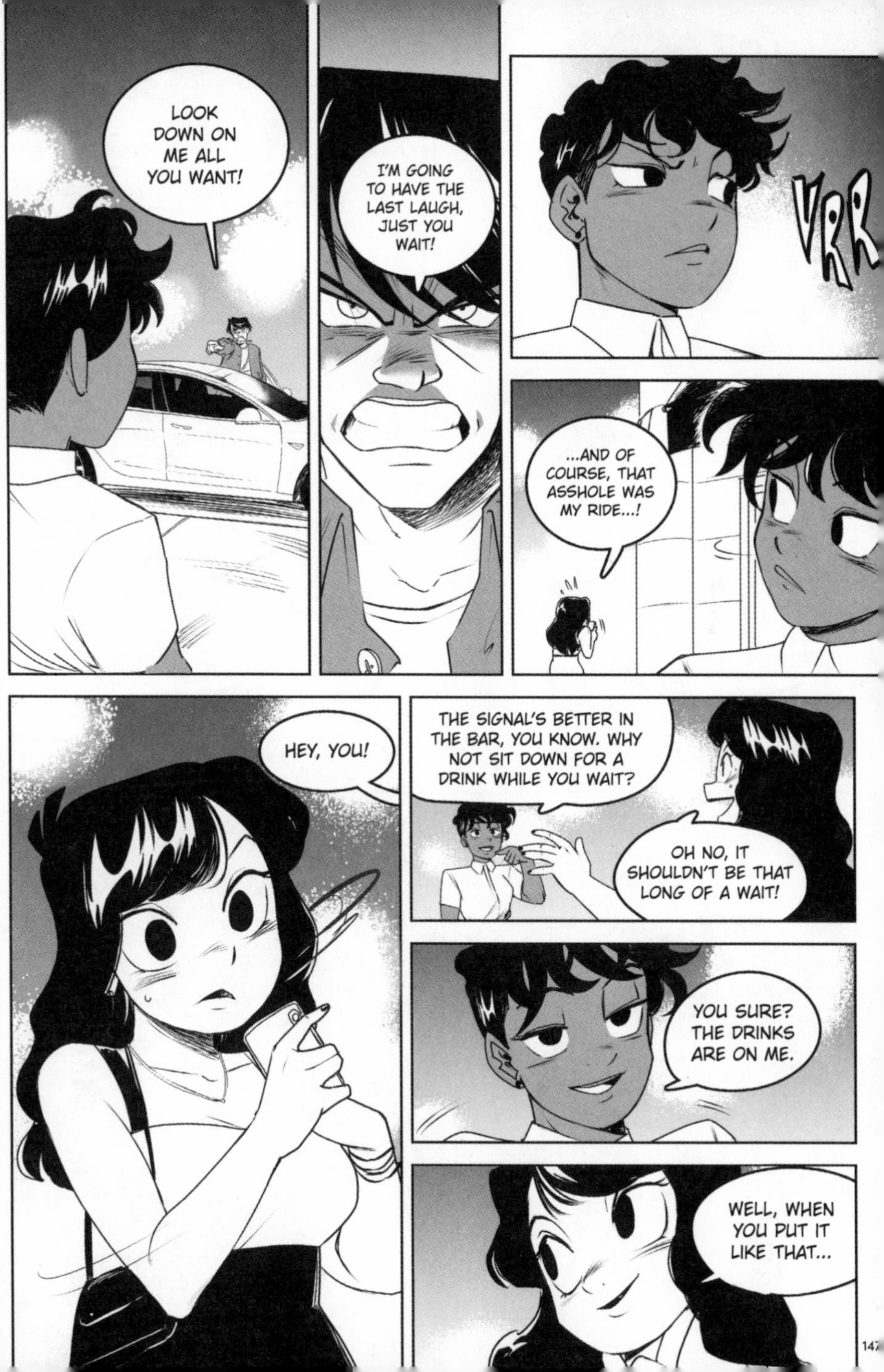
LOOK DOWN ON ME ALL YOU WANT!
I'M GOING TO HAVE THE LAST LAUGH, JUST YOU WAIT!
VRR
...AND OF COURSE, THAT ASSHOLE WAS MY RIDE...!
HEY, YOU!
THE SIGNAL'S BETTER IN THE BAR, YOU KNOW. WHY NOT SIT DOWN FOR A DRINK WHILE YOU WAIT?
OH NO, IT SHOULDN'T BE THAT LONG OF A WAIT!
YOU SURE? THE DRINKS ARE ON ME.
WELL, WHEN YOU PUT IT LIKE THAT...

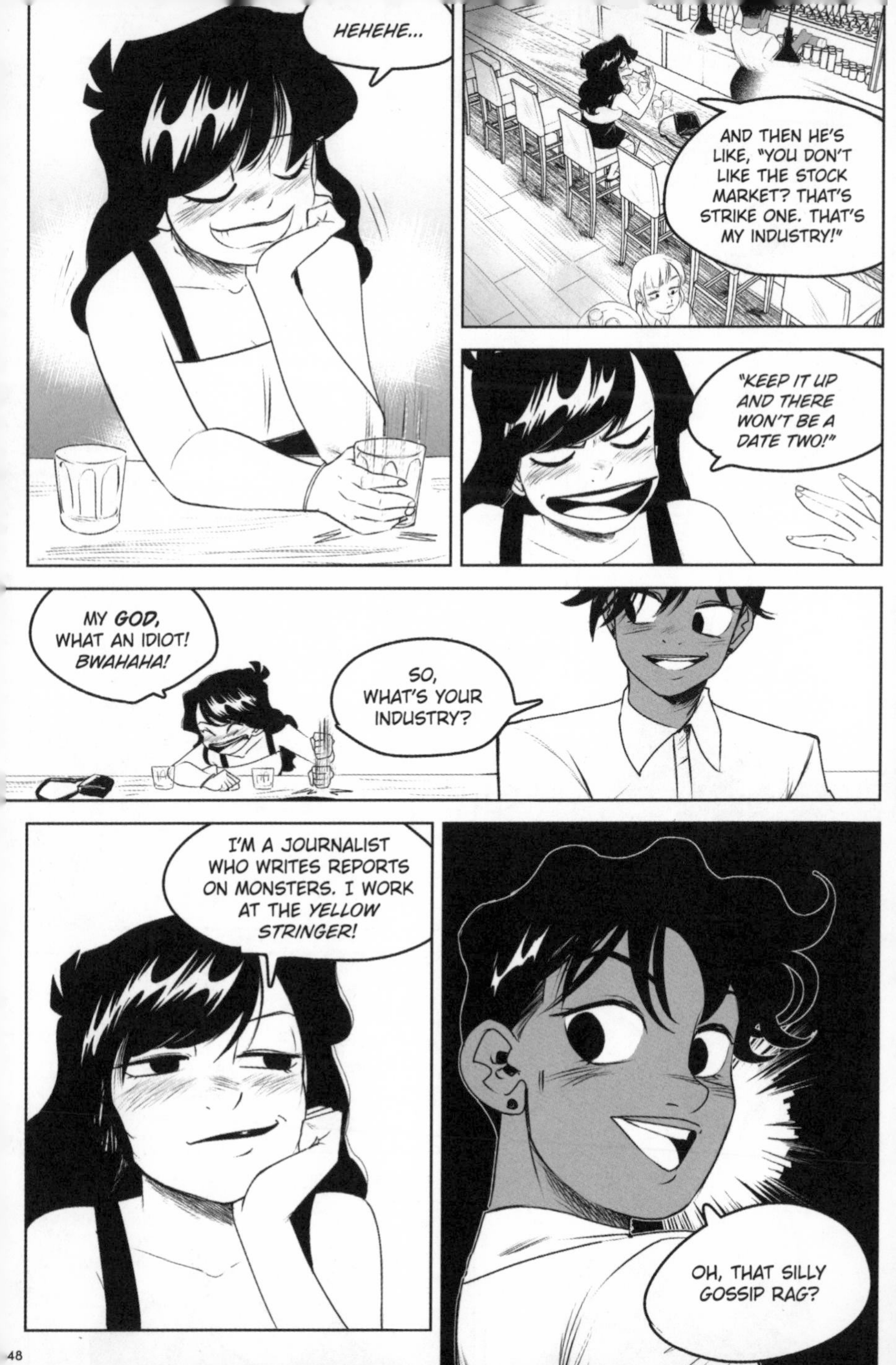
HEHEHE...
AND THEN HE'S LIKE, "YOU DON'T LIKE THE STOCK MARKET? THAT'S STRIKE ONE. THAT'S MY INDUSTRY!"
"KEEP IT UP AND THERE WON'T BE A DATE TWO!"
MY *GOD,* WHAT AN IDIOT! *BWAHAHA!*
SO, WHAT'S YOUR INDUSTRY?
I'M A JOURNALIST WHO WRITES REPORTS ON MONSTERS. I WORK AT THE *YELLOW STRINGER!*
OH, THAT SILLY GOSSIP RAG?

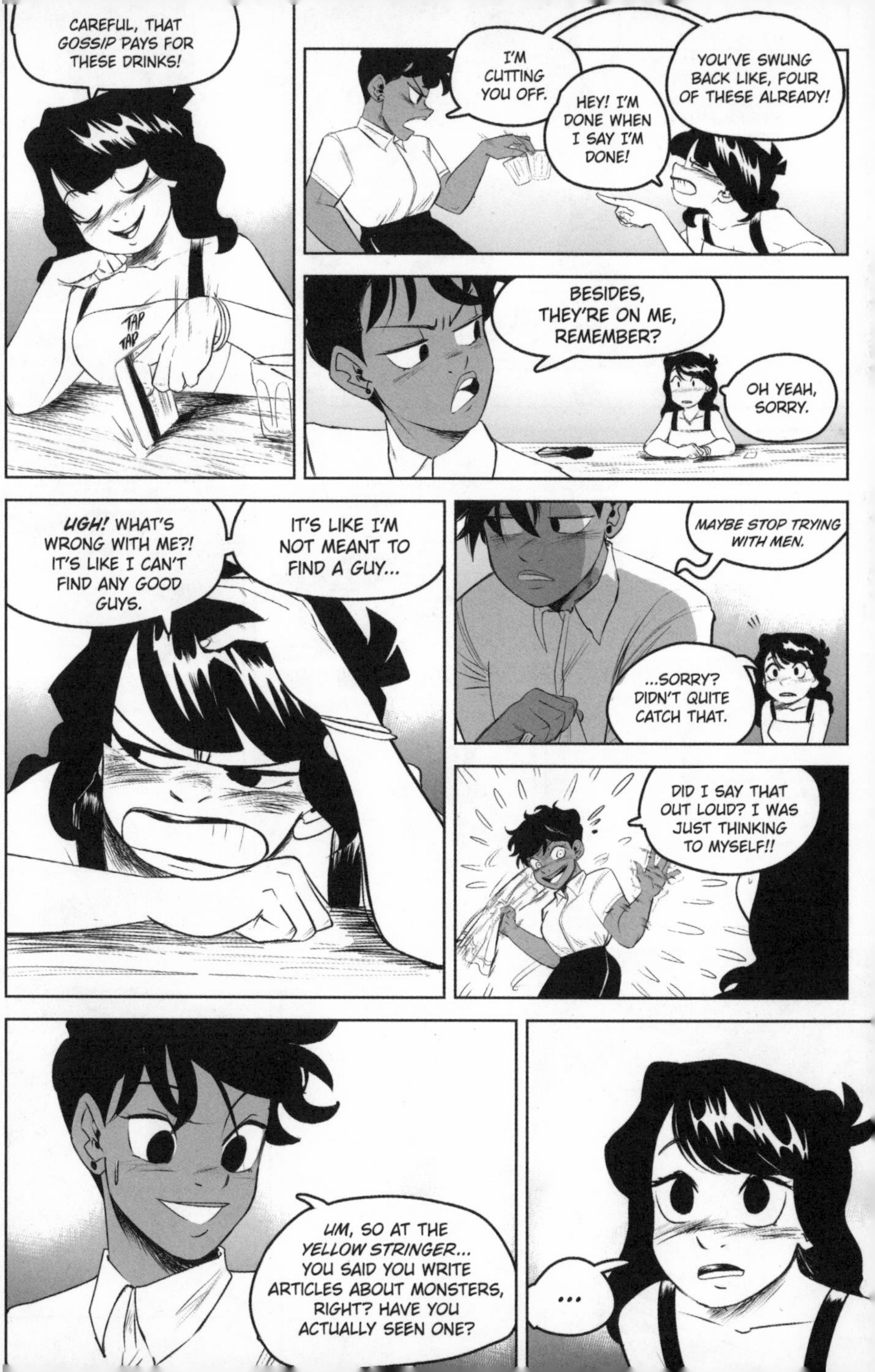
CAREFUL, THAT *GOSSIP* PAYS FOR THESE DRINKS!
TAP TAP
I'M CUTTING YOU OFF.
HEY! I'M DONE WHEN I SAY I'M DONE!
YOU'VE SWUNG BACK LIKE, FOUR OF THESE ALREADY!
BESIDES, THEY'RE ON ME, REMEMBER?
OH YEAH, SORRY.
UGH! WHAT'S WRONG WITH ME?! IT'S LIKE I CAN'T FIND ANY GOOD GUYS.
IT'S LIKE I'M NOT MEANT TO FIND A GUY...
MAYBE STOP TRYING WITH MEN.
...SORRY? DIDN'T QUITE CATCH THAT.
DID I SAY THAT OUT LOUD? I WAS JUST THINKING TO MYSELF!!
UM, SO AT THE *YELLOW STRINGER*... YOU SAID YOU WRITE ARTICLES ABOUT MONSTERS, RIGHT? HAVE YOU ACTUALLY SEEN ONE?
...

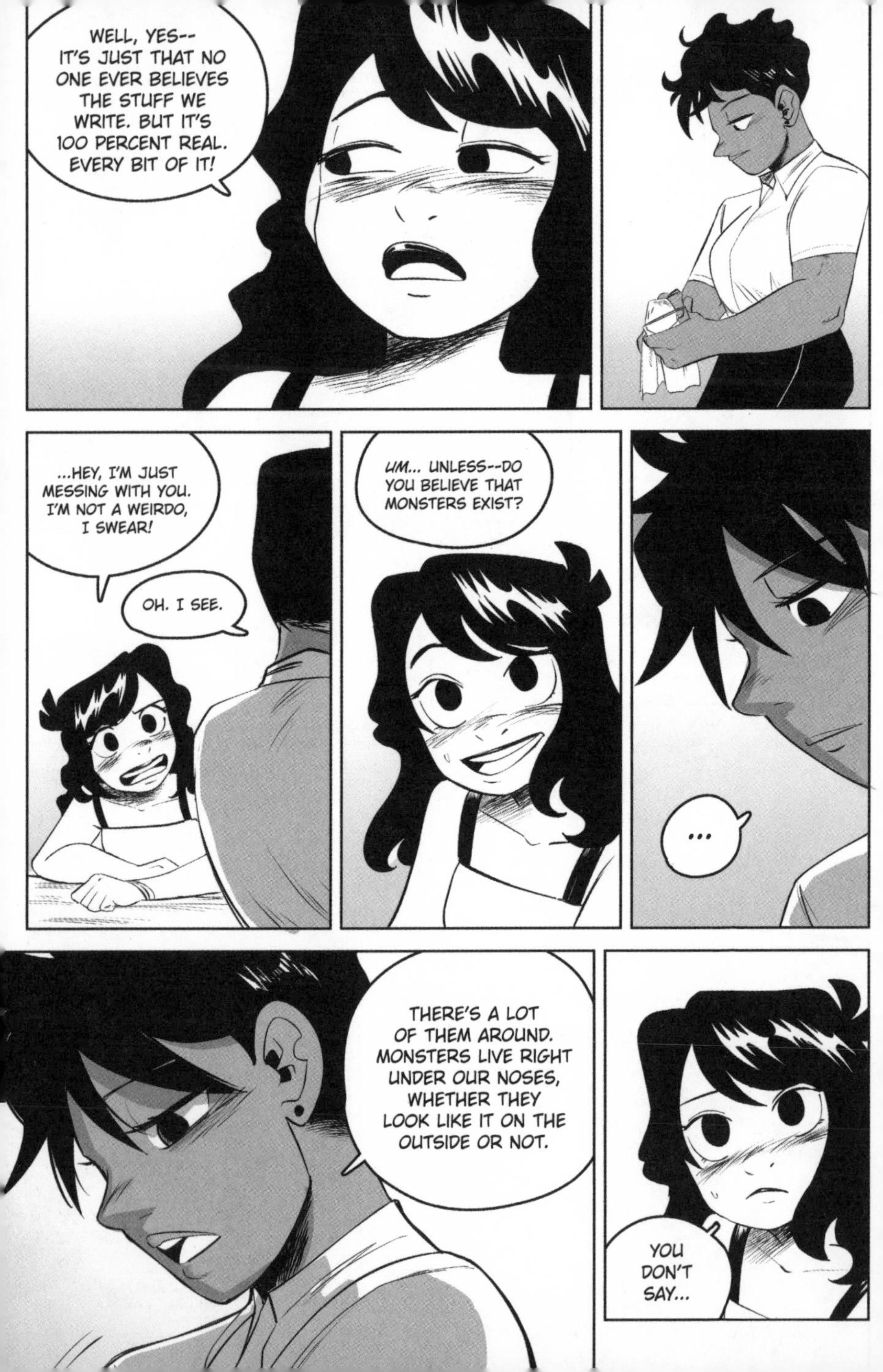
WELL, YES-- IT'S JUST THAT NO ONE EVER BELIEVES THE STUFF WE WRITE. BUT IT'S 100 PERCENT REAL. EVERY BIT OF IT!
...HEY, I'M JUST MESSING WITH YOU. I'M NOT A WEIRDO, I SWEAR!
OH. I SEE.
UM... UNLESS--DO YOU BELIEVE THAT MONSTERS EXIST?
...
THERE'S A LOT OF THEM AROUND. MONSTERS LIVE RIGHT UNDER OUR NOSES, WHETHER THEY LOOK LIKE IT ON THE OUTSIDE OR NOT.
YOU DON'T SAY...

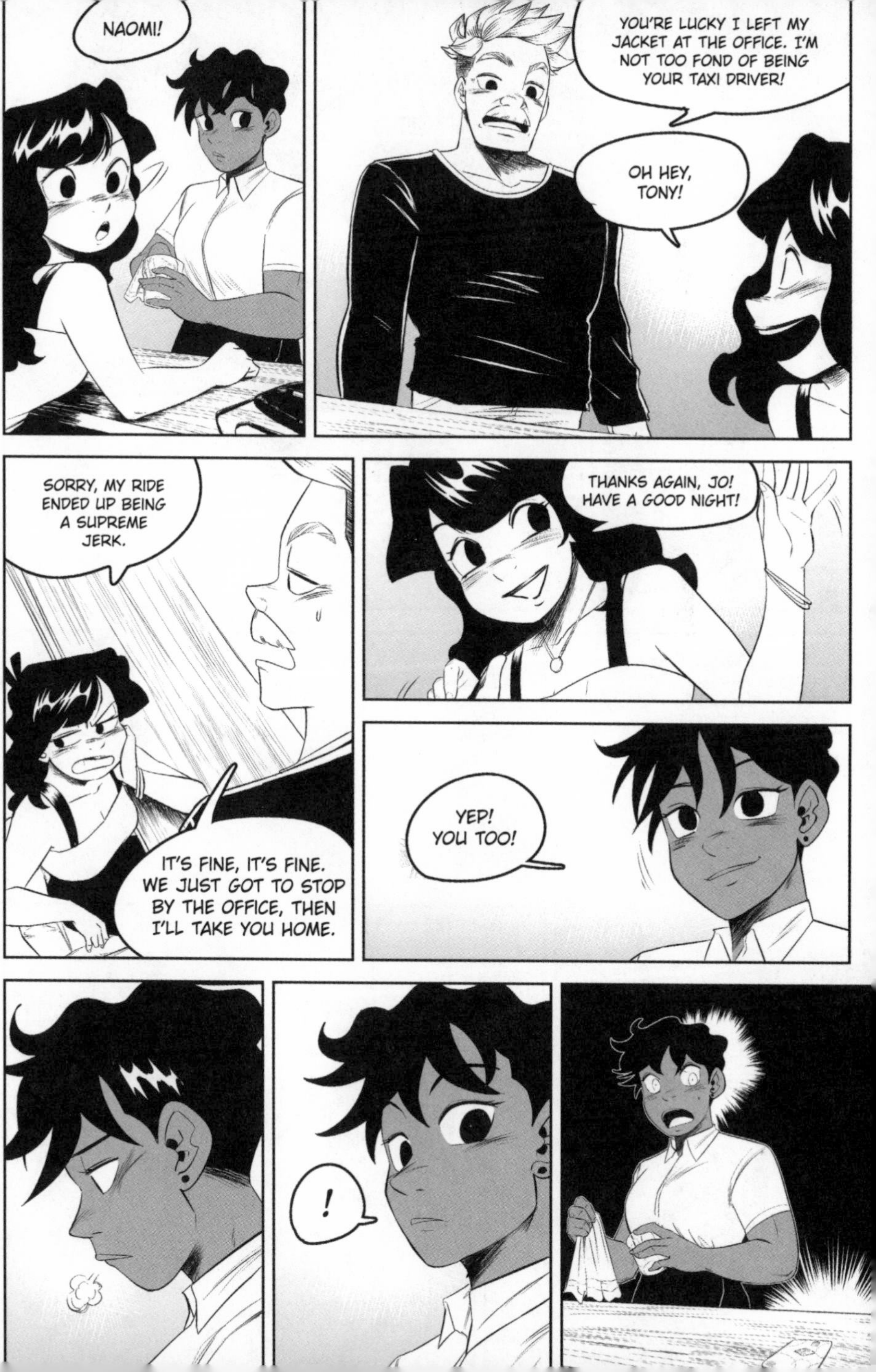
NAOMI!
YOU'RE LUCKY I LEFT MY JACKET AT THE OFFICE. I'M NOT TOO FOND OF BEING YOUR TAXI DRIVER!
OH HEY, TONY!
SORRY, MY RIDE ENDED UP BEING A SUPREME JERK.
IT'S FINE, IT'S FINE. WE JUST GOT TO STOP BY THE OFFICE, THEN I'LL TAKE YOU HOME.
THANKS AGAIN, JO! HAVE A GOOD NIGHT!
YEP! YOU TOO!
!

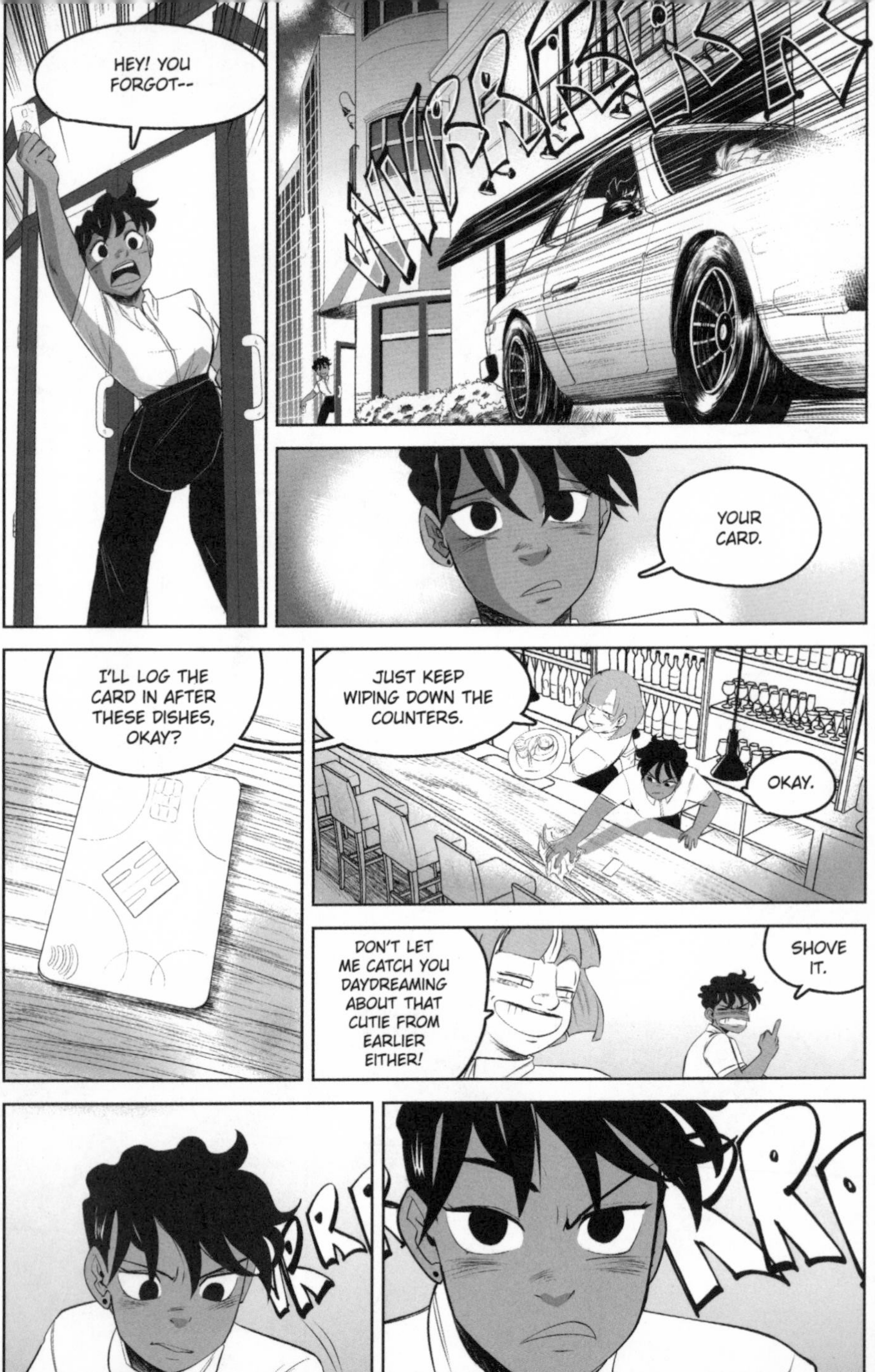
HEY! YOU FORGOT--
YOUR CARD.
I'LL LOG THE CARD IN AFTER THESE DISHES, OKAY?
JUST KEEP WIPING DOWN THE COUNTERS.
OKAY.
DON'T LET ME CATCH YOU DAYDREAMING ABOUT THAT CUTIE FROM EARLIER EITHER!
SHOVE IT.

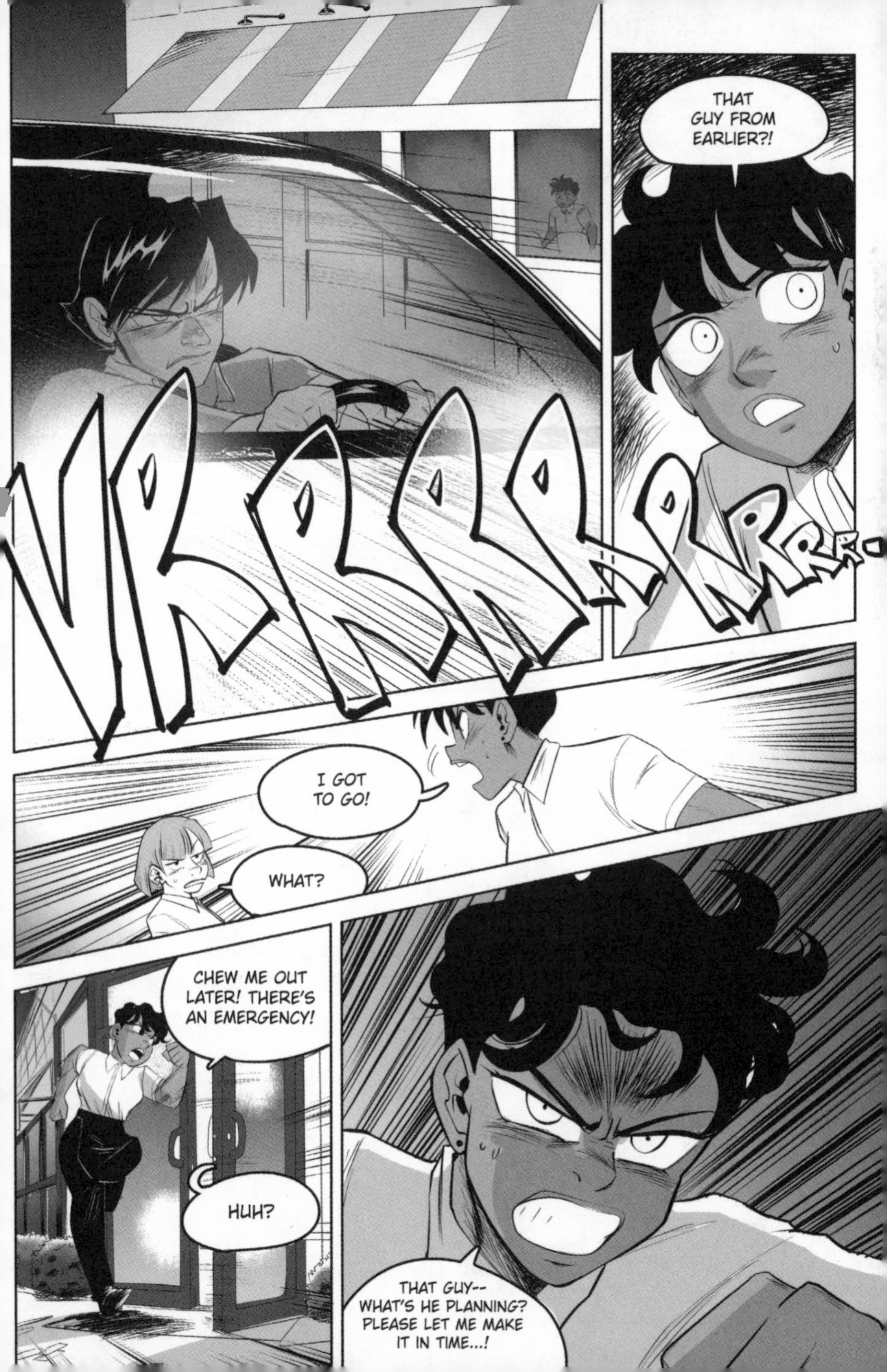

VRRRRRRRR
THAT GUY FROM EARLIER?!
I GOT TO GO!
WHAT?
CHEW ME OUT LATER! THERE'S AN EMERGENCY!
HUH?
THAT GUY-- WHAT'S HE PLANNING? PLEASE LET ME MAKE IT IN TIME...!

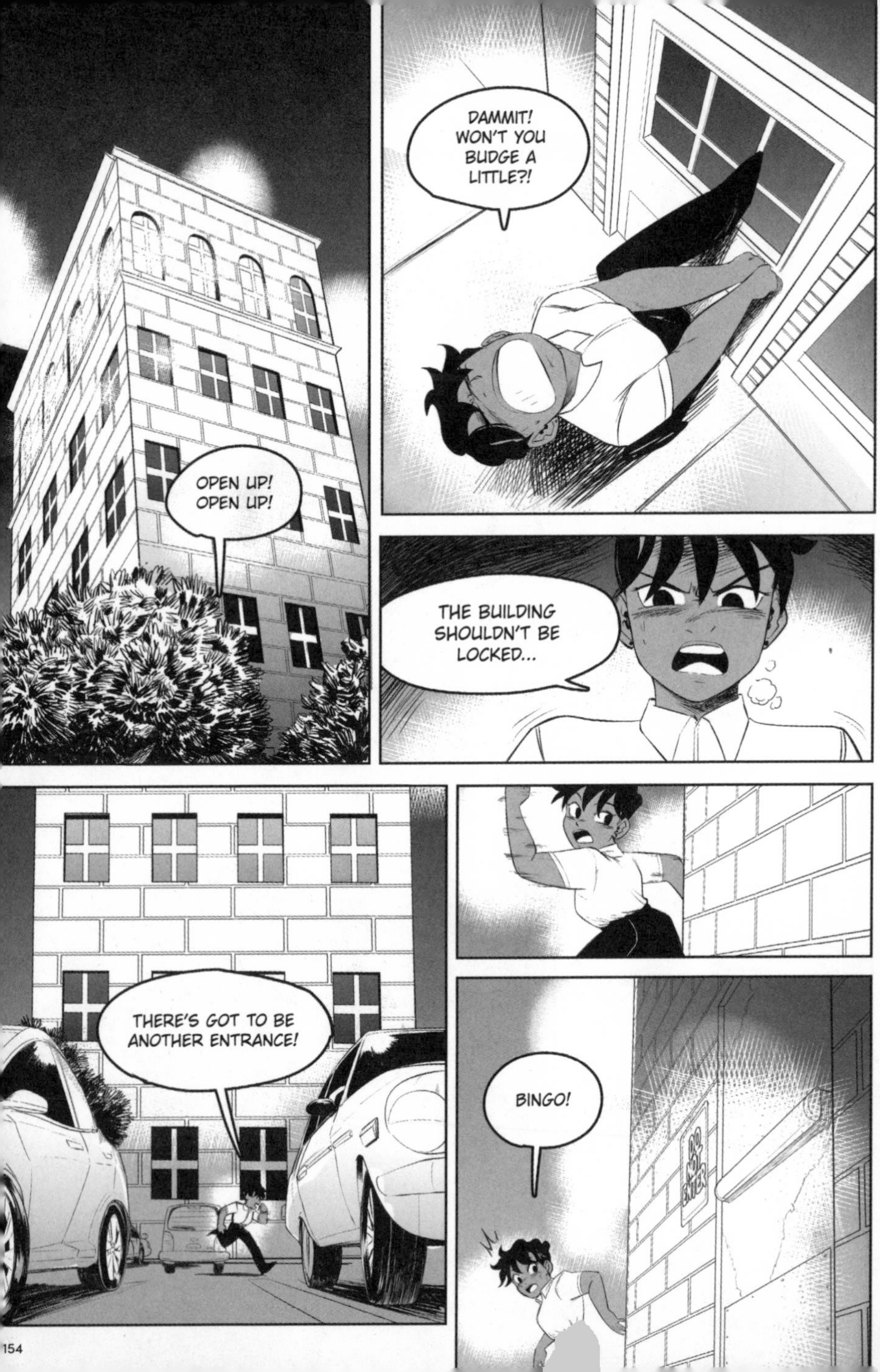
OPEN UP! OPEN UP!
DAMMIT! WON'T YOU BUDGE A LITTLE?!
THE BUILDING SHOULDN'T BE LOCKED...
THERE'S GOT TO BE ANOTHER ENTRANCE!
BINGO!

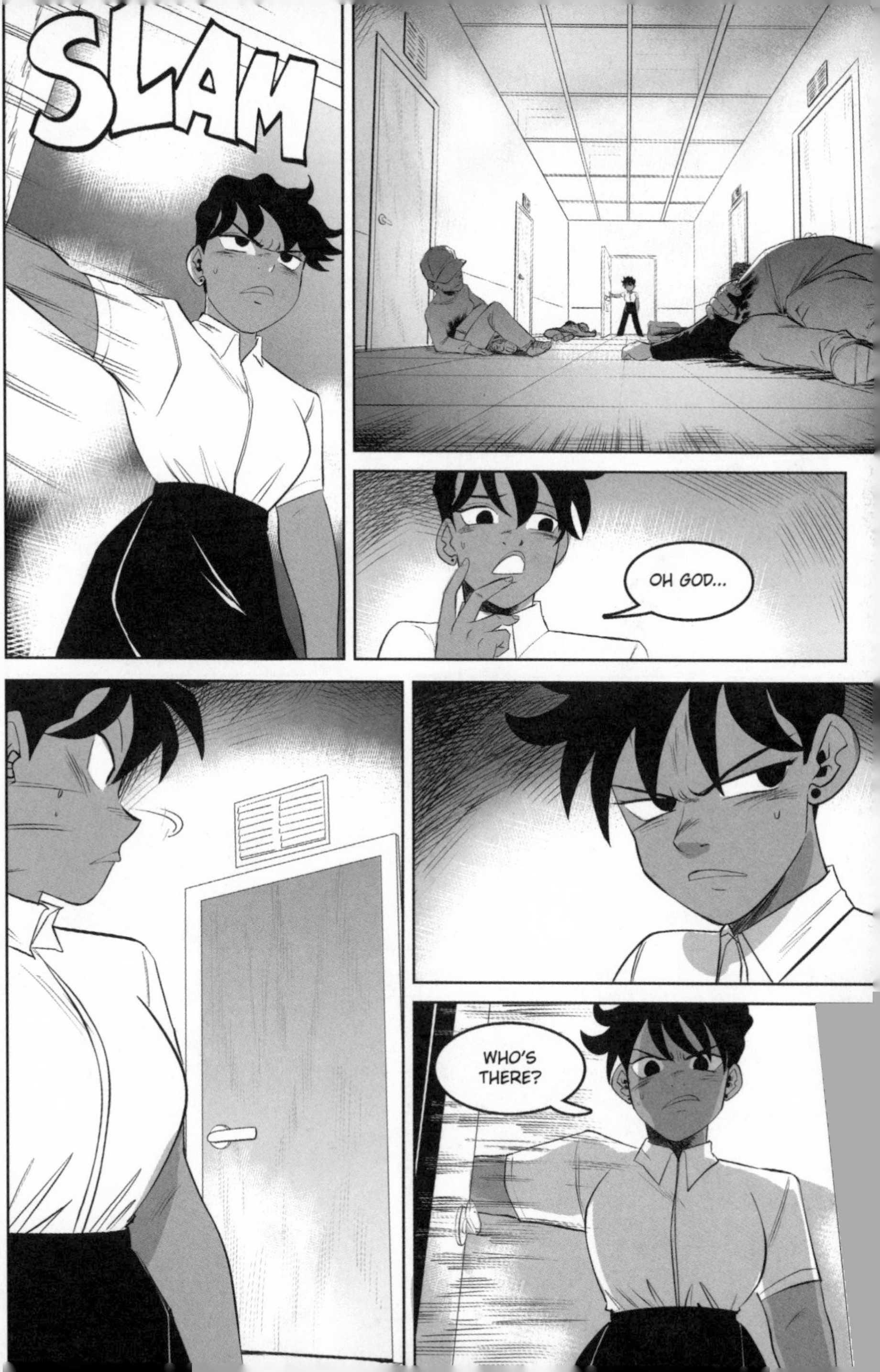
SLAM
OH GOD...
WHO'S THERE?

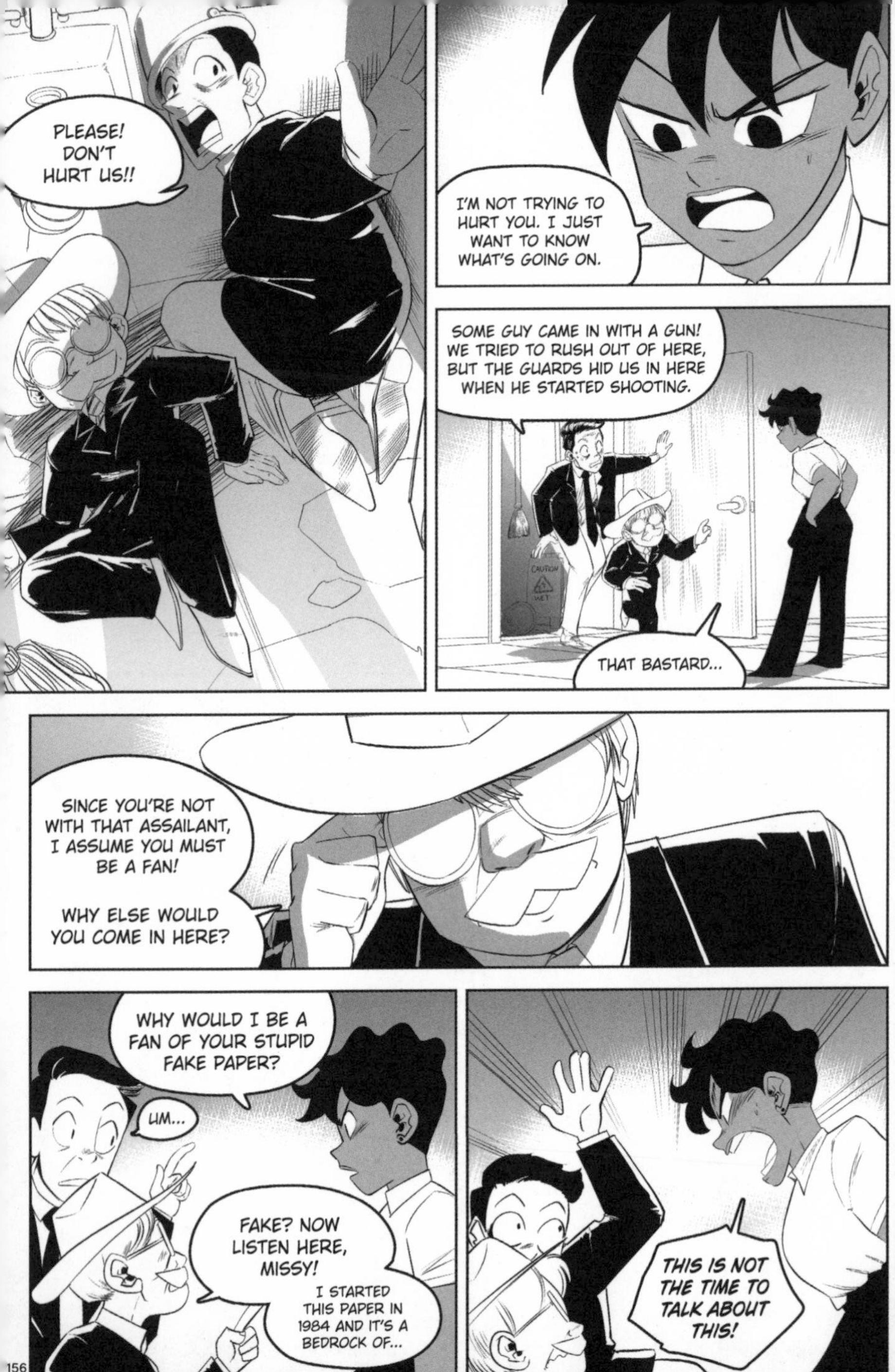
PLEASE! DON'T HURT US!!
I'M NOT TRYING TO HURT YOU. I JUST WANT TO KNOW WHAT'S GOING ON.
SOME GUY CAME IN WITH A GUN! WE TRIED TO RUSH OUT OF HERE, BUT THE GUARDS HID US IN HERE WHEN HE STARTED SHOOTING.
CAUTION WET
THAT BASTARD...
SINCE YOU'RE NOT WITH THAT ASSAILANT, I ASSUME YOU MUST BE A FAN!
WHY ELSE WOULD YOU COME IN HERE?
WHY WOULD I BE A FAN OF YOUR STUPID FAKE PAPER?
UM...
FAKE? NOW LISTEN HERE, MISSY!
I STARTED THIS PAPER IN 1984 AND IT'S A BEDROCK OF...
THIS IS NOT THE TIME TO TALK ABOUT THIS!

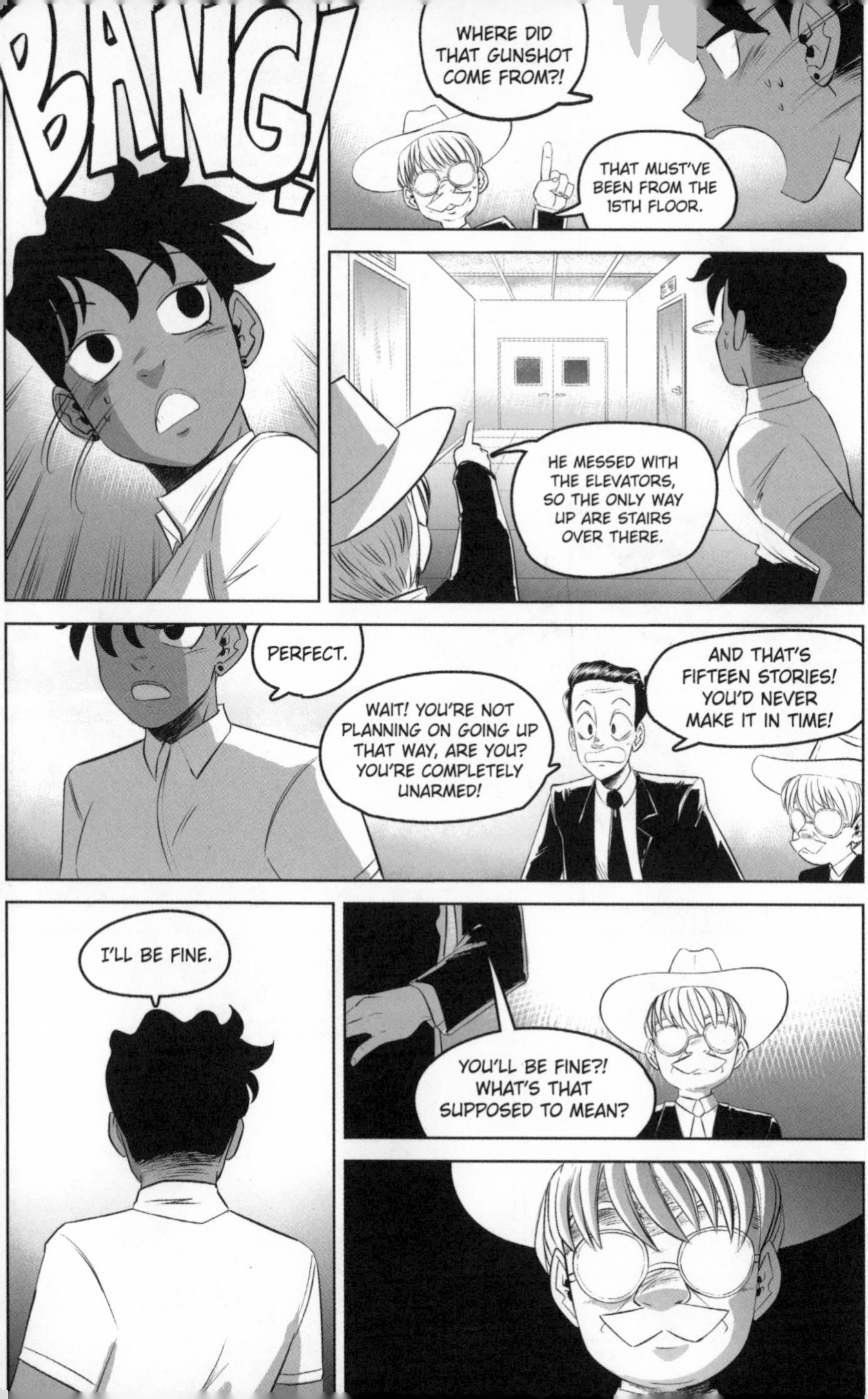
BANG!
WHERE DID THAT GUNSHOT COME FROM?!
THAT MUST'VE BEEN FROM THE 15TH FLOOR.
HE MESSED WITH THE ELEVATORS, SO THE ONLY WAY UP ARE STAIRS OVER THERE.
PERFECT.
WAIT! YOU'RE NOT PLANNING ON GOING UP THAT WAY, ARE YOU? YOU'RE COMPLETELY UNARMED!
AND THAT'S FIFTEEN STORIES! YOU'D NEVER MAKE IT IN TIME!
I'LL BE FINE.
YOU'LL BE FINE?! WHAT'S THAT SUPPOSED TO MEAN?

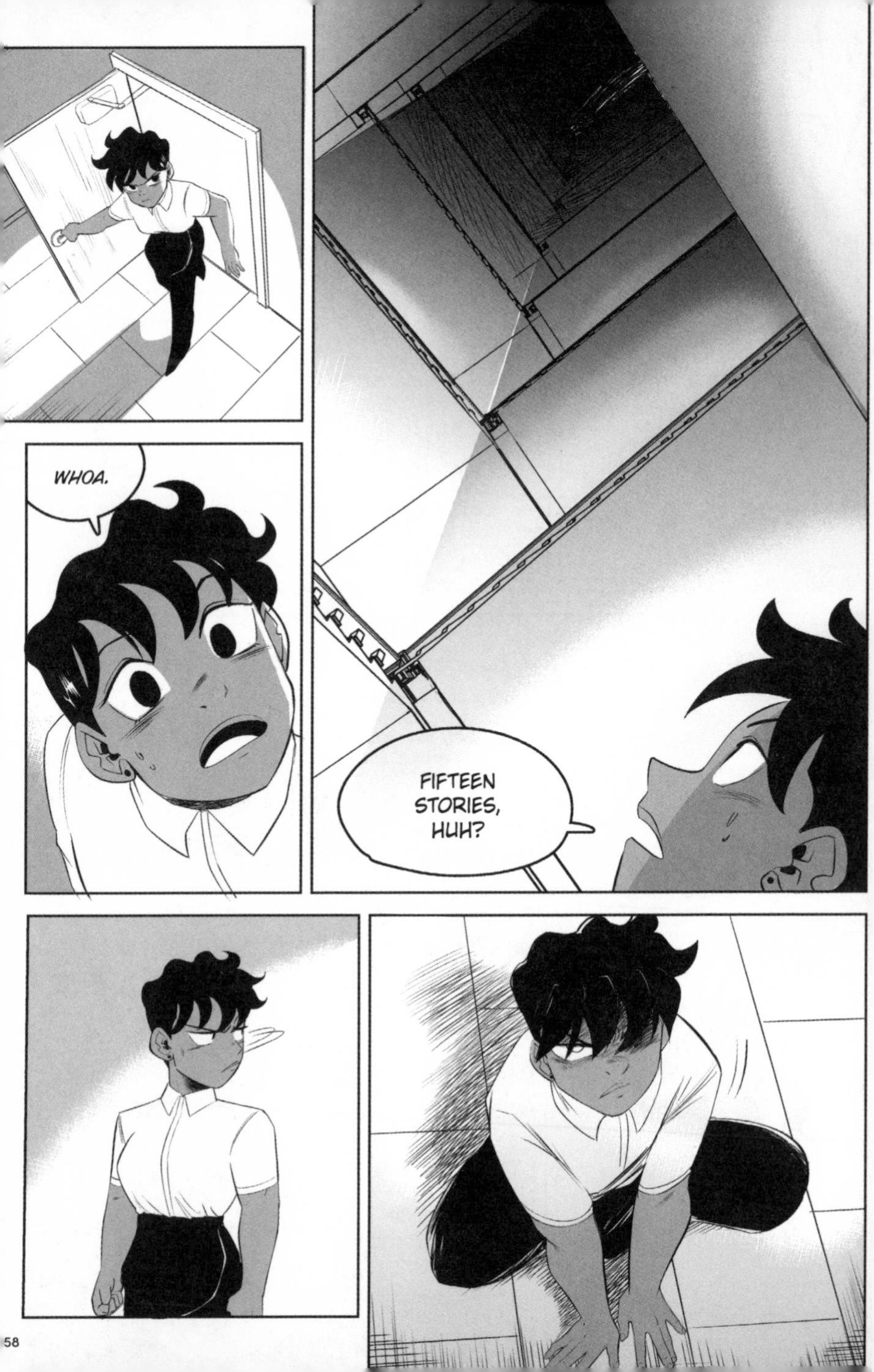
WHOA.
FIFTEEN STORIES, HUH?

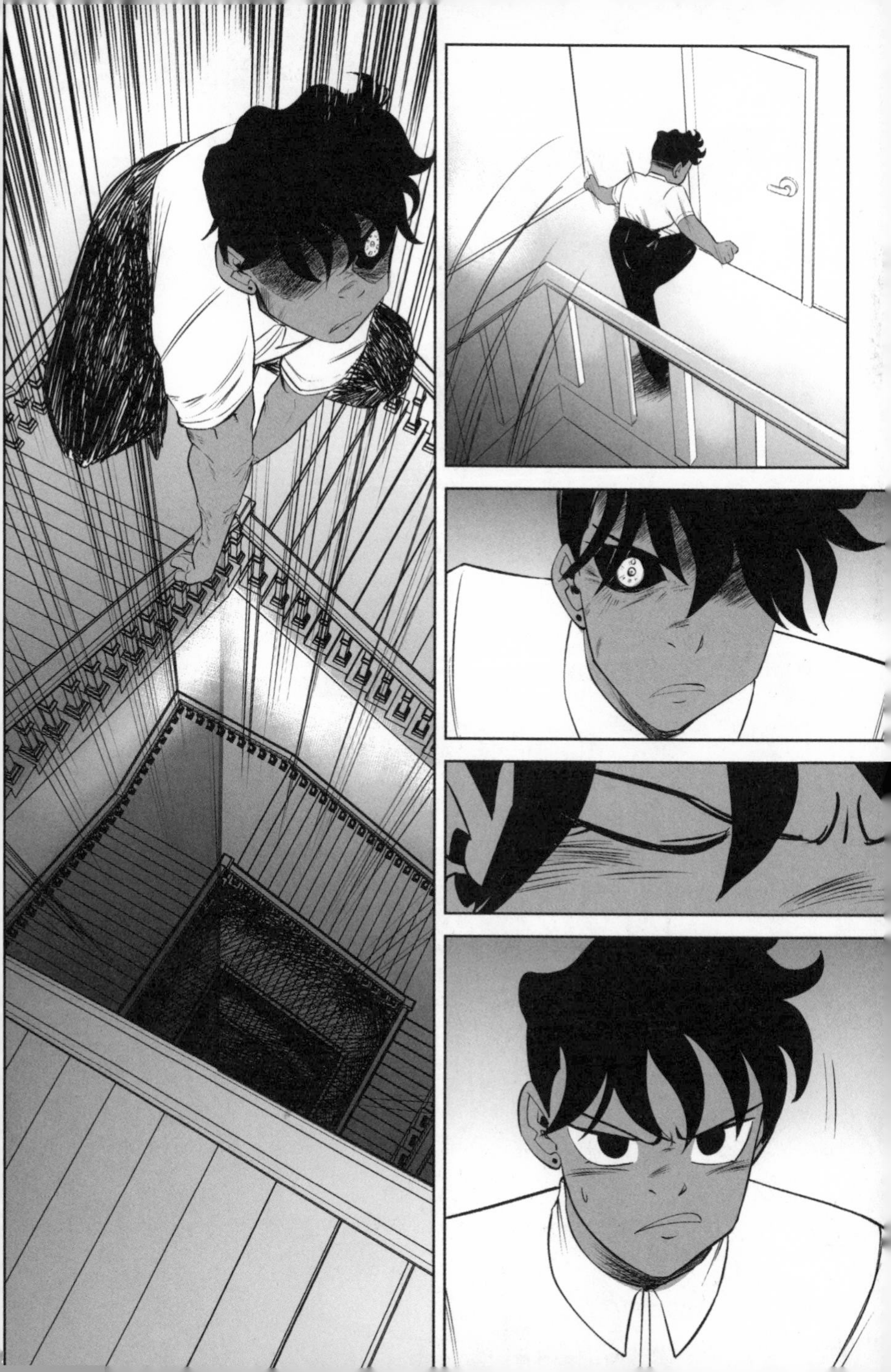

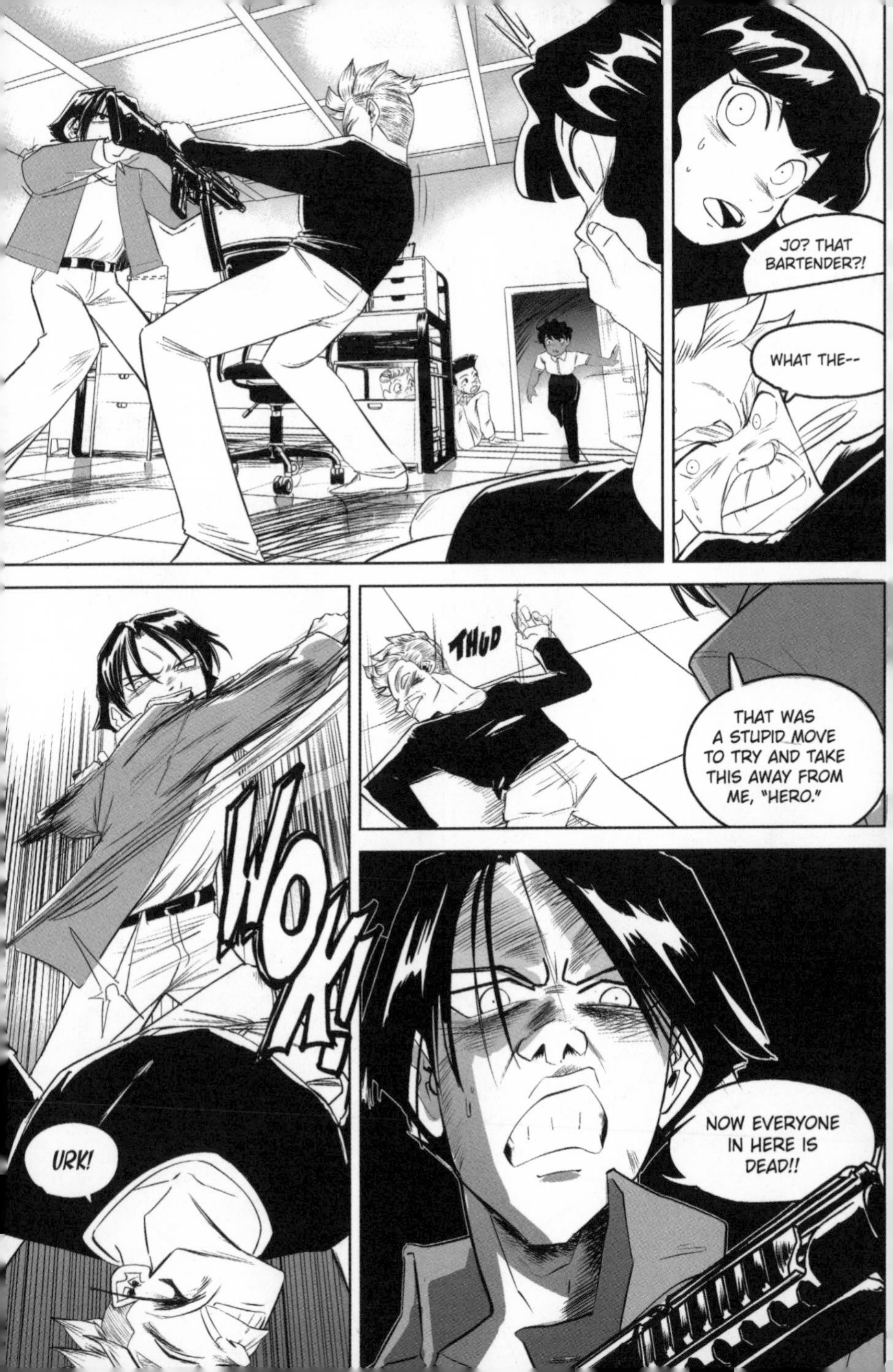
JO? THAT BARTENDER?!
WHAT THE--
URK!
THUD
THAT WAS A STUPID MOVE TO TRY AND TAKE THIS AWAY FROM ME, "HERO."
NOW EVERYONE IN HERE IS DEAD!!

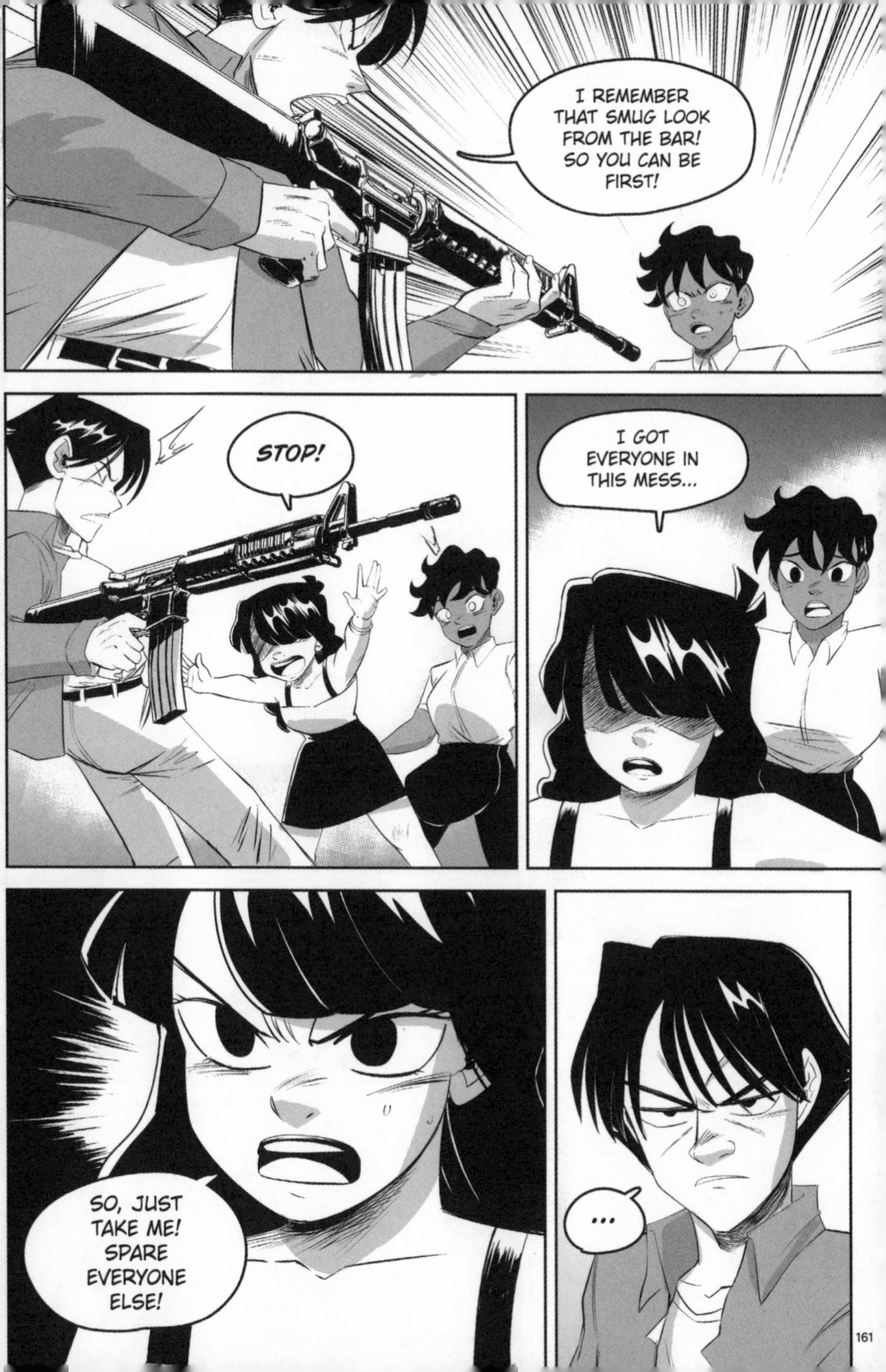

I REMEMBER THAT SMUG LOOK FROM THE BAR! SO YOU CAN BE FIRST!
STOP!
I GOT EVERYONE IN THIS MESS...
SO, JUST TAKE ME! SPARE EVERYONE ELSE!
...

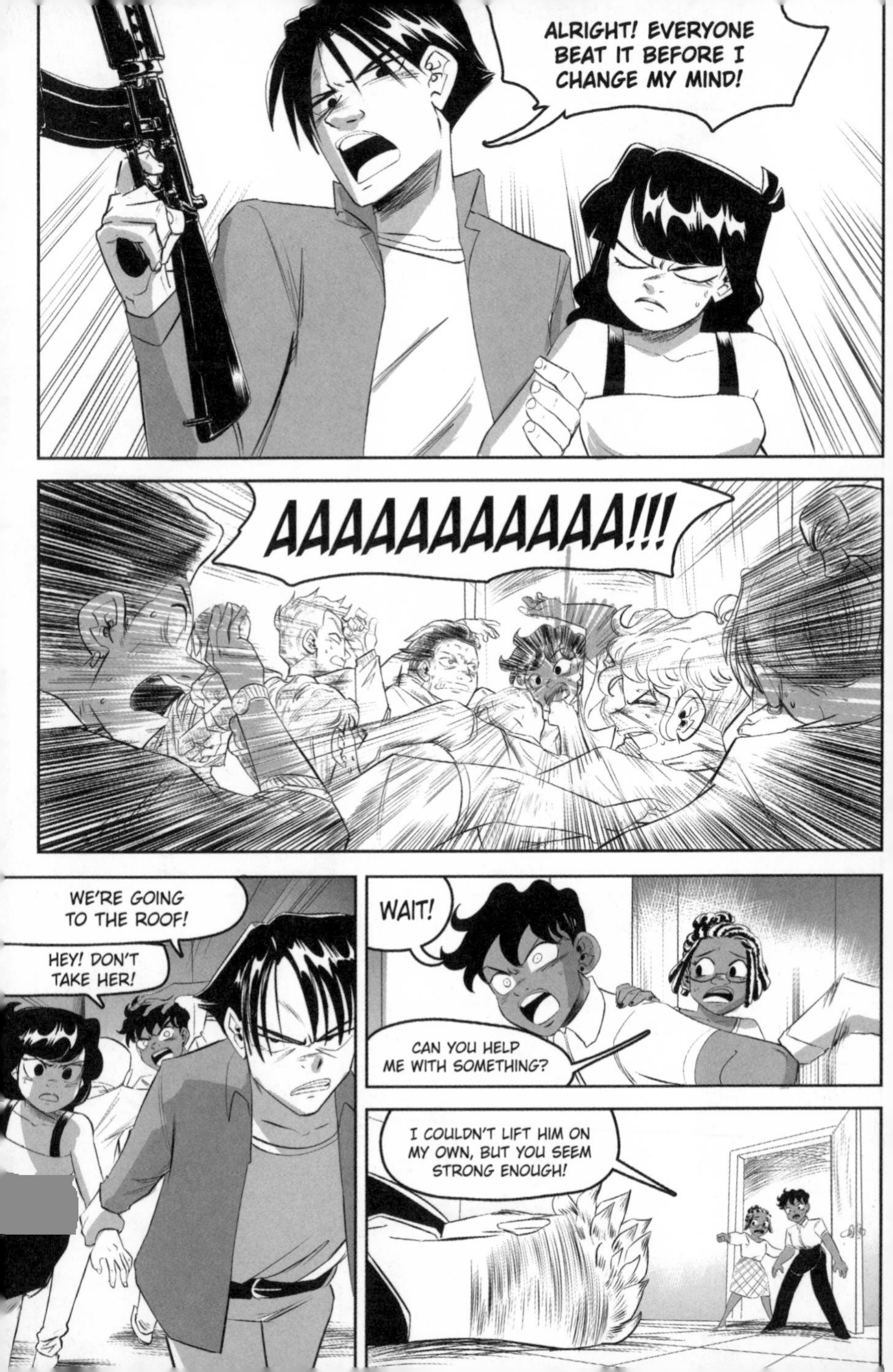
ALRIGHT! EVERYONE BEAT IT BEFORE I CHANGE MY MIND!
AAAAAAAAAAA!!!
WE'RE GOING TO THE ROOF!
HEY! DON'T TAKE HER!
WAIT!
CAN YOU HELP ME WITH SOMETHING?
I COULDN'T LIFT HIM ON MY OWN, BUT YOU SEEM STRONG ENOUGH!

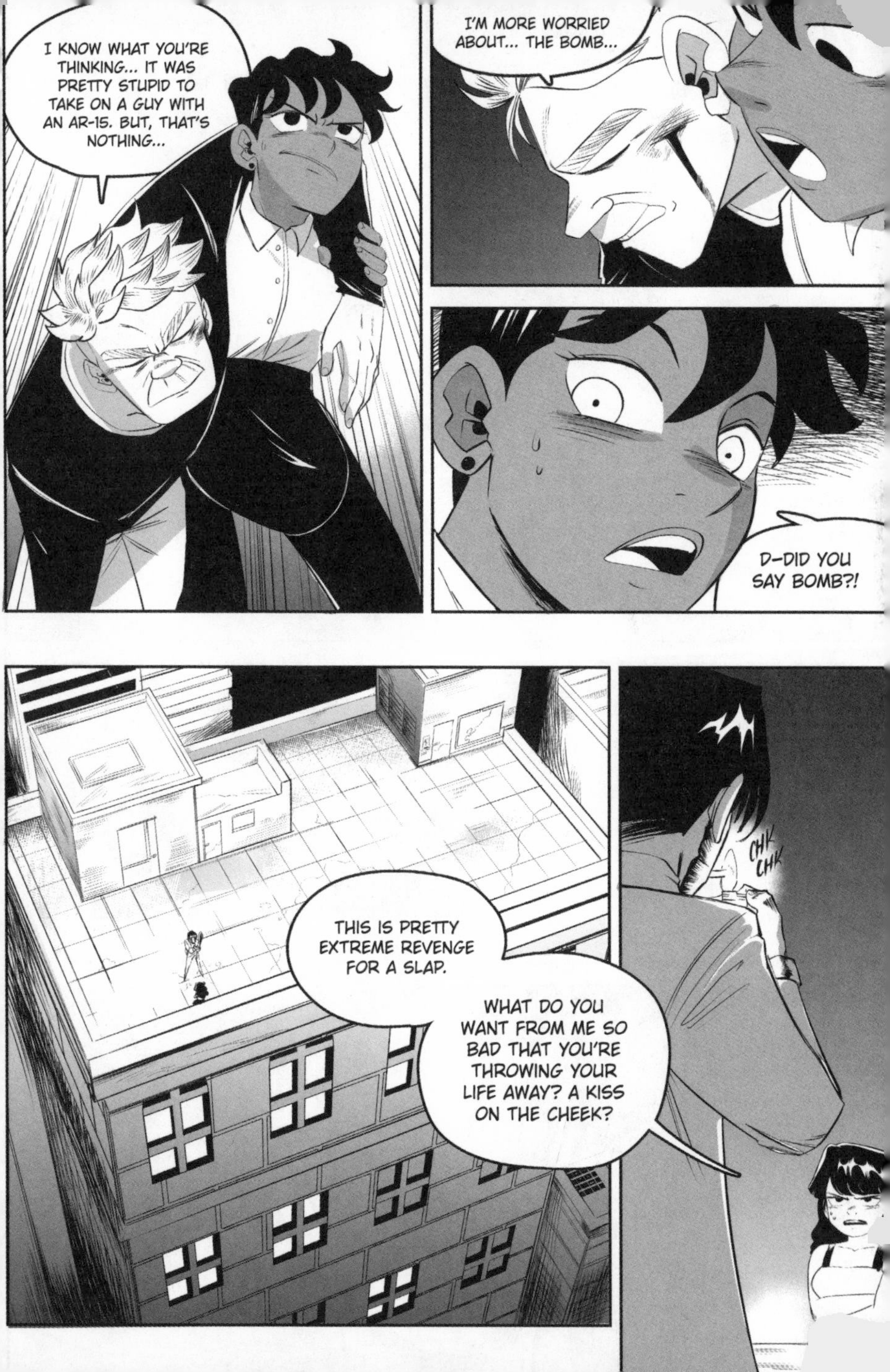
I KNOW WHAT YOU'RE THINKING... IT WAS PRETTY STUPID TO TAKE ON A GUY WITH AN AR-15. BUT, THAT'S NOTHING...
I'M MORE WORRIED ABOUT... THE BOMB...
D-DID YOU SAY BOMB?!
THIS IS PRETTY EXTREME REVENGE FOR A SLAP.
WHAT DO YOU WANT FROM ME SO BAD THAT YOU'RE THROWING YOUR LIFE AWAY? A KISS ON THE CHEEK?
CHK CHK

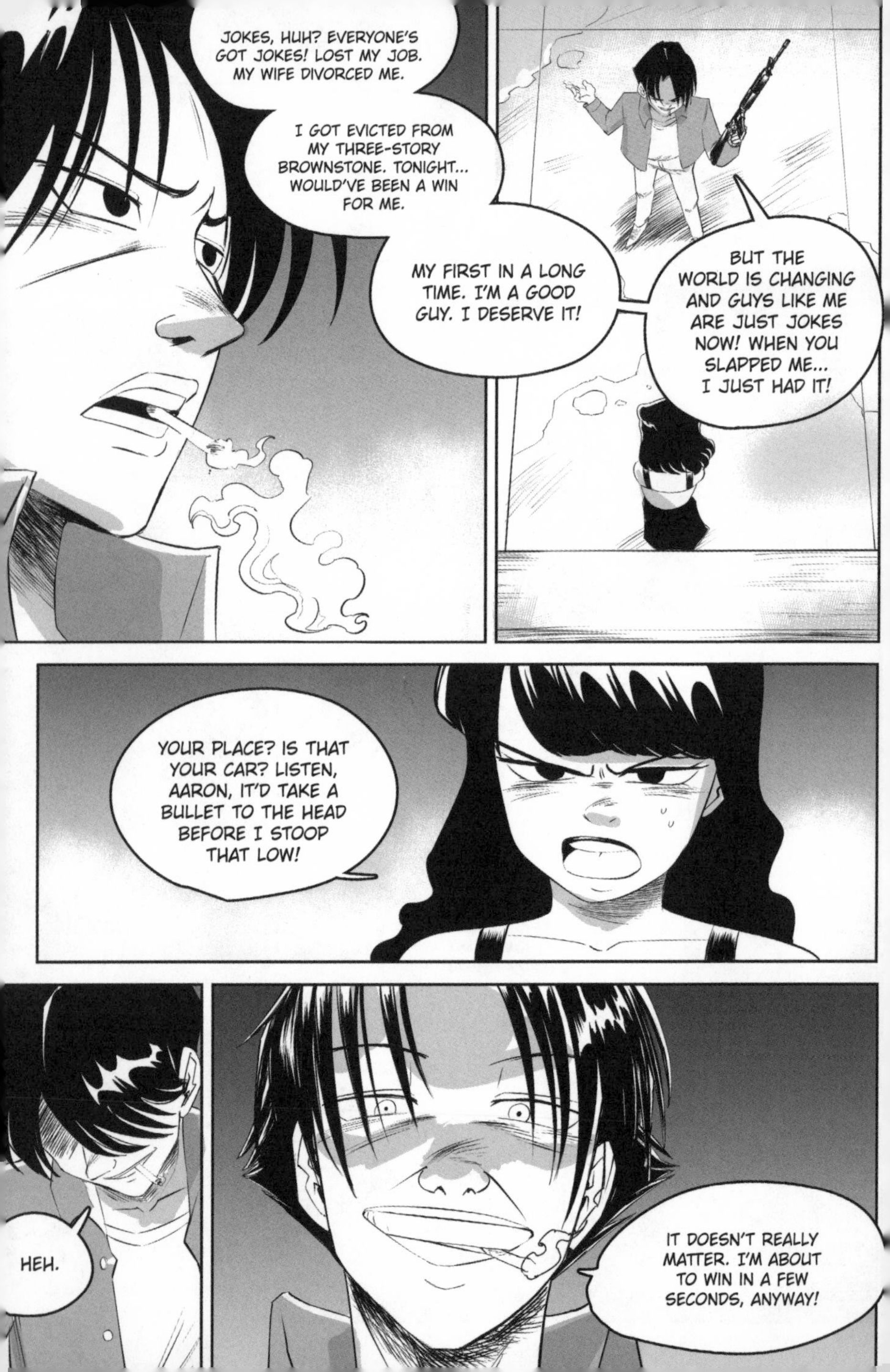
JOKES, HUH? EVERYONE'S GOT JOKES! LOST MY JOB. MY WIFE DIVORCED ME.
I GOT EVICTED FROM MY THREE-STORY BROWNSTONE. TONIGHT... WOULD'VE BEEN A WIN FOR ME.
MY FIRST IN A LONG TIME. I'M A GOOD GUY. I DESERVE IT!
BUT THE WORLD IS CHANGING AND GUYS LIKE ME ARE JUST JOKES NOW! WHEN YOU SLAPPED ME... I JUST HAD IT!
YOUR PLACE? IS THAT YOUR CAR? LISTEN, AARON, IT'D TAKE A BULLET TO THE HEAD BEFORE I STOOP THAT LOW!
HEH.
IT DOESN'T REALLY MATTER. I'M ABOUT TO WIN IN A FEW SECONDS, ANYWAY!

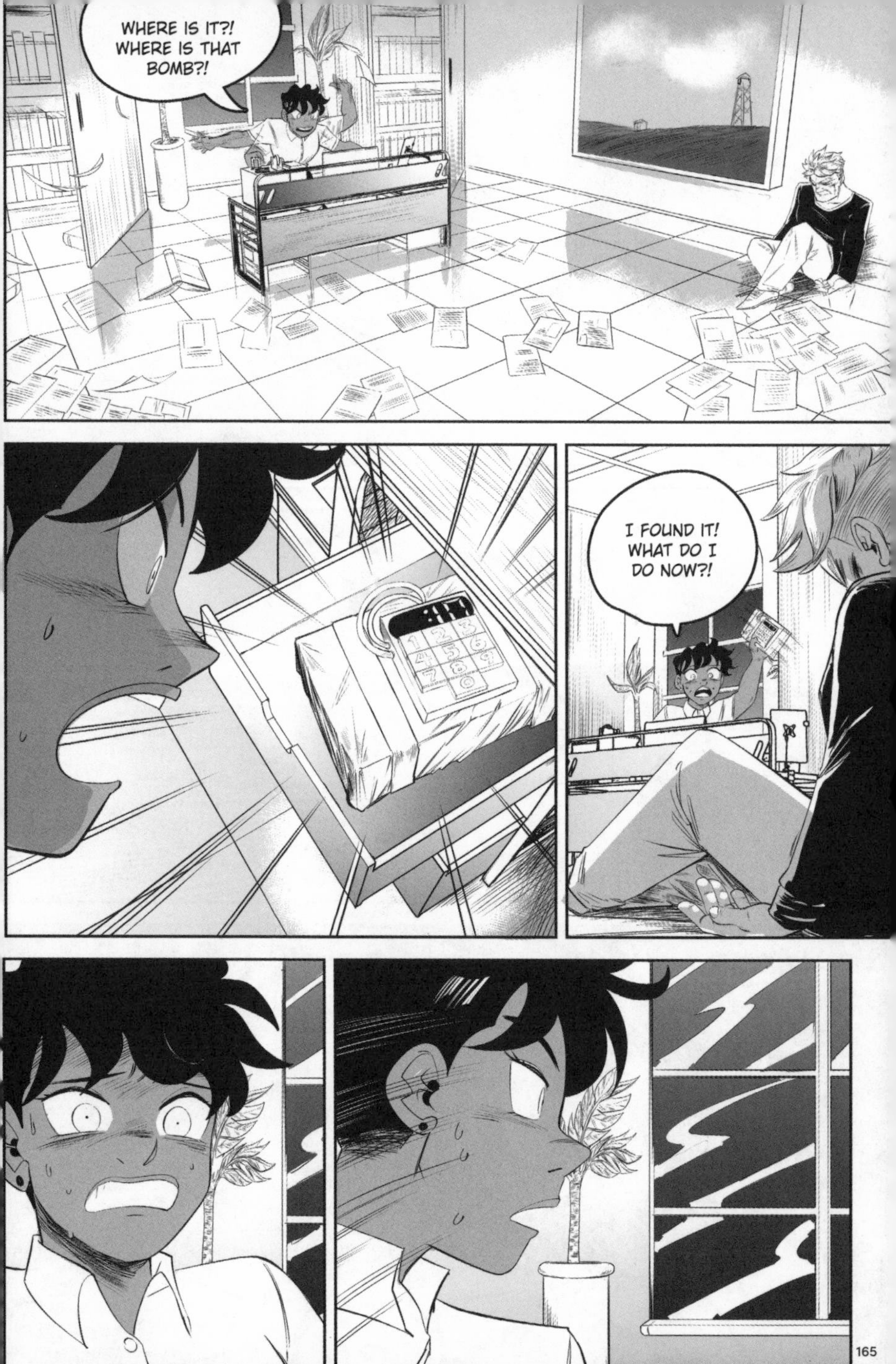
WHERE IS IT?! WHERE IS THAT BOMB?!
I FOUND IT! WHAT DO I DO NOW?!

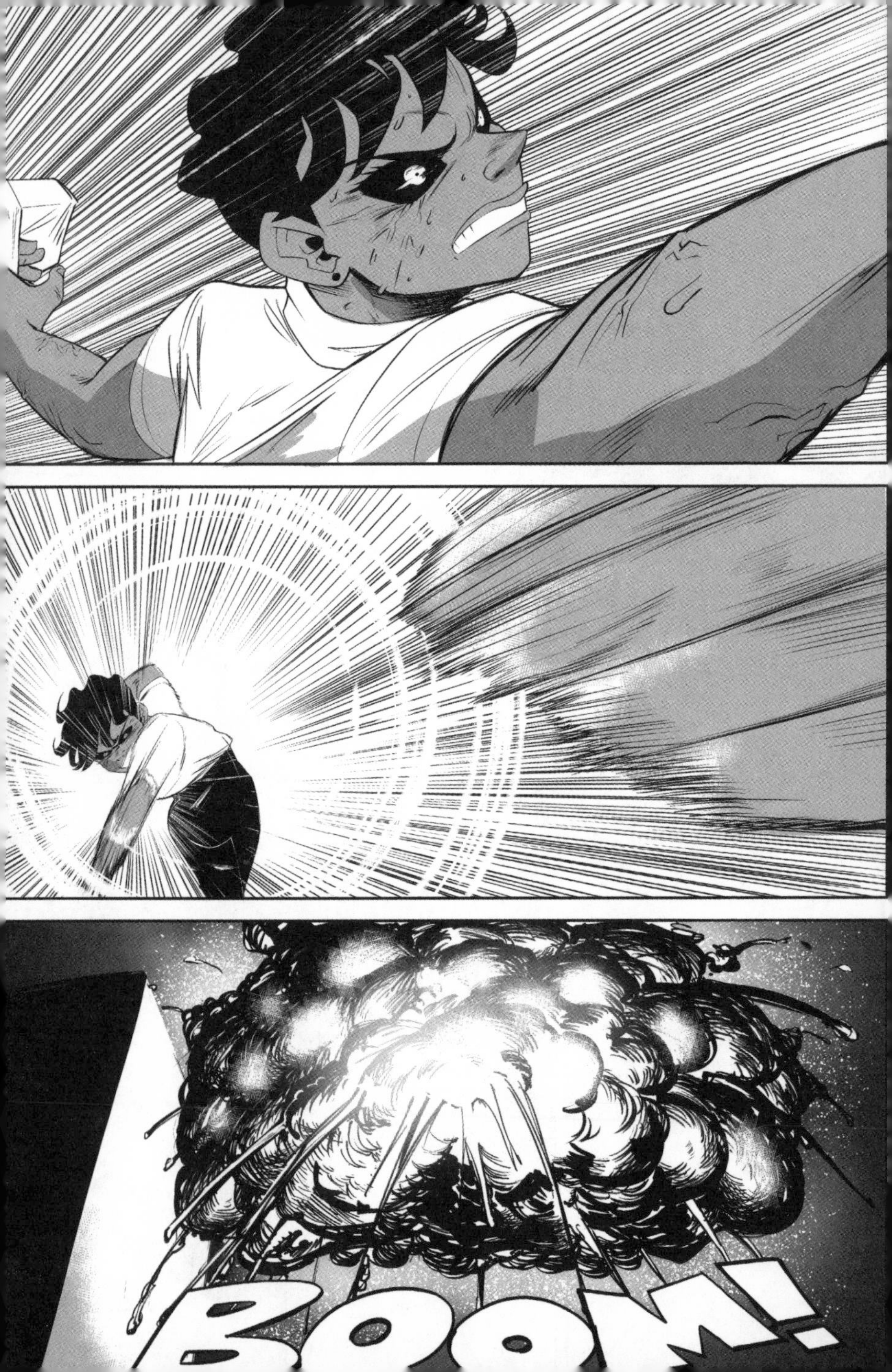
BOOM!

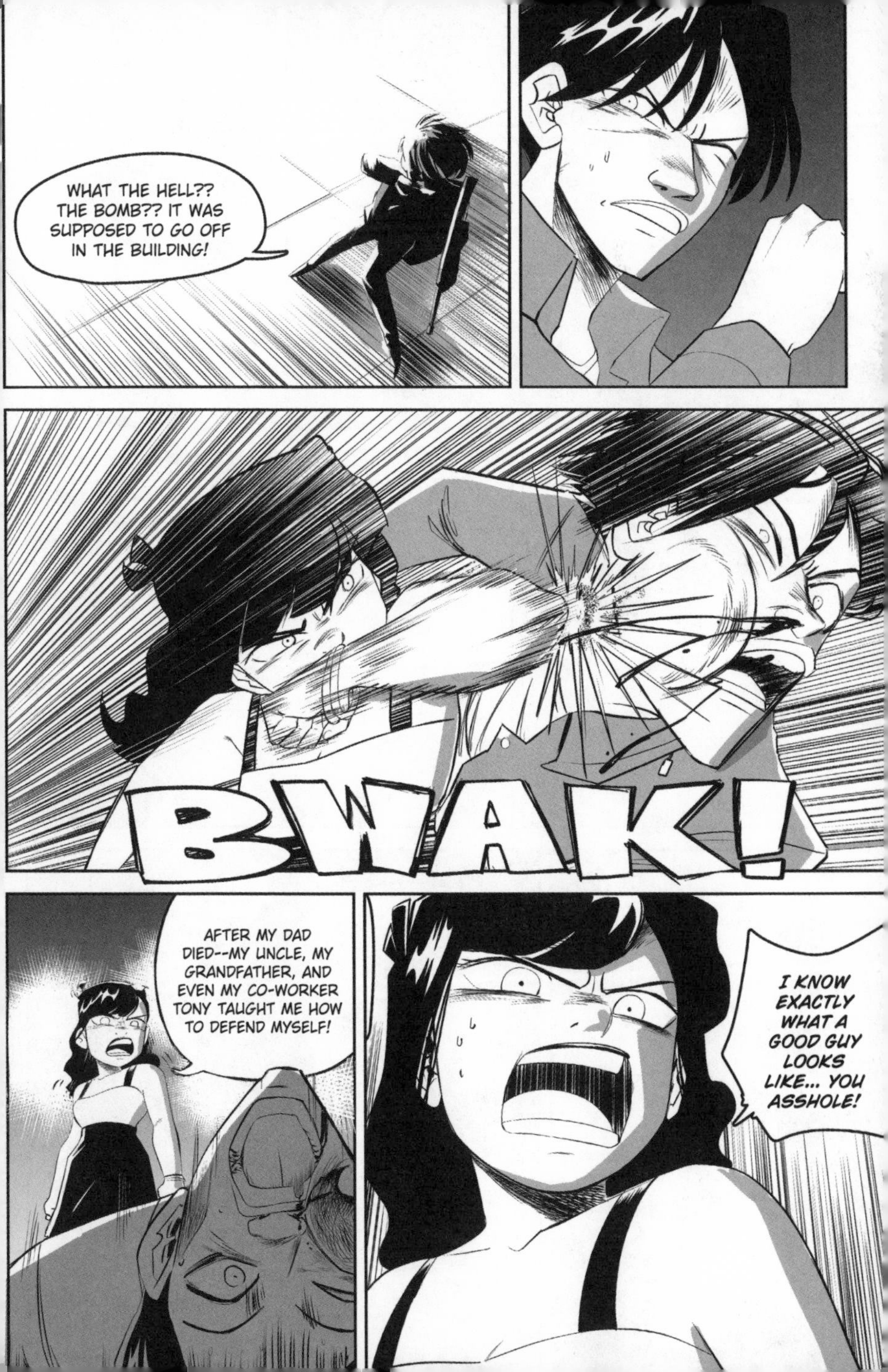
WHAT THE HELL?? THE BOMB?? IT WAS SUPPOSED TO GO OFF IN THE BUILDING!
BWAK!
AFTER MY DAD DIED--MY UNCLE, MY GRANDFATHER, AND EVEN MY CO-WORKER TONY TAUGHT ME HOW TO DEFEND MYSELF!
I KNOW EXACTLY WHAT A GOOD GUY LOOKS LIKE... YOU ASSHOLE!

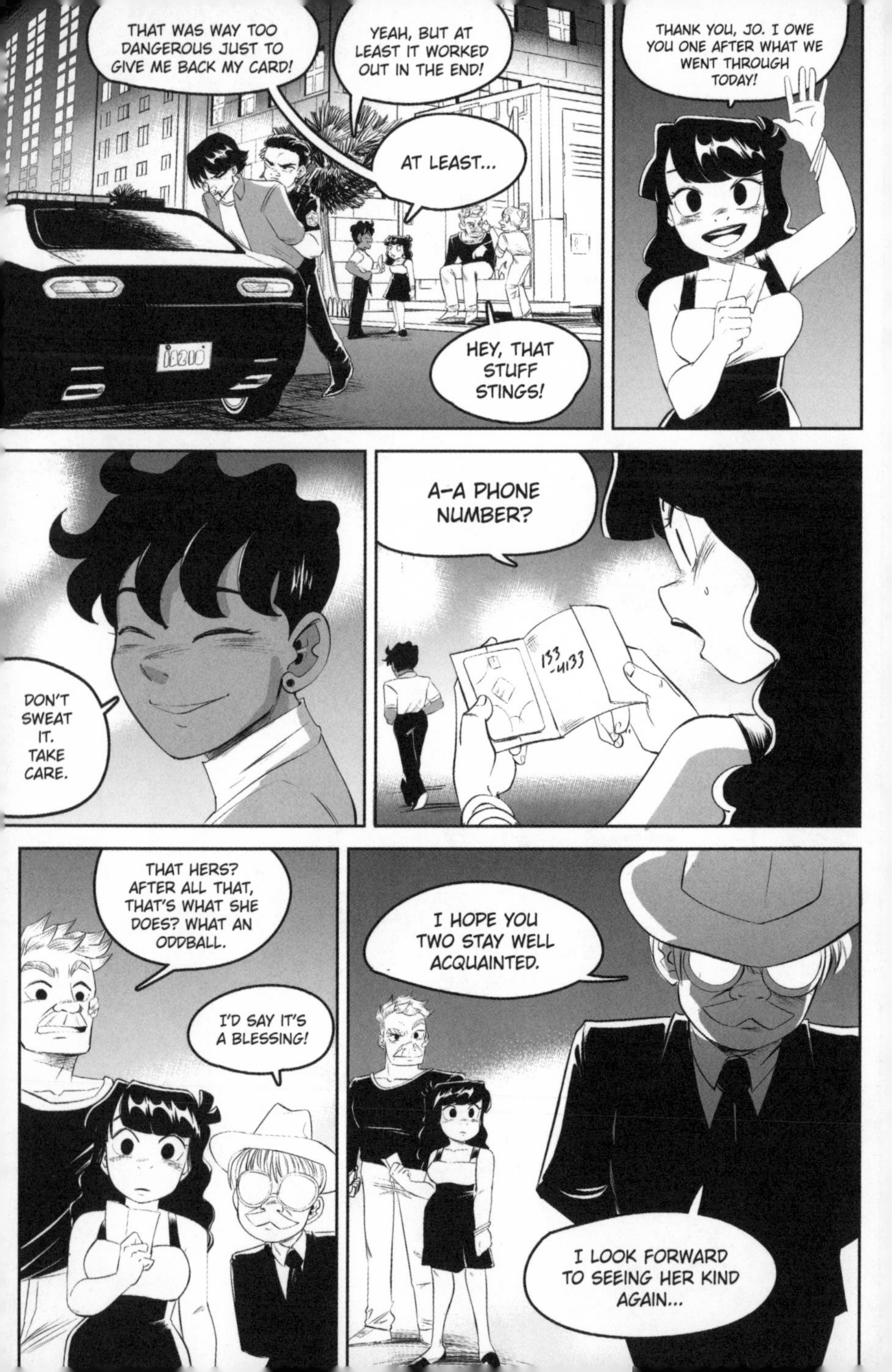
THAT WAS WAY TOO DANGEROUS JUST TO GIVE ME BACK MY CARD!
YEAH, BUT AT LEAST IT WORKED OUT IN THE END!
AT LEAST...
HEY, THAT STUFF STINGS!
THANK YOU, JO. I OWE YOU ONE AFTER WHAT WE WENT THROUGH TODAY!
DON'T SWEAT IT. TAKE CARE.
A-A PHONE NUMBER?
133 -4133
THAT HERS? AFTER ALL THAT, THAT'S WHAT SHE DOES? WHAT AN ODDBALL.
I'D SAY IT'S A BLESSING!
I HOPE YOU TWO STAY WELL ACQUAINTED.
I LOOK FORWARD TO SEEING HER KIND AGAIN...

YELLOW STRINGER

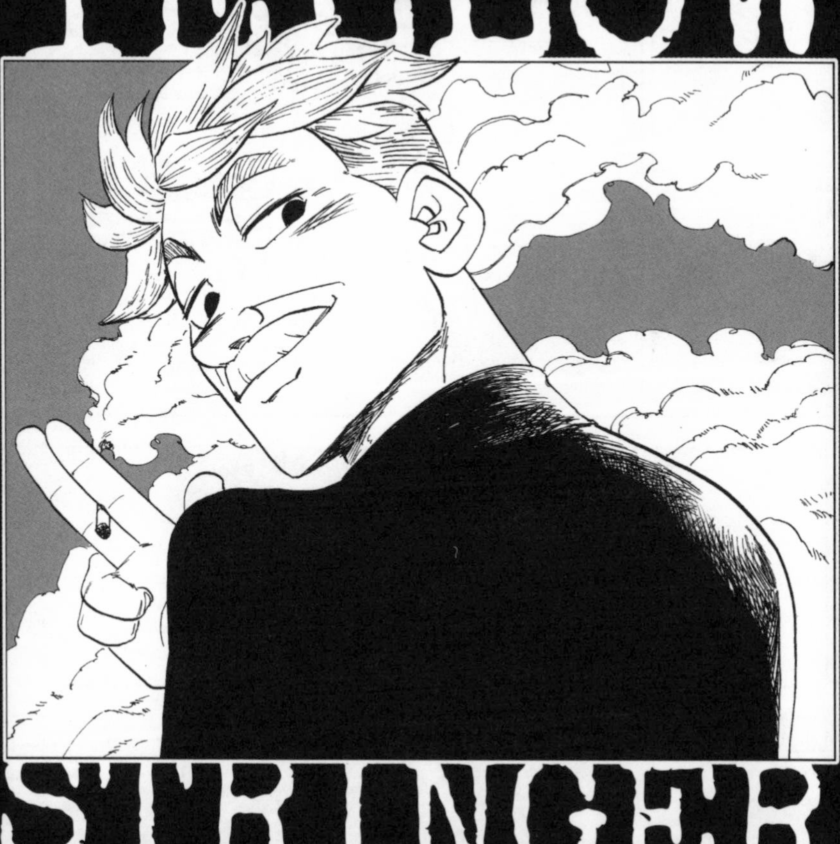

Article 7: Birthday Boy

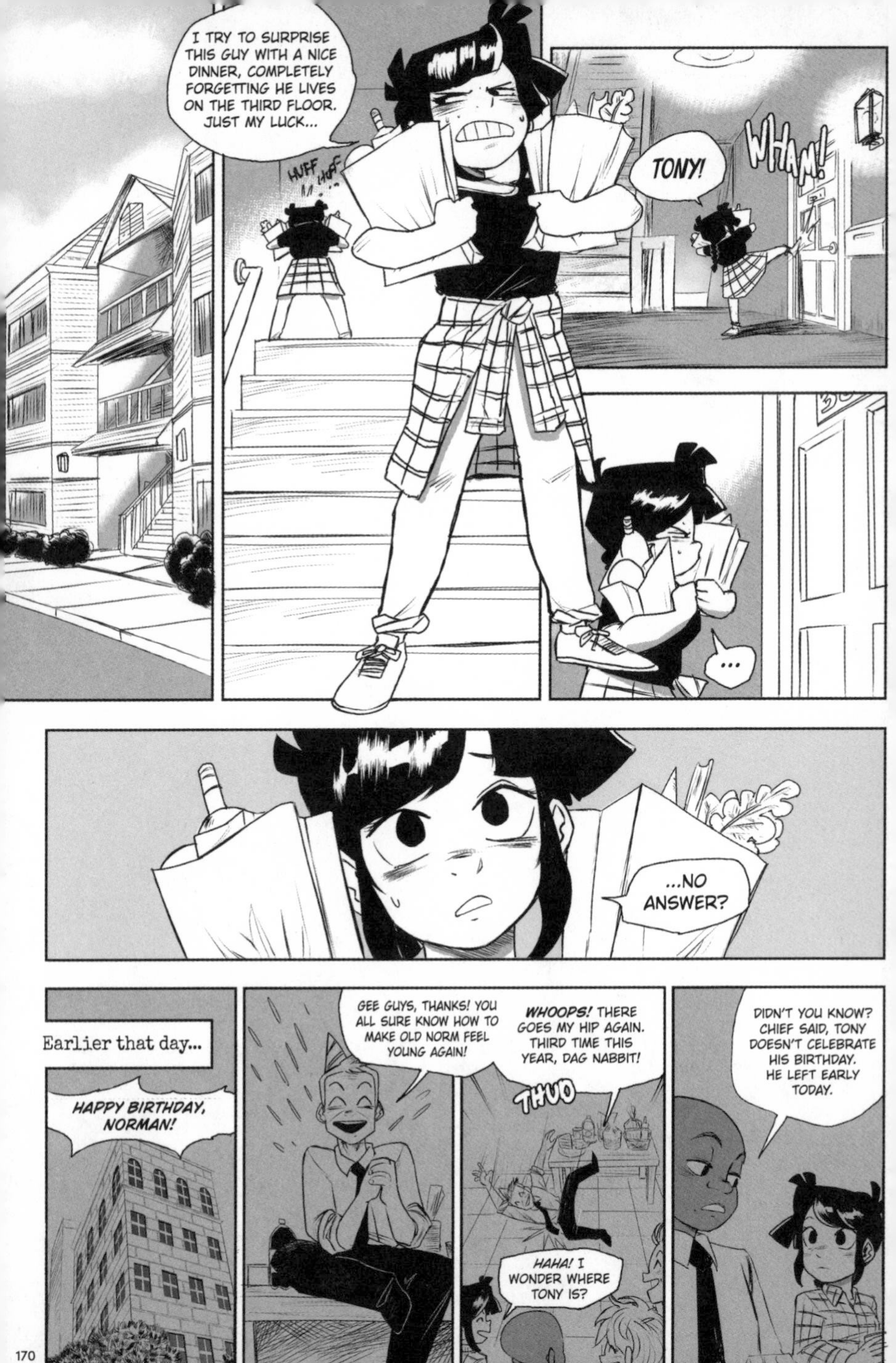
I TRY TO SURPRISE THIS GUY WITH A NICE DINNER, COMPLETELY FORGETTING HE LIVES ON THE THIRD FLOOR. JUST MY LUCK...
HUFF HUFF
TONY!
WHAM!
...
...NO ANSWER?
Earlier that day...
HAPPY BIRTHDAY, NORMAN!
GEE GUYS, THANKS! YOU ALL SURE KNOW HOW TO MAKE OLD NORM FEEL YOUNG AGAIN!
WHOOPS! THERE GOES MY HIP AGAIN. THIRD TIME THIS YEAR, DAG NABBIT!
THUD
HAHA! I WONDER WHERE TONY IS?
DIDN'T YOU KNOW? CHIEF SAID, TONY DOESN'T CELEBRATE HIS BIRTHDAY. HE LEFT EARLY TODAY.

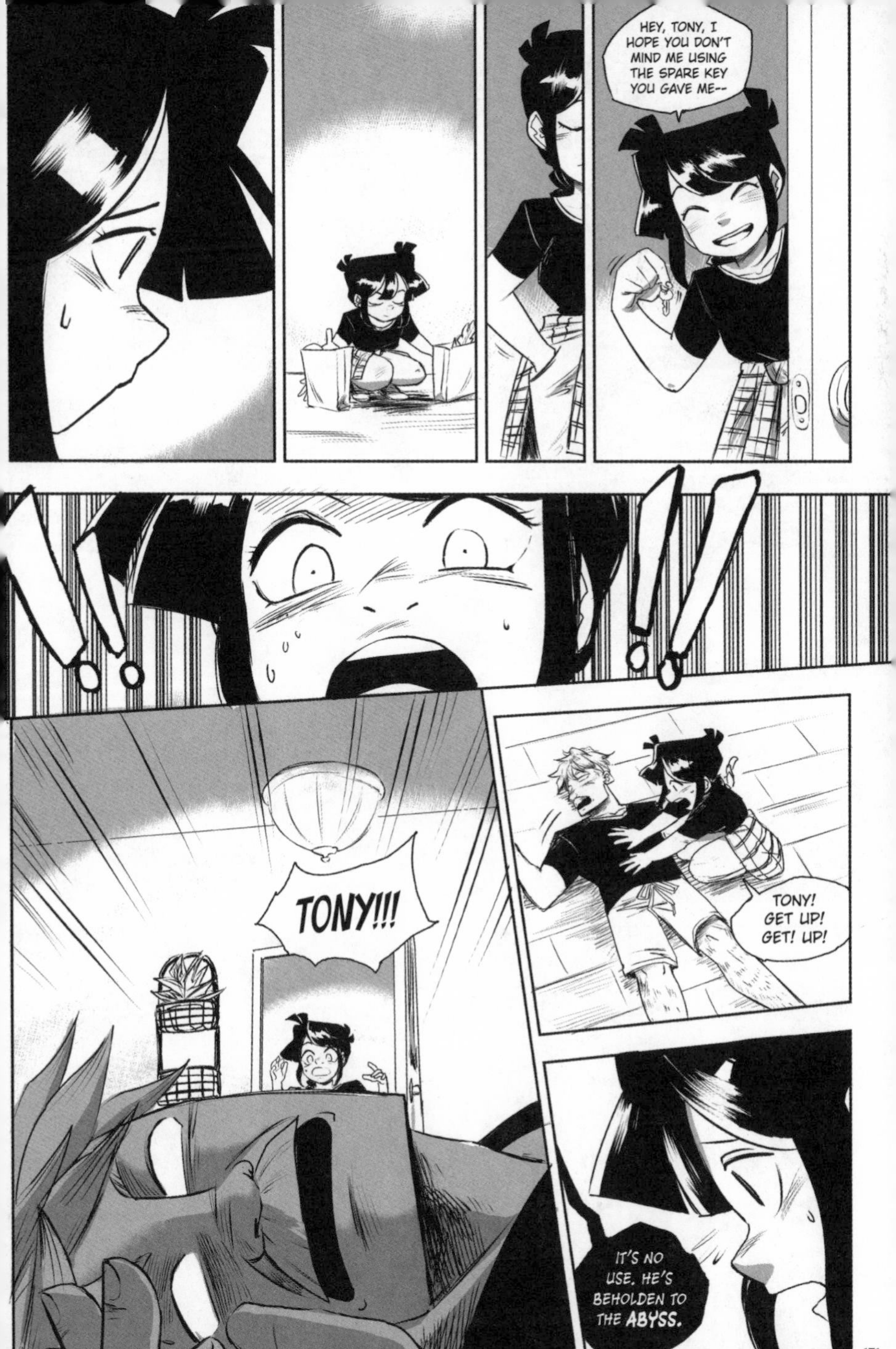
HEY, TONY, I HOPE YOU DON'T MIND ME USING THE SPARE KEY YOU GAVE ME--
TONY!!!
TONY! GET UP! GET! UP!
IT'S NO USE. HE'S BEHOLDEN TO THE ABYSS.

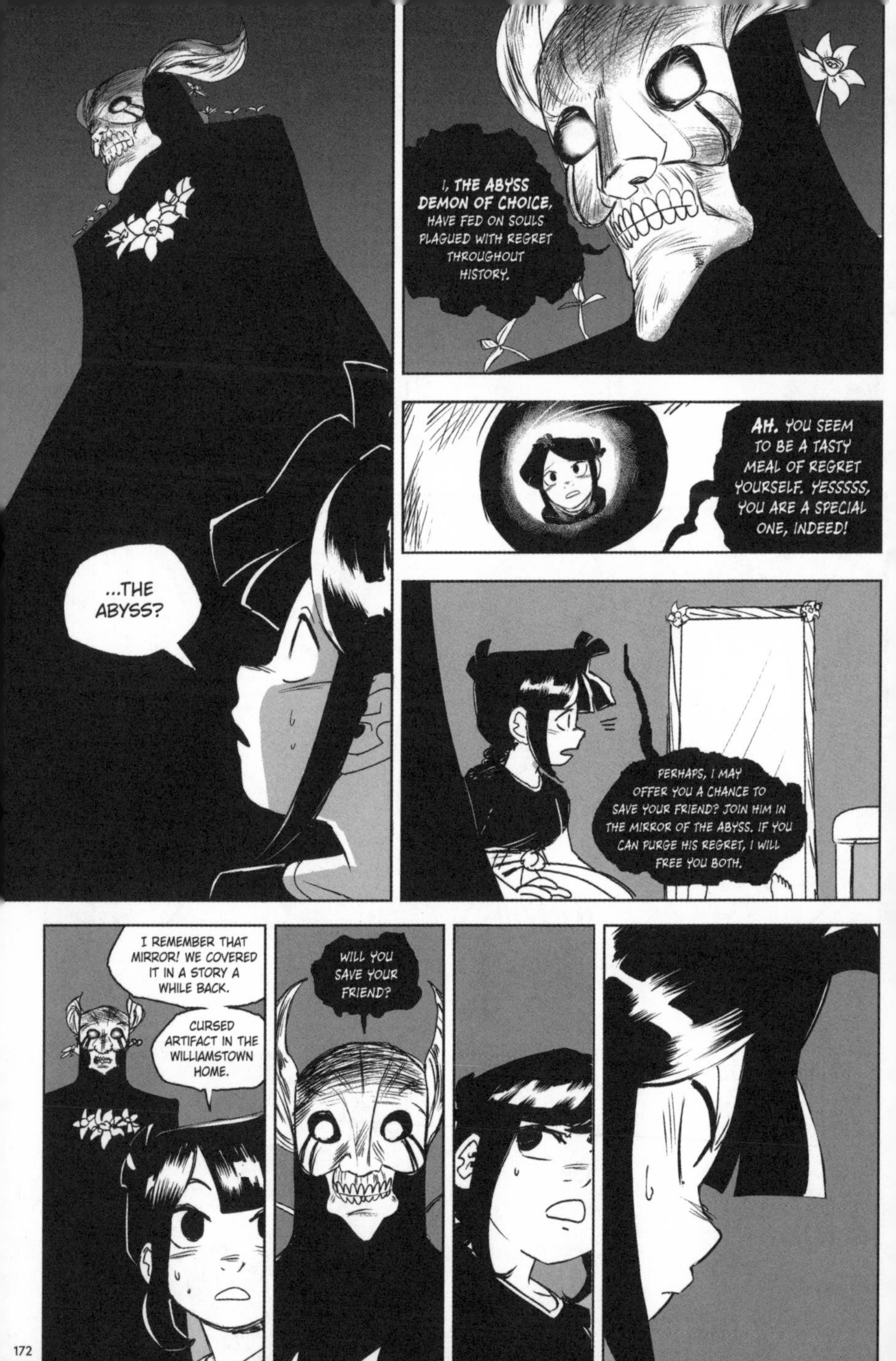

I, THE ABYSS DEMON OF CHOICE, HAVE FED ON SOULS PLAGUED WITH REGRET THROUGHOUT HISTORY.
...THE ABYSS?
AH. YOU SEEM TO BE A TASTY MEAL OF REGRET YOURSELF. YESSSSS, YOU ARE A SPECIAL ONE, INDEED!
PERHAPS, I MAY OFFER YOU A CHANCE TO SAVE YOUR FRIEND? JOIN HIM IN THE MIRROR OF THE ABYSS. IF YOU CAN PURGE HIS REGRET, I WILL FREE YOU BOTH.
I REMEMBER THAT MIRROR! WE COVERED IT IN A STORY A WHILE BACK.
CURSED ARTIFACT IN THE WILLIAMSTOWN HOME.
WILL YOU SAVE YOUR FRIEND?

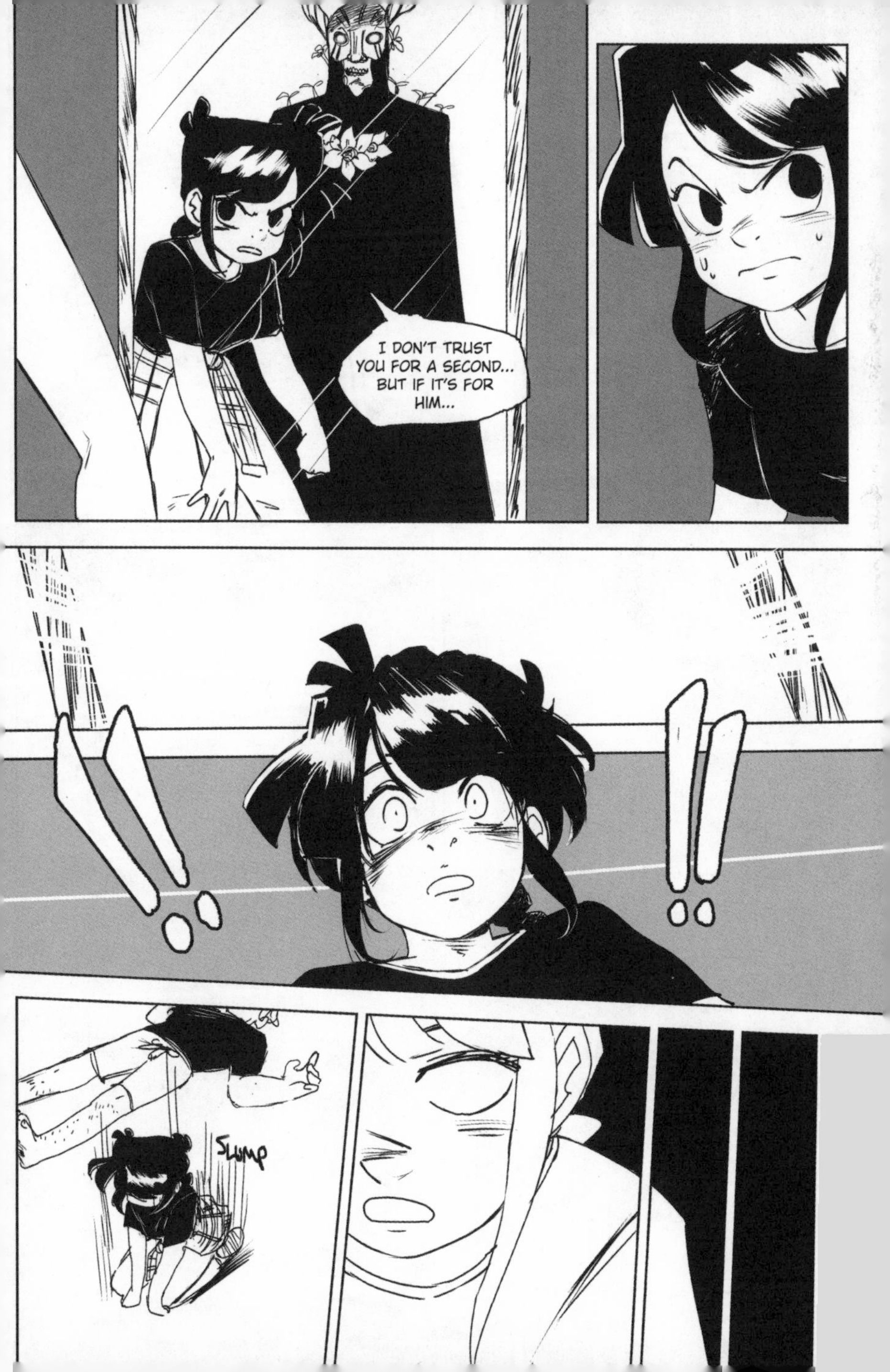
I DON'T TRUST YOU FOR A SECOND... BUT IF IT'S FOR HIM...
!!
!!
SLUMP

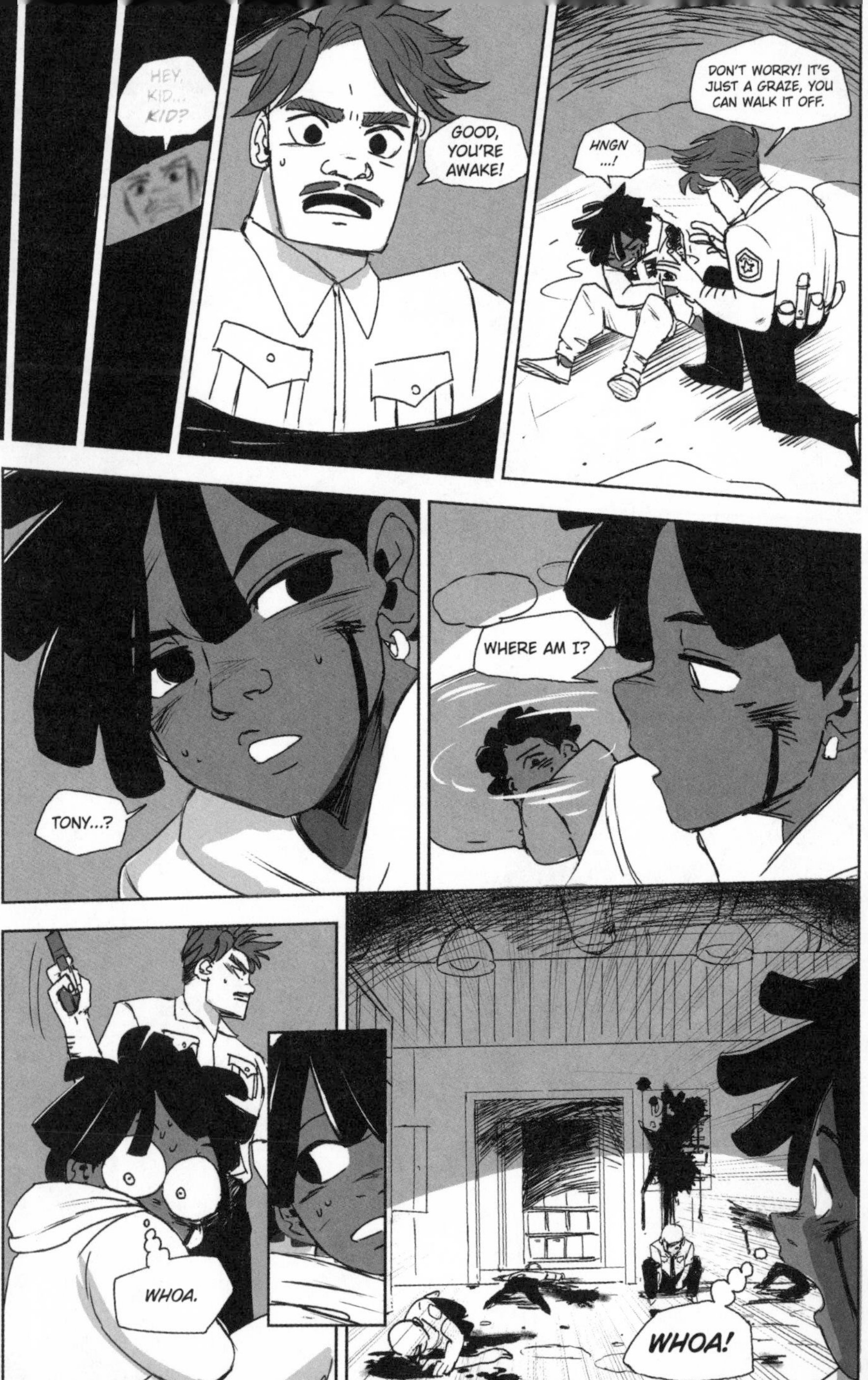

HEY, KID... KID?
GOOD, YOU'RE AWAKE!
DON'T WORRY! IT'S JUST A GRAZE, YOU CAN WALK IT OFF.
HNGN ...!
TONY...?
WHERE AM I?
WHOA.
WHOA!

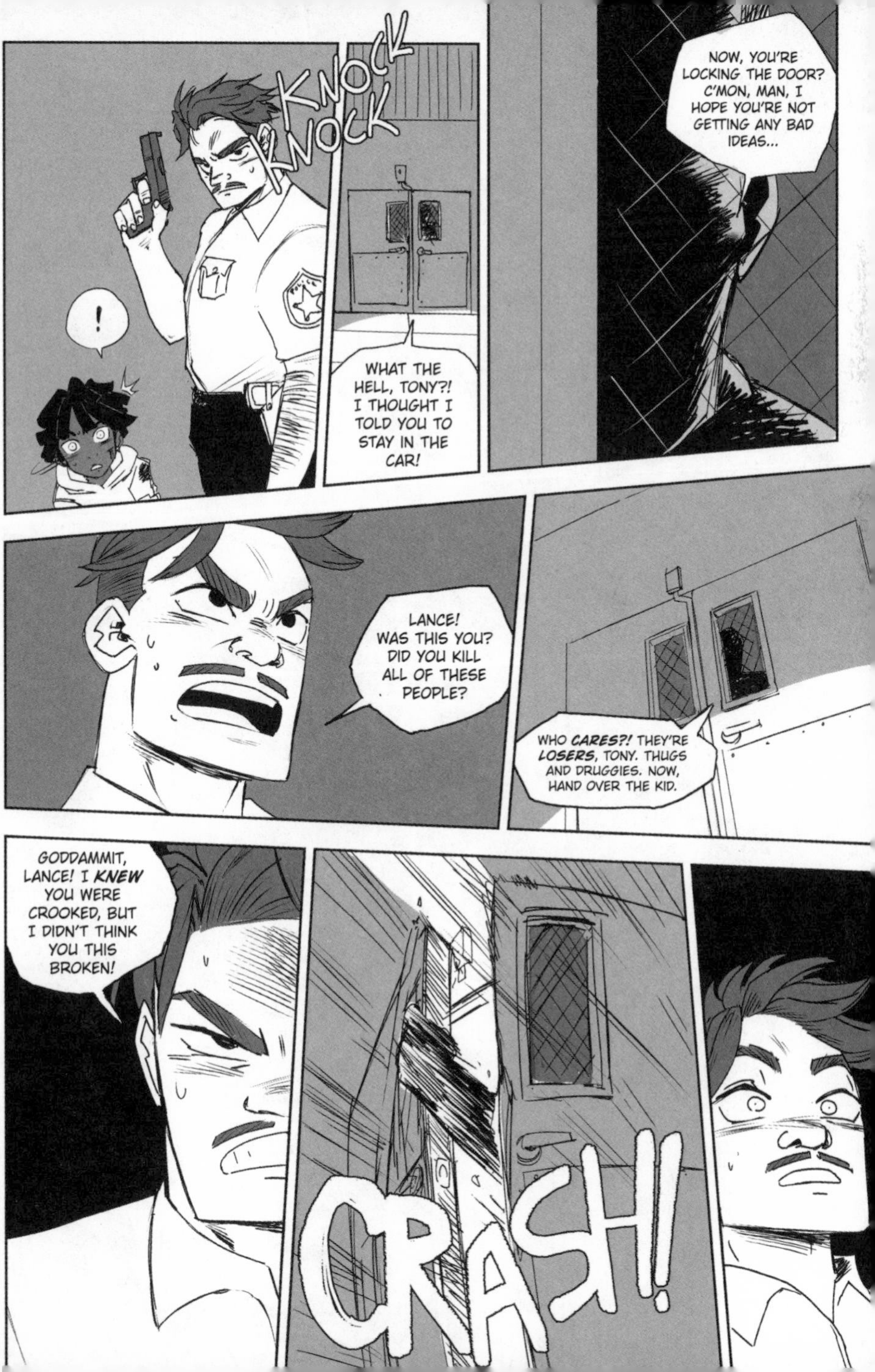
KNOCK KNOCK
!
WHAT THE HELL, TONY?! I THOUGHT I TOLD YOU TO STAY IN THE CAR!
NOW, YOU'RE LOCKING THE DOOR? C'MON, MAN, I HOPE YOU'RE NOT GETTING ANY BAD IDEAS...
LANCE! WAS THIS YOU? DID YOU KILL ALL OF THESE PEOPLE?
WHO *CARES?!* THEY'RE ***LOSERS***, TONY. THUGS AND DRUGGIES. NOW, HAND OVER THE KID.
GODDAMMIT, LANCE! I ***KNEW*** YOU WERE CROOKED, BUT I DIDN'T THINK YOU THIS BROKEN!
CRASH!!

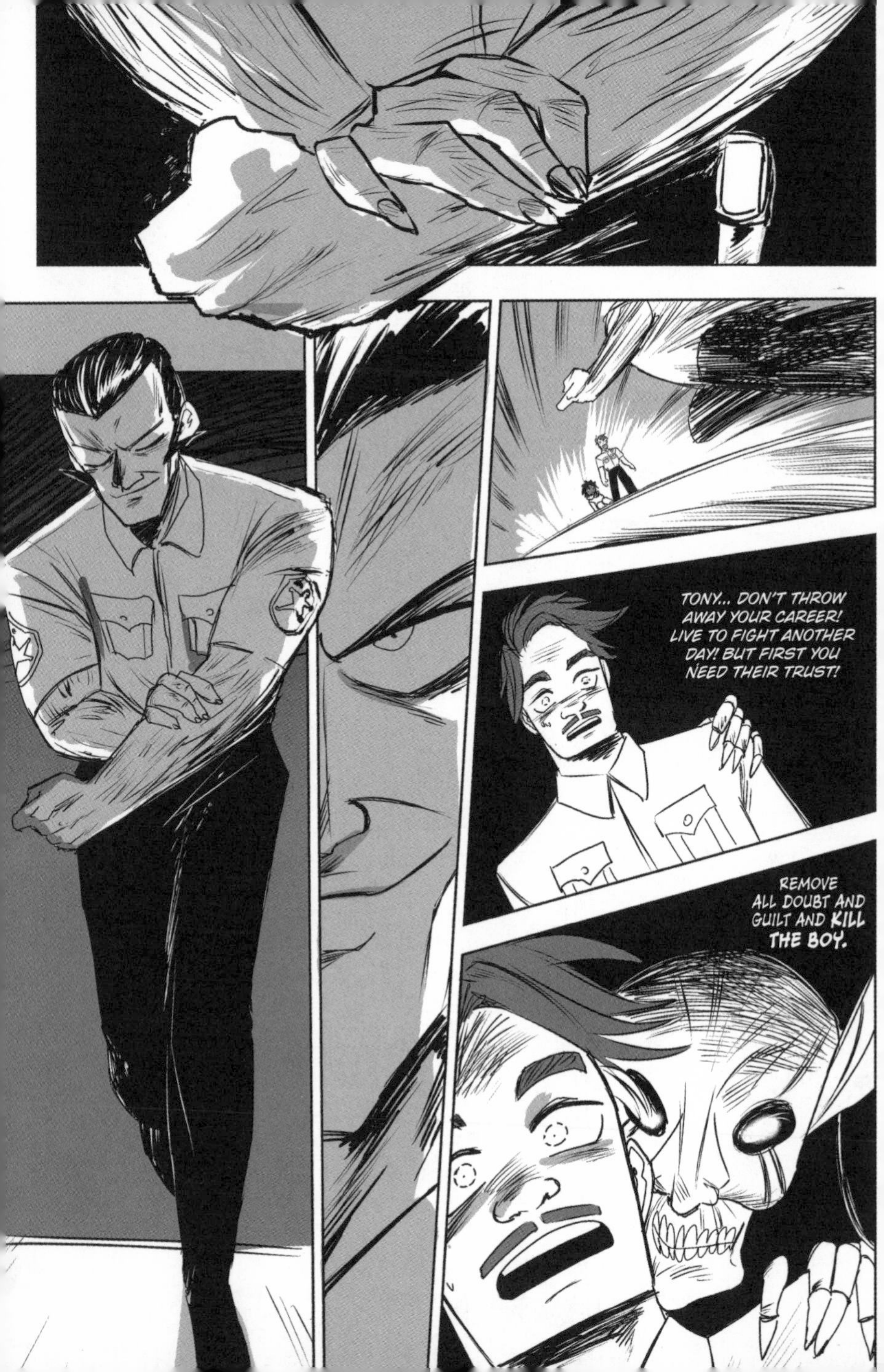
TONY... DON'T THROW AWAY YOUR CAREER! LIVE TO FIGHT ANOTHER DAY! BUT FIRST YOU NEED THEIR TRUST!
REMOVE ALL DOUBT AND GUILT AND **KILL THE BOY.**

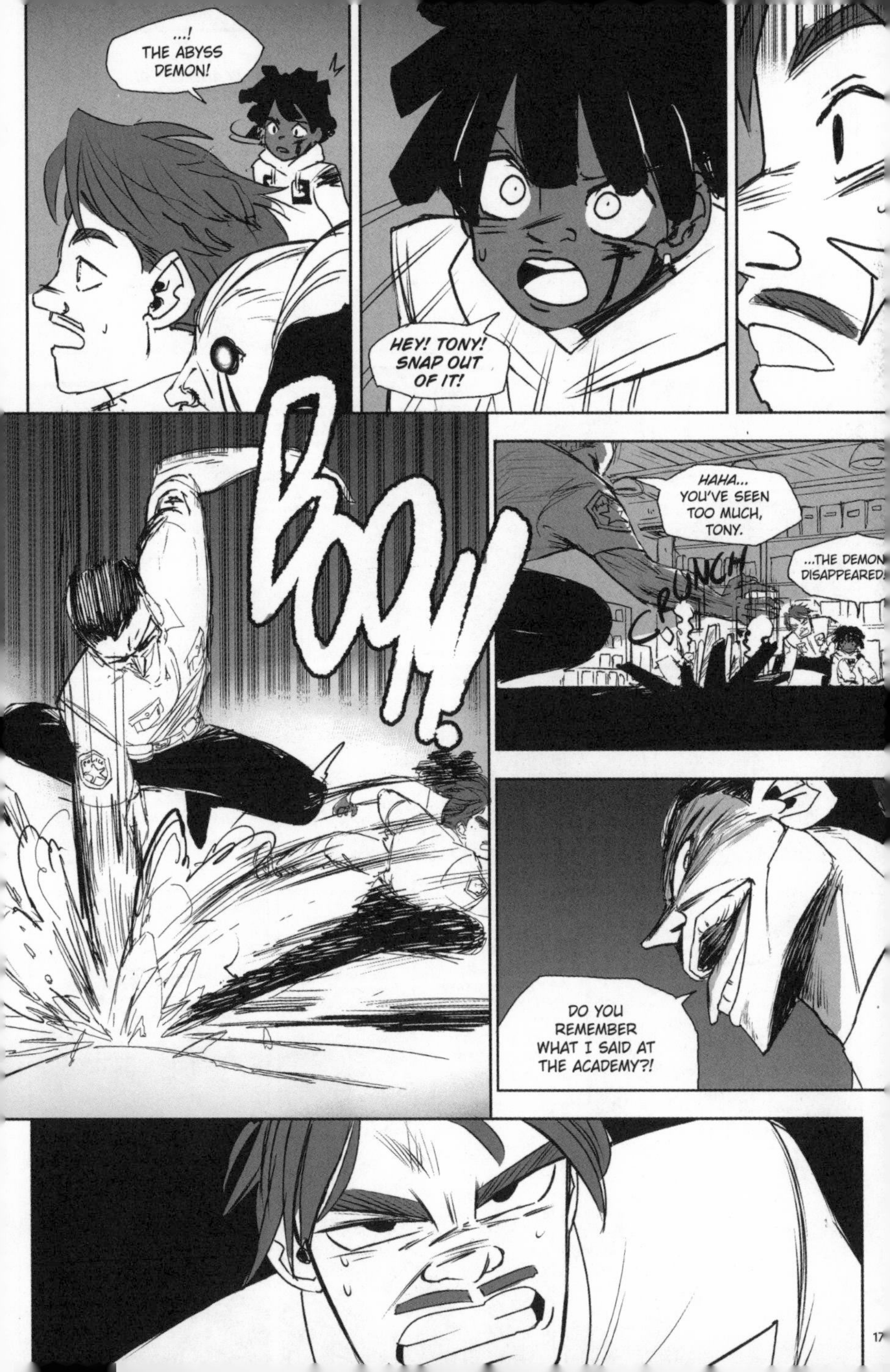
...! THE ABYSS DEMON!
HEY! TONY! SNAP OUT OF IT!
BOOM!
HAHA... YOU'VE SEEN TOO MUCH, TONY.
CRUNCH
...THE DEMON DISAPPEARED!
DO YOU REMEMBER WHAT I SAID AT THE ACADEMY?!

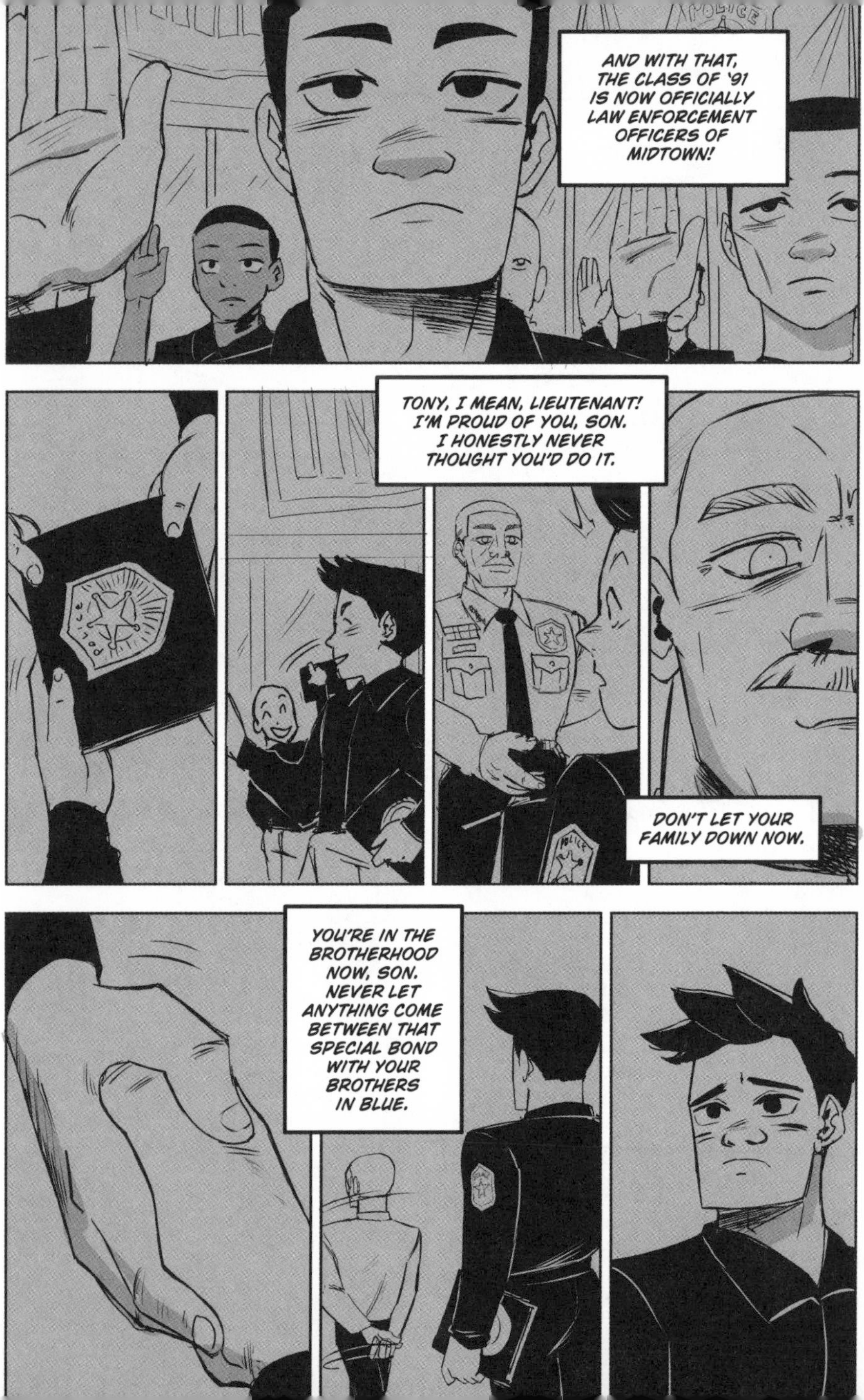
AND WITH THAT, THE CLASS OF '91 IS NOW OFFICIALLY LAW ENFORCEMENT OFFICERS OF MIDTOWN!
TONY, I MEAN, LIEUTENANT! I'M PROUD OF YOU, SON. I HONESTLY NEVER THOUGHT YOU'D DO IT.
DON'T LET YOUR FAMILY DOWN NOW.
YOU'RE IN THE BROTHERHOOD NOW, SON. NEVER LET ANYTHING COME BETWEEN THAT SPECIAL BOND WITH YOUR BROTHERS IN BLUE.

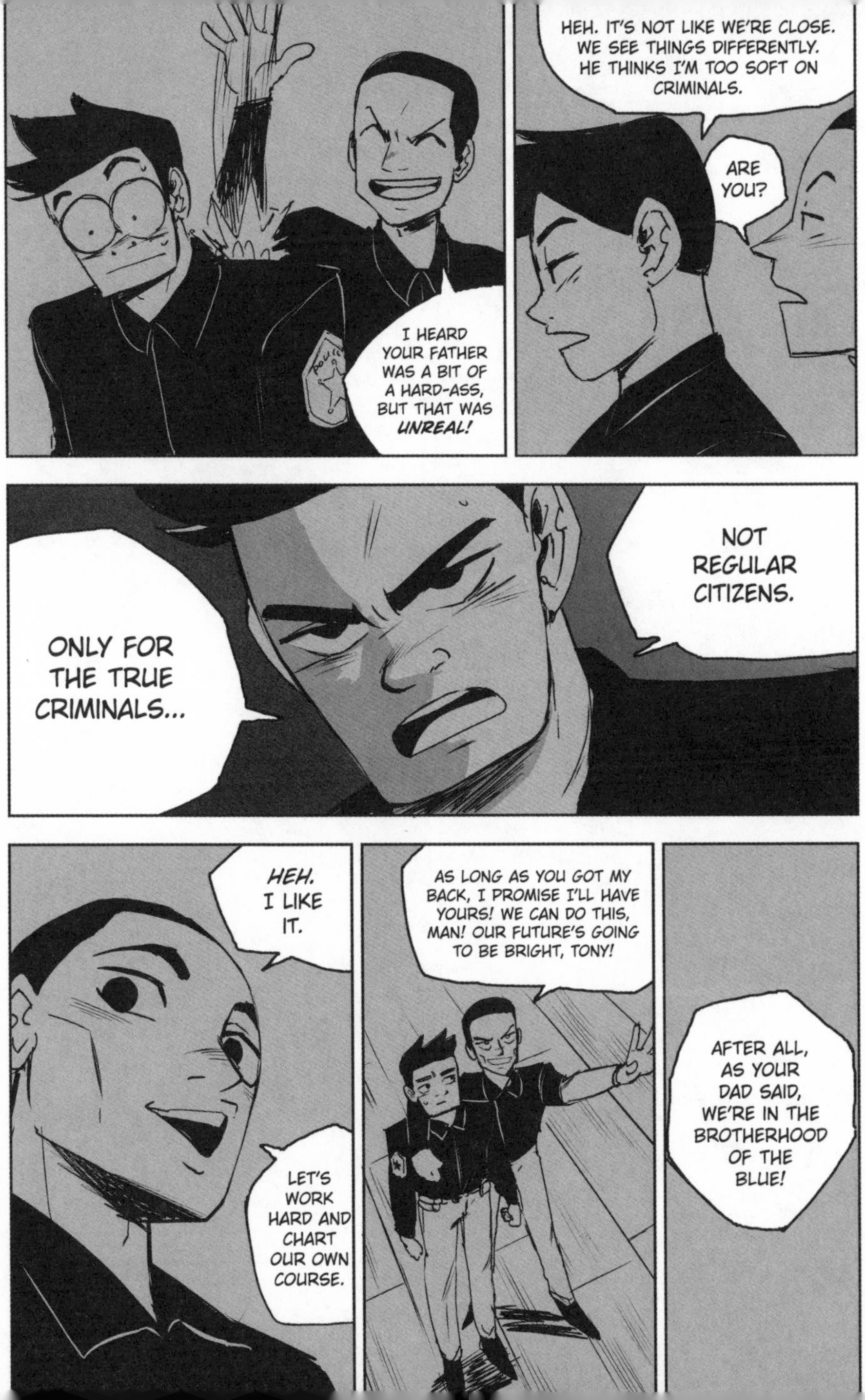
I HEARD YOUR FATHER WAS A BIT OF A HARD-ASS, BUT THAT WAS *UNREAL!*
HEH. IT'S NOT LIKE WE'RE CLOSE. WE SEE THINGS DIFFERENTLY. HE THINKS I'M TOO SOFT ON CRIMINALS.
ARE YOU?
ONLY FOR THE TRUE CRIMINALS...
NOT REGULAR CITIZENS.
HEH. I LIKE IT.
LET'S WORK HARD AND CHART OUR OWN COURSE.
AS LONG AS YOU GOT MY BACK, I PROMISE I'LL HAVE YOURS! WE CAN DO THIS, MAN! OUR FUTURE'S GOING TO BE BRIGHT, TONY!
AFTER ALL, AS YOUR DAD SAID, WE'RE IN THE BROTHERHOOD OF THE BLUE!

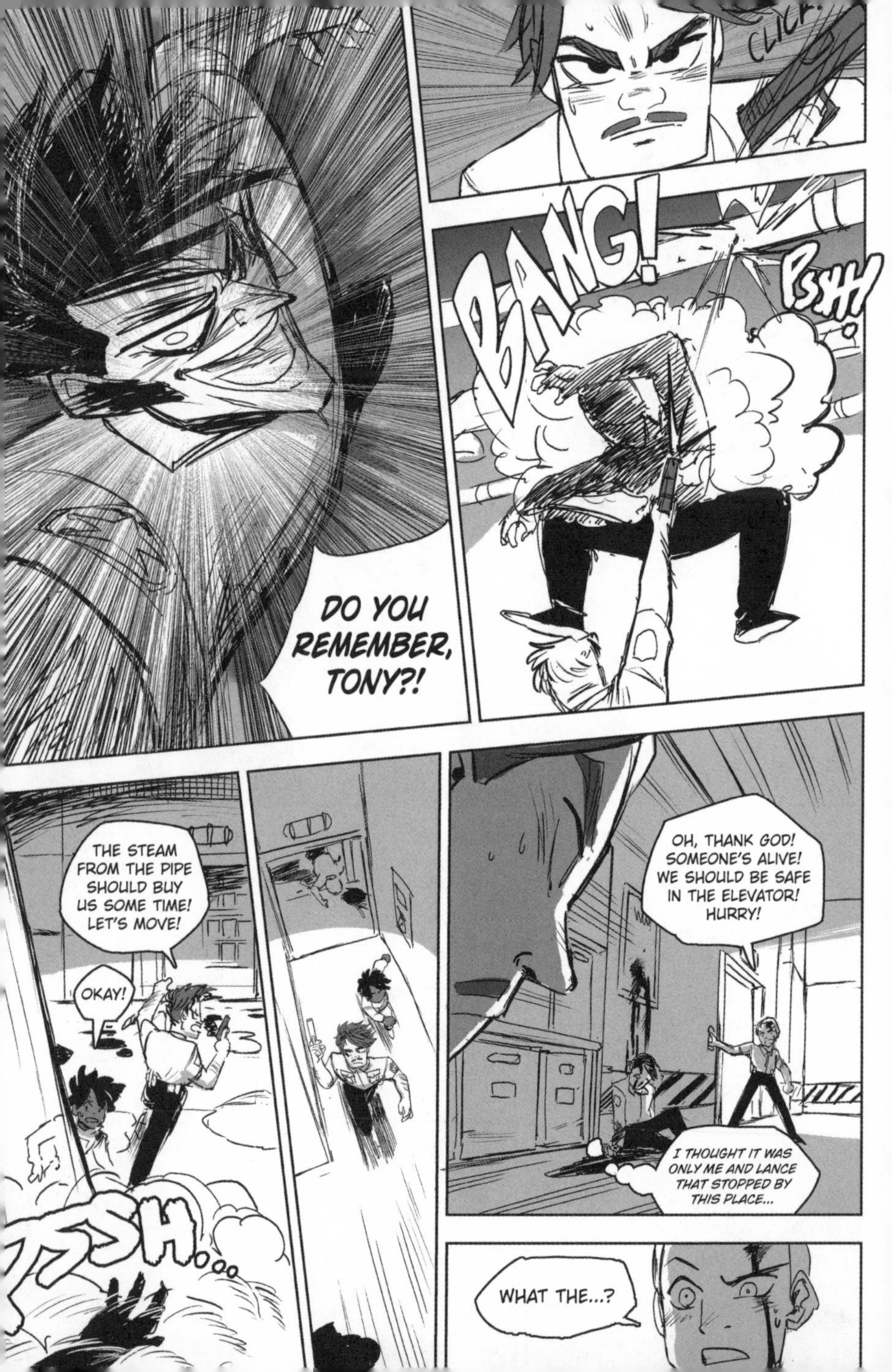
DO YOU REMEMBER, TONY?!
CLICK
BANG!
PSSH
THE STEAM FROM THE PIPE SHOULD BUY US SOME TIME! LET'S MOVE!
OKAY!
SHHH...
OH, THANK GOD! SOMEONE'S ALIVE! WE SHOULD BE SAFE IN THE ELEVATOR! HURRY!
I THOUGHT IT WAS ONLY ME AND LANCE THAT STOPPED BY THIS PLACE...
WHAT THE...?

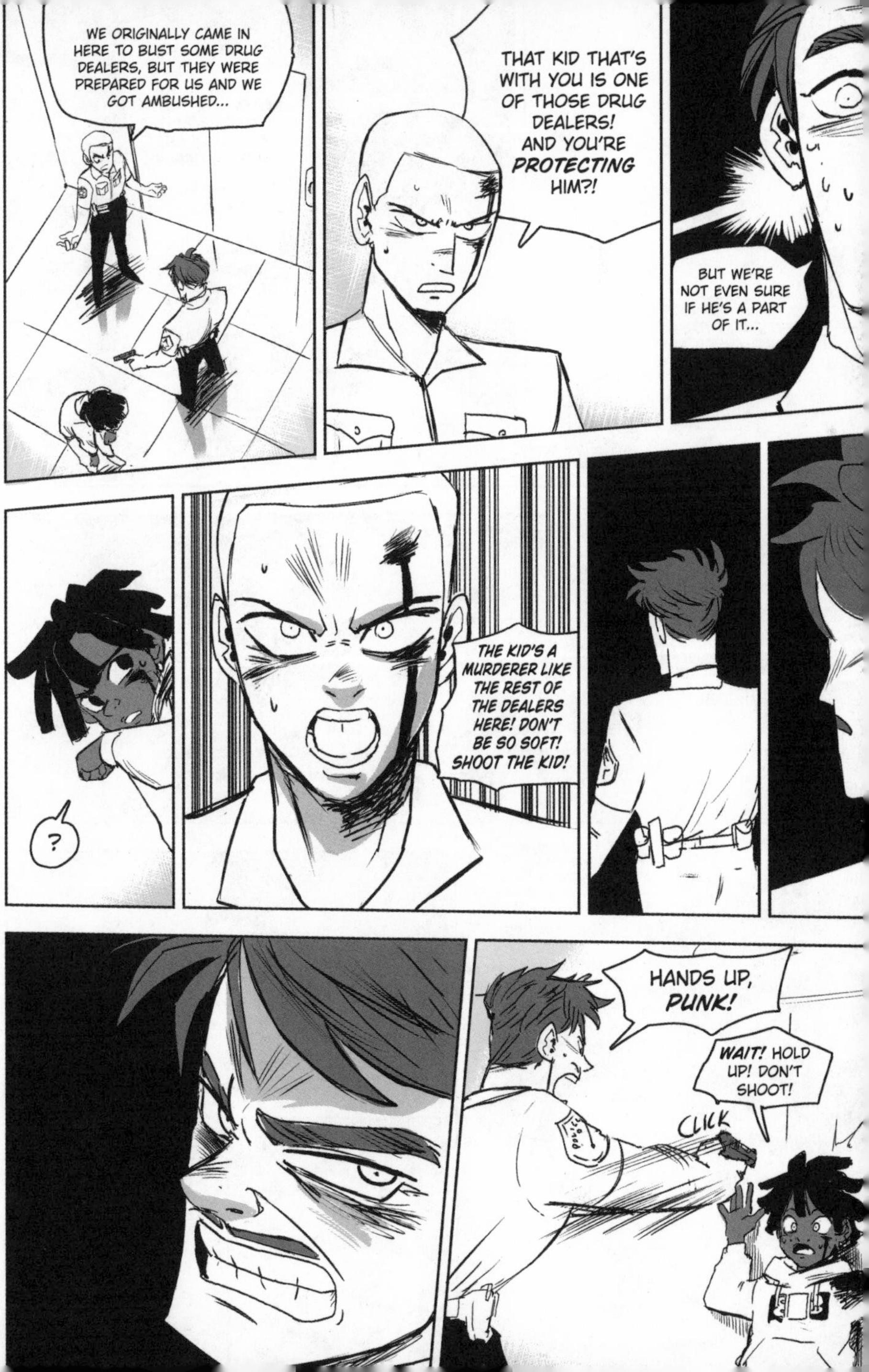
WE ORIGINALLY CAME IN HERE TO BUST SOME DRUG DEALERS, BUT THEY WERE PREPARED FOR US AND WE GOT AMBUSHED...
THAT KID THAT'S WITH YOU IS ONE OF THOSE DRUG DEALERS! AND YOU'RE PROTECTING HIM?!
BUT WE'RE NOT EVEN SURE IF HE'S A PART OF IT...
?
THE KID'S A MURDERER LIKE THE REST OF THE DEALERS HERE! DON'T BE SO SOFT! SHOOT THE KID!
HANDS UP, PUNK!
WAIT! HOLD UP! DON'T SHOOT!
CLICK

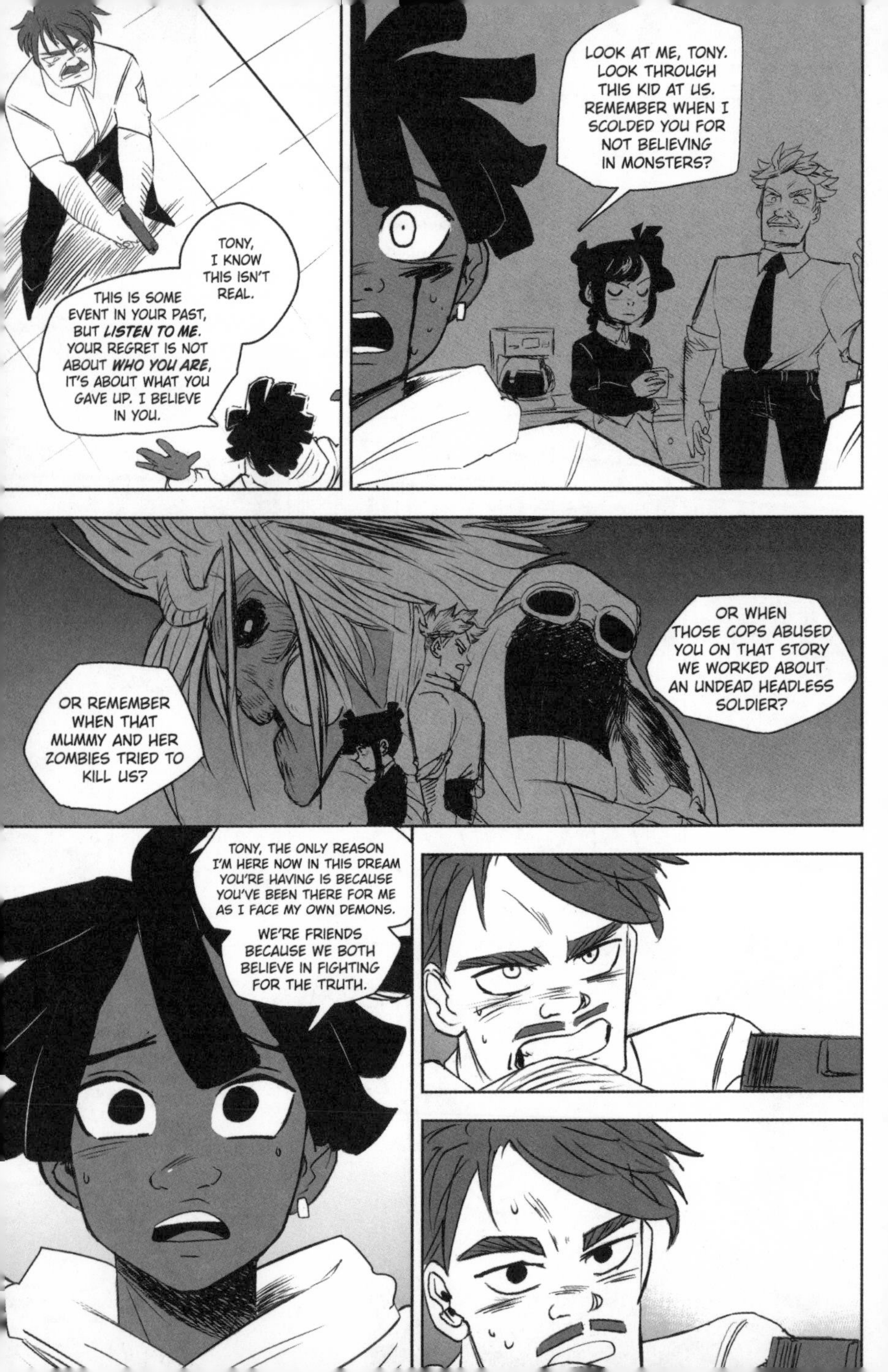

TONY, I KNOW THIS ISN'T REAL.
THIS IS SOME EVENT IN YOUR PAST, BUT ***LISTEN TO ME***. YOUR REGRET IS NOT ABOUT ***WHO YOU ARE***, IT'S ABOUT WHAT YOU GAVE UP. I BELIEVE IN YOU.
LOOK AT ME, TONY. LOOK THROUGH THIS KID AT US. REMEMBER WHEN I SCOLDED YOU FOR NOT BELIEVING IN MONSTERS?
OR REMEMBER WHEN THAT MUMMY AND HER ZOMBIES TRIED TO KILL US?
OR WHEN THOSE COPS ABUSED YOU ON THAT STORY WE WORKED ABOUT AN UNDEAD HEADLESS SOLDIER?
TONY, THE ONLY REASON I'M HERE NOW IN THIS DREAM YOU'RE HAVING IS BECAUSE YOU'VE BEEN THERE FOR ME AS I FACE MY OWN DEMONS.
WE'RE FRIENDS BECAUSE WE BOTH BELIEVE IN FIGHTING FOR THE TRUTH.

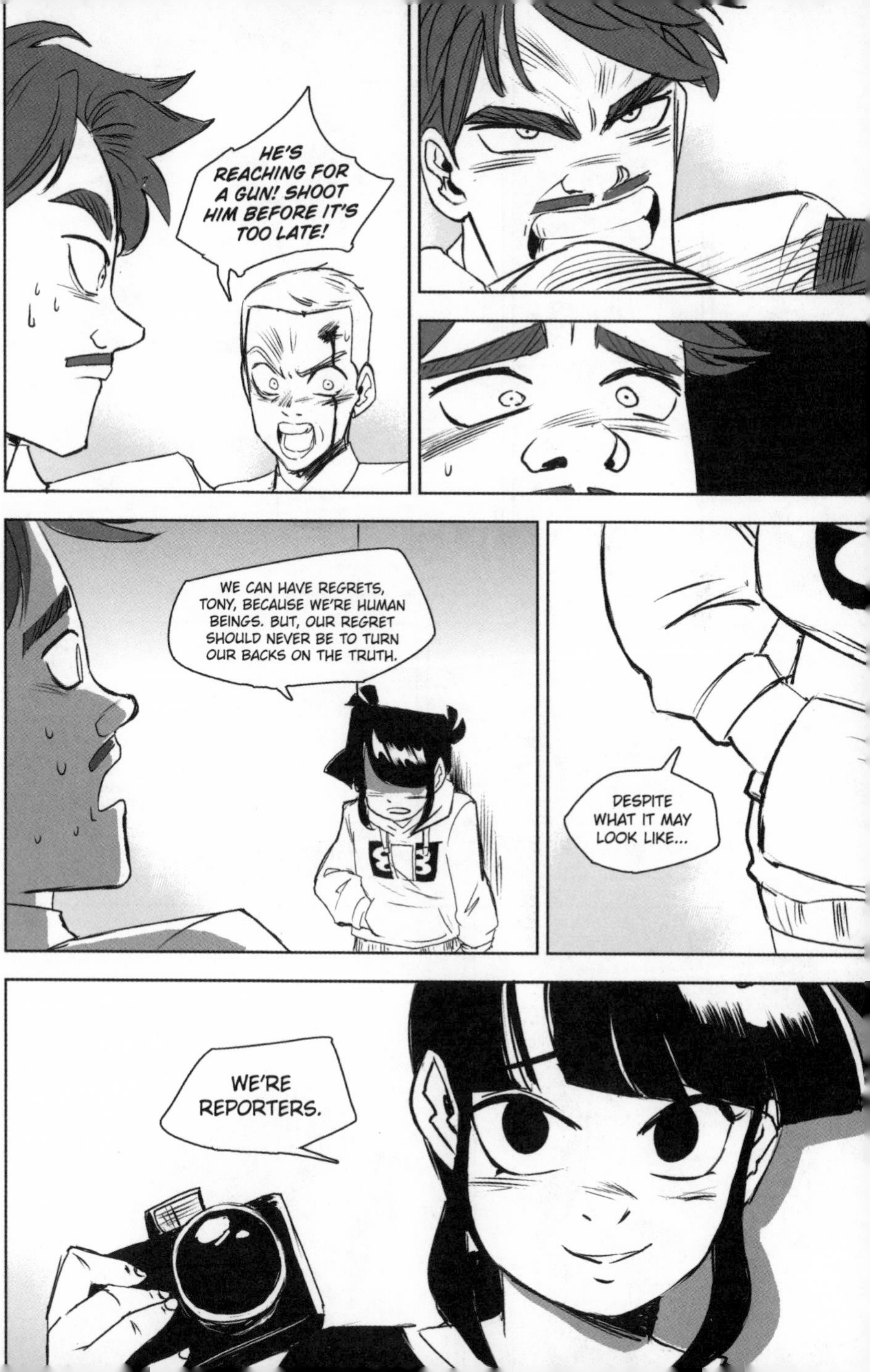
HE'S REACHING FOR A GUN! SHOOT HIM BEFORE IT'S TOO LATE!
WE CAN HAVE REGRETS, TONY, BECAUSE WE'RE HUMAN BEINGS. BUT, OUR REGRET SHOULD NEVER BE TO TURN OUR BACKS ON THE TRUTH.
DESPITE WHAT IT MAY LOOK LIKE...
WE'RE REPORTERS.

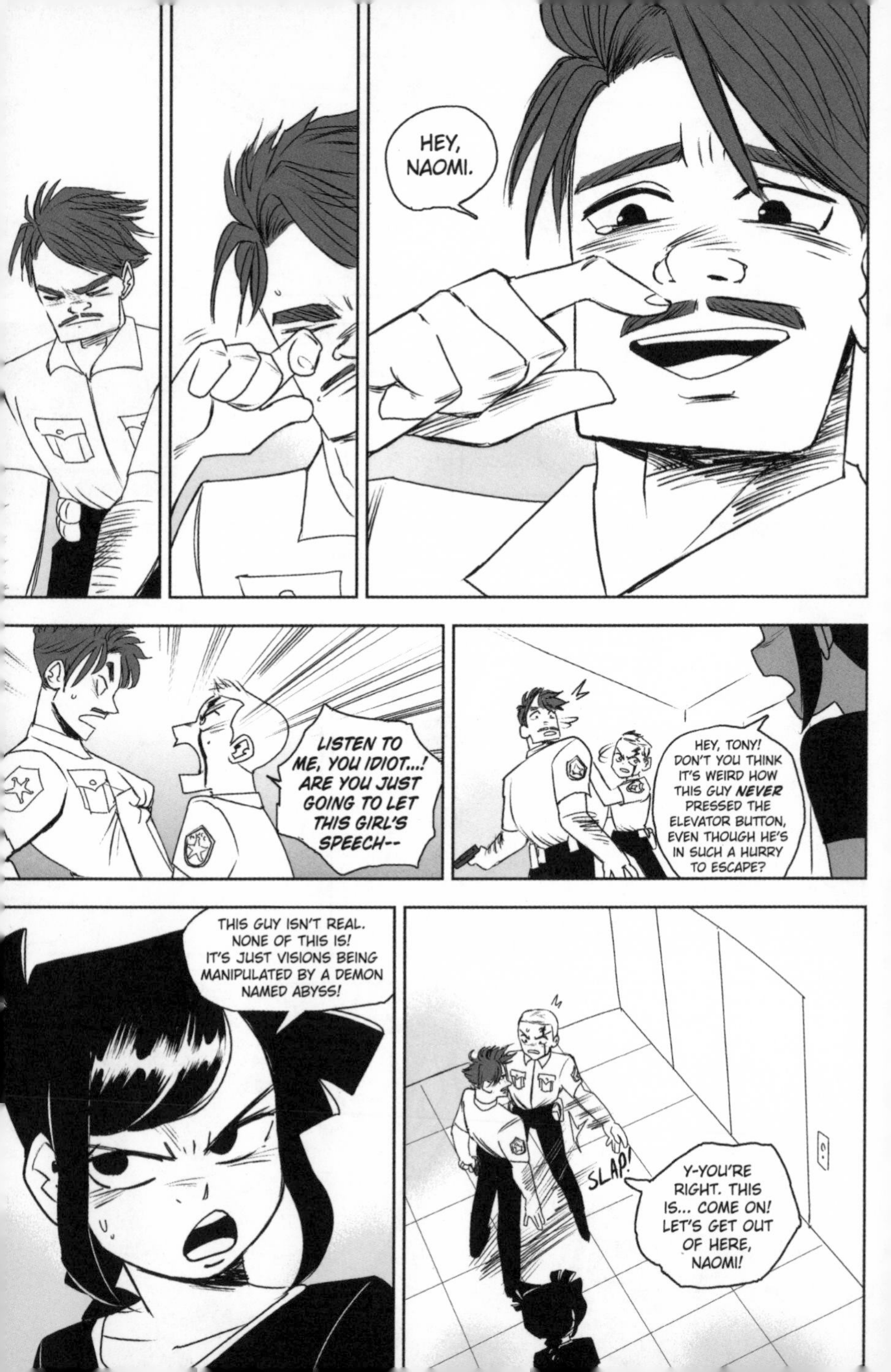
HEY, NAOMI.
LISTEN TO ME, YOU IDIOT...! ARE YOU JUST GOING TO LET THIS GIRL'S SPEECH--
HEY, TONY! DON'T YOU THINK IT'S WEIRD HOW THIS GUY NEVER PRESSED THE ELEVATOR BUTTON, EVEN THOUGH HE'S IN SUCH A HURRY TO ESCAPE?
THIS GUY ISN'T REAL. NONE OF THIS IS! IT'S JUST VISIONS BEING MANIPULATED BY A DEMON NAMED ABYSS!
SLAP!
Y-YOU'RE RIGHT. THIS IS... COME ON! LET'S GET OUT OF HERE, NAOMI!

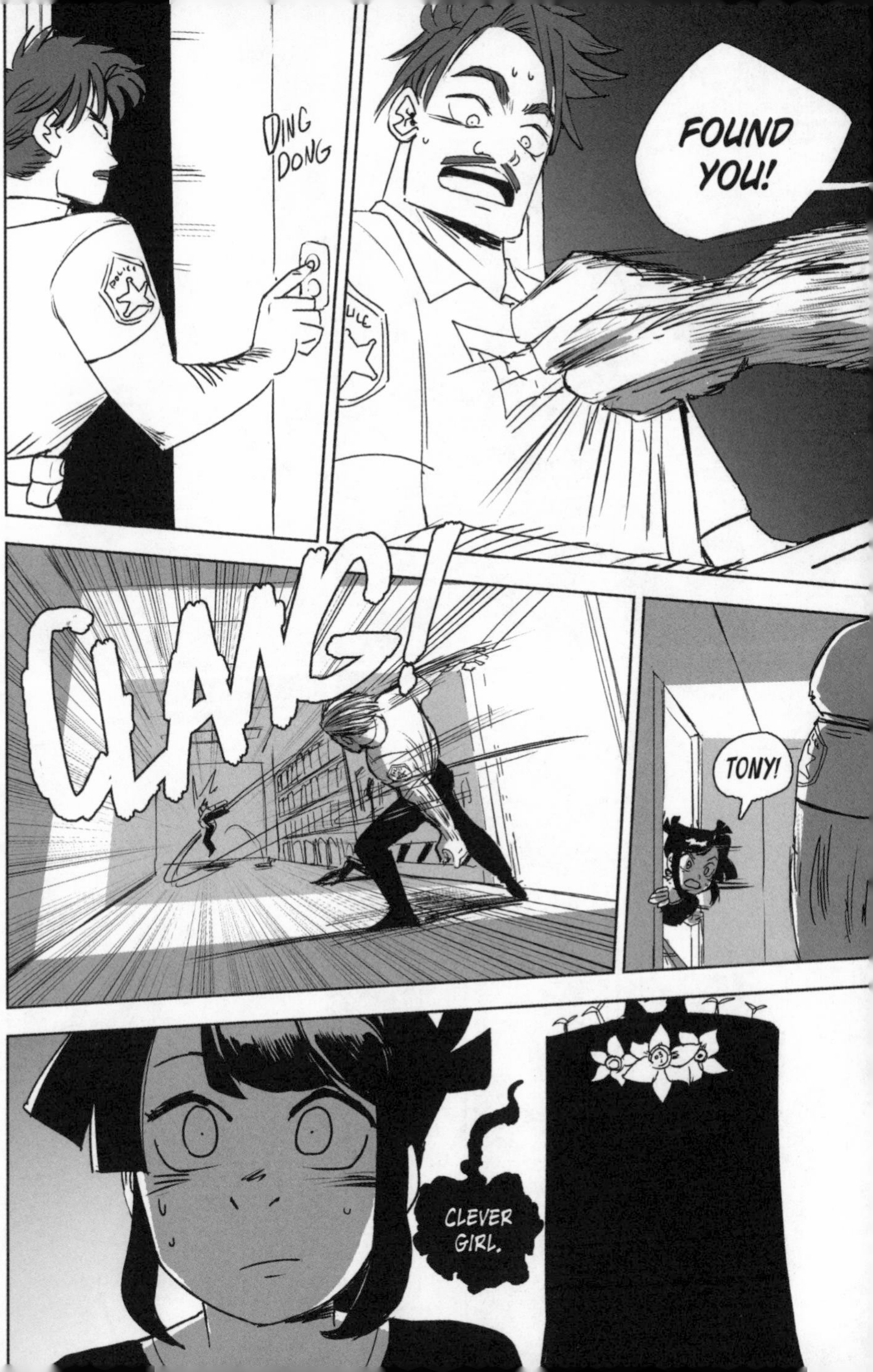
DING DONG
FOUND YOU!
CLANG!
TONY!
CLEVER GIRL.

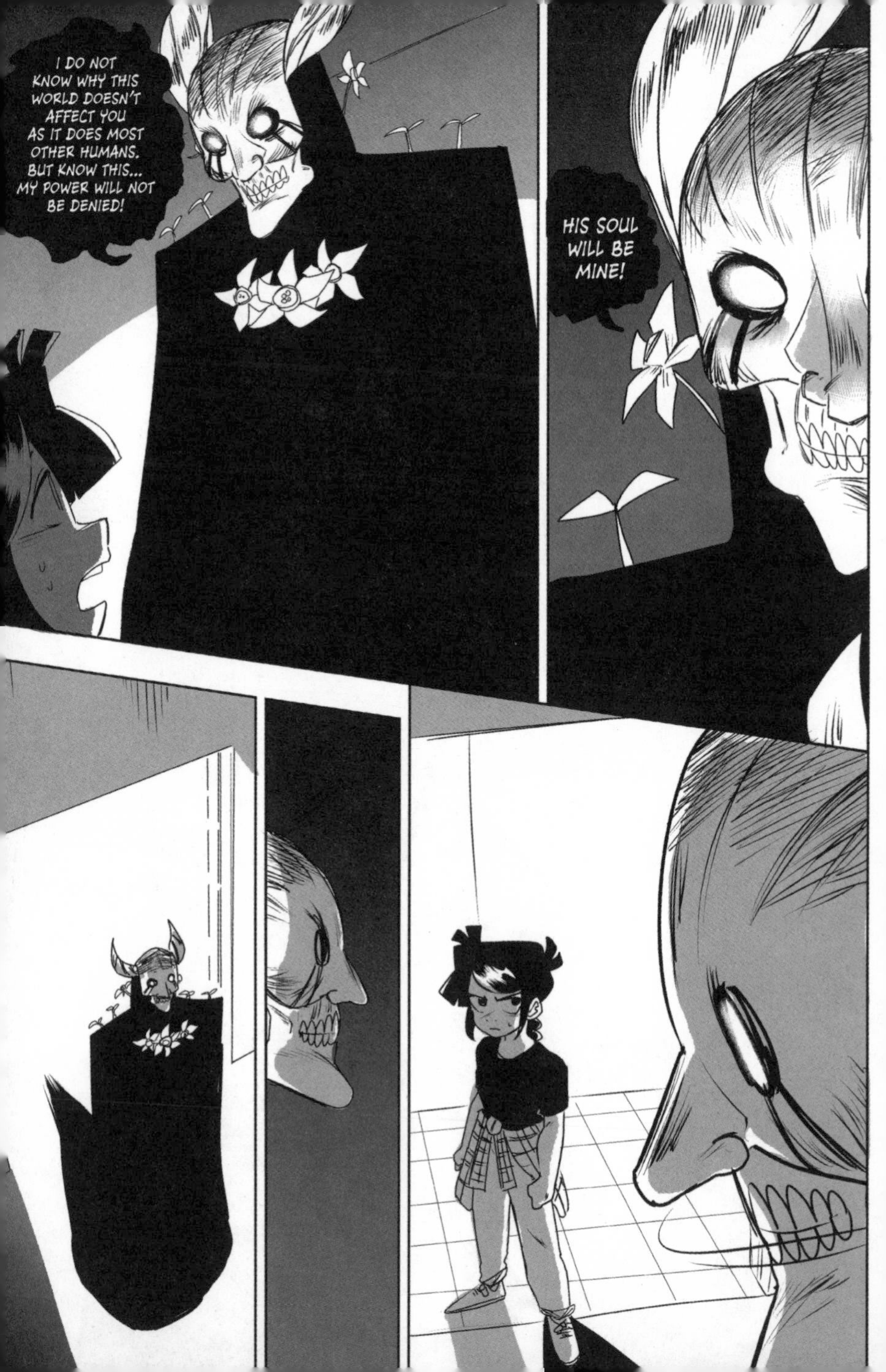
I DO NOT KNOW WHY THIS WORLD DOESN'T AFFECT YOU AS IT DOES MOST OTHER HUMANS. BUT KNOW THIS... MY POWER WILL NOT BE DENIED!
HIS SOUL WILL BE MINE!

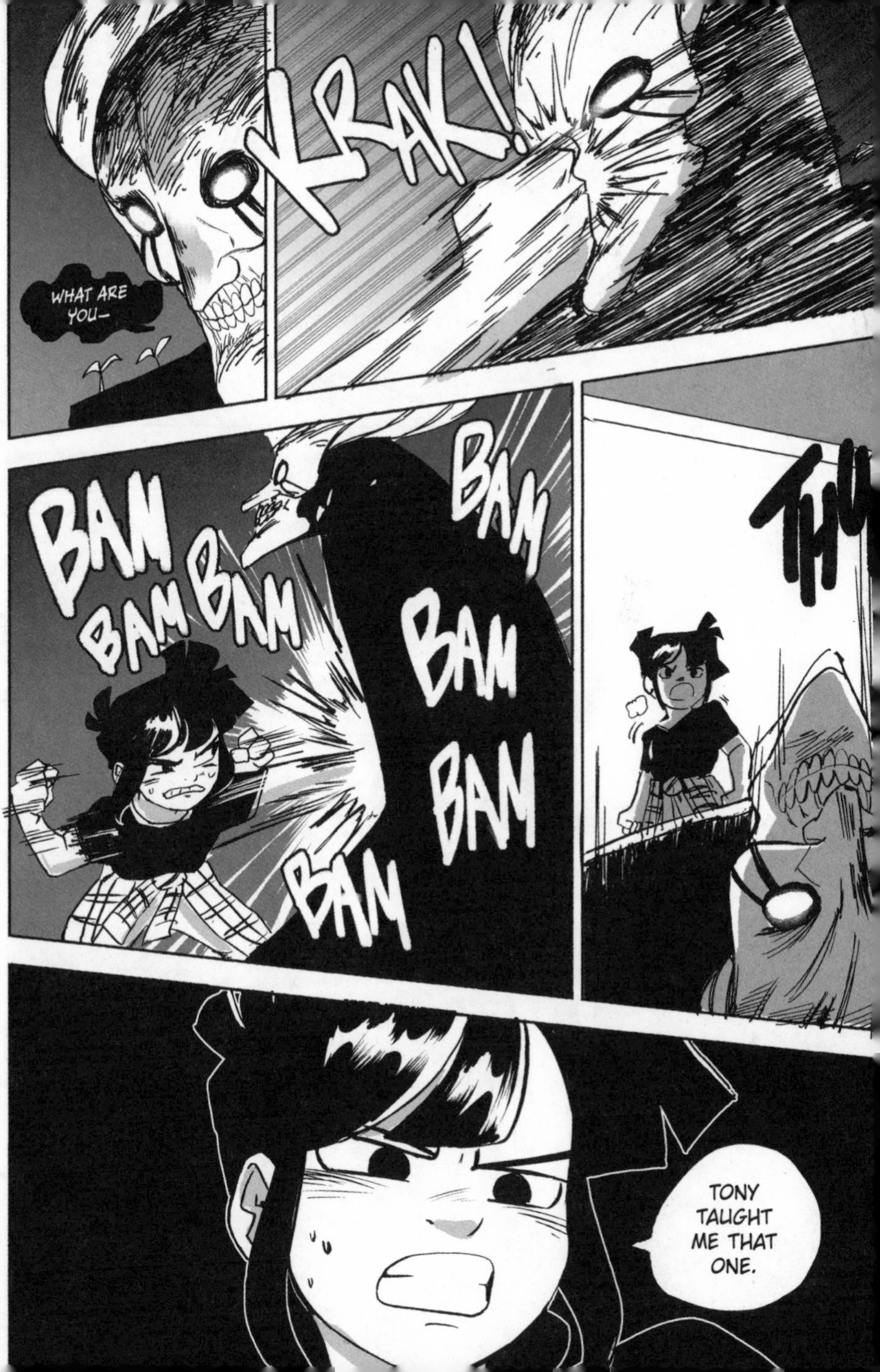
WHAT ARE YOU—
KRAK!
BAM BAM BAM BAM
BAM BAM BAM BAM
TONY TAUGHT ME THAT ONE.

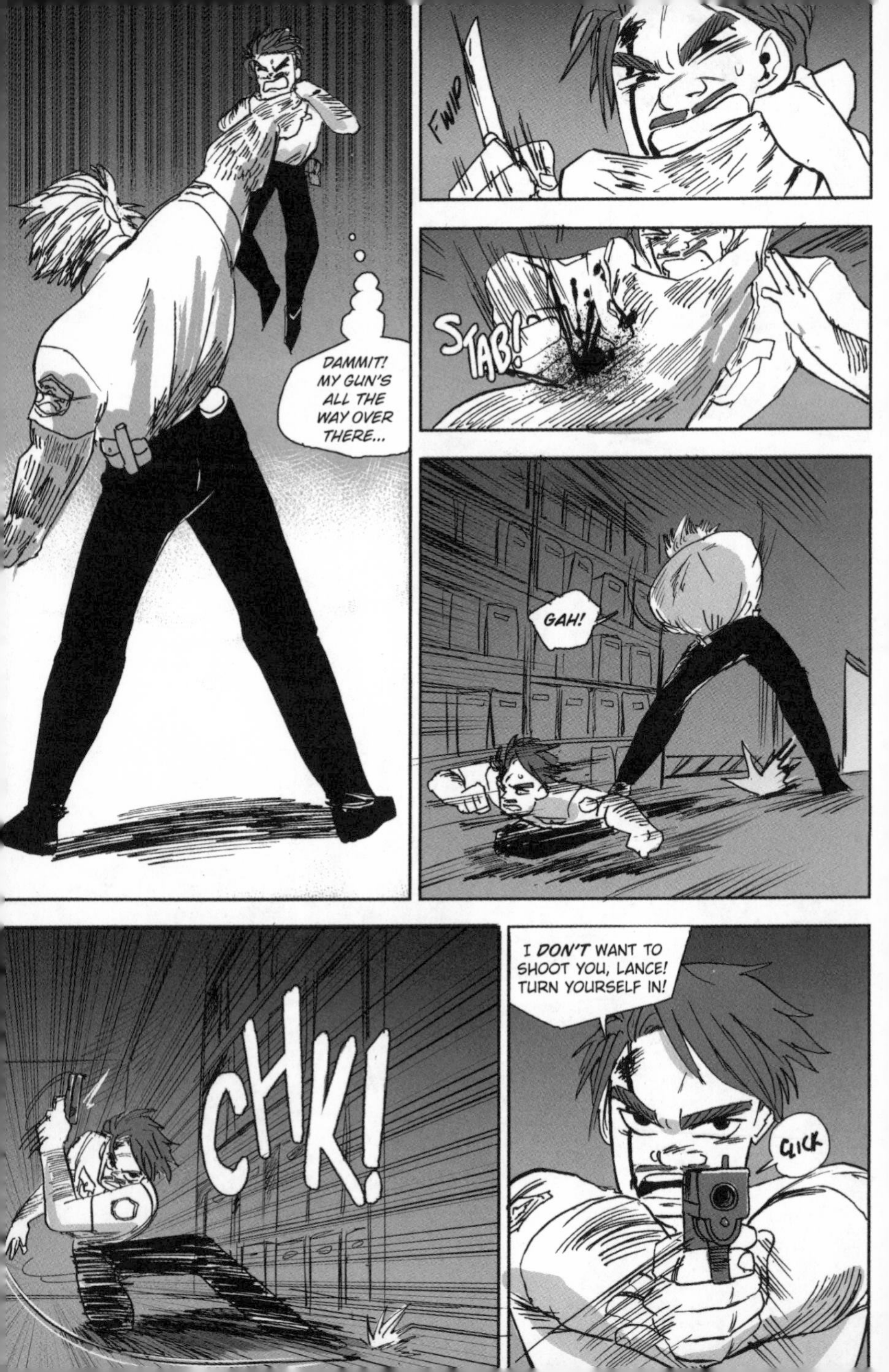
DAMMIT! MY GUN'S ALL THE WAY OVER THERE...
FWIP
STAB!
GAH!
CHK!
I DON'T WANT TO SHOOT YOU, LANCE! TURN YOURSELF IN!
CLICK

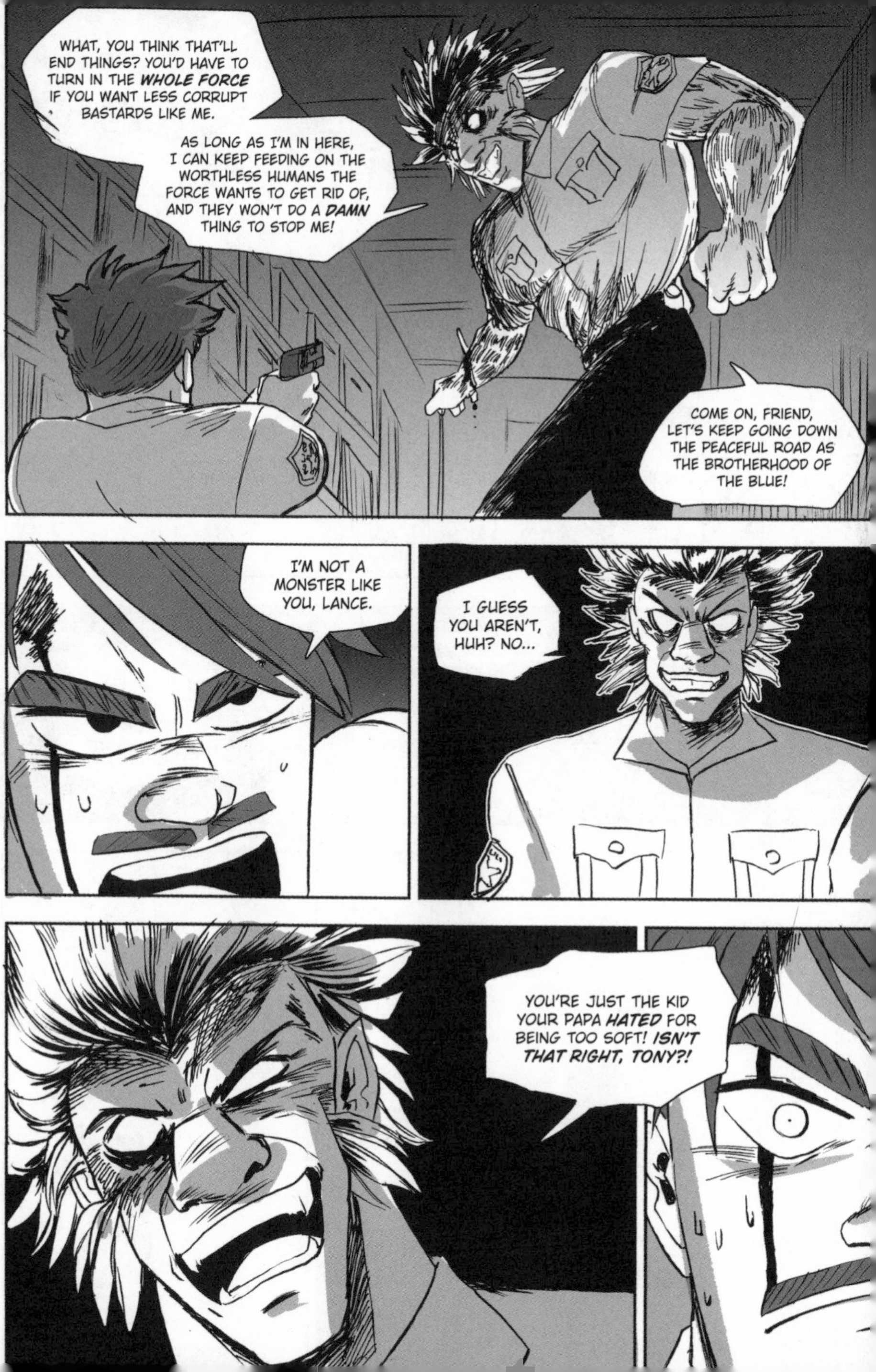
WHAT, YOU THINK THAT'LL END THINGS? YOU'D HAVE TO TURN IN THE **WHOLE FORCE** IF YOU WANT LESS CORRUPT BASTARDS LIKE ME.
AS LONG AS I'M IN HERE, I CAN KEEP FEEDING ON THE WORTHLESS HUMANS THE FORCE WANTS TO GET RID OF, AND THEY WON'T DO A ***DAMN*** THING TO STOP ME!
COME ON, FRIEND, LET'S KEEP GOING DOWN THE PEACEFUL ROAD AS THE BROTHERHOOD OF THE BLUE!
I'M NOT A MONSTER LIKE YOU, LANCE.
I GUESS YOU AREN'T, HUH? NO...
YOU'RE JUST THE KID YOUR PAPA ***HATED*** FOR BEING TOO SOFT! ***ISN'T THAT RIGHT, TONY?!***

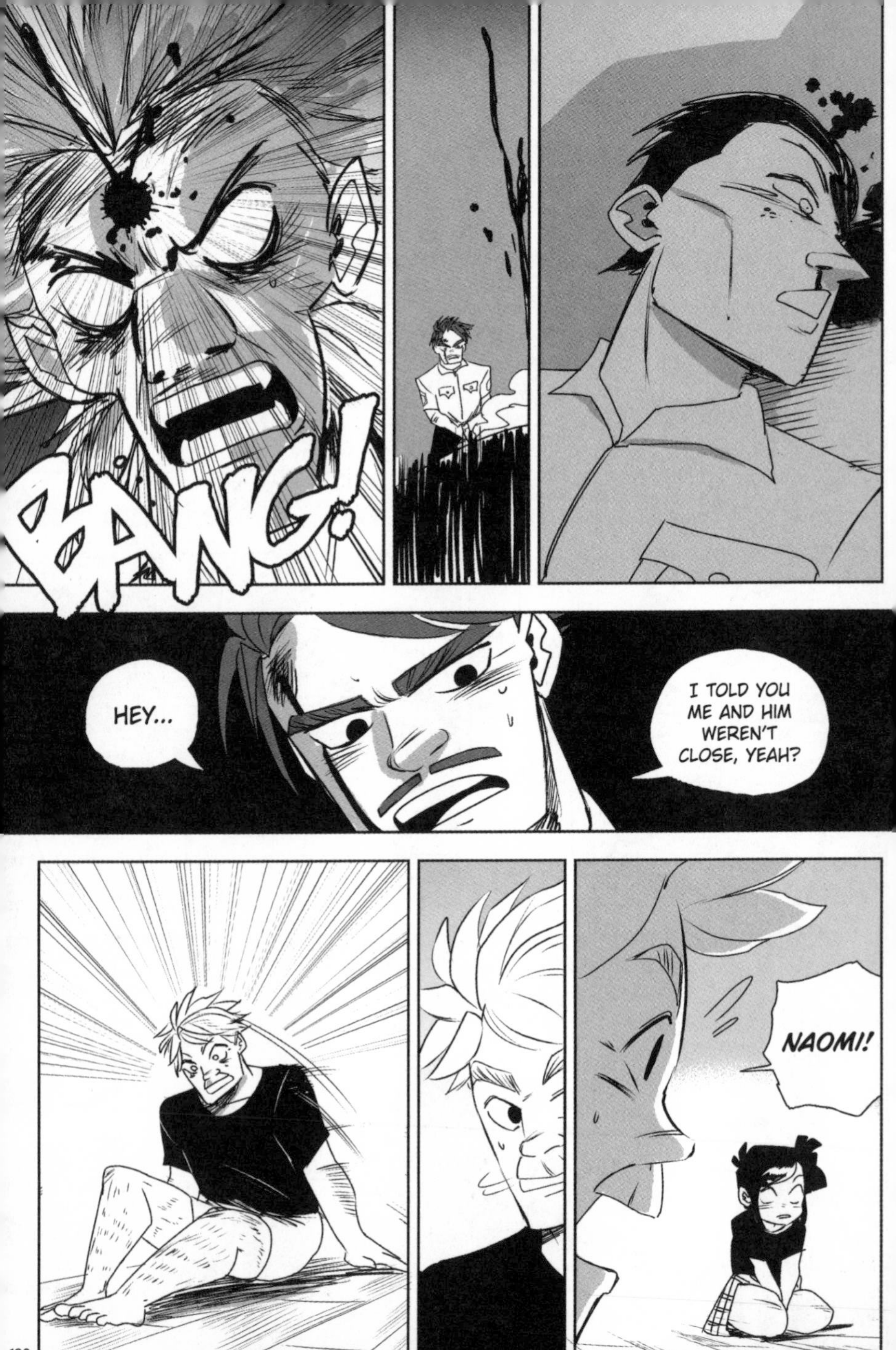
BANG!
HEY...
I TOLD YOU ME AND HIM WEREN'T CLOSE, YEAH?
NAOMI!

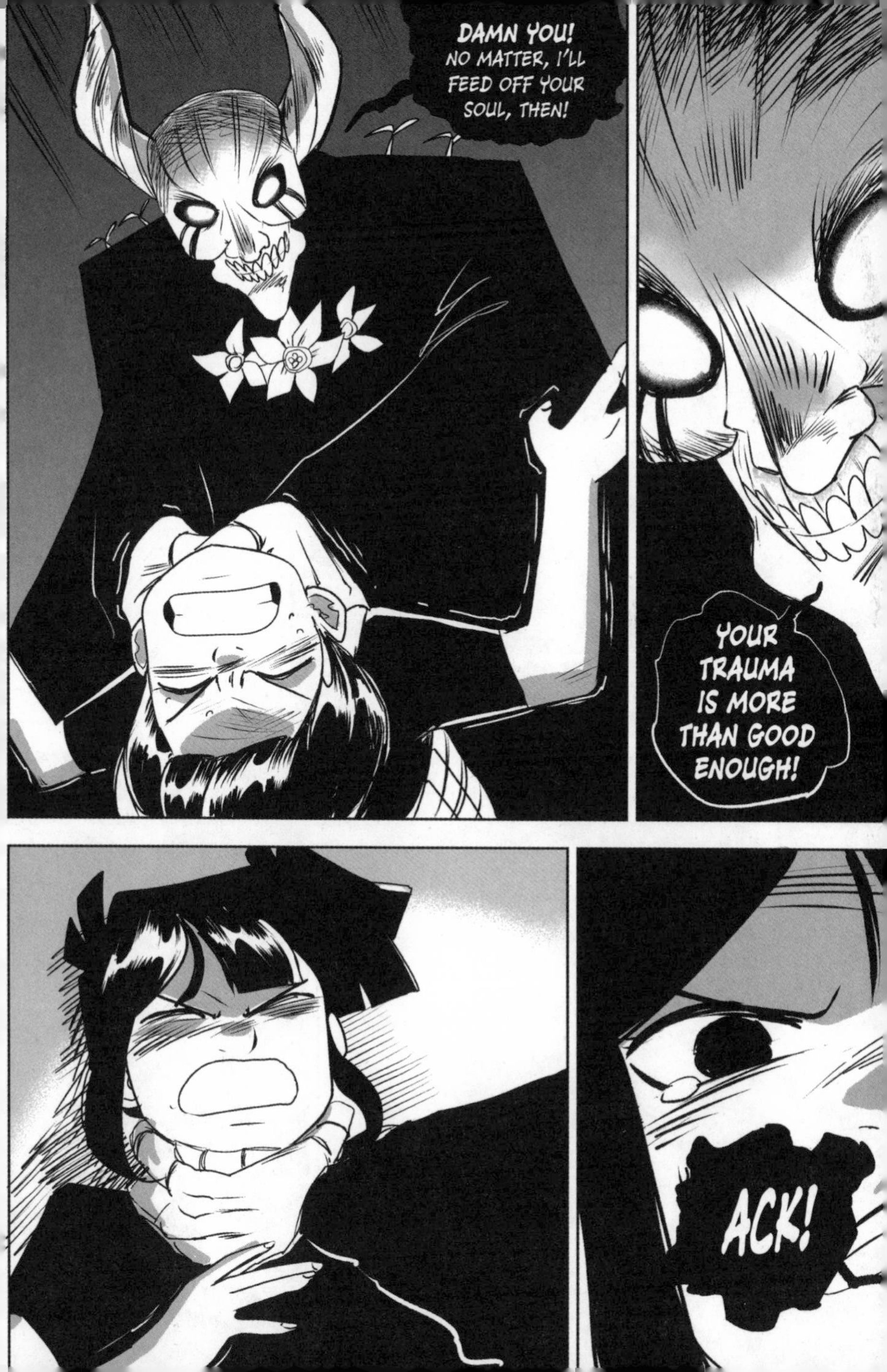
DAMN YOU! NO MATTER, I'LL FEED OFF YOUR SOUL, THEN!
YOUR TRAUMA IS MORE THAN GOOD ENOUGH!
ACK!

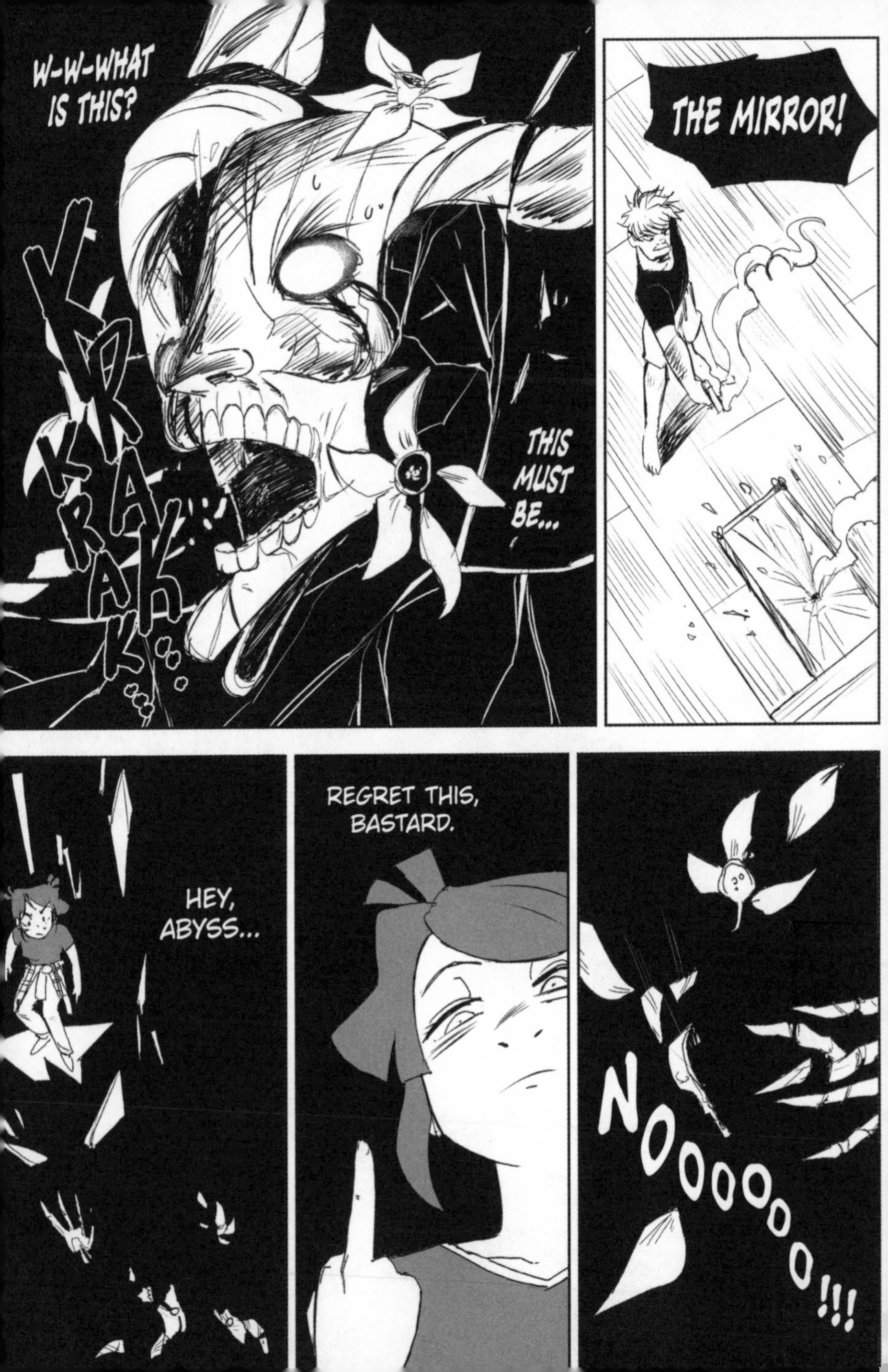
W-W-WHAT IS THIS?
KRAK KRAK
THIS MUST BE...
THE MIRROR!
HEY, ABYSS...
REGRET THIS, BASTARD.
NOOOOOOO!!!

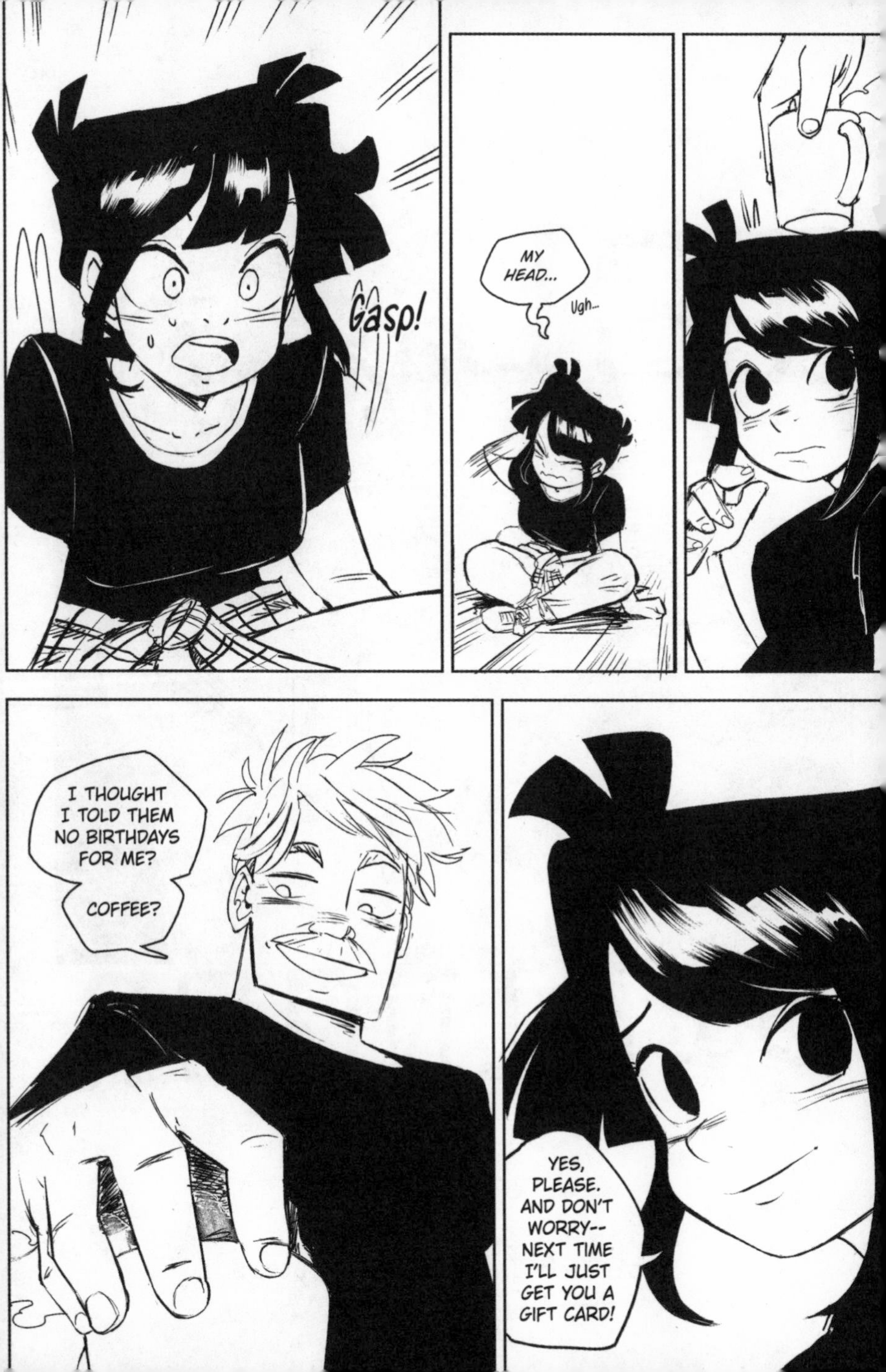
Gasp!
MY HEAD...
Ugh...
I THOUGHT I TOLD THEM NO BIRTHDAYS FOR ME?
COFFEE?
YES, PLEASE. AND DON'T WORRY-- NEXT TIME I'LL JUST GET YOU A GIFT CARD!

YELLOW

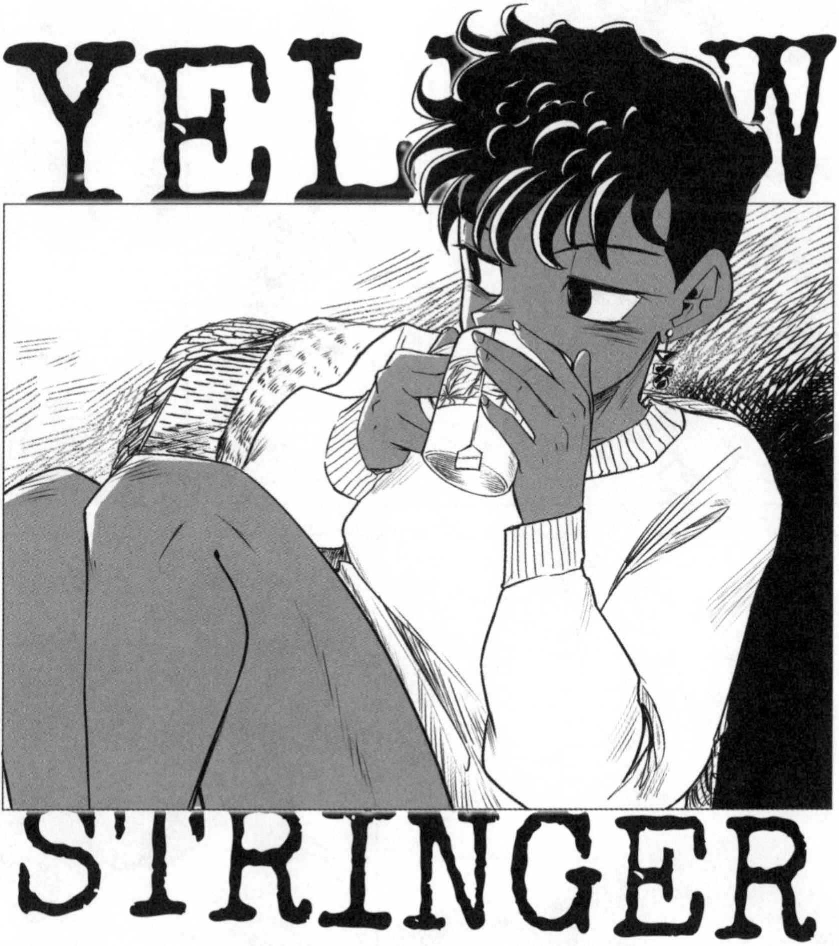

STRINGER

Article 8: Date-Night Jitters

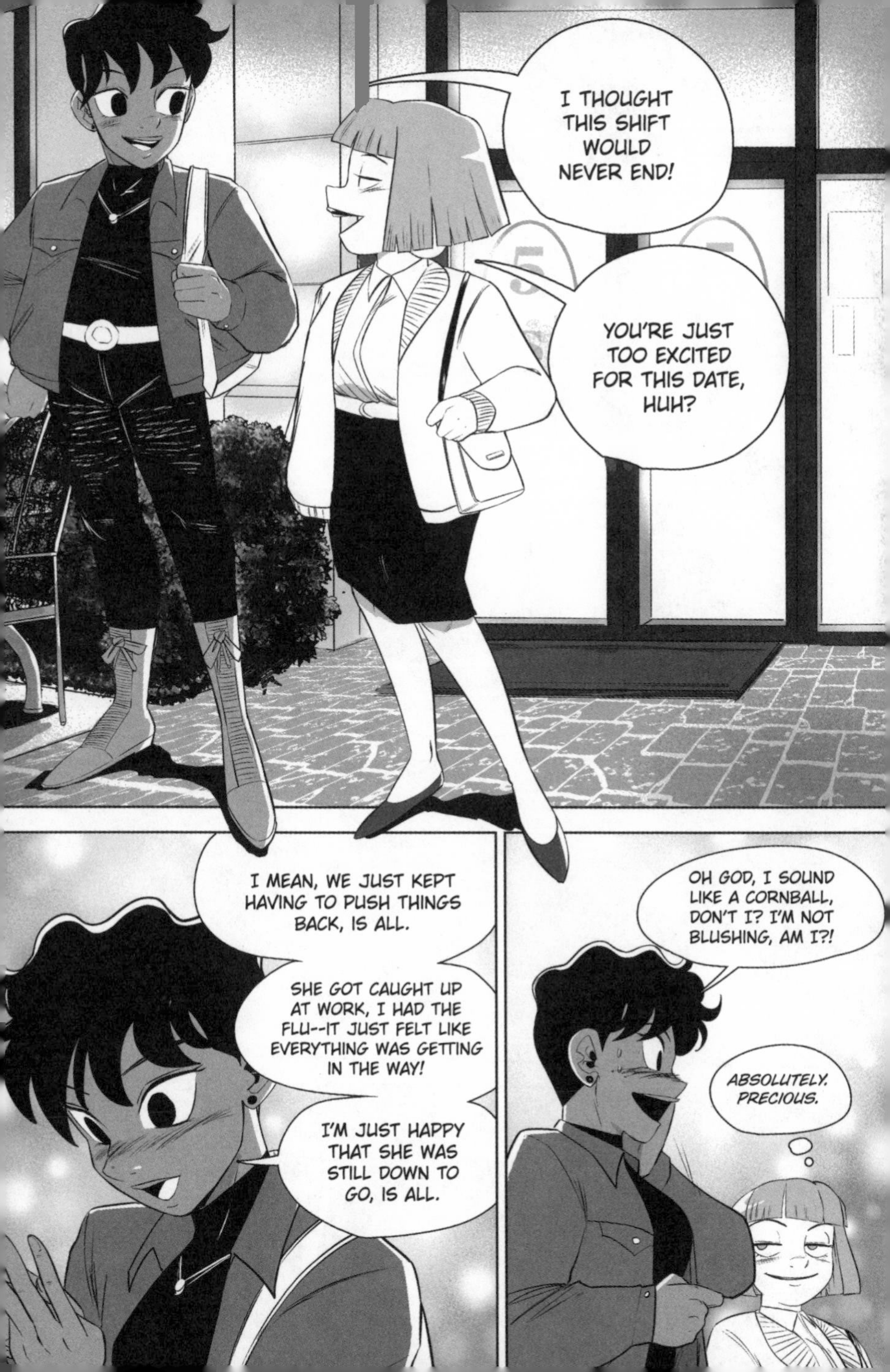

I THOUGHT THIS SHIFT WOULD NEVER END!
YOU'RE JUST TOO EXCITED FOR THIS DATE, HUH?
I MEAN, WE JUST KEPT HAVING TO PUSH THINGS BACK, IS ALL.
SHE GOT CAUGHT UP AT WORK, I HAD THE FLU--IT JUST FELT LIKE EVERYTHING WAS GETTING IN THE WAY!
I'M JUST HAPPY THAT SHE WAS STILL DOWN TO GO, IS ALL.
OH GOD, I SOUND LIKE A CORNBALL, DON'T I? I'M NOT BLUSHING, AM I?!
ABSOLUTELY. PRECIOUS.

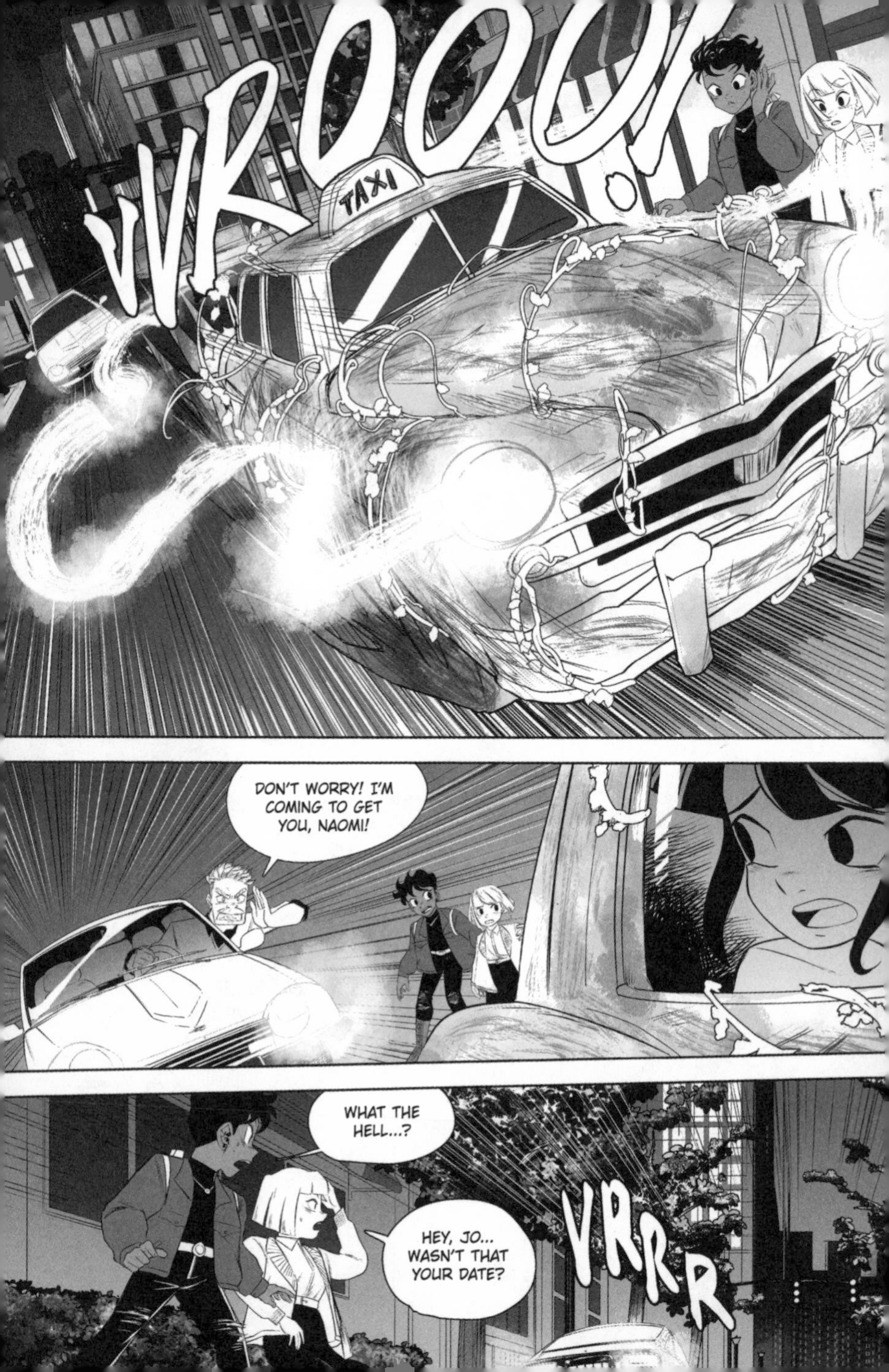
VVROOOM
TAXI
DON'T WORRY! I'M COMING TO GET YOU, NAOMI!
WHAT THE HELL...?
HEY, JO... WASN'T THAT YOUR DATE?
VRRR

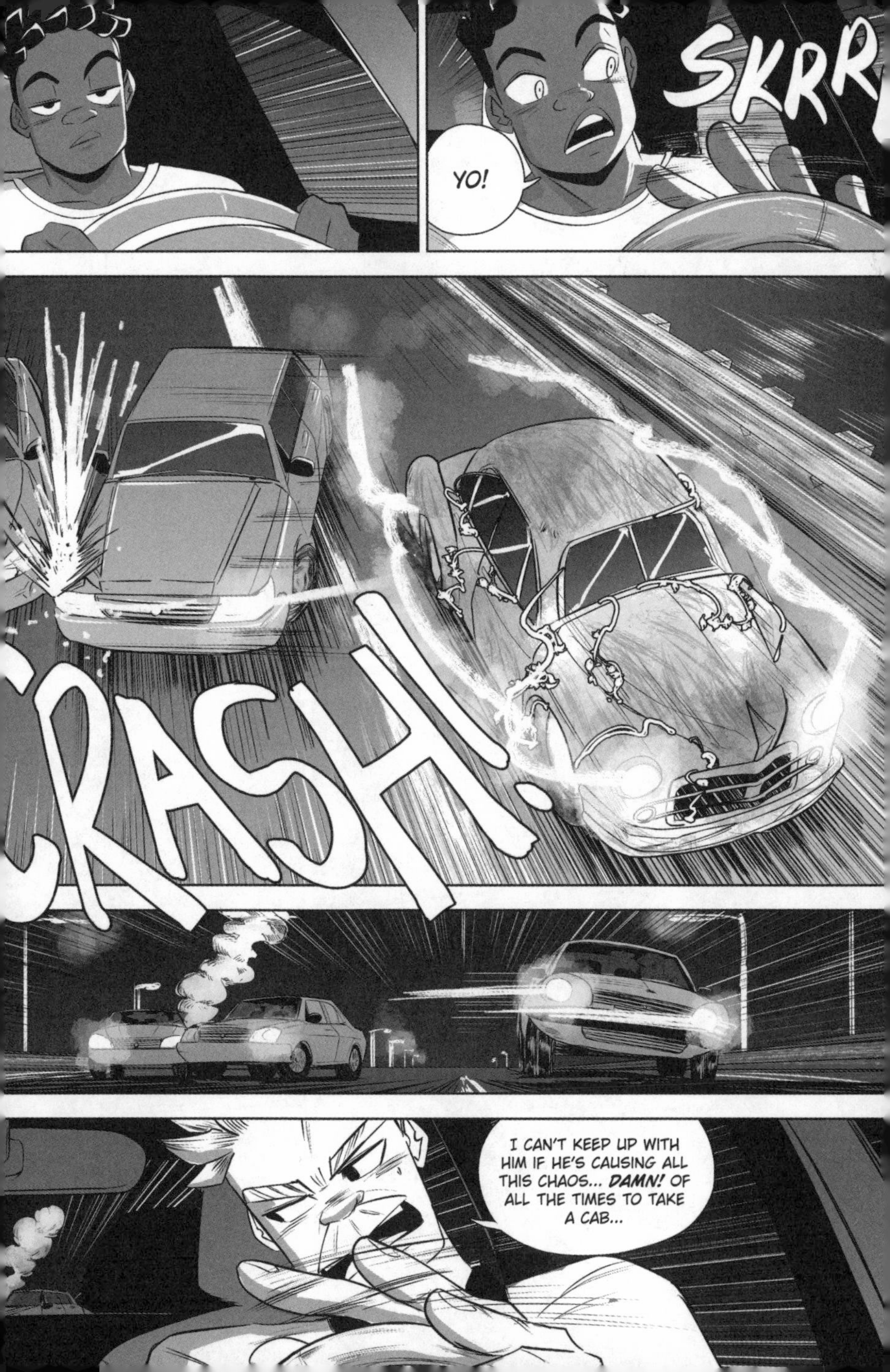
YO!
SKRR
CRASH!
I CAN'T KEEP UP WITH HIM IF HE'S CAUSING ALL THIS CHAOS... *DAMN!* OF ALL THE TIMES TO TAKE A CAB...

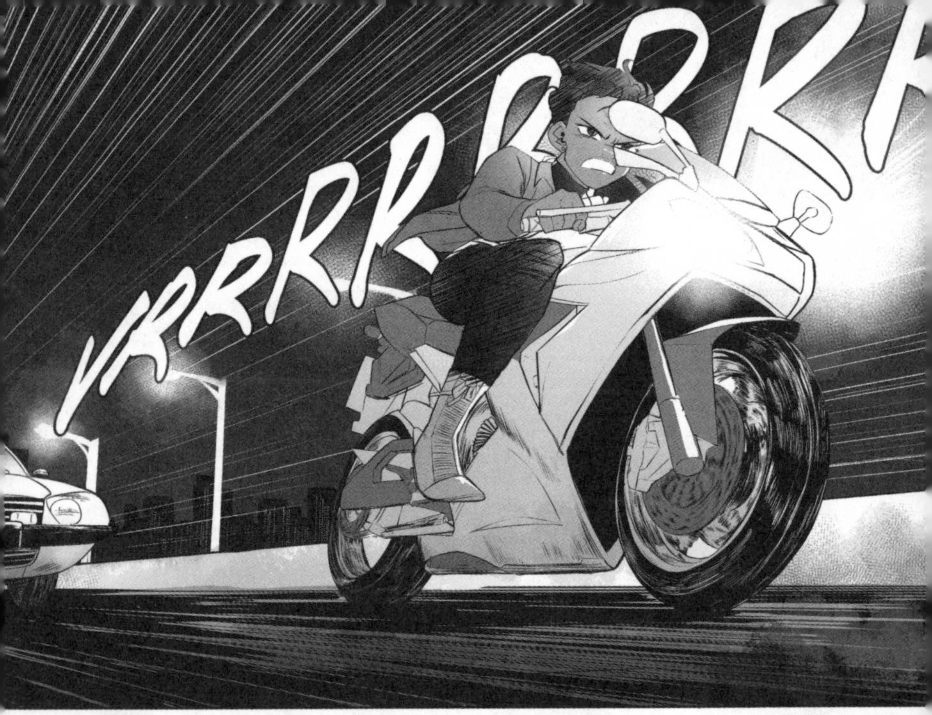

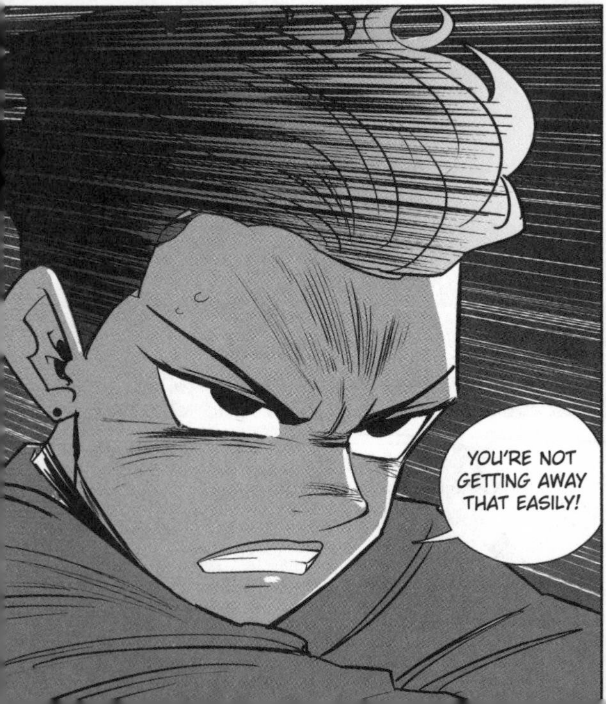
YOU'RE NOT GETTING AWAY THAT EASILY!

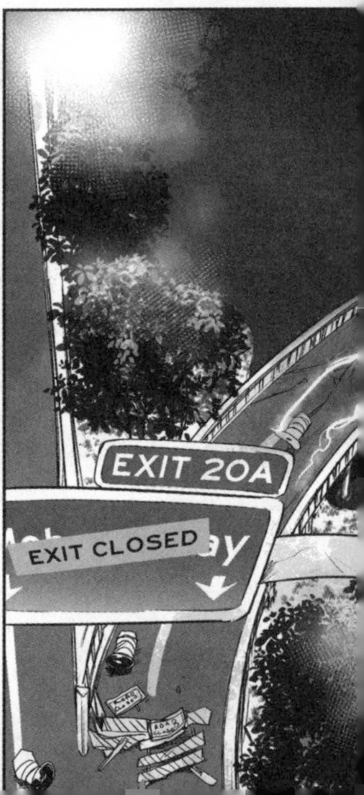
EXIT 20A
EXIT CLOSED

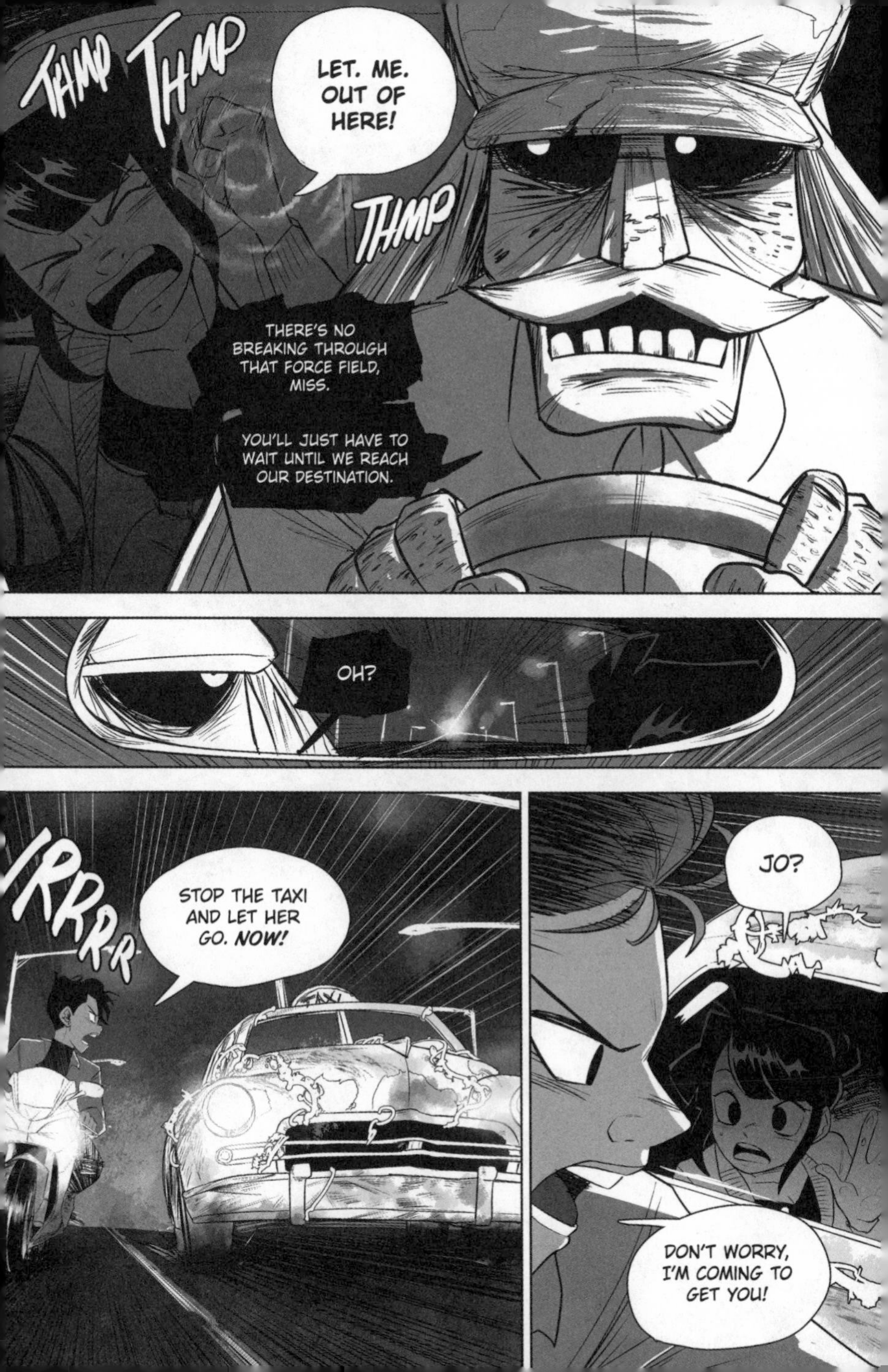
THMP THMP
LET. ME. OUT OF HERE!
THMP
THERE'S NO BREAKING THROUGH THAT FORCE FIELD, MISS.
YOU'LL JUST HAVE TO WAIT UNTIL WE REACH OUR DESTINATION.
OH?
RRRRR
STOP THE TAXI AND LET HER GO. NOW!
TAXI
JO?
DON'T WORRY, I'M COMING TO GET YOU!

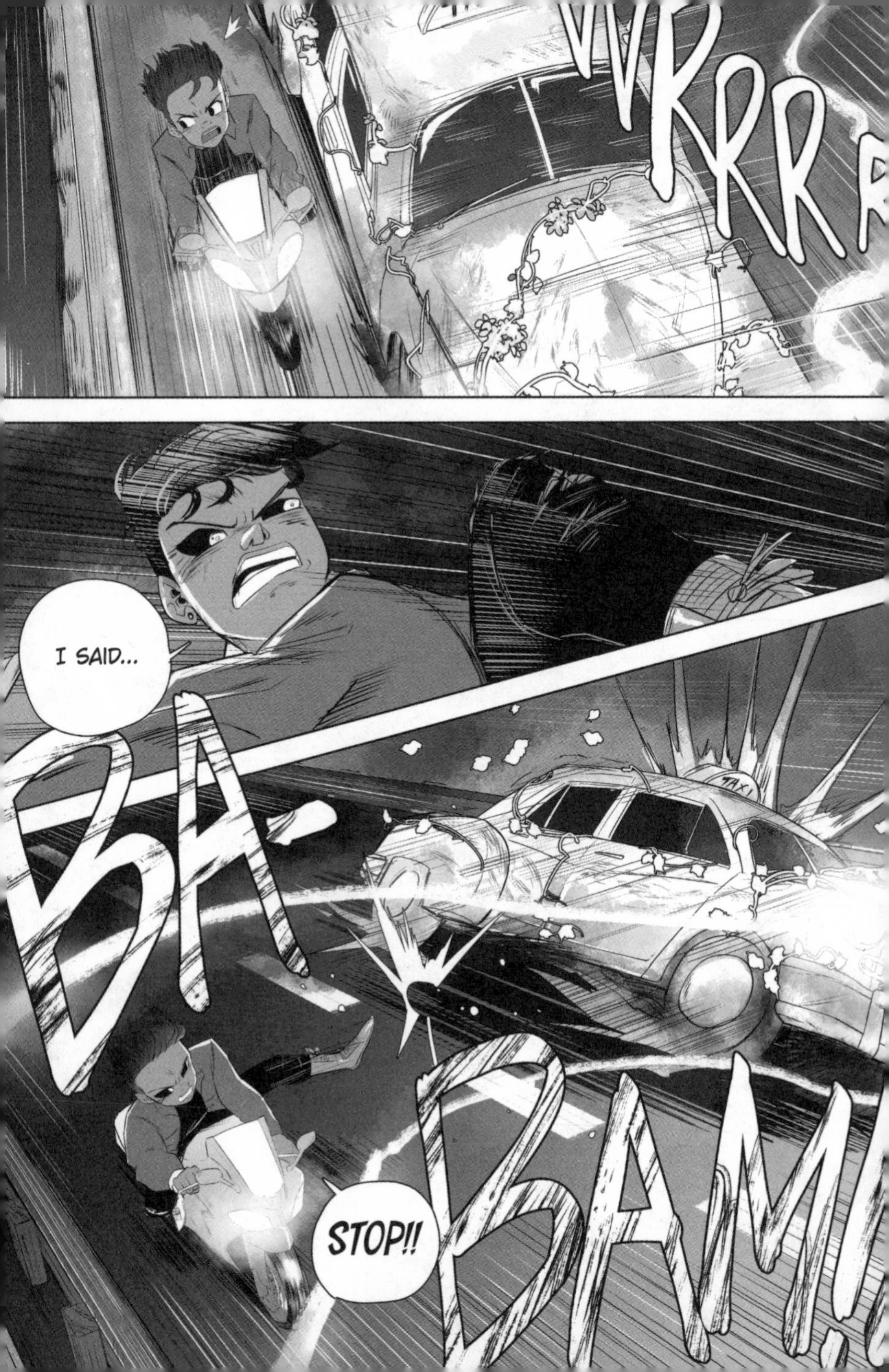
VVRRRR
I SAID...
BA
STOP!!
BAM!

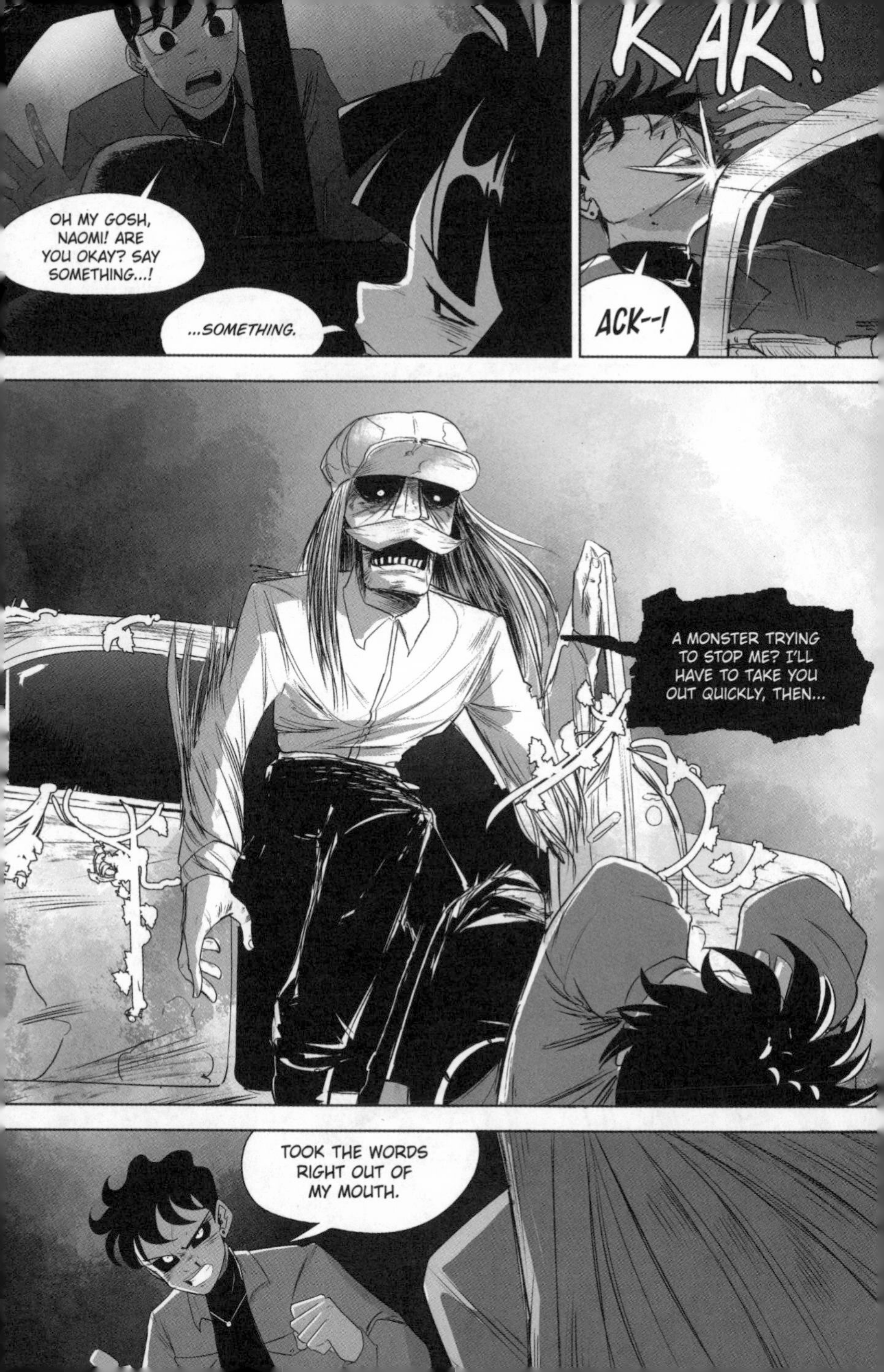
OH MY GOSH, NAOMI! ARE YOU OKAY? SAY SOMETHING...!
...SOMETHING.
KAK!
ACK--!
A MONSTER TRYING TO STOP ME? I'LL HAVE TO TAKE YOU OUT QUICKLY, THEN...
TOOK THE WORDS RIGHT OUT OF MY MOUTH.

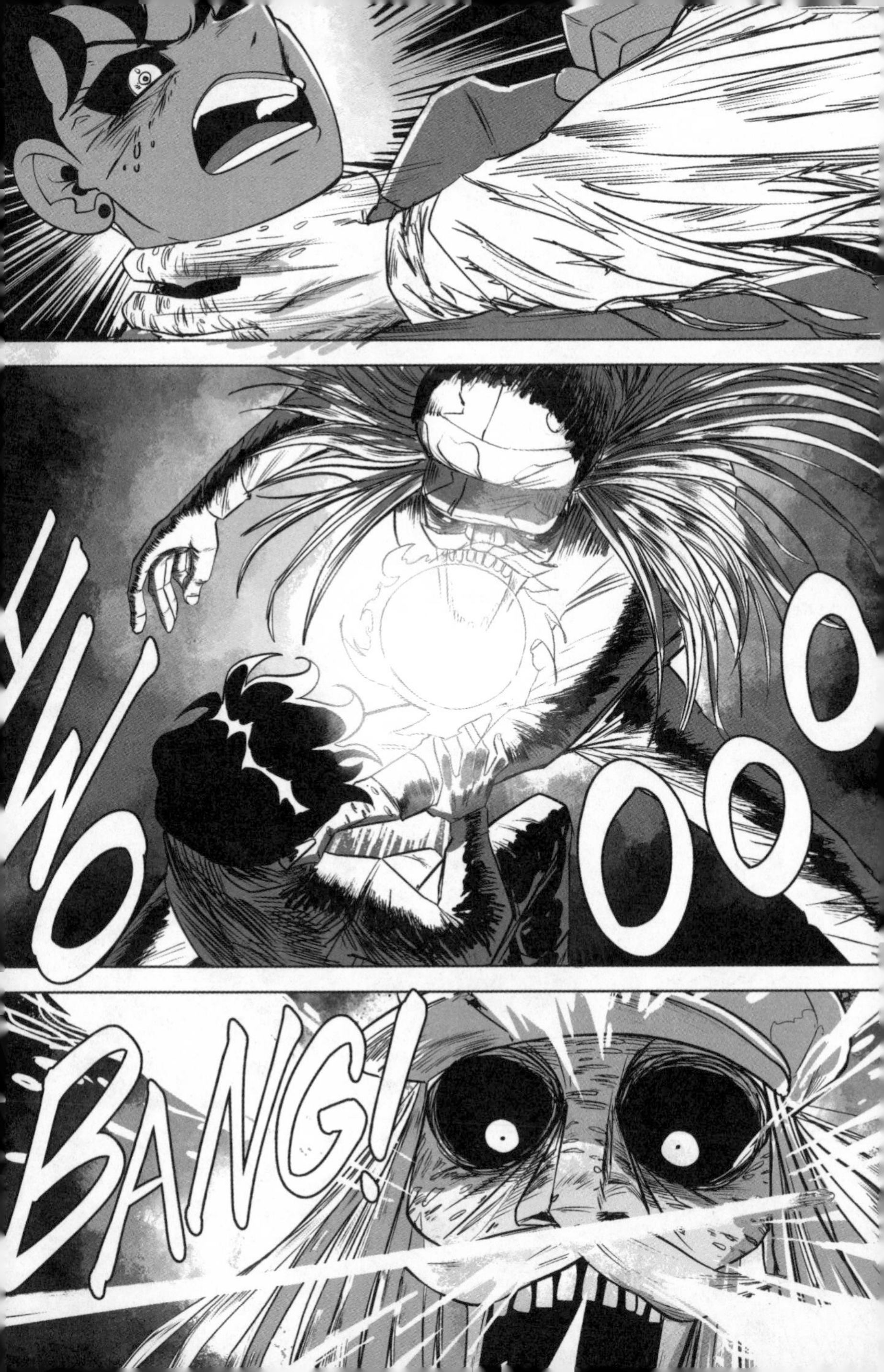
WOOOOO
BANG!

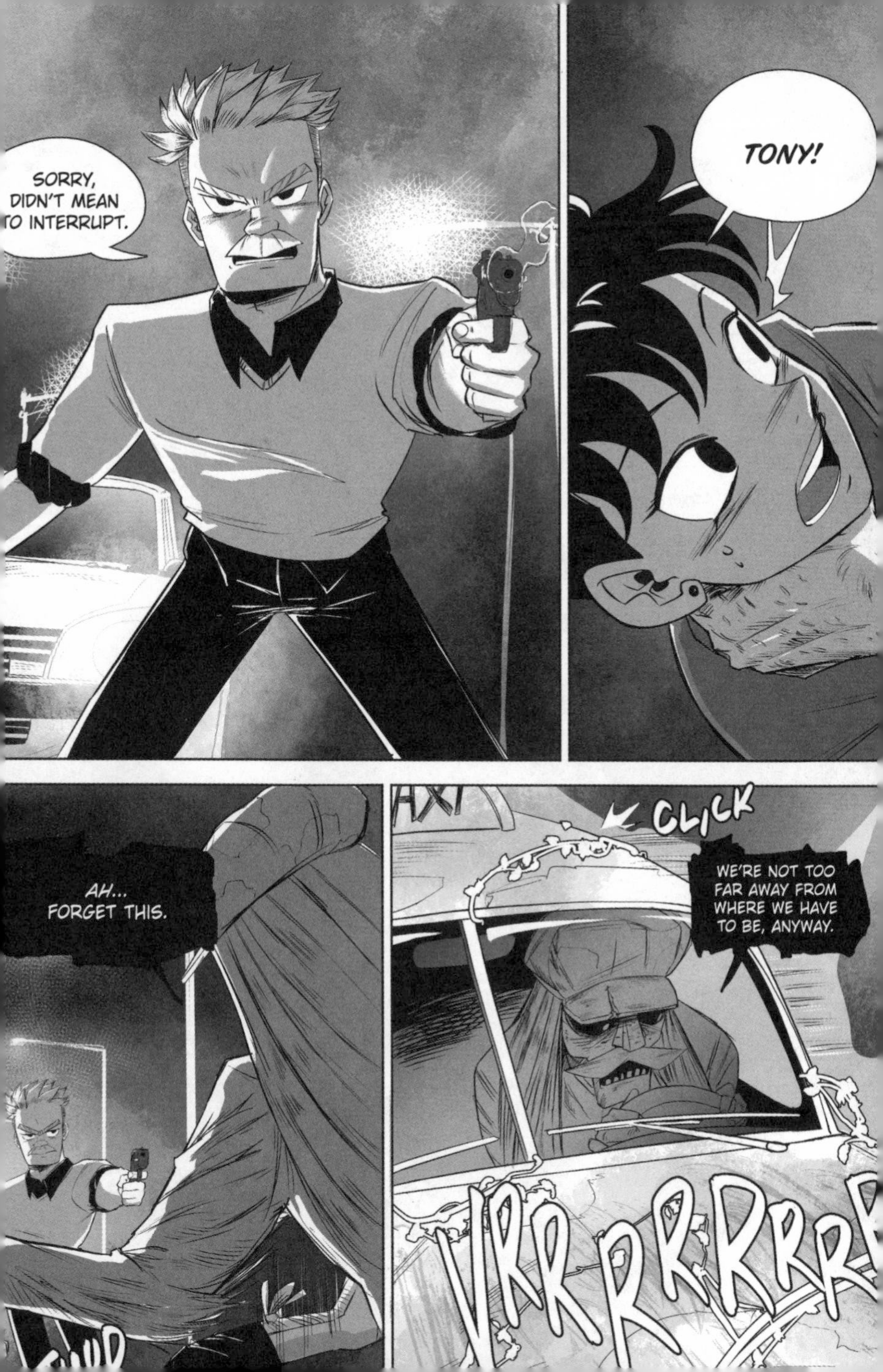

SORRY, DIDN'T MEAN TO INTERRUPT.
TONY!
AH... FORGET THIS.
CLICK
WE'RE NOT TOO FAR AWAY FROM WHERE WE HAVE TO BE, ANYWAY.
VRRRRRRR

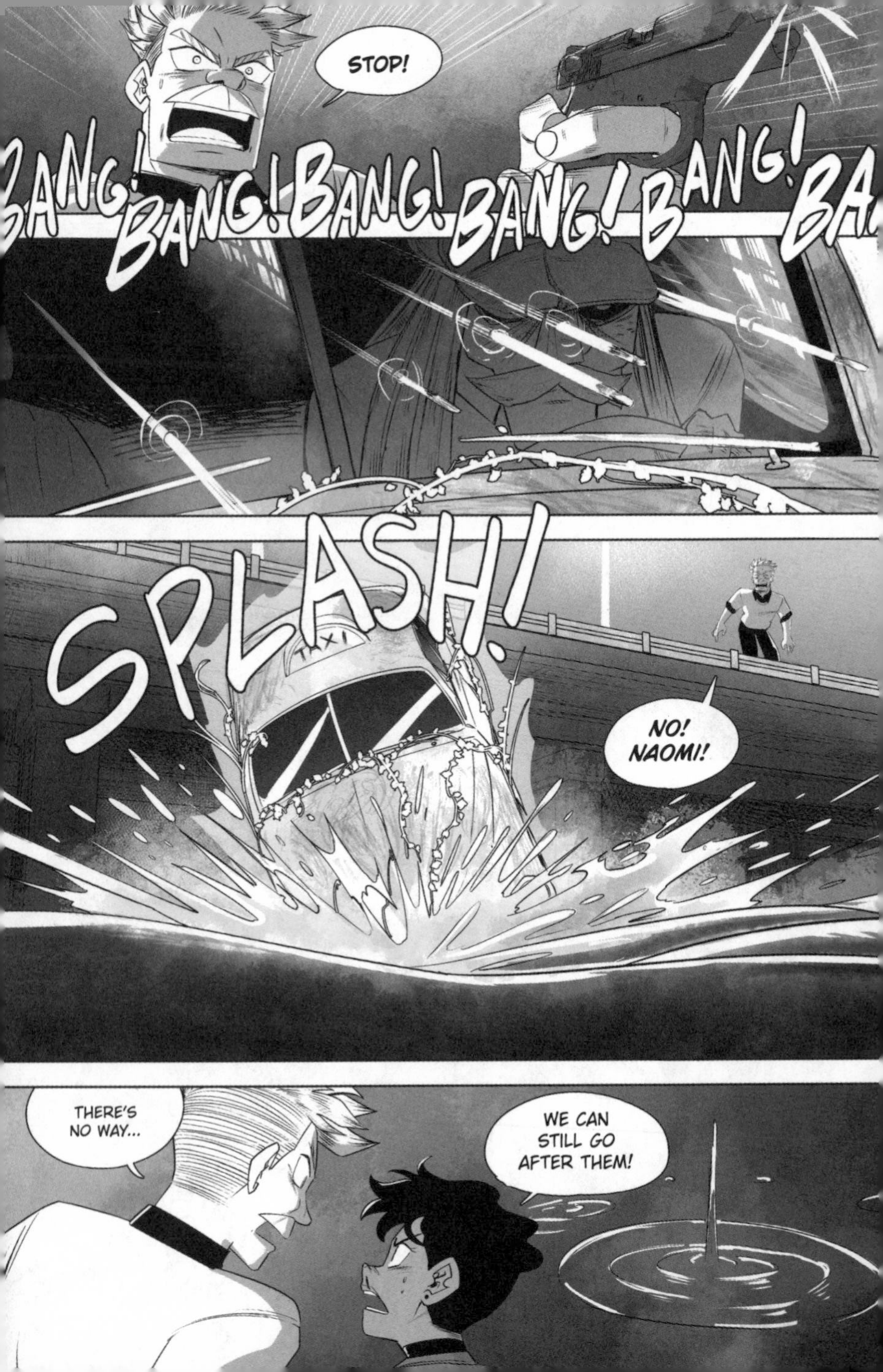
STOP!
BANG! BANG! BANG! BANG! BANG! BA
SPLASH!
NO! NAOMI!
THERE'S NO WAY...
WE CAN STILL GO AFTER THEM!

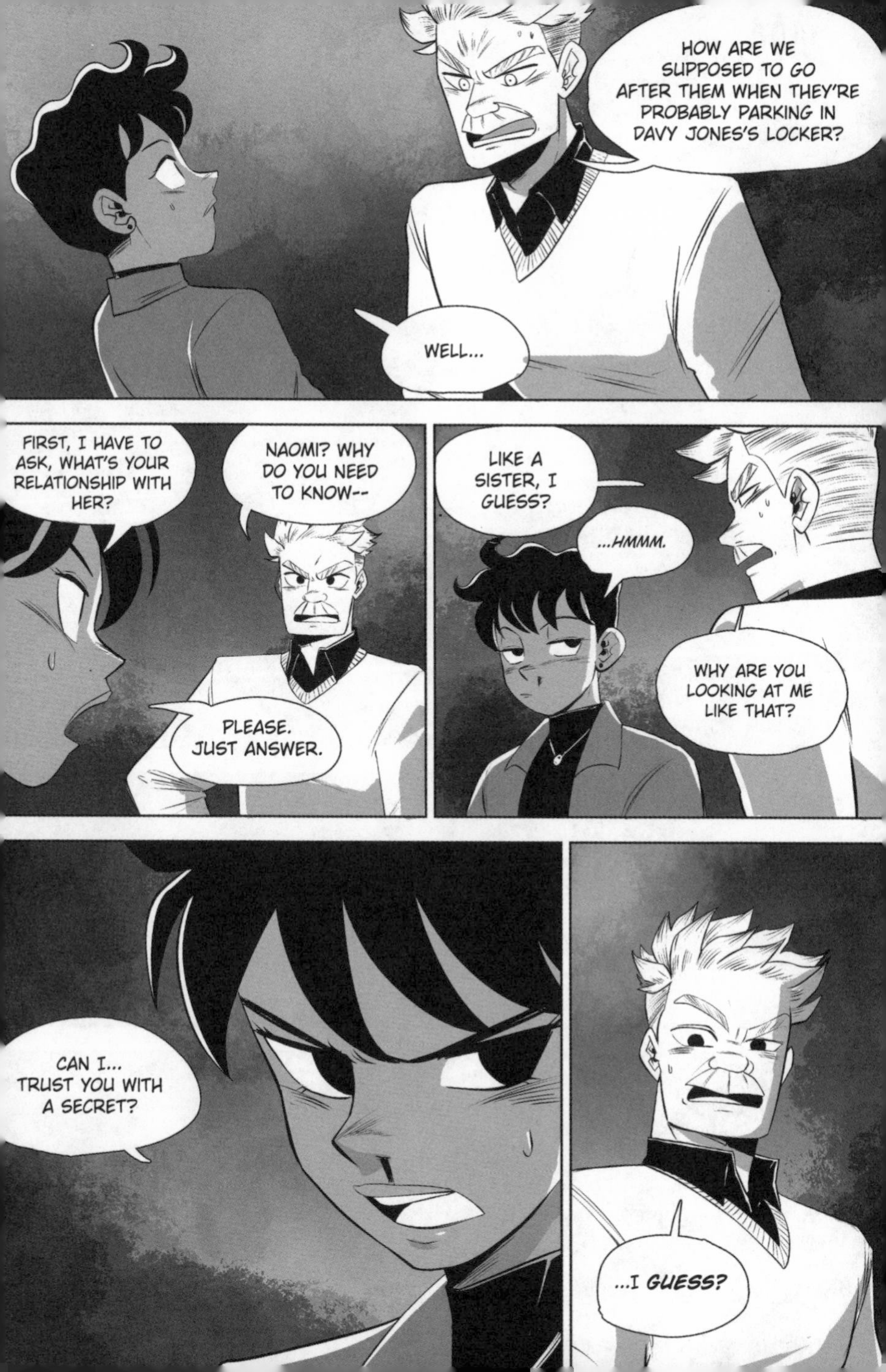
HOW ARE WE SUPPOSED TO GO AFTER THEM WHEN THEY'RE PROBABLY PARKING IN DAVY JONES'S LOCKER?
WELL...
FIRST, I HAVE TO ASK, WHAT'S YOUR RELATIONSHIP WITH HER?
NAOMI? WHY DO YOU NEED TO KNOW--
PLEASE. JUST ANSWER.
LIKE A SISTER, I GUESS?
...HMMM.
WHY ARE YOU LOOKING AT ME LIKE THAT?
CAN I... TRUST YOU WITH A SECRET?
...I GUESS?

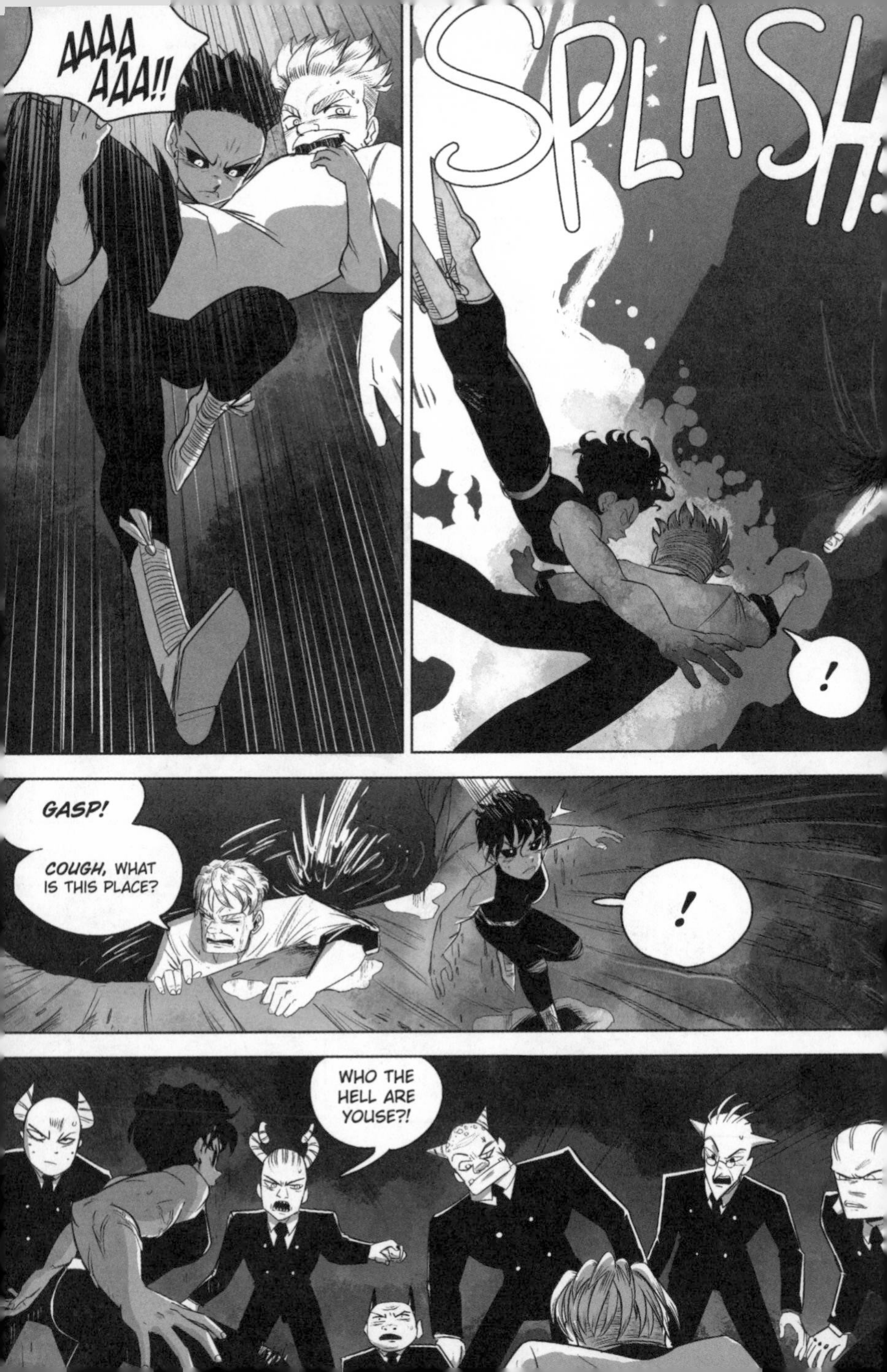

AAAA AAA!!
SPLASH!
!
GASP!
COUGH, WHAT IS THIS PLACE?
!
WHO THE HELL ARE YOUSE?!

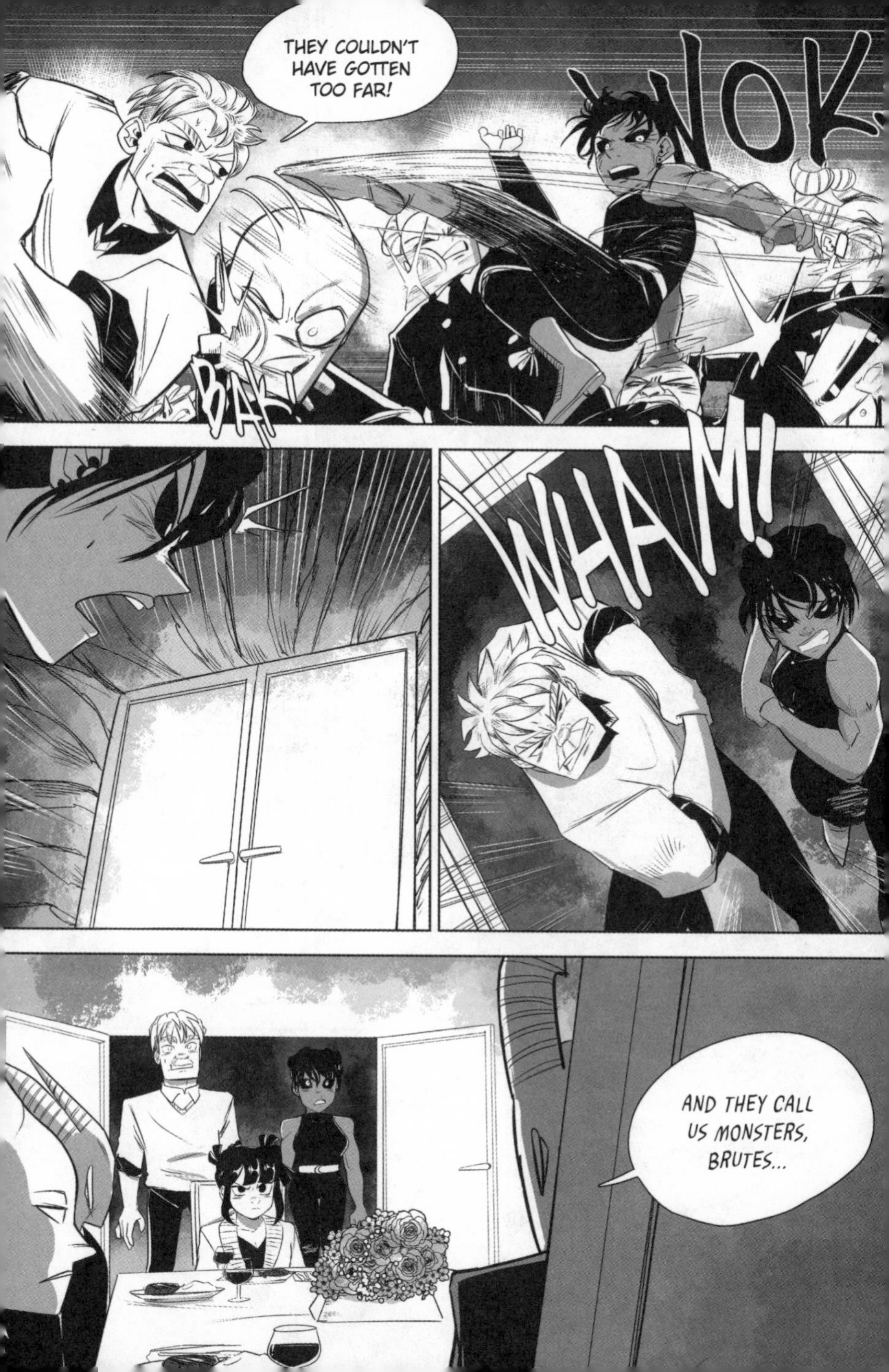
THEY COULDN'T HAVE GOTTEN TOO FAR!
WOK!
BAK!
WHAM!
AND THEY CALL US MONSTERS, BRUTES...

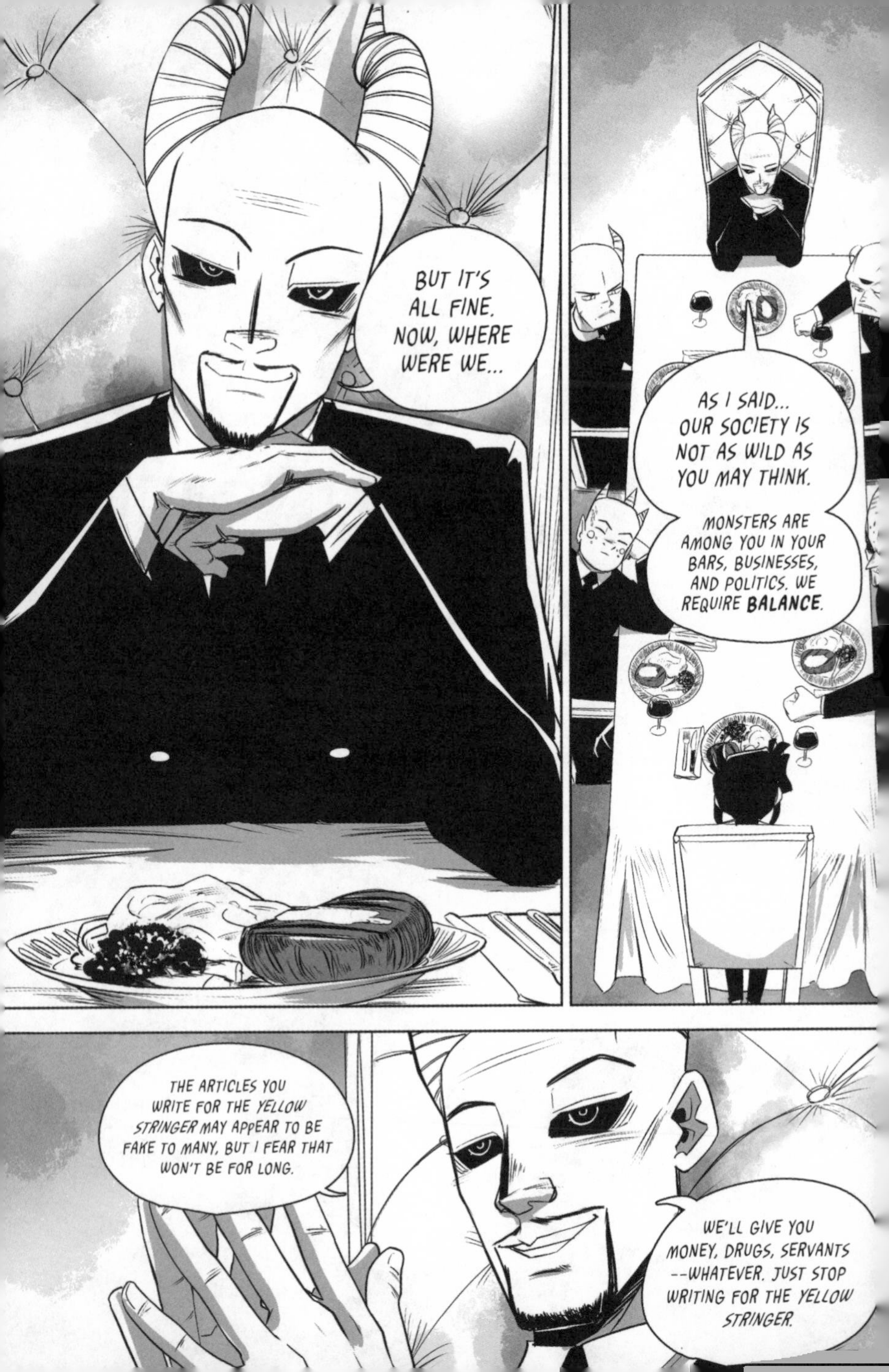
BUT IT'S ALL FINE. NOW, WHERE WERE WE...
AS I SAID... OUR SOCIETY IS NOT AS WILD AS YOU MAY THINK.
MONSTERS ARE AMONG YOU IN YOUR BARS, BUSINESSES, AND POLITICS. WE REQUIRE **BALANCE**.
THE ARTICLES YOU WRITE FOR THE *YELLOW STRINGER* MAY APPEAR TO BE FAKE TO MANY, BUT I FEAR THAT WON'T BE FOR LONG.
WE'LL GIVE YOU MONEY, DRUGS, SERVANTS --WHATEVER. JUST STOP WRITING FOR THE *YELLOW STRINGER*.

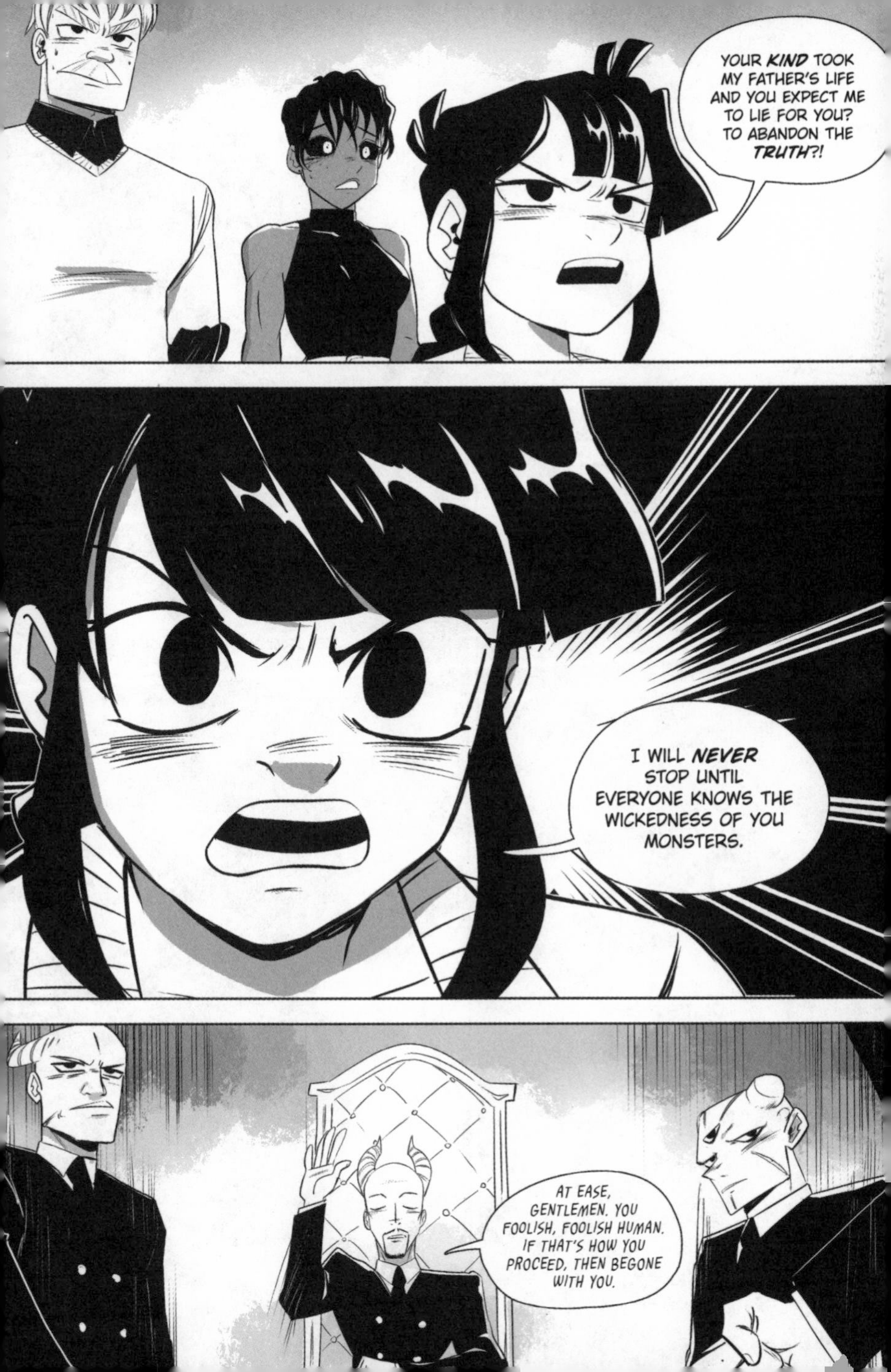
YOUR KIND TOOK MY FATHER'S LIFE AND YOU EXPECT ME TO LIE FOR YOU? TO ABANDON THE TRUTH?!
I WILL NEVER STOP UNTIL EVERYONE KNOWS THE WICKEDNESS OF YOU MONSTERS.
AT EASE, GENTLEMEN. YOU FOOLISH, FOOLISH HUMAN. IF THAT'S HOW YOU PROCEED, THEN BEGONE WITH YOU.

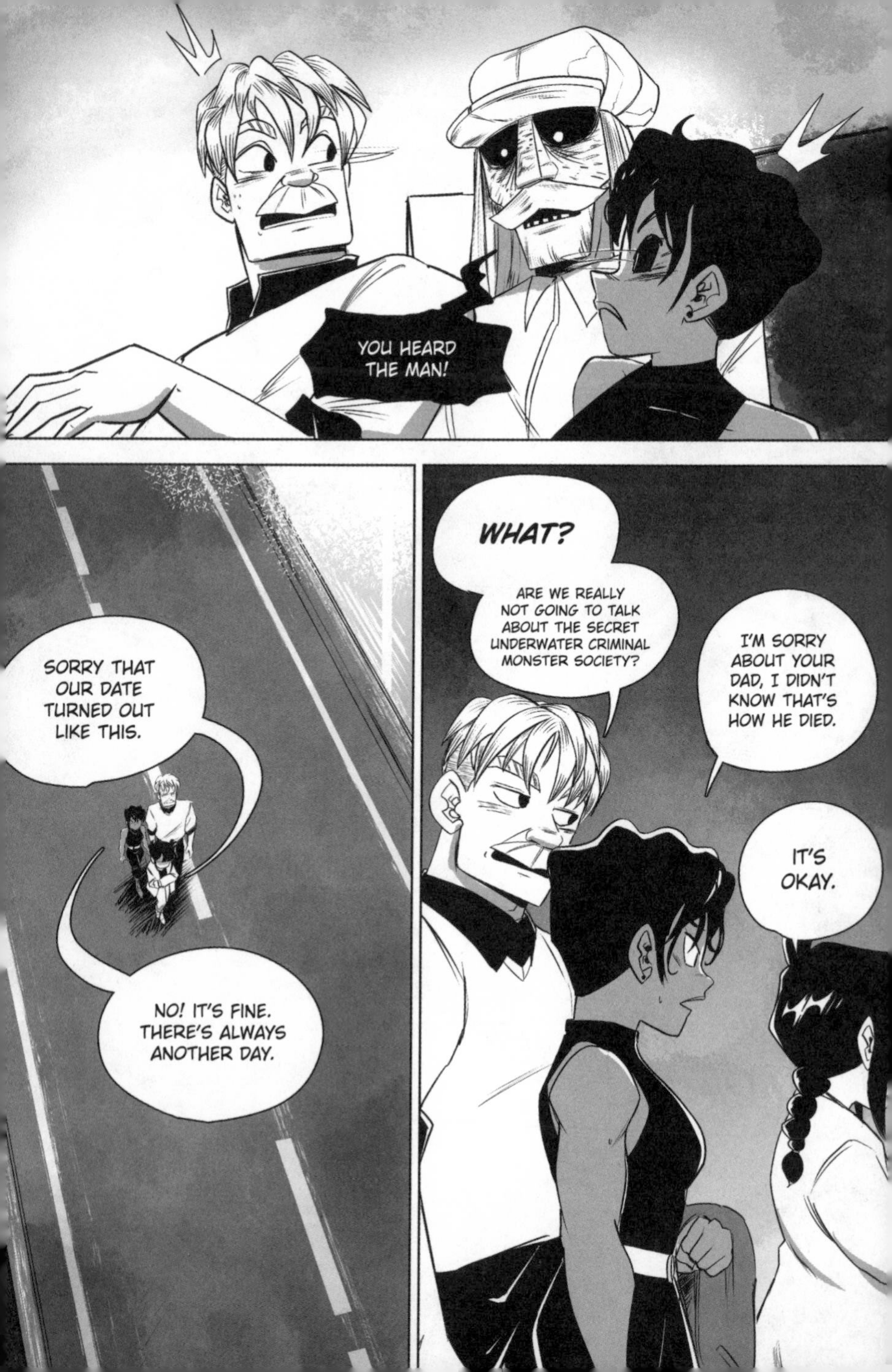
YOU HEARD THE MAN!
SORRY THAT OUR DATE TURNED OUT LIKE THIS.
NO! IT'S FINE. THERE'S ALWAYS ANOTHER DAY.
WHAT?
ARE WE REALLY NOT GOING TO TALK ABOUT THE SECRET UNDERWATER CRIMINAL MONSTER SOCIETY?
I'M SORRY ABOUT YOUR DAD, I DIDN'T KNOW THAT'S HOW HE DIED.
IT'S OKAY.

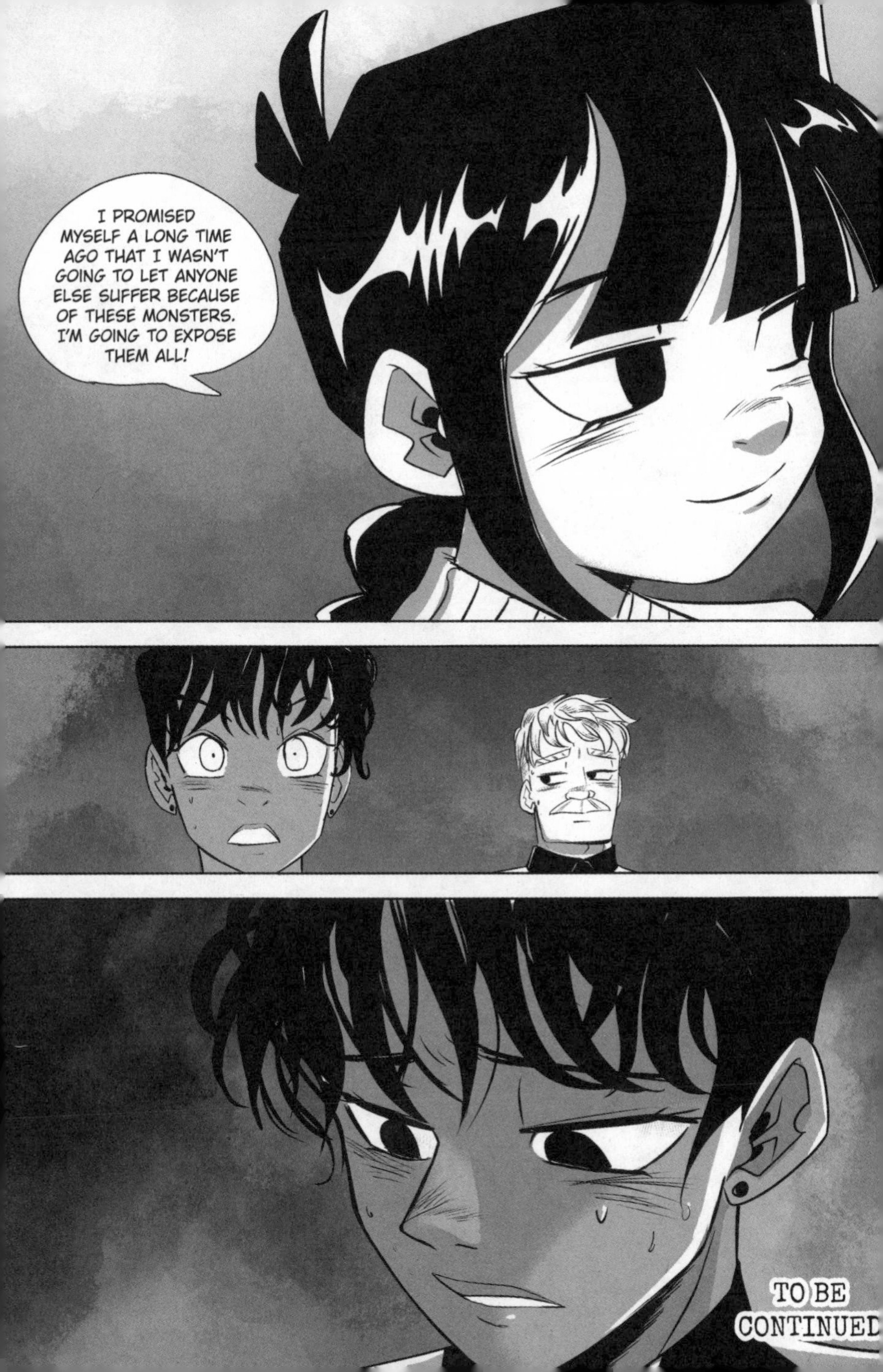
I PROMISED MYSELF A LONG TIME AGO THAT I WASN'T GOING TO LET ANYONE ELSE SUFFER BECAUSE OF THESE MONSTERS. I'M GOING TO EXPOSE THEM ALL!
TO BE CONTINUED

YELLOW
STRINGER

END OF VOLUME 1

GOEFFREY JEAN-LOUIS

Haitian American artist Goeffrey Jean-Louis was born in White Plains, New York, and raised in Orlando, Florida. After appearing in the 2017 edition of #SummerOfManga with his short story "Mara the Martian," he was tapped to illustrate and co-plot the *seinen* supernatural mystery series *Yellow Stringer*.

FREDERICK L. JONES

Frederick L. Jones graduated from the University of North Carolina at Chapel Hill with a BA in communication studies. After a decade as an executive in the video game industry, Frederick combined his experiences in product marketing, product development, and brand management with his lifelong love of anime to create the diverse manga brand Saturday AM in 2013.

ACKNOWLEDGMENTS

"I WANT TO THANK MY MOM, BROTHER, FRIENDS, AND THE SATURDAY AM STAFF FOR BELIEVING IN ME (AND PUTTING UP WITH ME)."

—Goeffrey Jean-Louis

"THIS BOOK IS A LABOR, AND I MEAN THAT IN ALL THE WAYS ONE WOULD THINK! AFTER GOEFFREY WOWED US WITH HIS *MARA THE MARTIAN* SHORT STORY DURING OUR 2016 SATURDAY AM #SUMMEROFMANGA EVENT, WE KNEW WE HAD TO OFFER HIM A CHANCE TO WORK WITH US OVER A MORE PROLONGED ENGAGEMENT. IT WAS TOUGH IN THE FIRST TWO YEARS AS GOEFFREY WAS STILL GROWING AS BOTH AN ARTIST AND PROFESSIONAL, BUT I'M SO PROUD TO HAVE WITNESSED HIS GROWTH AS A PERSON AND A COLLEAGUE.

LIKEWISE, I'M VERY THANKFUL TO MY FAMILY (SISTER, BROTHER, PARENTS, AND MORE), WHO GAVE ME PEACE OF MIND. SIMILARLY, I'D LIKE TO THANK OUR FANTASTIC TEAM AT THE QUARTO GROUP, WHO HAVE BELIEVED IN US FROM THE BEGINNING. LASTLY, OUR FANS ARE SO INCREDIBLY DESERVING OF OUR APPRECIATION. YELLOW STRINGER HAS AN EXCITING FUTURE (TRUST US!!), BUT WE KNOW THAT THE PATIENCE OF THOSE WHO FOLLOW SATURDAY AM HAS BROUGHT US TO THIS POINT. WE HOPE YOU ENJOY THIS BOOK AND CONTINUE TO FOLLOW US AS WE BUILD THE SAGA OF NAOMI, TONY, JO, AND OTHERS ON A FUNNY, THRILLING, AND EYE-OPENING JOURNEY."

—Frederick L. Jones

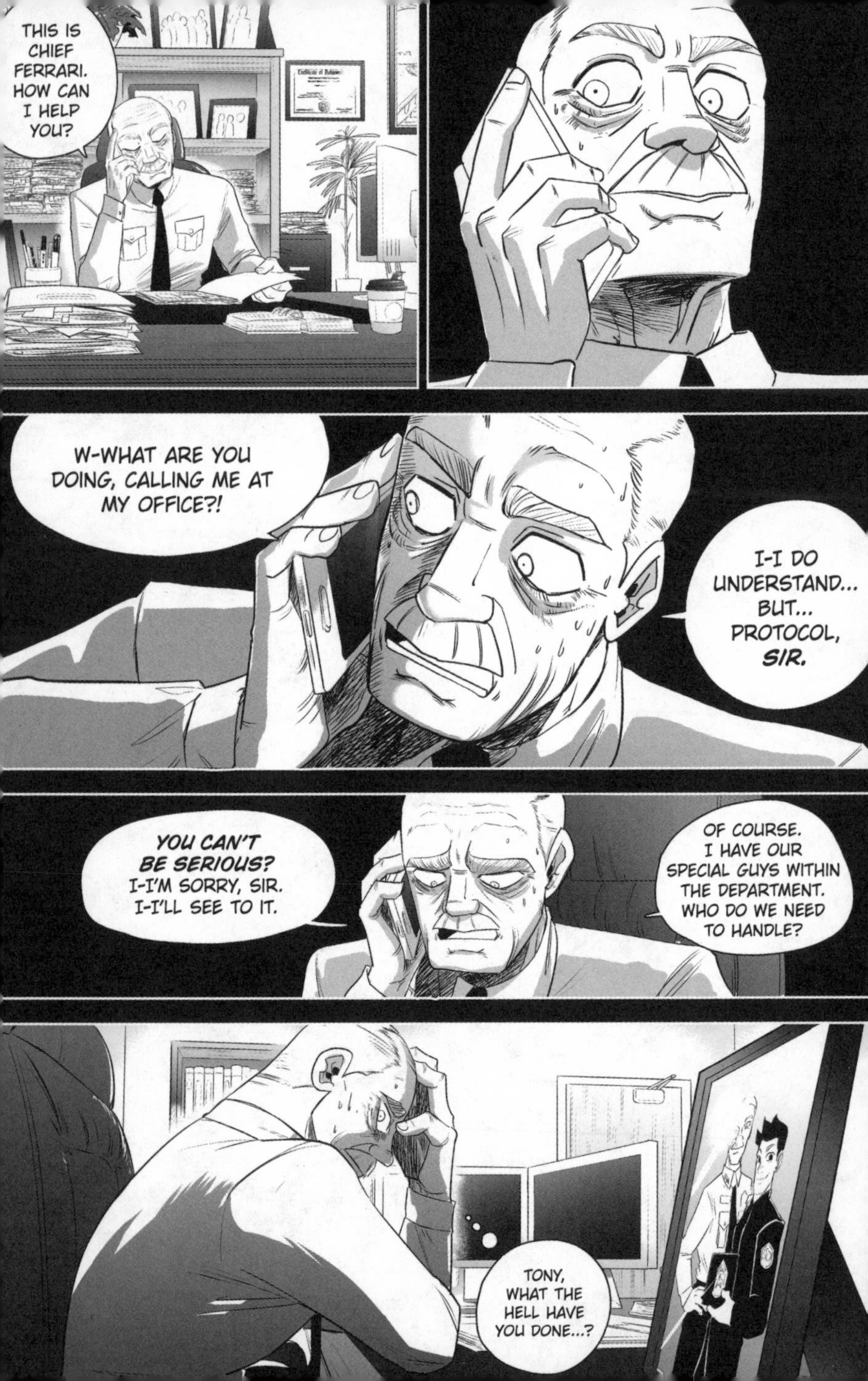
THIS IS CHIEF FERRARI. HOW CAN I HELP YOU?
W-WHAT ARE YOU DOING, CALLING ME AT MY OFFICE?!
I-I DO UNDERSTAND... BUT... PROTOCOL, SIR.
YOU CAN'T BE SERIOUS? I-I'M SORRY, SIR. I-I'LL SEE TO IT.
OF COURSE. I HAVE OUR SPECIAL GUYS WITHIN THE DEPARTMENT. WHO DO WE NEED TO HANDLE?
TONY, WHAT THE HELL HAVE YOU DONE...?

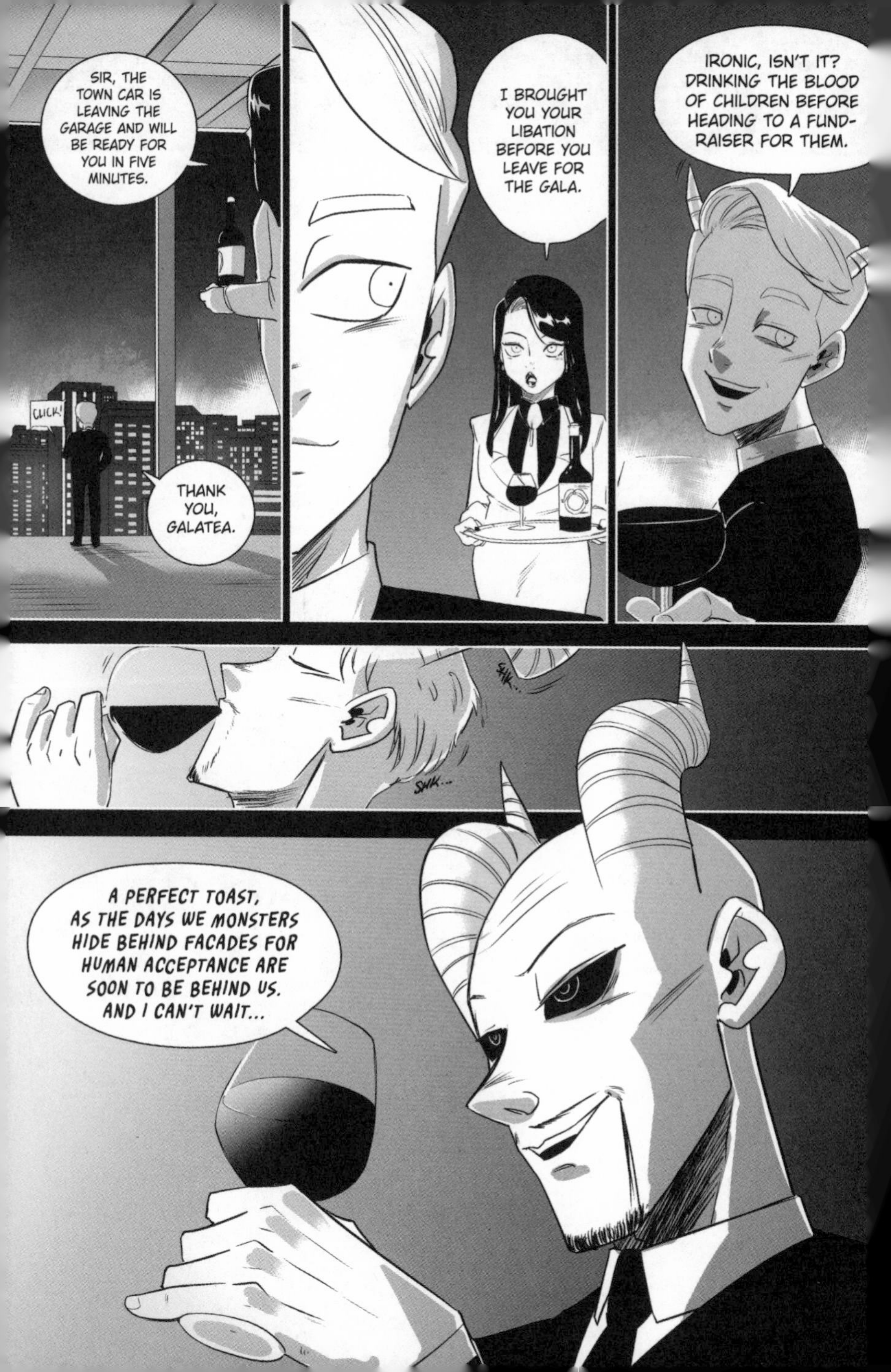
SIR, THE TOWN CAR IS LEAVING THE GARAGE AND WILL BE READY FOR YOU IN FIVE MINUTES.
CLICK!
THANK YOU, GALATEA.
I BROUGHT YOU YOUR LIBATION BEFORE YOU LEAVE FOR THE GALA.
IRONIC, ISN'T IT? DRINKING THE BLOOD OF CHILDREN BEFORE HEADING TO A FUND-RAISER FOR THEM.
SHK...
SHK...
A PERFECT TOAST, AS THE DAYS WE MONSTERS HIDE BEHIND FACADES FOR HUMAN ACCEPTANCE ARE SOON TO BE BEHIND US. AND I CAN'T WAIT...

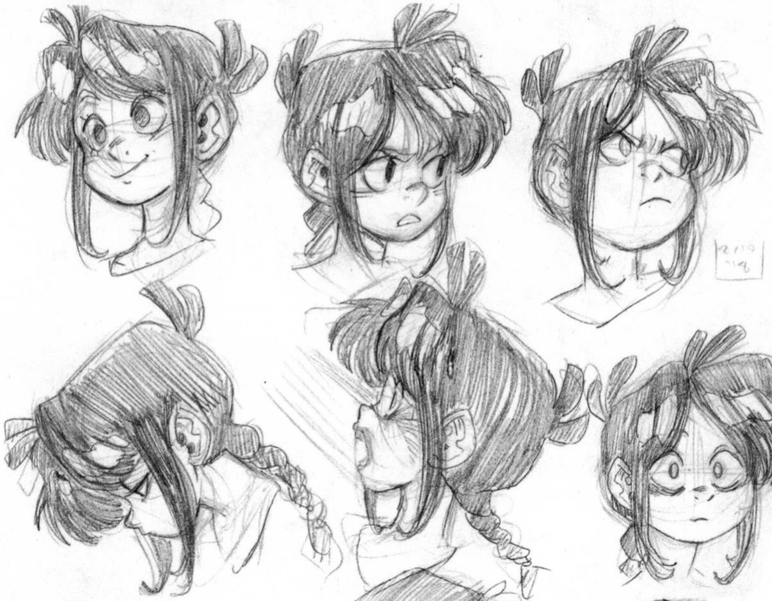

Naomi

"I HAD THE HARDEST TIME DESIGNING NAOMI'S HAIR. I TRIED TO MAKE IT LOOK UNIQUE BUT GROUNDED AT THE SAME TIME. I'M STILL NOT SURE IF I GOT THERE, BUT IT'S FUN TO DRAW!"

-Goeffrey Jean-Louis

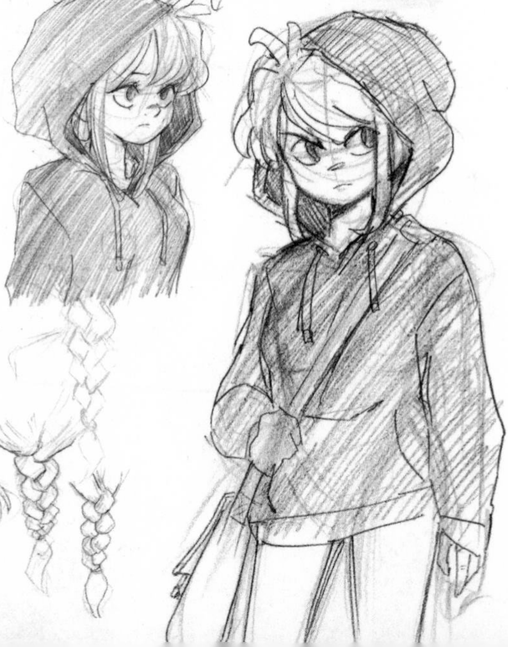

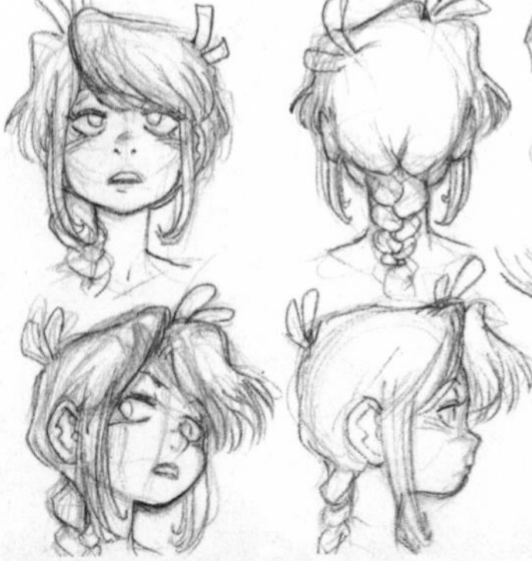

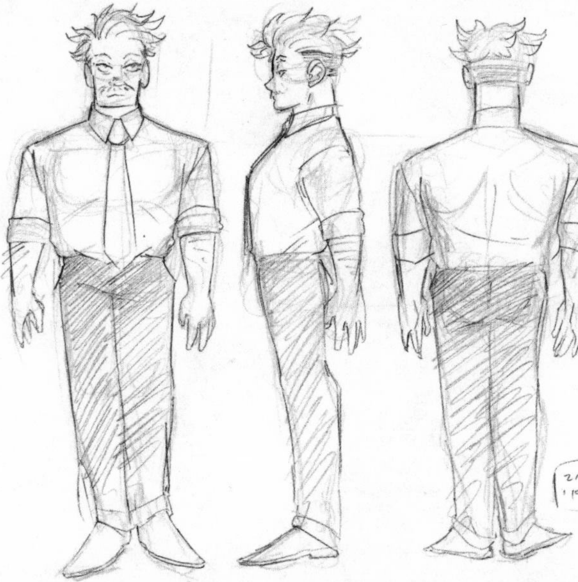

Tony

"TONY TOOK MANY TURNS TO GET TO WHERE HE IS NOW, BUT HIS BASE DESIGN HAS ALWAYS BEEN THE SAME. CHARACTERS THAT ARE HEAVY IN BODY SHAPE AND MASS MAKE FOR A REALLY COOL DESIGN."

-Goeffrey Jean-Louis

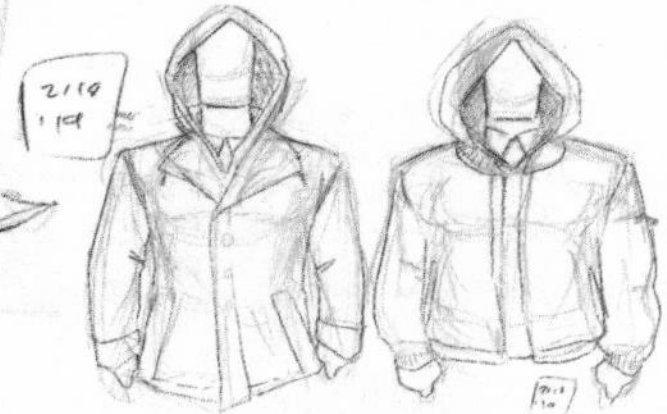
2/18
'19

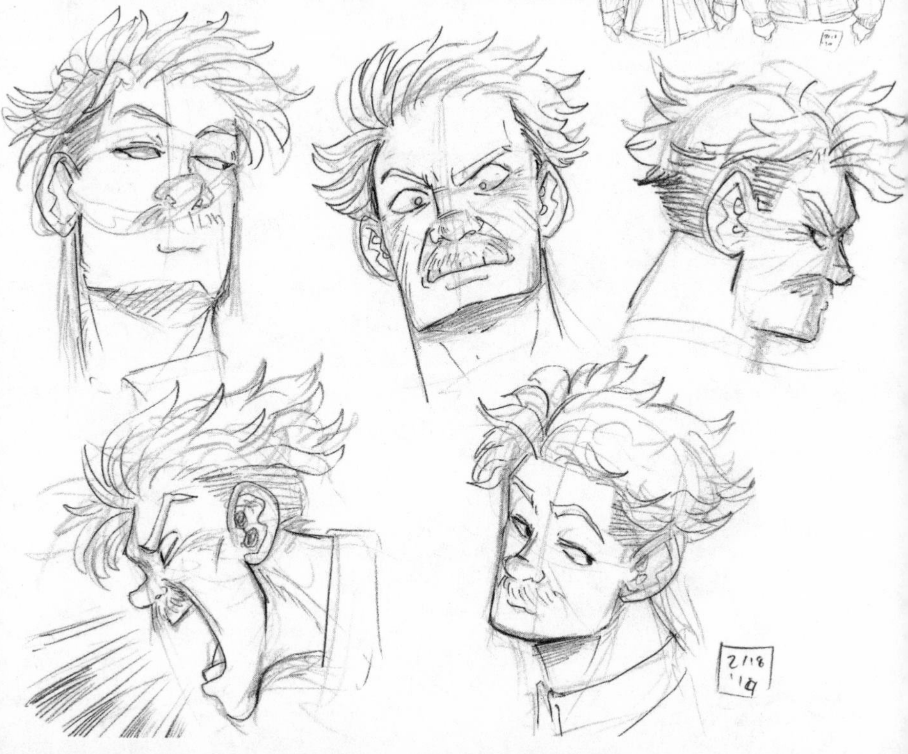
2/18
'19

Abayomi

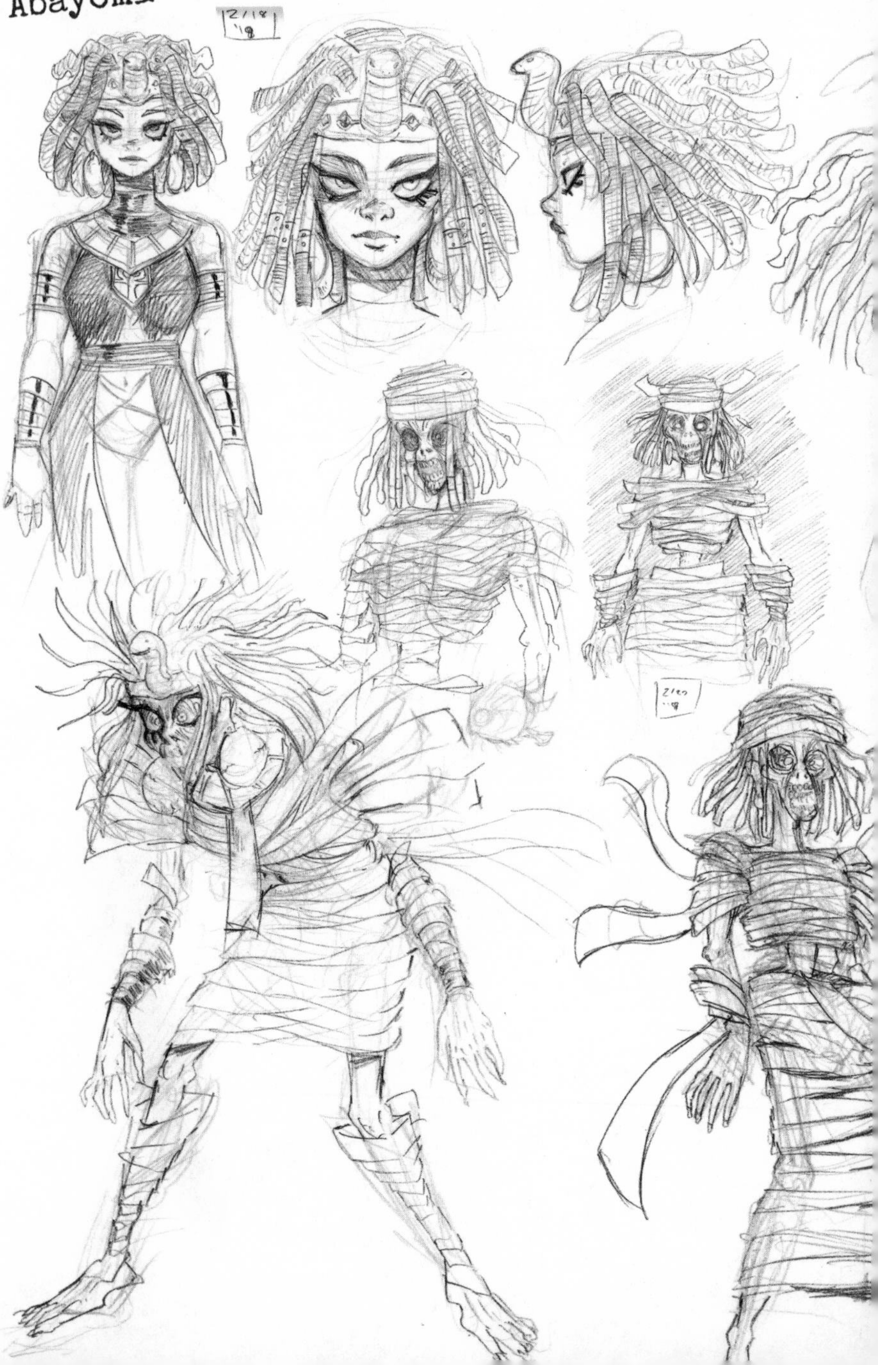
2/18 '18

The Curator

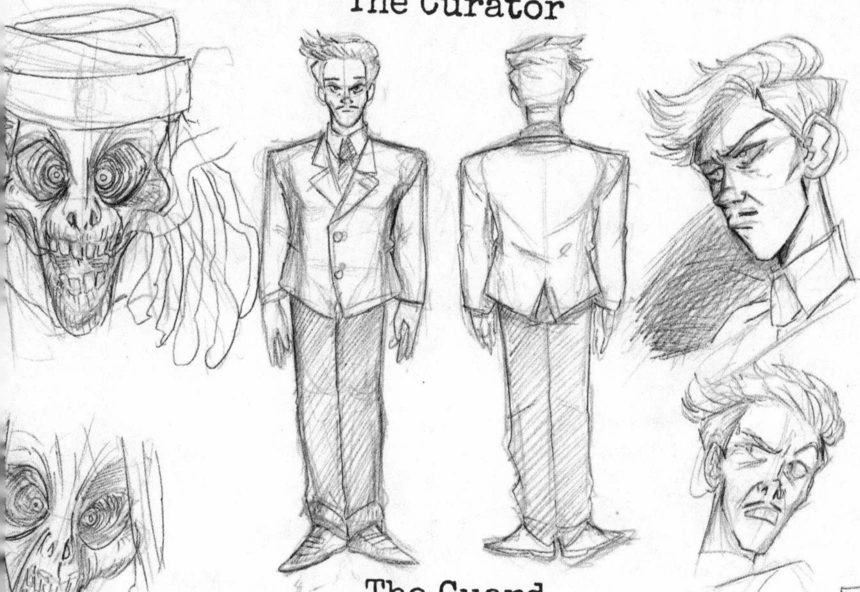

The Guard

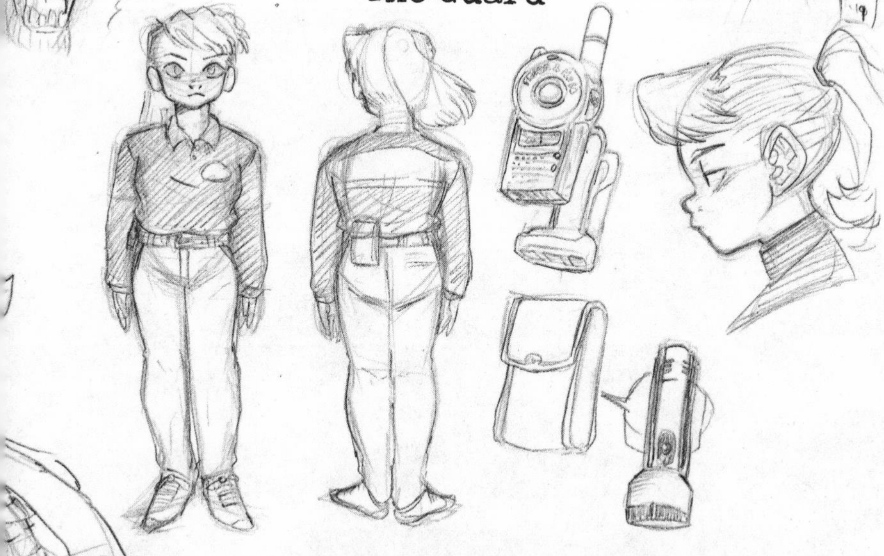

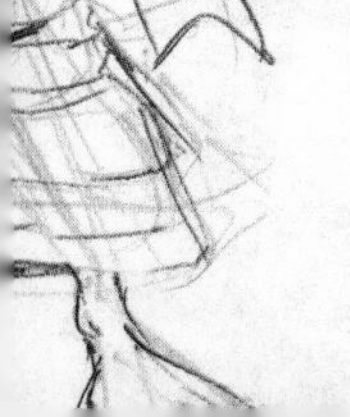

"I SKETCHED THESE IN THE BREAK ROOM OR IN BETWEEN CLASSES AROUND 2018. I HAVE A LOT OF FUN DRAWING EXPRESSIONS, AND SKETCHING THESE WERE A GOOD WAY OF FIGURING THAT OUT. ESPECIALLY WITH NAOMI SINCE HER EYES MAKE IT DIFFICULT FOR ME TO DRAW HER IN A SCARY WAY. I'M STILL TRYING, THOUGH!"

-Goeffrey Jean-Louis

Brimming with creative inspiration, how-to projects, and useful information to enrich your everyday life, quarto.com is a favorite destination for those pursuing their interests and passions.

First published in 2022 by Rockport Publishers, an imprint of The Quarto Group, 100 Cummings Center, Suite 265-D, Beverly, MA 01915, USA. T (978) 282-9590 F (978) 283-2742 Quarto.com

Rockport Publishers titles are also available at discount for retail, wholesale, promotional, and bulk purchase. For details, contact the Special Sales Manager by email at specialsales@quarto.com or by mail at The Quarto Group, Attn: Special Sales Manager, 100 Cummings Center, Suite 265-D, Beverly, MA 01915, USA.

10 9 8 7 6 5 4 3 2 1

ISBN: 978-0-7603-7690-4

Library of Congress Cataloging-in-Publication Data is available.

Created by: Frederick L. Jones
Story by: Frederick L. Jones and Goeffrey Jean-Louis
Art by: Goeffrey Jean-Louis
Lettering: Kai Kyou
Design and additional lettering: Mitch Proctor
Editors: Frederick L. Jones and Austin Harvey

Printed in USA
Printed in China

Yellow Stringer, Volume 1 is rated OT for Older Teens and is recommended for ages 16 and up. It contains strong profanity and graphic violence.